Hemlock Falls

Book Two of the Covens

CiCi Myers

To my friends who believe in me.
My family always supports me.
To my Hubby for being by my side through the good and the bad.
To the readers who always bring me up when my days are dark.
Without all of you, none of this would be possible.

Chapter One

I kept reading the line over and over again. "Your move?" What was this, a damn chess game to him? My fingers shook. My mouth felt like sandpaper. I was too shocked to even speak. What the hell were we going to do?

The future seemed dim from where I stood. How could we defeat someone we couldn't even see and who was always one step ahead of us?

Bash's arms tightened around my waist as if I would run if given a chance. The police sirens were getting closer every second, making my stomach knot in anticipation.

Tristian and Aden spoke in a flurry of words around us, arguing about what we needed to do. Aden's eyes were a fiery blaze of red, not his normal steel gray. Tristian kept running his hands through his hair and gripping it tightly.

"I texted Ella, Ethan, Coco, and James... Do I send one to Morgan?" Tristian looked to Bash for an answer, but Bash just sat in silence with his arms around me, staring into the fireplace, watching the flames dance around. It was as if he had already accepted his fate.

"Bash..." I whispered.

"Yes, Princess?"

I swallowed hard. "It's bad, isn't it?"

He sighed. "Yeah, baby, it is."

I looked up at his face. "I just got you back. I can't..."

He snapped his eyes up to mine and shook his head. "Never. You won't, Lexi."

Outside, a car door slammed shut, and a shuffle of shoes made their way up the porch stairs.

Aden began to pace the room. His fangs slid out, and his eyes set ablaze. In every jerky movement, I could see the thousands of demons fighting to get free from underneath his skin. He wanted to protect his own. His anger hit me like a hot iron, and I feared what he would do for Bash when the police came to arrest him. I feared what they would do to him and the rest of us if he didn't remain calm.

"Aden?"

He snapped his head toward me and scanned my face. A look of worry overcame him, and his features dropped into desperation to save his friend.

I raised my chin and looked into his eyes. The glowing red faded away, and the cool steel gray reappeared. I could feel his hostile anger melt away. The hopelessness in his eyes pressed into my heart.

"I need you to go and quickly hide everything we have on The Wishmaker. All the files, the boxes we've received, and any photo evidence. We can't let the FBI get their hands on it."

He jumped into action using vampiric speed and ran through the

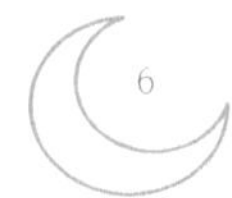

house, leaving nothing linking us to The Wishmaker out in the open. I stared at the door with dread washing over me. They would take Bash away from me just when I got him back. That was the ache I felt for my Devils. It made it harder to breathe. My heart wrenched with the thought of losing him.

"Bash... I..."

A loud knock came on the door. "FBI, open up!" Agent Rengard's smooth, baritone voice came through the other side.

Tristian moved to answer, but he was stiff in his movements. Fury rolled off him so intensely it felt like a slap against my face. I feared how he would react, so I called his name. He tilted his head to me with a questioning look in his eyes.

"Tristian, let me get the door."

His steps faltered, but he nodded in agreement and clenched his fist at his side, fighting the demons within him.

I looked up at Bash and softly kissed him one more time. I didn't want it to be the last kiss I ever had with him, and I knew I would walk through fire for this man I swore to hate.

"We'll find a way, Bash."

He tilted his head as he let me go. I slid out of his lap and walked to the door, opening it to Agent Rengard, who stood next to two large police officers from the Providence PD.

"Agent Rengard," I coldly greeted him.

"Ms. Rose." He paused and cleared his throat. "Lexi, we're here for Sebastian."

I opened the door wider, showing him where Bash was sitting in the armchair.

Rengard handed me a warrant. "We need to search the property for possible murder weapons."

"You know he had nothing to do with this," I hissed, glaring at him and the two police officers behind him.

The first officer looked young. He had a round baby face with wide eyes and the lightest blond hair I had ever seen. He stared at

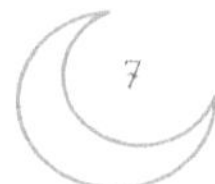

me in awe, and I glanced down and realized I was still in my bikini.

I narrowed my eyes at him. "Officer...?"

He flashed me a boyish smile. "Officer Watson."

I sweetly returned the smile as I let the venom drip into my words. "If you could kindly not stare while you try to arrest my friend, I would appreciate it. I know it might be hard, but let's keep our eyes above the chest and keep your dick in your pants, shall we?"

Agent Rengard laughed and covered it with his hand. "Ms. Rose has a point, Watson. Even if she is a siren, you should respect her regardless of how she's dressed."

I raised an eyebrow at Rengard, surprised he even agreed with me.

"Ma'am, are we going to have a problem?" one of the officers asked.

I could tell he was a giant of some type, not only because of his size, which was probably closer to seven foot seven, but because of the tattoos climbing up his arms with his tribe's symbol shining in bright-gold ink—a symbol only worn by members of the giant clans. His short dark hair and thick beard made him look even more intimidating. His eyes were as dark as chocolate, narrowing in a menacing way. His cold stare was the worst of it all. No sense of empathy or even concern rolled off him. This man was a dangerous threat. We would have to be careful with this one. But I was the Silver Pearl Coven's leader, and I wasn't going to back down. I would go down screaming and clawing for my Devils.

Crossing my arms, I glared at the officer, and my frown became a smirk. *Okay, big boy, if you want to tango, let's go.*

I glanced at his tag. "Officer Hyde, I have two words for you—"

But before I could get my words out, I was lifted from behind and twisted around.

I saw tattooed hands that read "Open Book" across their knuckles. I growled. "Tristian, put me down."

He put me on the couch and sat next to me, then pulled me close and whispered in my ear, "Easy, Lil' Star, you don't want Bash to have more problems, hmm? So shut your mouth, darling."

He smiled at me, which may have looked flirty to everyone else, but his words held a bite. I knew he was saving our asses. I crossed my arms and glared at Agent Rengard and the officers.

Aden led Rengard and his men into the living room. Rengard narrowed his eyes like he was trying to find something in this room to use against us.

He turned to me in an instant and glared, snarling through clenched teeth. "Where's Ryder?"

I looked around for Bash. Where the hell did he go?

"Relax, Agent Rengard. I'm right here," Bash said coolly as he walked from the hallway that led to my room.

Rengard straightened and frowned at him. "Sebastian Ryder, you're under arrest for the murder of Steven Daniels and Nyx Lu."

Officer Hyde rushed behind Bash, picked him up, and threw him against the counter with a hard thud that echoed throughout the room. Hyde slapped a pair of handcuffs on him with a smug smile on his face. Tristian and I shot up from the couch in an instant.

"He isn't resisting arrest. You don't have to shove him!" Tristian shouted, and Aden bared his teeth in a fury.

I bit my tongue so hard that the taste of blood filled my mouth.

"Tristian, get the fucking lawyer on the phone to meet us down at the station," Bash grunted with a chuckle that would make any fae shudder.

Hyde held his face against the counter as his own fear skirted out around me. A ruthless grin formed around my lips. I should have known better. Sebastian Ryder never needed help. He made even the giants shiver in fear. He was their nightmare, evil incarnate.

They hauled Bash to his feet and led him to the front door. Watson opened the door, and Agent Rengard looked back as I followed them.

"He'll need a few hours to be processed. Get the lawyer to meet us there. He might be home tonight." His voice lowered. "Lexi, the evidence is overwhelming against him at this point. I would expect the worst."

I took a deep breath. "You're all being played, and you know it. Arresting the wrong person won't stop the drugs or the killings." I held the door open as they walked out. "Good night, and I hope you all rot in hell." I slammed the door in his face and moved to the window where Aden and Tristian stood murmuring in low voices. "What's going on?"

Aden wrapped his arm around me as he pulled back the curtain to see out the window. The officers led Bash down the steps to where multiple police cars sat with all their lights on. A few news crews were set up along the fence, along with many of our neighbors with their mouths agape. I could sense the excitement in them. Newscasters and camera operators were running around trying to get the best vantage point. "The Prince of the Blood Moon Coven arrested" was a story for the masses.

I hissed in frustration.

"It's a goddamn circus," Aden spat.

I shook my head and pulled the curtains tight. "Come on. We aren't hiding from this. We will stand united."

They both looked a bit shocked but agreed. We walked outside, and I crossed my arms as Aden and Tristian stood at my side.

"Agent Rengard!"

He turned to me. "Yes, Ms. Rose?"

I let the anger that I was holding onto finally seep out toward him, and his eyes widened in surprise at me. "Your promises are small compared to what we did for you and yours. They mean nothing to me now. When I find out who The Wishmaker is—and trust me, I will find out—I will drag them into the depths of hell and set their soul on fire. We are The Covens of Providence Village. Do not mistake us for being weak. You and your people will not destroy us."

Agent Rengard's eyes tightened with anger for a brief second, but he recovered quickly and composed his face. "I truly hope you do, Ms. Rose. But until then, Mr. Ryder will come with us. I'll see you at the station."

The officers threw Bash into the back of a black SUV. Agent Rengard slid into the driver's seat and started the car. My eyes stayed on Bash, and I tried to banish the worry from them. He turned his head to me, his green eyes staring into my blues. Before I could stop myself, a tear escaped, falling to the ground. His eyes flashed with pain, but he shook his head as if telling me not to show weakness.

I swallowed my tears back and took a deep breath. I needed to focus on controlling my emotions. I wished I could flip a switch and turn all the feelings off. The millions of emotions surrounding me were overwhelming. My shield was solid on the best days, but tonight, I felt all the emotions from everyone standing around. Anger, shame, guilt, despair, and hopelessness—it was overwhelming.

"Lexi! Lexi, can we get a quote?" called the local news anchors.

The one thing I remember from Daniels was that the news was never on your side. They wanted a story. It was their sick form of entertainment, but I wasn't here for their amusement. Annoyed, I glared at one of the anchors with her cropped hair and badly fitted suit.

"The Covens have no comment at this time," I bit out.

I turned to the crowd and scanned the yard, memorizing each and every one of their faces.

"Lexi, let's go inside." Aden nudged me back toward the door.

I slid a glance to him, and he held out his hand.

"Okay, let's go." I gripped his hand tightly in mine.

I turned to the door but caught a glimpse of white-blond hair in the crowd. Franklin stood with his arms crossed, wearing a sharp suit and a smug look on his face. I glared at him and let the invisible force of my siren's gift hit him. It wrapped around his body, and his eyes snapped to mine. He smirked and waved his hand, then moved back and disappeared into the crowd.

"Was that...?" Tristian shifted his gaze from me to where Franklin had stood.

"Yeah, the slimy salamander, probably reporting back to Daddy Dearest."

I walked in behind Aden and Tristian and locked the door with a hard click. I wanted to collapse on the floor and crawl into myself. I felt helpless. Dyna walked out, winding her tail around Tristian and me.

Tristian finally gave in, picked her up, and snuggled her fur. "I think she wants you, Lexi."

I looked down at Tristian's arms. Dyna's big light-blue eyes found mine, and she gave me a cute meow with a stretch of a paw.

I smiled at her. "I know, I know, Dyna." I pulled her from Tristian's arms into mine, and she purred loudly.

I moved to sit on the couch and brought her close to me, burying my face in her fur. Tristian and Aden followed me and sank into the armchairs—Tristian's elbows were on his knees as he hung his head low.

Aden was stiff in his seat as his eyes grew cold, staring at the wall behind me. "What's our next move? You two have a plan, don't you?"

I looked around the room. The house felt empty without Bash here. His presence brought us all a sense of comfort, and with him gone, we all sat in despair.

Aden walked into the kitchen and pulled out crystal glasses. He filled them with the Dragon Whiskey. "First, we take a drink to clear our heads, then make a plan," he snarled.

I sighed, nuzzling my head down into Dyna, kissing her head as she purred loudly.

Aden rejoined us and handed out the glasses. "First, we need to call Anderson. He'll want to know what's going on."

I nodded in agreement.

"I have a lawyer on his way down to the police station, too." Tristian pulled out his phone and sent a message.

I sipped the Dragon Whiskey, trying to relax, but the longer I sat there doing nothing, the angrier I would become. Because *fuck* The

Wishmaker. Fuck them. I picked up my phone and looked at the news alerts.

Sebastian Ryder, a high member of the
Blood Moon Coven, arrested for murder.

"Great, just great," I spat out.

"Lex, you okay?"

As I showed them the news article, Aden's and Tristian's phones dinged at the same time.

"It's Morgan." Tristian sighed.

"Franklin probably already told Morgan," I pointed out. I took a huge sip of my whiskey because I couldn't believe I didn't think of it first. "Morgan already knows about Bash, thanks to Franklin."

Both groaned and took a huge sip of their whiskeys. Tristian's phone rang.

"Speak of the Devil, and he shall appear," he murmured as he put the phone on speaker. "Mr. Ryder, Aden and Lexi are here as well. You're on speaker."

Morgan's deep, smooth voice came through the phone. "I won't say this is a pleasant call for me to make in the middle of the day, Tristian. Would you like to explain why my eldest is being hauled away for murder?"

Tristian clenched his jaw before reining in his emotions. The hardness returned to his eyes, and that made my heart weep. Tristian was the one who was always levelheaded and relaxed, and I could tell his control was waning.

"We just found out about this ourselves, Morgan. We got tipped off just thirty minutes before the police came to the door. We were waiting until we had a plan before calling you." He looked up from the phone and placed a finger over his lip, telling us not to speak.

"I see, and the lawyer?" Morgan sounded indifferent that his son was arrested.

Aden cleared his throat. "He'll meet Bash at the precinct."

Morgan cleared his throat. "Good, I'll meet you there in forty-five. Ms. Rose, we have much to discuss."

The phone call ended with a click.

I downed the rest of my glass and glared at the ceiling. *He doesn't even care if anything happens to his son.*

"Fuck Morgan Ryder!" I screamed. I stood abruptly, sending Dyna scurrying off into my room. "I'm not going to sit here waiting for him to tell us what to do like a goddamn soldier."

Aden scoffed. "Lexi, we aren't Morgan's soldiers. We're the fucking generals. We say who does what, and we can end it just as quickly," he snapped as he stood in front of me with a speed unlike I'd ever seen before. His teeth were bared, and his anger licked at me.

I wasn't backing down now, though. "Screw you, asshat. You *are* Morgan's sheep. Yes, you may gain control of a few things, but Morgan is the puppet master, and you are his puppet, Aden. Once a soldier, always a soldier."

Aden's face turned into a scowl, and he got in my face, his fangs elongated. "Lexi Rose, if you think I'm the same little boy you knew years ago, then think again. I take what I want when I want, baby, and that includes you."

I heard the slap before I realized I had struck him.

"Ouch." I looked down at my hand, feeling a sting of pain. A line of blood dribbled down my palm from where Aden's fang had cut it.

I looked up. His head was jerked to the side, and a trickle of blood rolled from his lip. Aden leaned closer to me, his steel-gray eyes alive with anger and lust dancing in them. My eyes burned from the tears threatening to escape, but I held onto them, daring them not to fall.

He smiled down at me, licking his lip. "Careful, baby, I have fangs too, and they're sharp."

Tristian was instantly between us. He pulled me to him and

walked us to the door, his anger seeping. "Go for a walk, Lexi. Get out of here."

I shook my head, begging Tristian with my eyes.

His own filled with pain as he hissed in my ear, "You're emitting your emotions everywhere. Hold it together."

I looked between them and realized I couldn't take my anger out on them. Bash wouldn't want that, and it wasn't helping anyone in this situation. I turned to Aden.

"Aden... I'm sorry." I pressed a hand to my mouth to cover up the whimper that threatened to escape. "Trist... I don't... I didn't..."

He shook me enough to get me out of my head. His anger tasted bitter against my tongue. "And we both get it, Lexi. You fucking love him, not us!" he seethed as he turned and placed both hands on the countertop. "It doesn't change a damn thing to help in this situation." His voice was full of emotion, like he was trying not to break.

I had never seen Tristian angry, not with me, not like this. I wanted to run to him and wrap my arms around him, to tell him he was wrong, but I knew I needed to step away. They needed me to do that. So, I turned and walked out the door, closing it with a click.

I headed to the gate as people called my name and screamed questions at me.

"Do you think he did it, Ms. Rose? What will the covens do? Are the other Devils involved, too?"

I ignored them all and looked at the guards standing near the front.

Deke was pushing back a cameraman. "She said no comment!" He nodded to me, letting me pass as I murmured a thank you to them.

Sonny gave me a sad smile. "You good, Ms. Rose?" he yelled.

I waved him off as I headed to the back gate.

One cop car sat idle, watching me. I saw the tattoos of the giant Hyde. What the hell was he still doing here?

I walked over to the car and tapped on the window.

Officer Hyde looked up, annoyed, and rolled his window down. "What can I do for you, Ms. Rose?" His condescending voice carried over the noise around us.

"Officer Hyde, what are you doing here?" I eyed him suspiciously.

"I was told to watch the house and make sure no one left or came in."

I raised my eyebrows. "Are we all suspects?"

Hyde smirked. "Now, you know I can't discuss an ongoing investigation, but one of you is going down for murder. I can only hope it's Sebastian Ryder. That bastard deserves everything that's coming to him."

I rolled my eyes. "It's a vendetta, then?"

He said nothing; he just sat still.

"You should be wary of the green-eyed monster. It'll destroy your soul."

He scoffed at me and huffed a laugh.

"You aren't even half the man Sebastian Ryder is," I snapped out, turning on my heel and walking away, heading back through the side gate down to the beach.

The car door slammed. "Ms. Rose! Put your hands up, now!"

I turned around, and Hyde had drawn his gun, aiming for my chest. I put my hands in the air.

"You've got to be kidding me," I bit out at him.

He smiled cruelly. "No. I'm following orders, Ms. Rose. You're under arrest for obstruction." As he walked toward me, he holstered his gun and pulled out a set of cuffs. "I can do this the hard way or the easy way, Ms. Rose. I'm begging you to make it hard, please." He snarled at me, his hatred for me clear.

I looked from the cuffs to him, knowing that he had no problem reaching for his gun again.

Aden and Tristian bolted out the door, yelling my name. Hyde pulled me in front of him.

"What the hell?!" they yelled. "Let her go!"

Hyde whispered so low that I barely heard him, "I see their guns, Ms. Rose. I'm sure they're good shots, but they won't dare do that with you standing in front of me. Now, me? I'm an excellent shot. I will put a bullet in each of their pretty little heads."

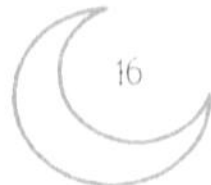

I glanced back at Aden and Tristian and slightly shook my head not to interfere.

"It's done. I'll go with you, Hyde," I growled as I held out my hands to him.

He slapped a pair of handcuffs on me. The cold iron felt heavy against my skin. The magic within them hummed at my wrist.

"Why are they spelled?" I grunted as the tingle worsened.

"The cuffs? Your powers won't work until I remove them."

I still shook my head at Tristian and Aden, telling them to back off. They both cursed and stood with their arms crossed, glaring at Hyde.

"Glad you see it my way." He moved behind me as the bile rose in my throat.

I looked back at the house as he led me away.

Aden hadn't moved, and even from this distance, I could tell his jaw was clenched. "We're right behind you," he reassured me.

I took a deep breath as I walked to the police car.

Hyde pushed me into the back, smiling a crooked smile. "Don't get too comfortable, darlin'," he drawled, slamming the door.

He whistled as he walked around the car and slid into the driver's side.

During the ride to downtown, he glanced at me in the rearview mirror. "Perfect little Rose, all tied up. It's a beauty to see."

I met his gaze in the mirror, tilting my head to the side. Only one person has ever called me "perfect little Rose."

"What did you call me?"

"Nothing," he muttered as he drove.

He looked back at me a few times, but I ignored him and stared out the window. Hyde just gave away one important clue: he knows The Wishmaker.

I started to laugh, and he glared at me with a deep frown.

"What's so funny?"

I grinned. "Oh god, you are so screwed, dude. You messed up big time. You know that, don't you?" I watched him, my eyes narrowing.

My siren wanted to come out, but the magic in the cuffs stopped her from doing so. I felt the ache deep in my stomach. "We'll come for you, so you might want to let your boss know that the Devils will be collecting soon."

I laughed to myself as his eyes filled with fear of what he had just said.

And then they turned hard, and a dark shadow spread throughout them until they were a solid black orb. I felt the temperature in the car drop, and the windows began to fog up. My breath came out in puffs.

He snarled at me. "You think you're special?" His cold laugh taunted me. "I want to know one thing. You grew up with everything. Your life was set. Then you threw it all away... for *them*? Rich boys with pretty faces? And you don't think they won't break you into a million pieces again? You're either the stupidest girl I have ever met, or your pussy must be made of fucking gold to keep the three Devils of Providence Village on their knees."

I bit my tongue, denying him a comment, because that's when I realized it wasn't just about me choosing one of my Devils. We were a unit of strength for the covens, and we worked because we were meant to all be together. The Devils and their siren were going to bring the entire force of their power down onto The Wishmaker and their followers. The only question was, would we all survive?

Chapter Two

Hyde drove down the pewter cobblestone streets and approached the Providence Village Police Building, which had been completely updated thanks to the Ryder family's massive charity donation last year. The sun glistened against the glass before Hyde pulled into an underground garage, where a dark iron-caged security area awaited us. He parked and pulled me out of the back seat, then spoke to another uniformed officer while he processed me into the system. We quietly rode the elevator. The doors opened into the precinct, which had an open floor plan with computers and desks in straight rows. Surprisingly, it seemed like any ordinary office building. In the back, a row of rooms were set for interviews. The interview rooms had dark glass so no one could peek in, and white blinds covered them.

"This way, Ms. Rose." Hyde pushed me to a desk close to the back. "Sit," he snapped, pointing to the chair.

My gaze roamed over him as I arched an eyebrow. I bit the inside of my cheek to keep the quirky comeback at bay and sat on the cold plastic seat, trying to get comfortable. I shifted my legs, crossing one over the other.

A deep voice spoke from behind me, "Ms. Rose?"

I turned to see a stunned Agent Rengard. Next to him was a very handsome but annoyed-looking vampire. Bash's eyes flashed crimson, his hands flexing against the cuffs.

"What the hell, Princess!?"

I stiffened and raised my chin. "Agent Rengard... Sebastian." I turned back, looking straight ahead as Hyde finished his process work.

"Why is she here?" Bash's deep, gravelly voice echoed throughout the room.

I glanced at the windows, and his reflection stared back at me. I shook my head at him, indicating he shouldn't cause a scene. The last thing I needed was more charges added to his already complex murder allegation. He glared at me, and fire burned in his eyes as he fought against his instinct to protect me.

"This way, Mr. Ryder, to the interview room. Your lawyer is waiting." Rengard started to move him to the room across from me.

"If you lay a finger on her, Hyde, I swear..."

Rengard pulled Bash along. "This. Way. Mr. Ryder." He spat each word in a warning.

Bash walked away, but his eyes never left mine. Between his tense shoulders and tightly balled fists, his whole body broadcasted his distress.

I kept my face blank, giving him nothing. He shook his head, his rage returning, and walked into a room where a young man stood in a costly suit, his arms crossed, with a severe look on his face.

Once inside the room, Rengard turned, his face betraying a hint of concern. He nodded to me and closed the door.

Hyde's phone buzzed, and he glanced down at the text message he had received, cursing under his breath. "Fucking Blood Moon whore."

I turned my head to him with an icy stare. "Excuse me, did you need to say something to me, officer?"

Hyde looked up from his phone and turned toward me, sneering. "Agent Rengard wants you to go to an interview room and answer a few questions."

Before I could protest, he stood, pulled me by my elbow, and quickly moved us to the interview room farthest from Bash's.

"Officer Hyde, please remove your hands from my client."

A smooth, baritone voice I recognized fell over the lobby. A few fae turned their heads as he strutted toward Hyde and me. I smiled to see Trinity's second-in-command walk into the precinct. Hudson James was a tall, handsome werewolf. He was out of his normal clothes and donned a charcoal suit. He strolled down the hall straight toward us. His dark hair was messy, as if he had gotten dressed in a rush, and a dark five o'clock shadow graced his face.

"Hudson James, nice to see you again." I smiled at him.

Hudson extended his hand to me. "Tristian called Grayson since their coven's lawyer is occupied with Bash tonight. But lucky for you, I've been practicing for years." He gave me a wolfish grin and winked at me.

"Trinity Coven's secret weapon, huh?" I mused as I shook his hand.

"You have no idea," he replied, smiling down at me.

Hyde puffed an annoyed breath, crossing his arms and glaring at Hudson with disgust written all over his face.

Hudson straightened his jacket and looked at Hyde. "Do not question my client without me present, Hyde, or I'll have your badge. And, as second-in-command of your coven, I'd suggest you heed my warning."

Hyde narrowed his eyes at him. It was obvious he hated Hudson.

"And Grayson told me you should report to him after your shift."

Hyde crossed his arms but nodded.

Hudson clapped his hands together. "Now, let's do this, shall we?" He smiled, making him look younger.

We walked into the interview room. The plain room had a metal table in the middle with a few matching chairs around it. Hudson pulled out my chair and offered me his hand as I sat down.

"Always a gentleman," I joked, and he turned to me, smirking.

"Not always, Ms. Rose," he said teasingly.

Hyde walked in, glaring at us. He stood in the corner and looked like he was about to spout smoke from his nose. Hudson took the seat next to me. His body looked relaxed, but he scanned the room, on alert. He studied Hyde from the corner of his eye, strategically keeping his body between us.

"Don't you have paperwork to do or something? Ms. Rose isn't going anywhere. She has no reason to flee."

"Doubtful. She could easily use her compulsion to let anyone set her and Mr. Ryder free."

I tilted my head and raised my hands, showing him the cuffs. "I can't use my siren gifts or magic with these on, so I think we're fine, and even if I could, I would have already done it." I smirked at him and sat up straighter, setting my hands together on the table and narrowing my eyes at him. "But it is interesting that you think that's a problem, officer, when your ways to get me here were... let's call them 'unorthodox.'"

Hudson's smile fell, and he turned to me, his wolfy eyes turning an icy blue. "Lexi, did he threaten you or hurt you?"

The air in the room grew heavy with silence as Hudson's eyes landed on mine.

I shook my head. "No, Hudson, I don't think Officer Hyde would be that dumb."

Hyde looked like I hit him in the face, but before he could open his mouth, the door clicked open, and Agent Rengard walked in with a pad of paper and sat across from me. "Ms. Rose, do you need water, a bathroom, or food?"

I shook my head. "I just want to go home and possibly take... my bodyguard with me."

Rengard's smile was anything but pleasant. "Your bodyguard? Is that what you call Sebastian Ryder? What about Mr. Cassium and

Mr. Charmante?"

Before I could answer, Hudson cleared his throat, sat back, took a folder out, and placed it on the table. "Ask Ms. Rose your questions, Agent, regarding the case. Then let her go. You have no evidence to hold my client, or do I need to call Agent Cillian?"

Rengard stiffened at the demand, and for a moment, he showed nothing but contempt for Hudson. "Right," he bit out. "Ms. Rose, do you understand your rights?"

I forced myself not to roll my eyes. "Yes."

Rengard laid a folder down and sat poised with the pad of paper and a pen. "Can you tell me about the night Ms. Lu died and the events that led up to Sebastian Ryder's arrest?"

I glanced at Hudson, and he nodded for me to answer. I took a deep breath. "Bash, Tristian, Aden, and I had dinner with Coco and Jason that night."

The agent looked up from taking notes, narrowing his eyes at me. "They can confirm you were in the house the whole time?"

Heat rose in my cheeks as I thought of what Aden and I had done earlier that evening. "Yes, they can. I was in the conservatory at one point picking up a few things I left the night Daniels died, but Aden was with me."

I tried my damndest not to let a blush creep into my cheeks. The memories from the night in the conservatory still played in my head. Finding the riddle and the knife meant we were one step closer to finding out who The Wishmaker was and how to stop them.

Rengard began to scribble on the pad. "Then?" He sounded annoyed.

I skipped over the whole "finding the pixie dust clues" and the whole Aden and myself being with each other. What I did in private wasn't anyone else's business, and technically, this was about Nyx and Daniels, not pixie dust, so I decided to only keep with the relevant facts.

"Then we went home. The guys talked about security and the next steps for us to take to keep everyone safe. As you recall, I was almost a murder victim myself." I glared at Rengard.

Officer Hyde huffed. Hudson turned around with an arched eyebrow. "Do we need him in the room?"

Agent Rengard didn't even look up from his pad of paper. "You can go, Hyde. Check on Mr. Ryder."

Hyde pushed off the wall and glared at me. "Yes, sir."

Hudson turned back to me. "Lexi, please continue." He smiled gently at me, and I returned it.

I definitely needed to send Grayson a big old basket of treats for sending Hudson. What the hell does a werewolf-dragon shifter like? Moon pies or chocolate gold coins? I looked back at Rengard, and his eyes narrowed on me.

"Yes, please continue."

"Then we worked to try and figure out who my stalker was and what they wanted. That was until about three in the morning. At that point, I went to sleep. Bash, Aden, and Tristian stayed up, and from what I know, they were there the whole night. I'm sure they can confirm."

He smirked. "And the next morning, did you wake up alone?"

I folded my arms, looking at him with a raised brow.

Hudson held up his hand to stop anything further. "What are you getting at, Rengard?"

He leaned back, crossing his arms over his chest, resembling a spider looking for a fly to trap. "Nothing at all. I'm just wondering if Ms. Rose was or was not an accomplice to Mr. Ryder. Maybe she saw him leave. Maybe she saw him with Ms. Lu and got jealous, and maybe she murdered Ms. Lu instead. Is Mr. Ryder taking the fall for our newest coven leader?"

I laughed. "You're kidding me. That is the most ridiculous statement anyone has ever made. I was asleep. You can check with Tristian and Aden, as they were next to me most of the night." I let the words hang in the air.

"Most of the night?" Agent Rengard questioned me.

I placed my hands on the table, clasping them together, and

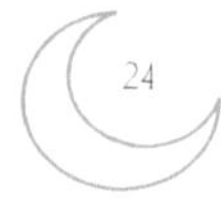

looked at Rengard, snarling. "Yes, I went to bed early, as I told you."

He straightened his back and lifted his head to me. For a moment, I saw a sheen to his eyes as if he had lost focus for a minute. "Yes, I'm sorry, Ms. Rose, you are correct. Forgive me, Lexi, I haven't slept much in the last few days."

My shoulders dropped. "Look, Agent. I get it. You now have two murders and probably an entire department down your throat, but Sebastian didn't kill Nyx. As for me? I wouldn't. I couldn't; she was my friend." The tears threatened to spill over. "She was also part of my coven. It was my duty to bring her home, and I didn't. I couldn't save her." I let my eyes brim, and Hudson pulled a handkerchief from his pocket.

"Here, Lexi," he said gently.

I took it from him and dabbed my eyes before the tears could fall. *I will not cry; I will not give Rengard the satisfaction.*

Rengard tapped his pen on the pad and sighed. "See, the thing is, Lexi—"

Hudson interrupted him. "Probably best to use Ms. Rose, Agent Rengard, as this isn't a social call," he pointed out.

Rengard looked over at Hudson and chuckled nervously. "Yes, Mr. James, you're correct. As I was saying, Ms. Rose, it's not off the table. Morgan Ryder suggested it."

I tightened my hands and growled, "He did what?!"

Rengard straightened his tie, looking uncomfortable. "He said maybe you wanted the title and killed Daniels to take his place. The stalker and letters are an act to help you take over the covens to get other leaders on your side."

Hudson clenched his jaw and stood, leaning on his palms as he loomed over Rengard. "That's hearsay, Rengard, and you know it. Stop baiting Ms. Rose."

Rengard glared up at Hudson. "Mr. Buford even suggested that you might know more about pixie dust than you're letting on. So please prove me wrong. I'll ask one more time: who can tell me you were in bed all night?"

My mouth hung open at the fucking ridiculous allegations thrown against me.

Hudson looked like he was about to go full wolf on Rengard but turned to me and sighed. "Ms. Rose, please answer the question." He straightened his suit and sat back down.

Grinding my teeth, I bit out, "I wasn't alone. Aden came in first, then Tristian, and Sebastian next. All three of them were in bed with me this morning."

Hudson cleared his throat to cover up a laugh. I hit his foot with mine under the table.

"Sorry, Lexi, sorry," he mumbled.

Rengard looked a bit shocked, but I continued. "When I woke, I took a swim in the ocean to clear my head. Losing half of your family can cause a bit of stress. I needed to call on my siren and replenish whatever was lost from the night before. When I came out, Bash was there, then we sat and talked for a while."

Rengard leaned forward, hands clasped, tilting his head. "About what?"

I almost let out a hiss but bit my lip from letting it escape. "Very personal things, Agent Rengard."

He scribbled on the pad. "That it?"

I closed my eyes in frustration because what Bash and I had was more than words. It was ours. It was our tiny escape, and no one had the right to take that away from us.

So, I thought about how much I wanted to say. "Bash and I finally... look, we finally came to an understanding of each other. It's ten years too late, and we finally figured our shit out. We found common ground and understanding of each other. We want what's best for our covens, and we agreed that we would protect not just our own Silver Pearl and Blood Moon but also Trinity." I glanced at Hudson, whose eyes beamed, and I could tell he wanted to hug me. I shrugged and bumped my elbow with his in solidarity. I looked back at the sphinx across from me. "Then we made it back to the house where Tristian said you were on the way to arrest Sebastian. Thanks for the call, by the way." I gave a coy smile that said *go fuck yourself.*

Agent Rengard narrowed his eyes. "I thought it was only right for you to heed a warning since Sebastian is a leader of our community."

Hudson stood. "Are we done here? Ms. Rose has answered your questions about your case and even more personal questions. That does not leave this room," he growled. "You have no evidence against my client, and the obstruction is laughable because your officer can't control his temper. I have already filed a complaint against him to the department, but don't worry, I heard through the grapevine that Agent Cillian is on his way to help you out." He gathered his phone and helped me up, then held out my hands for Agent Rengard to uncuff.

Rengard returned Hudson's menacing stare. "If you think of anything, give me a call, Ms. Rose. We are done... for now. Well played, Ms. Rose." He stood and uncuffed me.

I stood and straightened my body. "Agent Rengard, I don't know who The Wishmaker is. For all we know, it could be anyone. We don't know what he or she truly wants from us, but I do know one thing. When you find them, I want to be there to watch them fall." My eyes shifted into my siren's form, the lavender haze washing over my vision and casting the room into a violet fog.

Rengard's eyes widened at the shift. "I sure hope you get to see that one day, Lexi. Let's just hope it doesn't cost you something dear in return."

He turned and walked out the door, not looking back at us, leaving us questioning, "If The Wishmaker could be anyone, how much chaos could they ensue?"

I smiled at Hudson. "Thank you, Hudson James, and please thank Grayson."

He held up his phone. "No worries, he knows." He smiled mischievously.

I rolled my eyes and waved to the camera in the interview room. "Let me guess. Aden, Tristian, and Grayson hacked the police station camera."

Hudson gave a full belly laugh. "Maybe... who knows, I'm just some paranoid lawyer."

I smiled at him. "So... you're a lawyer?" Because this gorgeous, rough, tall man in front of me did not look like a lawyer.

He grinned. "Why? Because I have tattoos, a beard, and am Grayson's second? I think that makes me the perfect lawyer."

"But in all seriousness, Hudson, thank you both."

He blushed slightly. "Lexi, can I be honest with you?"

I stopped halfway out of the door. "Of course, Hudson."

He moved close to me and whispered low enough for only the two of us to hear. "You're a breath of fresh air to the covens. I know you have issues with the Devils, but I see your powerful bond with them. I think it's the best thing for everyone involved." He laid a warm hand on my shoulder, giving me a gentle squeeze.

I smiled at him and turned, walking out of the room to see two of the Devils waiting for me.

Hudson laughed. "Lexi, you got it bad, but if you want to thank anyone, then you should thank those two. They're the ones who got all of this into motion, Bash's lawyer and yours. The only thing Grayson did was send me." He smiled and did a little twirl, looking like a cocky wolf. He hugged me and kissed my cheek. "Look, I gotta run, but I would wait with them. Sebastian's lawyer should have him out soon."

Chapter Three

I waved goodbye to Hudson and walked over to two of my Devils. Tristian had a worried look on his face, but as soon as he saw me, he stood.

I ran my last few steps and wrapped myself up in his arms, which were warm and comfortable, like home.

"You good, Lil' Star?"

I sniffed. "Yeah, I'm sorry, you guys. I'm good now."

He smiled down at me, examining my face. "Braver than you seem." He kept his arm around me as I looked for Aden.

Aden stood back, looking down, giving us space. I didn't want space, so I reached out for his hand. He gave me a small smile as he took hold of it. I pulled him closer to us.

"I'm okay. Any news on Bash being released?"

Tristian frowned. "Hopefully soon. All we can do is wait right now."

The sliding doors opened on the far side. Morgan and Franklin walked through the doors, their heads held high with a sense of privilege oozing from them. Then to my surprise, Ella and Ethan walked in behind them. Ethan held Ella close to him as if he was her only savior.

The memory from the night of the masquerade ball sprung to mind, and how her face looked when she found Aden, Tristian, and me in the library. I released Tristian and Aden in an instant, stepping away from them. Not knowing where Ella and I stood, I stared at the ground until I heard the slap of her flip-flops.

I glanced up, and she saw us. Sadness filled her features, which made my heart break. I let the tears fall, and her face mirrored mine. She pulled from Ethan, and we started to run toward each other. I met her halfway as her body slammed into mine.

"Lexi! I'm so, so sorry. You deserve to be happy," she sobbed into my shoulder.

I sniffed and hugged her tighter. "No, Ella, I'm sorry; I should have told you first. I was stupid." I hugged her so tightly, I didn't think she could breathe.

"Let's never fight again," she cried.

"Never again, I promise."

The guys greeted each other, and Ethan hugged his brother and Tristian in a bro-ish way.

He looked over at us and smiled, giving me a tiny wave.

I smiled back and rolled my eyes, clearing my throat. "Hey, Ethan, wanna take Sniffles over here?"

He laughed. "Says the girl who once cried over a dog commercial."

I laughed with him as I wiped a tear from my face. "Well, just take the blonde one, then."

Ethan took her under his arm and kissed her cheek. "It's gonna be okay, babes. He has the best lawyer in town, and it's Bash."

I rolled my eyes and turned to Aden as he wrapped an arm around my waist. "You want anything, Lex? Maybe food or coffee?"

I turned in his arms, looking up at him. "Maybe a coffee, if you don't mind."

He smiled. "Nope, I don't. I'll get everyone some in a second, but

I really want a greeting. Trist got a hug. What do I get?"

I bit my lip as I leaned closer to him. "What do you want?"

He grinned as he leaned in and kissed me softly, slowly, with such care I thought I would melt. He pulled back before I could deepen it, smirking. I frowned with a pout.

"Let's get Mr. Dark and Broody out first, baby. Then you can have me." He let go of me.

I stepped back and saw that we had every eye in the room on us.

I murmured, "Look at what you did now."

Aden laughed as he walked away to get the promised coffees, and I looked across the room to see Morgan watching us with interest. Franklin was shooting daggers at Aden. You could almost see his anger forming around him. It was a deadly game we were playing with him.

Tristian flanked my side as I stepped closer to Ella. "What did your dad tell you about Bash?"

Ella's sad eyes turned angry. "He says Bash has nothing to worry about, but I overheard the evidence they have. It's scary how much it looks like he did it."

Ethan ran a comforting hand up and down her arm.

I frowned. "You don't think he…?"

Ella pinched my arm. "Lexi Briar Rose, If I ever hear you talk like that again, I'll be joining Bash in jail too. I know you two don't get along, but he didn't kill…"

I shook my head. "First, ouch." I pointed to my arm. "Second, I didn't think he did anything of the sort. I know he didn't because Bash was with me most of the night. He was in my bed this morning."

I bit my lip as I spilled my truth out to her. I realized I had just confessed to Bash's little sister that I was sleeping with him, too. Which wasn't technically true—Bash and I hadn't slept together in over ten years—but I wasn't going to go into that little detail with her.

Ella's eyebrows shot up. "Well, shit… that's, ummm… all three? You gotta tell me how the hell that works?"

Ethan barked out a laugh. "Ella!"

Tristian's breath caught in his throat, and I laughed. "I am not talking to you about that! It's your brother!"

She laughed. "Ewww, not like *that*. I meant, like, relationship-wise. Get your siren mind out of the gutter!" She smacked my arm.

I sighed and looked back to the door where Bash was being held, wishing I could see him. That's all I wanted: for him to escape from this hellish situation.

"I'm not sure how it'll work, Ella, but it will because this is how it's supposed to be." I turned back to Ella and saw her eyes shining. "No more tears." I pointed to her. "I have cried enough."

She shook her head at me. "These are happy tears because you deserve all the happiness in the world. I'm sorry I didn't realize it sooner."

I blushed slightly, grabbing her hand and squeezing it.

Luckily, Aden returned with a tray of coffees for everyone. I let the warmth of the coffee bring me the energy I was dying for.

"I love you!" I whispered.

Aden cleared his throat, looking over at me with a hidden smile.

Ethan laughed and patted his brother on the back. "Bro, she's talking to the coffee, not you." He winked at me, and my blush deepened.

Aden moved closer to me and put an arm around my shoulders. "Yes, but can coffee keep you warm at night?"

I rolled my eyes. "You know coffee keeps me warm morning, noon, and night, sir."

He was quiet for a minute, and I tilted my head to look up at him. Did he really think I was talking to him? I knew I loved him as a friend, and I knew we were more than that, but love? Love is so different for everyone, especially my Devils.

"Aden..."

He shook his head. "Nope, Lex, we're all good." He leaned closer to me, whispering, "If or when we do say it, I know it'll be just for us."

I smiled shyly as Aden Charmante lived up to his name and made me swoon for Prince Charming. I knew he was, deep down.

He kissed my cheek. "Come on, gotta talk to Trist."

We walked over to Tristian, who hung up his phone as we approached.

Aden stood close and whispered, "I walked by Morgan and Franklin. Franklin is talking of bringing a necromancer in to see if they can get Nyx back to question her."

I gasped. "They can't!"

Ella turned to me with a frown playing on her lips. "I know necromancers can be dangerous, but why would that be a bad thing? Maybe it could help us."

We turned our heads back to Ella as she and Ethan stood beside us with their arms folded.

She huffed. "What? I'm tired of being left out of the Scooby gang."

I mimicked her posture, crossing my arms. "Ella, I really don't think you—"

She held up her hand. "Hear me out. Ethan and I talked about it. We want to help." Before I could argue, she continued. "In a nonlethal way. We want to be behind the scenes. We'll help with research and scope out anything we can. Plus, Ethan is a sharp shot, and I'm a powerful, badass vampire. We can do this."

Aden, Tristian, and I exchanged a glance and shrugged. "Fine, but research first before you start getting all Sherlock on us."

Tristian grinned at them. "I, for once, agree with you, Ella."

She grinned at him. "See, Trist agrees."

Tristian crossed his arms and faced Ella. "To answer your question about necromancers, though. When we die and fade into the Veil, our souls can go a few different ways. A necromancer interferes with that transference, causing a rip in the Veil, and the soul is lost in a purgatory-type state. So, returning Nyx from the Veil for a question means she would be lost and forced to roam for eternity. Lexi is worried about what will happen to not only the witch who performs the spell but to Nyx herself. Necromancy is dangerous, and there are only a few witches in the world who can perform it."

Ella's big eyes widened at the horror. "No. I won't let him do it." She glared over at Franklin, who had his phone up to his ear.

Aden closed his eyes. "Bash won't let them do it. I can still hear them talking. God, Rengard is a maunderer." He shook his head. "He has the video showing Bash with Nyx, and when he left, she was alive. They don't have enough evidence, but Agent Rengard is sure he's complicit somehow." He let out a groan and sighed. "They're going to station a cop at the house to watch his movements. We need to prepare for a car to tail us when we leave too."

Tristian cursed under his breath. "They'll have undercovers on us too. Damn it. This is going to fuck everything up with the pixie dust."

I glared over at Morgan and Franklin, who were talking closely. Aden raised a finger to his temple, and Tristian shut his lips.

"They're bringing him out now." He sipped his coffee, turning to me. "Act normal, Lex. Go sit down. Look worried, not pissed, because you look like you're gonna set Morgan on fire the way you're staring at him."

Ella grabbed my hand and pulled me to the chairs. I took a deep breath and sat on the closest chair, crossing my legs and looking at the blank wall across from me.

A shadow fell over me, and I looked up to see Kane Anderson, CEO of Anderson & Ryder, but he didn't look like a CEO today. He was in jeans and a dark-maroon sweater with a collared shirt peeking out beneath.

"No suit today?" I asked.

He shook his head. "Can I sit, Ms. Rose?"

"Sure." I gestured to the chair, and we sat silently for a minute.

I stared into my almost empty coffee cup, unsure what to say, so I asked the most straightforward question, "Why are you here, Kane?"

He stiffened as if I had hit him. "I heard about Sebastian, and I just needed to come down here to ensure everything was okay. I know he didn't do this. I just wanted to see if I could help somehow." He sat with his arms on his knees, running a hand through his hair in a familiar way I had seen before.

I turned to him. "Why do you care what happens to Bash?"

He looked up at me with the truth sitting behind his eyes. "I…"

A door clicked open, and I whipped my head to see Bash walking out with his hands still cuffed. I opened my siren's magic to feel him, and even though he was weak, he held his emotions in check, keeping a wall up. But relief leaked from him when he saw us waiting for him.

He looked exhausted. His skin was gaunt and colorless, his eyes were bloodshot from lack of sleep, and his normally perfectly styled hair was messy and unkempt. The last thing I saw made me gasp, and I narrowed my eyes at Agent Rengard and Hyde. Bash had a light purple bruise forming across his jaw.

Grinding my teeth, I walked over to Tristian and Aden. "You see it, right?"

Tristian grunted in response, and Aden's hands tightened around his cup. "Bastards fucking worked him over, then healed him just enough."

Hyde pushed Bash toward the front, jerking his wrist and un-cuffing him. The officer whispered something in his ear, and Bash looked at him like he was ready to carve him up and hang him out to dry. I started to walk toward him, but a tiny blonde pulled me back and ran at him, wrapping her arms around his neck. He quickly caught Ella and hugged her back, assuring her he was okay as she started to cry again.

Ethan promptly rushed over to take her from Bash, and she sobbed quietly into his shoulder as he comforted her. Morgan was next, clasping his shoulder and talking to him in a low tone, but Bash's eyes found mine. He said something to his father, who looked over at me. Morgan nodded. I waited for him to approach me, unsure where he and I stood at the moment.

Tristian pushed me toward Bash. "Go, Lil' Star."

I looked at Tristian with unshed tears in my eyes.

"Let the world know that you own him."

I opened my mouth and turned back to look at Bash. I started toward him. It felt like it was all in slow motion, but I knew I was running down the hall as I leaped onto him, wrapping my legs around his waist and clasping his neck, bringing my lips down to his in a scorching kiss. I kissed him like I always wanted to. It wasn't sweet, not a chaste kiss at all. I kissed him as if I needed to breathe him into me, his scent still there, that woodsy pine I loved.

I let the tears I had held all evening fall, hugging him tightly. I couldn't even bear the thought of what could have happened tonight if he wasn't who he was.

I pulled back and traced my fingers down his face. "You're okay?"

He nodded. "Yeah, Princess, I'm okay."

He smirked and kissed me again, running his hand to the back of my head, holding me as he searched my mouth with his.

A voice called my name, and I pulled away from Bash to look back at Ella, Ethan, Tristian, and Aden, who each sported huge grins.

"Fucking finally!" Ethan said, throwing his hands into the air.

I laughed. "What do you even mean?" I blushed and buried my face in Bash's chest.

I peeked up through my lashes to see Bash cockily grinning.

"I said fucking finally, you two have been circling each other for years. We've all seen it, and all we have to say is—"

"About goddamn time." Ella smiled like a Cheshire cat.

The heat returned to my face.

Bash brushed my hair to the side and gently lifted my chin. "Nothing to be embarrassed by, Princess, just the entire Providence Village Police Department and my entire family have seen you finally claimed me," he teased.

I laughed and playfully hit his shoulder. "Put me down, Bash."

He grunted and shifted his weight to keep me held in place. "Kind of hard to do," he muttered.

Bash pushed into me a bit more, and I felt all of him against me. Hard, yeah, that was a good word to use. I bit my lip.

"You and I have unfinished business, Princess."

I whispered in his ear, "I think all three of you might have unfinished business with me."

He let out a brassy growl.

Tristian and Aden surrounded us.

"*Frère*." Tristian placed a fist over his heart and bowed his head to show respect for the true leader of his coven.

Aden and Ethan followed suit, and Ella dropped into a curtsey, her head bowed.

"*Le sang de la lune et du ciel protégera notre chemin, et nous suivrons toujours la lumière*," they all said in unison.

I watched with admiration.

Bash smiled down at me. "The blood of the moon and the sky will protect our path, and we will always follow the light. It's our oath. Every Blood Moon Coven member says it when they're accepted into the coven."

I gazed around the room to see other officers and the precinct bowing their heads. The women in the room were all in a curtsey. Even a sex worker who was wasted had their head bowed to Bash. The entire room was showing respect, not to Morgan but to Bash. It was astonishing. This is how a coven should be led. I glanced over to Morgan, who stood with his arms crossed with a glimpse of pride for his son. A sheen of sweat covered Franklin's face, and it seemed as if he was about to be sick with disgust. A scowl further distorted his features.

Kane Anderson walked up to us as Bash let me slide to my feet. Anderson reached out and clasped my hand.

"Sebastian." He released my hand, then extended his to Bash.

Bash, looking a bit shocked, shook his hand. "Kane, I'm not sure why you're here, but…"

Kane shook his head. "I needed to be here to make sure it turned out okay. Look, I know this evening's events have been, well, eventful, but can we talk somewhere less out in the open?"

Sebastian, who looked wrecked, nodded.

I looked over to Ella, giving her an apologetic glance.

She shook her head. "Go. We'll distract anyone who comes looking for you."

I mouthed, "Thank you."

Tristian stretched his arms above his head, yawning. "Like, what is the worst that could happen?"

We all looked at him with raised eyebrows.

"You know what I mean," he said.

"You know you've cursed us now with that logic." I pointed out.

Bash laughed. "Princess, we've been cursed for years, so let the fire rain down on us, because Devils don't burn."

Chapter Four

Bash kissed my temple, and we all speed-walked through the emergency exit doors in the back.

Outside, I saw a small alleyway, and I nodded for everyone to follow me. The alley was full of trash cans, garbage, and muddy water. The smell of old Chinese food lingered in the air around us. Tristian walked around the alley, circling his hands, and a gold spark shone as ancient runes flashed and then disappeared.

I crossed my arms as Aden pulled me under his arm.

"What's Tristian doing?" I asked.

Aden hugged me closer, explaining, "He's placing an illusion spell so anyone who walks by only sees the alley. It's an advanced spell you probably would've learned if you continued your schooling. He's not as strong as a witch, but it will hold for a good thirty minutes."

I looked for Bash, and his arms were crossed, his eyes hard, as he looked out to the alleyway. Tristian finished the spell, his hands waving in an intricate pattern as the shimmer of magic flew around us.

"It's been a long fucking day, Anderson. What do you want?" Bash said in a gruff voice.

Kane walked into the alley, looking at each of us. He threw up his hands in a wide circle and cast a silencing spell around us. It glittered down and enveloped us into what felt like a small bubble. The size of the silence bubble let me know how powerful this man in front of us was, which made me wonder if we might have been standing in front of The Wishmaker himself, and if this was just a sick game he was playing.

He turned to us. "I have an informant who works within Morgan's trusted circle, and he's let me know that he thinks he's found the antidote spell for pixie dust."

We all straightened in surprise.

I stepped toward Anderson. "Where is the antidote?"

Anderson frowned. "Well, that's the problem, you see. It's in an armory buried deep in the earth, protected by a spell so only the worthy can pass. And we need to find the three keys."

I shook my head. "Kane, you're not making any sense. A place, a spell, and keys? Stop being so cryptic. We don't have time for riddles."

He chuckled. "You do have your mother's sass, Ms. Rose."

"Bullshit radar is more like it," I murmured.

Aden huffed out a laugh, and Tristian smirked at me. "She's right, Anderson; lay it out."

He frowned. "Okay, I know you have the coven grimoires that Daniels left you."

I raised an eyebrow. "*And,* pray tell, how do you know this?"

He laughed lightly. "Because I gave them to Daniels to give to you when he was ready, and I had a spell placed upon it to let me know when it was opened."

I tilted my head. "That's what you were doing in the conservatory. You knew about it all—the pixie dust origins from the beginning. But why not just tell us?"

He shrugged. "I needed to know that you weren't corruptible and that you were doing this for the covens, not revenge or power."

I moved closer to my Devils, and Anderson watched us closely. "Is that still the case? Do you want this for power and revenge, or are you ready to better the covens?"

I looked at him with disgust. "You think I only wanted this for vengeance?" He still looked unsure about what I wanted for the covens. I ran my fingers through my hair. "I lost my family, Kane. Then I lost a man who was not only a friend but like a father to me. Now I have coven members going missing and last, the man who I..." I shook my head and continued. "Bash is now being wrongfully accused of killing those people. Yeah, revenge is in the cards, but that's not the 'why.'"

Kane smiled. "Your courage might save us all, Ms. Rose."

"It's not courage, Kane. It's standing up for what's right. You don't need to be brave to do that." He started to open his mouth, but I interrupted him. "So, what do we need to get?"

Looking down at his phone, he pulled up an image to show us. "Here's an image of the three keys."

All of our phones dinged, and we pulled them out to see the picture.

"Three keys? Seems too simple," said Bash sarcastically.

Kane laughed. "Well, it would be if your father didn't have them scattered throughout the city. I have one, and I know your father is in possession of one. The third key's whereabouts are unknown, but some say it's lost in the depths of magic at the bottom of the sea. Even your father doesn't know where it's truly hidden."

"How does he not know?" I asked, feeling the pit of my stomach fill with dread.

Anderson glanced at me. "Because he gave the key to Daniels, and Daniels gave the key to a friend for safekeeping." His voice was low with uncertainty. "I'm unsure if it's true that the third key is truly lost, but it's not on this plane, that I'm sure of. I've searched for it for many years."

Bash crossed his arms, narrowing his eyes. "If my father has possession of one of the keys, we might be out of luck." He rubbed his chin, deep in thought.

Anderson's smile spread across his face in a wicked manner. "Well, lucky for you, young Ryder, I know your father well. I know where he's hidden the key."

Tristian rolled his eyes at Anderson. "You could've led with that, dude."

Aden snickered behind me and murmured, "Fae and their damn dramatics."

Anderson widened his stance and crossed his arms. "Are we done with the interruptions?" His eyes crinkled to keep in a laugh. "As I was saying, my problem is he has it hidden in his vault, and that place is locked up like The Iron Mountain. That's where you come in. I need you to retrieve both keys for me."

Bash snapped his head to Kane. "Why did my father have control of these keys?"

Tristian moved up to my side. "The better question is, *how* did Morgan Ryder get these keys?"

Kane shrugged. "I'm not sure of the why or how, I just know he wanted me to keep one safe with me, so I did."

He pulled a slim old sliver of key out of his breast pocket. The top was ornate and had the Trinity Coven's symbol inlaid in it. "This is one of the keys to the answers you've been searching for. This will help keep all our covens safe."

Aden ran a hand over his face. "I've been to the vaults. There's only one way in and one way out. It'll be nearly impossible to do."

I whispered to Aden, questioning him, "Nearly impossible?"

He grinned at me. "I said nearly, baby, but not impossible." He winked at me, causing me to shake my head at him.

"You know how to get in, don't you?"

Tristian put his arm around my shoulders and whispered, "I told you he's good."

"You're all a bunch of thieves," I teased.

Aden looked up at the night sky and groaned. "We'll need at least

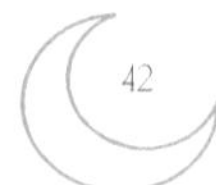

two more people to pull this off."

Tristian wiggled his eyebrows at Aden mischievously. "I know who can help."

"Who?" I asked.

"A half-dragon, half-wolf and his lawyer pup." He kissed my cheek.

I laughed, pushing him away. "Grayson and Hudson?"

Aden clapped Tristian on the shoulder. "That's brilliant, *mon frère*."

Anderson cleared his throat. "Sounds like you have a plan." He placed the silver key in my hand and furrowed his brows. "You promise only to use this for the good of the covens?"

Wrapping my fingers around the key, I looked up at him. "I do, Kane."

The magic of a promise passed between us as he dropped my hand. The silencing spell evaporated around us, and the world returned to focus. He turned and walked into the foggy street.

Bash came to my side. "I'm still not sure if he's friend or foe."

I looked toward Kane's dark shadow disappearing into the foggy clouds. "Me either, but he's our biggest ally against The Wishmaker right now."

Bash wrapped his arm around me, pulling me into his body. "Let's get home, Princess."

I turned and ran my hands over his jaw as I looked up at him. "God, yes, I need a hot shower to get the police-station stink off me and a stiff drink to forget about this day."

Bash bent lower. "Oh, I'll give you something stiff, Princess." He smiled at me like the wolf who had just found Little Red in the woods.

I hit his shoulder. "You're exhausted, Sebastian."

He nuzzled my neck. "Not for you, Princess, never for you."

Aden and Tristian chuckled behind us, and I rolled my eyes. "I want a milkshake. Let's go." I walked away from him, heading back to the street.

"Always thinking of food, aren't you, Lil' Star?" Tristian teased as we walked back.

I threw a finger in the air at him as they followed.

By the time we made it home, the sun had long since set, and the day slipped through our fingers. We all moved in silence like an army back from war. I guess, to an extent, that was what we were doing with the murders, the drugs, and the missing mermaids. We were fighting a war we didn't know if we could win.

I didn't think we could handle many more empty promises, but knowing the entire FBI was looking to blame us for everything that had happened kept me going. I wouldn't let them take us down that easily. Once I unlocked the door, Dyna, my sweet fluffy white cat, curled around our legs.

I picked her up and kissed her furry head. "Hello, my little murder paws." Her purr was deep and comforting as I held her in my arms.

Tristian came in behind me to pet Dyna's soft fur. "I was texting Grayson and Hudson in the car; they wanna meet with us tomorrow. Hudson already has the original building plans for Anderson & Ryder," he said.

Bash huffed out a laugh. "Must be nice to have those connections."

I tilted my head in question to Bash. "Huh? What does that mean?"

Aden closed the door. "Hudson's family is... well, let's say they're high in the criminal circles."

Shock rolled through me. "Like the Mob?"

Tristian took Dyna from my arms; and she curled around him, snuggling down farther. "No, Lil' Star, not *like* the Mob. They *are* the Mob. Al Capone, Lucky Luciano, Meyer Lansky, that kind of mob."

Holy shit. I coughed. "But he's a lawyer..."

Aden chuckled. "Perfect cover. Really, I should have thought of it."

Tristian smiled. "Yeah. Maybe then your family wouldn't be so disappointed in you."

I pointed to Aden. "The Charmantes are one of the most likable families in Providence Village. Even with Aden's bad-boy attitude, he has the town fawning over him every time he walks into a room." I rolled my eyes.

Aden smiled at me. "Are you jealous, baby?"

I huffed. "No, but you can't deny that almost all the women here would spread their legs for you."

He grinned wickedly at me, stalking over to me as if he was a cat on the hunt. He bent his head to my ear, sending a shiver down my spine. "Hmmm, I can't help but think you would like me to spread your thighs in front of Tristian and my brother and let them watch me devour you."

I blushed as I remembered how much I liked that only a few days ago.

I was pulled back against Tristian, who caged my body into his. "And me, Lil' Star?"

My voice came out in a husky whisper. "You're the golden boy, Trist; everyone loves you, but no one knows how cunning you can be. The smile and flirty attitude is nothing but a facade."

I leaned back onto his shoulder as his fingers ran down my stomach. Goose bumps followed the path of his fingertips, sending heat from my neck to my cheeks.

"She's blushing." Bash smirked as he moved in front of me, wrapping his hand in my hair and tilting my head to meet his eyes. "And what about me, Princess? What do the town gossips say about me, huh?"

I looked into his green stare. My breath came out in short spurts. "You are the most dangerous out of the Devils but also the most desirable. They want the power, status, but most of all, the brutal sex you promise. Women want you to destroy them in the bedroom and in life itself." My voice came out so low I didn't recognize it.

He smirked. "Good girl."

Those two little words sent shivers down my back. He released his hold and stepped away from me, chuckling, and my stomach did a little flip.

"Think you have us all figured out then, Princess?" He walked into the kitchen, snatched a bottle of whiskey off the counter, twisted the cap, and took a deep drink from the bottle.

I watched his throat bob up and down as he drank deeply.

I bit my bottom lip. "I don't think anyone knows you, Sebastian. I like to think I know you, though, because a boy shared a secret with me ten years ago that I've never told."

Bash looked over at me as he poured a glass of amber liquid. As he sipped from the cup, he stared at me over the rim. "Well, Princess, sorry to inform you, but ten years was a long time ago. We've all changed since then."

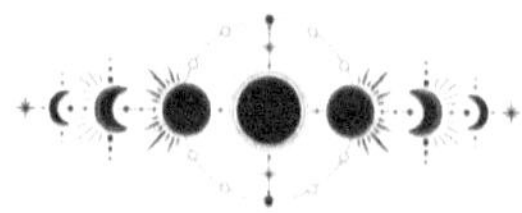

Ten years ago, on my sixteenth birthday, Ella was passed out on the bed with a bottle of Calypso Water and a whole bag of Cyprus chips. John Hughes's movie *Sixteen Candles* played in the background, and I smiled when Molly Ringwald walked out to see Jake by the shiny red car.

"Fuck, damn it, shit, shit, *shhhhhhhhh!*"

I peeked through Ella's slightly open door and saw a very drunk Bash walking by, swaying back and forth. I snickered as he stumbled and fell to his knees.

"Ouch," he groaned and fell forward on his face.

I walked to the door and threw it open. "Bash? You good?"

He rolled onto his back. "Helloooo, pretty mermaid."

I raised an eyebrow. "I'm a siren, idiot. What the hell? You smell like goblin's breath."

I reached out to help him, slipping my arms under him and lifting him. His body was heavy against mine, but the warmth made

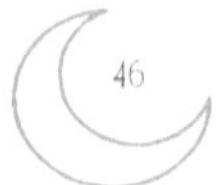

my heart skip a beat.

I set him into a sitting position as he drunkenly sang, "Part of your world."

I laughed, nudging him. "Okay, okay, vamp boy, come on, I'll help you to your room."

He was already six foot two, and I stood at five foot four. I wasn't sure how I'd manage, but if Morgan found him like this, I knew the punishment would be far worse than the hangover he deserved.

Through a glossy smile, he muttered, "You're so damn beautiful."

I blushed at his remark. "Bash, come on, you're drunk. You probably think I'm someone else."

He humphed. "Not that drunk, Lexi Rose." He booped my nose. "You're one of the most beautiful girls I've ever seen. You're the stars, and I'm the sun, never going to be able to touch you."

He sighed as he stood. I held on to him to steady him, and he pulled me under his arm. He smelled like the forest at night, woods with a sweet, crisp, clean scent.

"Let's get you to bed, okay? You'll forget this in the morning, but I'll mock you relentlessly about it."

He half smiled. "Maybe... but it doesn't make it less true."

We made our way down the hall, and he opened his room. I had never been in Bash's room, but it wasn't what I expected. I always imagined his room to be messy—with clothes everywhere and unkept—but it was far from that.

Exposed brick comprised one wall with a king-size bed in the center. The bed had a modern headboard and was neatly made with gray and black sheets. Next to it stood a nightstand bearing an industrial lamp and a journal that had been set aside. A small nook was set up on the other side of the room, with shelves full of books and a desk in the center with an open laptop. He had a small leather couch on the other side, where a large TV was attached to the wall, and a game console sat with the controllers laid out neatly.

It was immaculate and organized. I managed to drag him over

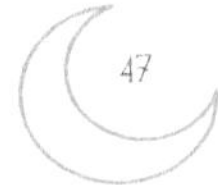

to the couch.

"There ya go, big guy."

"Thanks, Princess."

A book lay open on his bed, and I picked it up. "*The Art of War*?"

He ran a hand over his face. "It's good."

I walked over and smiled. "Will you read it to me?"

He looked shocked, and I was, too. Was I really asking him to read to me?

His face scanned mine, and he opened his mouth. "Lexi..."

I shook my head. "It's okay. I don't know what made me say that. I'm going to go now. Can you not mention this to Ella? I don't want her to think I have a crush on her older brother, not that I do. I just thought... Okay, I'm going to shut up now." My face heated with a blush.

"Bring me the book, Princess. It'll sober my ass up anyways."

I smiled, took the book over, and sat on the other side of the couch.

He picked it up and started to read. "'If you know the enemy and know yourself, you need not fear the result of a hundred battles. If you know yourself but not the enemy, for every victory gained, you will also suffer a defeat. If you know neither the enemy nor yourself, you will succumb in every battle.'"

I closed my eyes and listened to him read. I drifted off to sleep but woke up a little while later and found him sitting at his desk. "What are you still doing up?"

He turned to me. "Come here."

I walked over to him, and he reached out, pulling me until I straddled his lap. "Sebastian, what the...?"

He shushed me and wrapped his hands in my hair, bringing me down to him. His lips were soft as they carefully brushed mine. I felt him harden underneath me, and my breath hitched as he pressed up to me.

"Sebastian."

He pulled back, smiling. "Happy birthday, Princess."

I smiled back as he pulled me closer and kissed me intensely. His tongue separated my lips as he deepened the kiss. I moaned into him, wrapping my arms around his neck as he stood and walked us over to his bed. He laid me down, kissing his way down my throat.

"Bash, we need to stop."

He pulled away. "Yeah, we should. I don't want this to go further than you want it to."

I leaned up and kissed his lips lightly. "I just meant Ella will be up soon and looking for me. It might be weird to find her best friend in bed with her older brother."

He laughed. "True. Let's keep it quiet for a while."

"I like that idea." I smiled and kissed him again. "Will I see you later?"

He nodded, rolling onto his back. "I'll text you later."

I walked to the door. "You are the Devil. You know that?" I laughed.

"*Your* Devil, Lexi."

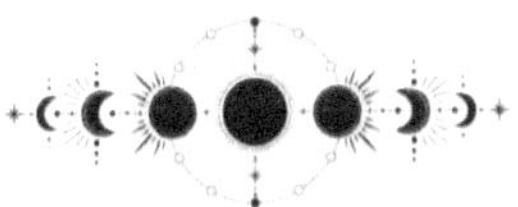

I pulled myself from the memory and touched my lips, still remembering that first kiss. I watched him take a drink from the crystal tumbler, still trapped in Tristian's arms, knowing he was thinking the same thing with the fire behind his eyes.

"You want him, don't you, Lil' Star?" Tristian breathed against my neck.

A shiver sent a shock straight down my stomach. I now knew why other fae became addicted to vampires. They were more addicting than a siren.

Tristian chuckled against my throat. "Your heart is beating faster than a hummingbird's. What are you thinking about?"

I shook my head. "Nothing." I pulled myself from Tristian's arms and gave Bash a coy smile. "Just a memory from a lifetime ago. I'm gonna go change," I said to the room.

I walked into my bathroom, trying to expel the thoughts from ten years ago, but I felt myself grow hot with every step. In the mirror, I saw the heat rise to my face, and my pupils dilated, turning violet.

"Get it together, Lexi," I said as I splashed water on my face to cool myself down.

I was drying off my face when I caught a figure leaning against the doorframe through the mirror. I jumped, but when I saw it was Aden, I threw the towel at him over my shoulder.

He let out a light chuckle. "You know you're adorable when you're flustered, right?"

I glared at him and stuck out my tongue.

"I see how you look at Bash; you two have been drawn to each other ever since I've known you. I was jealous of you two when we were younger. I wanted you to look at me the way you looked at him."

I pressed my lips together. "How did I look at him?" I asked, unsure if I wanted to hear the answer.

He moved closer to me. "Like you would set the world on fire for him."

I looked down as he embraced me, and heat raced down to my stomach. "What changed? How did you... why aren't you jealous now?"

He was silent for a moment, but then he rested his chin on my shoulder, and his voice came out in a whisper. "Because he's my brother, my *frère*, and I've never seen him more infatuated with anyone; even after everything he did to you, baby, after what we all did, he never stopped protecting you. From afar, he watched you. He would ask Ella how you were, and when you were in a situation where you might have run into him, he stayed away. He knew what we did hurt you, and I watched for ten years as his regret slowly killed him on the inside. I knew then he loved you. It doesn't excuse what we did, but I think it'll help you understand Bash's reasoning now. I would've put my happiness aside for my brothers, but, Lexi, there was never anyone serious, not for Bash. I think he was always waiting for you."

I looked at him through the mirror. "Waiting for me?" I whispered.

Sebastian Ryder didn't do relationships. He fucked. Girls were on a consistent rotation for him, but from what I knew, he never committed to any of them except for me. He was waiting for me the whole time, and my heart thumped harder in my chest. Sebastian Ryder was in love with me this whole time, and I think I might have been in love with him too.

He kissed my temple. "Baby, none of us have ever wanted or needed someone like you. We would have our assignments from Morgan, then we drank, partied, and fucked, but we never had relationships or any friendships besides the three of us. It's been just us three for so long. Bash had Ella, but he protected her from everything. She and I had Ethan, but my brother isn't the same as Trist or Bash. Then you came back into our lives and wrecked our souls to the core, and we fell under your spell."

I turned in his arms, wrapping mine around his neck. "Aden, you know I would never use my song like that, right?"

He smiled and kissed my nose. "We know. We choose to fall for your song willingly, little siren." He bent down and kissed my lips lightly, then trailed feather kisses down my neck.

I moaned as his tongue licked around my throat. But reality came crashing in when I was hit with a realization. "You all need blood, don't you?"

He pulled away. "I don't. I got yours the other day, so I'm filled up. I'm just being greedy because your blood is like the perfect mix of spicy and sweet. Tristian and Bash might need a fill-up. Bash, for sure. Did you see how pale his skin is?"

I nodded. Bash didn't have Aden's beautiful olive tone. He was gaunt, his cheeks a touch hollow, and the white of his skin looked sickly.

"Send him in here. I'll feed him. Tristian can... he can find someone if he wants." The jealousy ripped through me as I said it.

Aden raised his eyes. "I don't think he would, but I'll let him know."

I took a deep breath. "Send Bash back, then."

He unwrapped his arms from me and kissed me lightly one more time. "You got it, Lex, but I want extra cuddles for giving you up." He winked at me.

I shook my head, laughing. "Just go get Bash, please."

I found a pair of lacy cotton shorts and a matching crop top. I pulled my long chestnut hair into a bun on top of my head as I brushed my teeth, washed my face, and removed the day from my skin. Once I was done, I found Bash in the bedroom pulling his shirt off. I followed the perfect sculpt of his shoulders from his arms to his abs, each one perfectly stacked, and the V that directed the way to...

"Lexi?" His voice broke through my reverie.

I shook my head. "Yeah, what's up?"

He laughed. "Aden said you wanted to see me."

I cleared my throat. "You need to feed."

He shook his head. "I'm fine. I can find someone tomorrow."

"No!" I growled.

His eyebrows shot up in surprise. "No?"

I nodded. "No, you're my... you need to feed, so you'll do it from me."

I crossed my arms, preparing for a fight. He moved to sit on the bed, staring at me.

"Come here, Lexi."

I stepped between his legs. "I want to feed you, Bash. I don't want you to have anyone else's blood in you. I want to be the reason you feel powerful."

I straddled his lap, and he looked up at me as I tilted my head to the side, giving him permission. I felt his control slip.

He pulled me closer to him, his hands holding me firmly against his body. "Thank you, Princess."

He gripped my chin and softly placed a kiss on my lips. Then he trailed light kisses along my neck, and my body shuddered. I ran my fingers through his hair, loving the feather softness. As he sucked and kissed the tender spot behind my ear, I let out a soft moan. His grip tightened around my hips as he moved against me.

I hissed at his hardness beneath me, teasing me through my tiny shorts. The sweet sensations flooding me provided the perfect distraction before he struck. His fangs sank deep into my throat as he took greedy pulls, never stopping the friction between us. I gasped, and my fingers tightened in his hair, gripping the silky strands.

"Bash! Oh god…"

It felt amazing how he took and pulled from me. The ecstasy from a vampire's bite was like flying through the clouds. It was more intimate than sex. It was like having your two souls combined into one. A rumble came from his chest as he drew more of my blood into his mouth. A trickle escaped and ran down my throat into the valley of my breasts.

He pulled away quickly and healed my neck with his tongue. I could only pant as my desire for him grew. He focused on the blood trailing down my throat and chest.

"I made a mess," he snarled as he reached for a towel to clean it up, but I grabbed his hand.

"Clean it up then, Sebastian."

His eyes looked up in surprise, and he flipped us quickly. I landed on my back, looking up at the ceiling. He pulled my shirt off and licked the blood from my navel to my breast, pulling my nipple into his mouth as his hand trailed down my side to between my legs.

I arched into his hand and ran my hands along his back. I groaned at his touch, tightening one hand on his bicep. "Bash, please…."

He pushed my legs farther apart and ran his fingers up my inner thigh. I shivered from his touch.

He reached under my shorts, tracing my underwear with his fingers, and groaned. "Princess, you're killing me." He pushed two fingers into me and found me slick with need. "So fucking ready for me."

I arched my back as he tugged one of my nipples with his teeth, and I let out a whimper. I needed him now, and I was tired of dancing around us. I had my Devil back, and it was time for me to claim what was mine. Sebastian Ryder had been mine since the first day I met him. It just took us years to get here.

I pushed him slightly, and he sat up, removing his fingers. I immediately missed them but tugged on his boxers, freeing him. He was hard and ready for me. I moved back to the bed's edge and stood up.

He growled at me. "Where are you going, Princess?"

I turned back to him, pushing my shorts down and standing naked in front of him with a slight smile. "Coming?"

He shot up from the bed, a grin across his face. "Oh, I think you'll be coming first, Princess, probably lots of times on my fingers, lips, and with me inside of you." I let out a laugh. He gazed down at me, a look of worry on his face, and he traced where he had bitten me. "You're not weak, Princess."

"Should I be?" I bit my lip.

"Even some of the more powerful fae are weak after one of us takes their blood. It usually takes them a day or two to regain their strength."

"The only thing weak is my knees, Bash." I pulled him into the bathroom and turned on the shower.

He came up from behind, wrapping his arms around me and kissing my hair. "God, you're fucking beautiful."

Surprising me, he turned me around and lifted me, and I locked my legs around his waist as he kissed me the way he had in the police station, without any caution. It was hard, brutal, and what he needed. I pushed my tongue into his mouth, pulling his hair back, trying to taste every part of him. He moved us to the shower, letting the warm water fall over our bodies. Our kisses were frantic. He devoured me like a starving man and pushed me against the tile wall. His hands clasped my ass, shifting me so I could feel how hard he was. He growled into my neck.

"You need more, don't you?" I asked.

He shook his head. "I need you, Princess."

He moved to line himself up with me.

"Then take it, Bash. Claim me."

A pound on the door made us jump, and I groaned, "Nooo..."

Bash cursed. "We're busy! Fuck off!"

"It's your father." Tristian's voice came through the door.

"I'll call him back in an hour; I'm busy!" Bash bellowed.

"He's here, *frère*."

I sighed in disappointment as Bash froze before dropping me to the ground. His head fell against mine, and he kissed me softly. "Princess, I promise our time is coming."

I smirked as I got an idea. "Hey, Trist!"

"Yes, Lil' Star?"

I gave Bash a coy smile as he looked at me curiously. "Stall for ten minutes."

Tristian's laughter faded away as I sank to my knees.

Bash looked down and cupped my face. "Ten minutes?"

I gazed up at Bash through my lashes. "Better be quick," I teased as I grasped him in my hands, pumping him slowly.

He let out a needy moan and dropped his head back. I wrapped my mouth around the tip of his cock and let out a hum. Moving slowly, I sucked him down and curled my tongue around him.

He let out a string of curses.

"Lexi... shit..."

I moved back up and sucked gently on the end of his cock before pulling back. I sat back on my knees and grinned up at him. "Yes?" I batted my eyelashes innocently.

"Oh no, Princess, get that beautiful mouth back on me."

A husky laugh escaped me, and I kissed his tip, then swallowed him whole. Bash pulled my bun loose and ran his hands through my hair.

"Baby, I won't last long..."

I hummed in response as I sucked harder, moving my hands up

his thighs and wrapping my hand around him, moving up and down. I pulled him farther into my mouth. As I took his velvety shaft in as far as I could, his cock slipped into the back of my throat. I was so turned on that I moaned and was dying for him to have me so we could finally finish what we had started.

Bash began to push farther into my throat, his hands wrapped around my hair as he guided me up and down. He became larger with each thrust.

"Princess, god, do you see what you do to me?"

His thrusts became more frantic with each push. I started to taste his lust on my tongue, and I pushed back and slid my lips off him. He stared down at me in frustration.

I moved closer and whispered, "Do it, Bash. I know you want to."

His eyes were ablaze and blood red. "Princess…" He moaned and pulled my head back down as he pushed back into my mouth, and I took all of him in.

I pressed so close to him that it was hard to breathe. Then he moved rapidly, and all I could do was hold onto him.

"Lexi, I can't hold out much longer."

That was all the warning I got before he came with a roar and spilled himself down my throat. I had to rub my thighs together to ease the ache. I was two seconds away from saying screw it, pulling him from this shower back into my bed, and spending the rest of the night there.

Bash bent down, wrapping his arms around me to help me stand. I leaned into his smooth chest. We stood there for a minute before he lifted my head to him, cupping my cheeks. He held me gently, caressing my face with his thumbs.

"We can't go back. You know that, right, Princess? Because I'll walk through fire for your body, heart, and soul."

He kissed me deeply, and the thundering pounding returned.

"He's threatening to send Franklin in. Bash, get out here!" Aden yelled through the door.

I laughed and pulled a towel around me. "Okay, okay, we're coming!"

Bash smirked. "Already have, Princess," he teased as he wrapped a towel around his hips. I smacked his arm as he pulled me closer to him. "Shall we go see what Lord Douchery wants?"

I laughed as I dried off and tugged on leggings and a sweatshirt. "Was that a joke, Sebastian Ryder?"

Bash slipped on gray sweats and pulled a shirt over his head. "I got jokes," he said cockily.

"Says the grumpy vampire."

He came up behind me and wrapped his arms around me. "I'm still a grumpy vampire, Princess, but you just let me take your blood and then fuck your beautiful throat, so I'm in a good mood."

He wrapped his fingers around my neck, pulling me closer to him, and I moaned as I pushed myself against him. "Sebastian Ryder, you're a tease."

He chuckled and let go of me. "Let's go see what Lord Douchery wants." He bowed, sweeping his arms out for me. "After you, Princess, and once he's said what he wants, I'm bringing you back here and making you truly realize why they call me a Devil."

His eyes were alight with fire, and I knew he would make good on that promise.

We walked out to the living room, where we found Aden in the corner looking lethal and Franklin wiping his nose where a trickle of blood fell.

I lifted my gaze and looked at Morgan. "What's going on?"

Morgan turned to me. "Nothing. Franklin was just trying to explain to Aden why it's important to stay focused on the task at hand and not be distracted by other things or people." He gave me a pointed look.

I smiled sweetly at Franklin and used what Coco would call a "customer-service voice." I walked over to Franklin. "Sure, Franklin, I can see how that might bother you. It must be hard only jerking off to pictures of Morgan every day and not getting the real thing, but you're in *my* home. If you talk to anyone like that in my home again, I'll rip your throat out and feed it to the sharks. Mmkay?" I gently patted his face as he snarled at me.

I felt my Devils focus their attention on Franklin, and not in a cheerful way. "Careful what you say next, Franky. You don't want to piss anyone off," Tristian said casually, leaning against the wall and cleaning his nails with a knife.

"Sebastian, I spoke with the lawyer, and he agrees it would be best to stop your investigation now that you're a murder suspect."

Sebastian, who was eerily quiet, snapped his gaze to his father. "You're joking, right?"

Morgan sighed, pinching his nose. "Son, look, just lay off for a few days and stay out of trouble. Maybe even go to a few coven meetings and show them what the new leader will look like when you take my place. Show a united front so we don't lose any favor within the coven. Since you and Cassandra called your relationship quits, maybe you can spend time with the other members and show them what it's like to be loyal to us."

Sebastian's posture straightened, and mischief flickered in his eyes. "Isn't there a meeting in a few days?"

Morgan perked up. "Yes, Tristian is letting us hold the meetings at Belladonna, his new speakeasy."

Bash looked to Tristian, who seemed to be in on the idea, because he smiled with a sly glint in his eyes.

"Thank you, Tristian, that is so kind of you."

Tristian smiled like he was on the hunt. "Yeah, man, no problem. *Mi casa es su casa.*"

Morgan clapped Bash on the back. "Great! You'll come with me to the meeting then, and after, we can have dinner with Ella. Nice family night."

With the mention of Ella, Bash perked up more and turned to his dad, giving him a huge smile. "Perfect. Anything else?"

Morgan looked at his watch. "No, and best be on our way, Franklin."

Bash walked his father to the door as Franklin followed, uncrossing his arms and scowling at me.

Franklin turned and bowed his head slightly to me. "Always a pleasure, Ms. Rose."

I narrowed my eyes at him and flipped him the finger. "Go jump off a cliff, you scummy worm."

Franklin stormed up to me, a sneer on his face as he hissed in a whisper, "Tell me something, Ms. Rose. How does it feel to please all three of the Devils? I bet you can handle the three of them quite nicely."

A knife whizzed past Franklin's head and lodged in the wall beside us, barely skimming his cheek. A thin line of thick, dark, sluggish blood ran down his face, and he turned in shock to Tristian, who was staring at his phone.

"Oh no, did that slip, Franky? I really should remember that arm spasm I recently developed. It's weird. You know, it only happens when slimy frogs start talking and getting close to my Lil' Star." Tristian grinned evilly at Franklin, and shock crossed the man's face when he realized that my Devils would kill for me if needed.

Franklin straightened his jacket and glared. "Good evening. And I'll remember this, Devils. One day, your blood will pour, and I will bathe in it." He slammed the door, and we all stood silent before I started smiling like an idiot.

"Bash, you're brilliant."

Tristian glanced between us. "What are you talking about, Lil' Star?"

I turned to him. "The meeting. That's when we'll hit the armory. It's genius." Aden's smile broke through at the same time Tristian's did. "While all the higher-ups are wining and dining across town, they'll never know we're breaking in. It's just crazy enough to work, and you have an alibi." I grabbed four crystal glasses and moved over to the bar. After pouring the Dragon Whiskey, I handed one to each Devil. "To robbing Morgan Ryder!"

I laughed to a ring of cheers as we clicked our glasses together. I chuckled quietly, and all three turned to me.

"What?" Tristian tilted his head in question, and Bash looked at me in a confused daze.

I laughed louder. Aden doubled over in laughter, too.

"She's fucking lost it, *frère*," Tristian said to Bash.

Bash pulled me to him. "No, she's just the perfect kind of crazy for us."

He kissed my head as I continued to laugh at the ridiculous luck that dropped into our laps.

CHAPTER FIVE

The next few days passed as we laid out our plan to search for the key in Morgan's vault. Grayson and Hudson examined floor plans and worked to find exit strategies. Aden and Tristian spent time scoping out the building, writing down shift changes, and looking for any weaknesses we could use to our advantage.

Luckily for me, I was in charge of research with the help of Ella, Ethan, Anderson, and his assistant, Camille. Camille was sweet, but she kept flirting with Sebastian every time she stopped by with a folder of info for us. I wrapped myself in his arms to ensure she backed the hell off.

One day, she came in wearing a short black dress and dark-red lipstick, her curly hair cascading down her back. Bash was sitting at the bar in the kitchen when she strolled over and handed him a floor plan. She leaned so far forward that her breasts were about to spill out as she whispered something into his ear.

"Oh, hell no! Two can play this game," I whispered, moving from the hallway into the kitchen. I walked up behind Bash, wrapped my arms around his neck, and kissed his cheek. "Do you need anything, my Devil?" I whispered in a purr.

He took my hands and kissed them, trying to hide his growing grin. "No, little siren, but later, I can think of a few things."

Camille narrowed her eyes at me for a second, then leaned forward. "Think about the offer, Sebastian. I would love to see you at the party. Of course, it's Blood Moon only."

My eyes shifted as the lavender haze grew across my vision. I hissed low between my teeth as they begged to elongate.

"You better leave, Camille," Grayson said sternly as he pulled me back and walked me over to the dining room table, putting distance between Camille and me.

She looked up and saw my face. A flash of fear crossed through her, and she gathered her purse.

Hudson moved in front of me, putting a barrier between me and her.

"See you tomorrow with those files, Sebastian," she said in a hurry as she walked out the door.

Grayson held me tighter, and Hudson grinned down at me.

"Easy, little seductress..." Grayson said with a laugh.

I muttered, "I swear, I might rip her damn hand off next time."

Hudson laughed. "They say wolves are possessive, but don't mess with a siren and what she puts a claim on."

I folded my arms and glared up at him. "I swear, Hudson, I'll make you cry for your momma like a little pup."

He gave me a crooked smile. "Down, siren, down."

Bash walked over and looked at me with a frown. "What's wrong?"

I shook my head. "Nothing."

I walked away to the large table where we had set up shop with floor plans, computers, and slim black cases with fun spy gadgets. It was all very *Mission Impossible*.

I bent over the table, studying the floor plans for the vault. "The only elevator to get in is here. Are you sure Steve is okay to pull this off? He has a family, and I don't want anything to happen to him."

Bash brushed my hair off my shoulder. "Anderson's using him that day for security, so they will be away from the office. Camille as well."

I rolled my eyes. "She can stay. Maybe we could even lock her in the vault."

Bash looked at me with raised brows. "Princess, is that a tinge of green I see in your eyes?"

I huffed but didn't say more.

"Lexi."

I looked up at him, and he gazed at me with soft eyes.

"You know there isn't anyone else, Princess, only you. It was always you." He ran his knuckles down my cheek and turned me to face him. "Need me to prove it?"

I pushed away from him slightly so I was out of reach. "It's part of my siren. I get possessive about my... *belongings*."

I turned back to look at the vault's intricate doors and passageways where, if we weren't careful, we would wander around until we were lost.

He laughed, moving behind me and placing light kisses on my neck. "So, I belong to you, then? Just an object of your desire to play with?"

I let a small moan escape and leaned back into his body. "Hmm, no, you're my very hot belonging, my Devil. With magical fingers and lips." His teeth scraped my neck, and I bit my lip, needing his fingers on me. "Fuck, Sebastian." I reached up and wrapped my fingers into his hair to pull him closer.

"Greedy, greedy, greedy, Princess." He continued to suck and kiss my neck, his fingers trailing my arms. I pushed my ass into him, feeling him getting harder, and a whimper escaped me. He bit my neck playfully. "We have guests, Princess. Stop," he whispered.

I huffed. "One day." I sighed, moving away from him. "I hate this," I whispered.

"Me too," Bash said as he kissed my cheek.

I looked around and felt the blush rise.

Hudson pointedly ignored us by staring at his laptop, but Grayson's eyes were locked on me with a hint of amusement as I walked around the table to put space between us.

I cleared my throat. "Aden needs to work on the lock. Do we know what kind of vault we're looking at?"

Bash shifted his pants and sat down. "Anderson will give it to us tomorrow. He said they use magic, so it'll likely need a witch to open it."

"Bastard needs to hurry," Grayson muttered.

Bash nodded in agreement. "I'll stay here until I have to go to the meeting at the Belladonna."

I frowned at him. "How are you going to stay in communication with us?"

He gave me his cockiest smile. "Don't worry, Princess. I'll be able to hear you, just not see you all unless I can get to Tristian's office. I'll be able to stay in contact with you, and you'll be with me on all fronts. I don't want to lose any of you down there."

Aden walked in and sensed the sexual tension in the air between Bash and me. He looked over to Bash. "What's going on?"

Bash shook his head slightly. "Nothing, *frère*, just a little green beast coming from our siren."

Aden rolled his eyes. "Camille always wants one of us. Nothing new, baby. We only have eyes for you."

Bash's phone dinged. "I got the micro-cameras that you wanted. They'll be delivered today. I'll be able to hear what's going on. I'll monitor the cameras Steve gave us access to once you're in, too."

Aden snickered. "Good. I'm going to go set these up. Give him hell, Lex."

He picked up the small slim case that contained the micro-cameras, walked over, kissed my cheek, and headed outside again.

I looked at the floor plans, memorizing the exits and any place

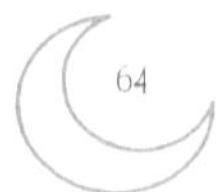

where we could find spots to hide a piece of equipment. Tristian had been going in and out of the building for business all week, scoping the ins and outs. We'd been running on little sleep, diving into planning the heist to get the key from Morgan.

I knew Bash feared what would happen if he had to take control of the coven. He would have to fight for his spot against Morgan. It was the way of the fae. When two fae were equally as powerful as each other, they would have to challenge one another for the seat of coven leader. It was usually a match of not only skill but also wit. It usually ended with someone's death. From what I could tell, Bash and Morgan were equally matched, but that didn't stop the deep primal fear that sat in the pit of my stomach—knowing that one day soon, Bash would have to challenge Morgan for his spot as a coven leader.

I turned to Hudson. "This is going to be a bigger problem, isn't it?"

He looked up, his intense gaze meeting mine. "You have no clue, siren. This shakes our morals and codes to the ground. Covens are supposed to be run equally. Morgan has taken these keys as a bargaining chip."

I ran my fingers over the blueprints and cross-referenced each key, trying to figure out the *why* behind it all. I looked at Bash. His shoulders were tense, and his face was set in determination.

"Why would he want the keys if he doesn't plan on using them?" I whispered under my breath.

Bash heard me and laughed. "Power, Princess. The one who holds all the keys holds power over the covens. It's always about power with Morgan Ryder." Shaking his head, he went and fixed another cup of coffee.

Bash closed his eyes and sighed. He looked exhausted. I glanced up at the clock. It was late already, and I knew he was running on little to no sleep right now. He would stay up working long after we were asleep and then only come to rest for a few hours before waking early the next day to start all over again.

"Bash, you gotta get some sleep."

He waved me off, and I looked to Grayson for some backup.

"Hey, if the vamp boy wants to go to sleep and leave you with me, I'm fine with that."

A throaty grunt came from Bash.

I threw up a hand. "Bash, you need sleep..."

Bash glared at me in a way that would scare the shit out of any normal fae, but good thing I wasn't normal. "No fucking way, Princess."

I marched up to him, my hands on my hips, and tilted my head back to look up at him. "Okay, Mr. Grumpy Pants, that's it. If you don't sleep now, I swear I'll sing you into a goddamn dream state."

He sipped his coffee, glaring right back at me. "You're a pain in the ass, Rose."

I smirked. "I'm *your* pain in the ass, so now, go."

He placed his coffee down on the table with an irritable huff. I bit my lip to keep a laugh from escaping. He walked over to me and lifted me up. It took me by surprise, and I laughed. His hands tightened around my butt, and I instinctively wrapped my legs around his waist.

"Now look who's jealous," I teased and kissed the tip of his nose. He grumbled under his breath about Grayson and his stupid Southern charm. I shook my head and leaned it against his. "Go, Bash. We'll keep working. Three hours of sleep won't hurt you."

"Fine," he said with a roll of his eyes.

"Okay, good. Now, put me down."

He grinned evilly. "Not a chance, Princess."

He captured my lips and kissed me hard, forcing my mouth open with his. His kiss was full of lust and want. I could feel his emotions moving through him, dying to escape. The lust was so powerful, it simmered beneath the surface, his skin warming at my touch. He pulled me closer, wanting more. His kisses were fervent. I moaned into his mouth, wishing I could join him in the bedroom as well.

Bash pulled back with an arrogant grin. "Good night, Princess," he said as he dropped me to the ground.

I moved my hair away from my face and looked up at him. "Now *that* was a good-night kiss."

He smirked and turned his back to me, whipping his shirt off his narrow waist and broad shoulders. "Good night, Princess. I'll dream of you."

I sat down, breathless and a bit wobbly.

"Damn." Hudson whistled. "That boy has it bad."

I touched my mouth and smiled. "Yeah, I think we both do."

Grayson looked over at me. An uncomfortable moment passed between us and filled the room. "Sebastian, huh?"

I bit my swollen lip. "It's... well, we have history... we all do."

Grayson arched his eyebrows. "All?" He laughed and clapped his knee. "Wait, you gotta be shitting me. You're with *all* of the Devils?"

My lips popped open. "Ummm, it sorta, I mean, it just kind of happened. Hell, I didn't even know it was happening until it did." I blushed, headed to the kitchen, and looked around for Dyna to give her dinner.

My fluffy white monster walked into the living room, looking over at me like, "Yeah, girl, three dudes, that's on you," as she circled Hudson's legs.

"Shouldn't cats hate you, wolf boy?"

Hudson laughed. "Wolf boy?"

I shrugged and gave him a small smile.

"I guess they should, but for some reason, I love cats. I have three of my own at home. My partner, Wes—"

I raised an eyebrow. "Wes?"

Hudson's face flushed. "Yeah, he's a witch, mostly air magic." He waved his hand. "He says two are his familiars, but they hang around me most of the time, so I guess they're mine, too."

His smile grew sweet when speaking about Wes. His shield dropped, and his emotions brushed my skin. I felt his love for his partner and saw it in his eyes. He picked Dyna up, placed her on his

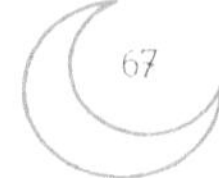

lap, and rubbed her ears as she purred loudly at him. I only hoped that one day I would find someone who looked that way when they spoke about me.

The front door opened, and Aden and Tristian walked in arguing. "You are so wrong. If we go in from the east side, we'll have an easier time finding the vault."

Aden was fuming. "Tristian, *frère*, if you don't shut the hell up, I swear I'll pound you until you're nothing but a bloody mess."

Tristian walked up to me and bent me back into a dip. He smiled wildly. "Hello, beautiful."

I gasped a laugh and slapped his chest lightly. "Tristian, stand me back up."

He leaned closer. "Ahh, Lil' Star. You're gonna hurt my feelings." He righted me but kept a hand on my hip. "Okay, I'll forgive you. For a kiss."

He wiggled his eyebrows at me and leaned in, puckering his lips. I put my hand up and laughed as I danced away.

"Never!"

I raced around to Aden, hiding behind him. He smirked and crossed his arms. "Come and try to get her, douche. I'd love to see you try to take her from me."

His cocky smile made me poke him in the side.

"Hey! I'm not just some possession you two can fight over." I smacked Aden's arm playfully.

Aden lifted me up and grinned. "We don't own you, but baby, you own us, and you know what they say about dogs fighting over bones?"

I laughed. "Put me down, you big asshat."

He kissed the tip of my nose and set me back down. I blushed as I walked over to the sofa, Tristian looking at me like I was his prey.

I leaned toward him, giving him a flirtatious smile. "Did you have a good day at the office today, dear?"

Hudson chuckled as he picked up Dyna, rubbing her soft fur. "You sound like a 1950s housewife."

I laughed. "Never. I'm a strong, independent woman," I said.

I stretched out on the sofa, yawning, as Aden sat down and put my head in his lap.

Tristian rounded the couch and bent down, kissing my lips lightly. "It was good. I think I have an idea of how we'll get in, but you might not like it. Bash will hate it, but I think it might work." He tapped his chin as he considered his plan.

I raised an eyebrow at him. "What is it?"

He kissed me softly. "You, you're the key to it all." He wiggled his eyebrows up and down.

I smiled, laughing. "That was cheesy as hell."

"It worked, though, didn't it?" His eyes sparkled with mischief.

I shook my head and closed my eyes for a minute as Aden ran his hands down my hair. "Sleep, Lil' Star, we got you."

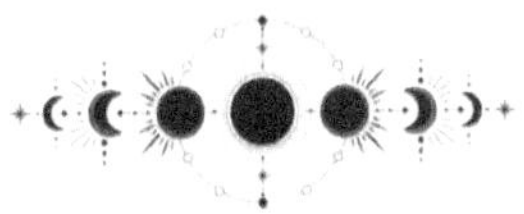

I woke up hours later in a dark room with my head tucked on a warm chest, a heavy arm wrapped around my waist, and a powerful leg tangled around mine. We had become a big puppy dog pile. I looked up into Aden's face. The harsh scowl he wore most of the time was noticeably absent. He looked younger, like the world hadn't damaged him yet.

I kissed his chest and listened to his heavy breathing.

"Fuck, what time is it?" A grumble came from behind me as Tristian reached across me and looked at the clock. I turned in to his arms.

"Shhhh, five more minutes of cuddles, then the real world and its bullshit."

He snickered. "Mmm, I can't say no to that." He wrapped both

arms around me, pulling me to his chest. I inhaled his soap, wood, and sweet vanilla scent. "Did you sleep well, Lil' Star?" he whispered and kissed my head.

I snuggled down into his chest and sighed. "Yes, I guess we all needed it. Grayson and Hudson?"

He smirked. "They went home to get some rest as well. I think Grayson is jealous of us."

I lifted my head and looked at Tristian. "I did see him looking at us, but why do you say that?"

Looking down at me, Tristian brushed my hair away from my face. "Because of the way he watches you. He watches you as we do."

I tried to remember the little touches we shared, how he flirted with me, and how I teased back. I was a siren, so it was natural, but I never thought it was more than a bit of fun.

I frowned and looked across the darkened room, worried I had given him the wrong impression. Grayson was handsome and powerful and the leader of one of the most powerful covens, but did I think anything more of him than beyond a friendship?

"You're thinking hard, Lil' Star. Should we be worried, or do you want to add a fourth to our group? Are the three of us not enough for your appetite?"

I looked up at him. "I... I don't know. As of right now, all three of you are a lot of work, but Grayson is a friend and an ally. I don't want to cause a rift with him and the covens."

He laughed. "Says a siren full of emotions."

I hit him playfully. "Hey!"

He pulled my hand into his and kissed the back. "Don't worry, Lexi. We don't mind sharing you among the three of us. Now, a fourth would be something we would need to talk about. For so many years, it's just been us, so sharing you seems natural to us. It's easy."

I sat up and looked down at him, biting my lip. "I like the three of you; you're each different, and that fulfills me. Sirens aren't always polyamorous. It's more based on a connection to the person."

I slowly traced his tattoos with my fingers. He had an eagle on his chest, and I outlined each wing, then trailed down to his stomach. His abs bunched with my touch, goose bumps scattering across his skin. I traced each tattoo: a diamond, a hand, a lion's head, and flowers from a gun that peeked out the top of his athletic shorts.

Tristian's breath became heavy, and his eyes followed my fingers. I gripped his shorts and pulled them off as he lifted his hips in frustration. He was straining in his boxers as I ran my fingers over each tattoo down his thigh, tracing the interlocking chains to a woman with intricate lace over her face.

"Lil' Star, if you stop…" he struggled to get out.

I smiled. "That's a challenge, Mr. Cassium. Don't wake up Aden yet."

I moved back up and leaned over to kiss his chest where the eagle sat. Slowly trailing kisses down to his stomach, I still paid close attention to each tattoo, licking and tracing them with my tongue.

"Lexi, good god."

I finally made my way to his boxers and sat up to pull them off. The tip of his cock bobbed up, and I wrapped my hands around his shaft, moving up and down slowly. I looked up at Tristian and held his gaze as I took the tip into my mouth. His hips lifted, and he dropped his head back, groaning in pleasure as I felt him grow with each pull.

He combed his hands through my hair and pulled slightly, guiding me down his length. I took him in, then teased his shaft with my tongue as I slowly came back up. Once I reached the tip, I circled it with my tongue, enjoying driving Tristian to the brink.

His voice was husky as he caressed my face. "Lexi, I need more, can I…"

The question hung in the air.

I moved back to nod. "Yes."

His eyes stared down at mine, full of lust, and he pulled my head gently as he thrust himself into my mouth until I felt him hit the back of my throat. His low groans filled the room, and he moved his hips until I had taken him completely down my throat as we pushed each other to the edge.

"You don't even know what you do to us. You make us whole, Lexi."

I moaned at his proclamation. He pulled me up and lightly traced my swollen lips with his finger.

"So fucking perfect, Lil' Star."

I grew wet with desire, begging for him to touch me. He lifted me so I lay beside him, and he placed light kisses across my neck.

"Tell me you're completely soaked, baby."

Before I could respond, he tilted my head and kissed me deeply. I matched his intensity as our tongues intertwined. We nipped and licked at each other, our lust completely taking over.

He moved his hands over the front of my shorts, and a whimper escaped my mouth. "Trist. Please."

He laughed as he slid my shorts off, tossing them to the floor. My shirt came off next, and I lay naked before him, ready to be devoured by the Devil in question. I ran my fingers slowly down my stomach. His eyes followed my every move as I circled my clit, sinking into the sweet warmth he caused.

Tristian licked his bottom lip and moved closer, placing his hand on top of mine and guiding my fingers in tiny circles over my clit.

"Do you think about us when you touch yourself, Lil' Star? Do you imagine what it would be like? How we would worship your body every damn day if we could?" He licked my ear as he took his hand away.

I pulled back, bringing my fingers from my clit up to his lips. "You tell me, Tristian."

He grinned and placed my fingers in his mouth, sucking on them gently. He moved his other hand to my inner thigh, teasing me slowly with his fingers. I looked over at Aden, who was on his side, completely asleep.

Tristian glanced over and chuckled. "You'll need to be quiet. We wouldn't want to wake him," he teased, and I nodded.

With his vampiric speed, he lifted me and twisted me around

until I hovered over his face. I gasped as I tried to hold myself up while facing away from him.

"Sit, Lil' Star. I need to taste you now."

I lowered myself, my knees digging into the bed. Tristian's magical tongue licked my clit to the center as he teased me.

I moaned loudly, and he pulled away with a laugh. "Shhh, or we have to stop," he murmured against my thigh.

I bit my lip, thinking there was no way I could be quiet. I looked down and saw him hard and wanting. I bent forward and took him into my mouth once again.

"Shit," he whispered but continued working slow circles around my clit.

I took him hard and fast, sucking down to his base until I had to come up for air. He chose then to push two fingers inside me.

"Tristian!" I gasped and gripped his thighs as I tightened around his fingers. I rolled into the depths of a mind-blowing orgasm.

Aden stirred and sat up sleepily, looking around. His eyes widened when he saw me in the throes of orgasm with Tristian's head buried between my legs. He moved closer to us as a lecherous smile stretched his lips.

"Good morning, Lex." His fingers found my hard nipples, and he pulled and teased me.

"Oh god, I'm so close, don't stop."

If Tristian noticed Aden, it didn't stop him. He kept working his tongue against me. Then his fingers started to play with my tiny hole. I tightened up as his finger circled and poked gently at my sensitive hole, sending me closer to the edge again.

I ground into his face as he hit that perfect spot.

"Don't stop!" I screamed.

He moved back, pushing two fingers inside me. "Never, Lil' Star, never."

He continued sucking my clit, and his fingers moved in and out steadily, spiraling me into an orgasm so profound that my back arched, making me see stars as I shook and came all over his face and hands. Tristian circled my clit faster with his tongue, and his fingers hit the right spot again.

"*Fuck! Fuck! Fuck!*" I came again as tears sprang to my eyes.

I panted his name as I rolled to his side. Darkness threatened to take me under as I came down from the high. I looked up, and they smiled with lust built up in their eyes.

"Lil' Star, are you still here with us? Because we aren't even close to being done."

I nodded. "Jesus, is that why you call me Lil' Star, Trist?"

He smirked. "Did you see stars, baby?"

I licked my lips and gasped. "Yeah, I saw the whole damn universe."

I lay there for a moment, coming back down to earth. I sat up and looked at Tristian, tilting my head to the side.

"You're still hard. We can't have that, can we?" I murmured as I moved and slowly straddled his legs.

He kissed me softly. "Are you sure? We don't have to."

I kissed him. "I want you, Tristian. I want you all."

Aden looked at us with hungry eyes. I could tell he wanted to join in. I started to reach out for him, but he shook his head.

"This is Tristian's time, baby, but I'll watch you send him to heaven." He grinned like a maniac.

He stood and adjusted his gray sweats. With his tattoos on full display, he moved quickly to sit on the chair near the window that cast him in the shadows.

"One day, it'll be all of us," he said.

The thought of having all three of them made me pant even harder. Tristian held onto my hips as I slowly lowered myself onto his hard length. I groaned and slowly rocked back. All my Devils were big, but Tristian hit me in my sweet spot with every thrust. I now knew why he was so damn cocky.

"Lexi, fuuuuccckkk, you're tight."

I met him with each thrust. I found his hand and wrapped my fingers with his, arching my back.

"Such a good girl taking me all the way. Isn't she, Aden?"

I turned my head to see Aden, his head resting in his hand, his eyes alight with lust.

"That she is, *frère*," he said in a gravelly rasp.

Tristian lifted me carefully, letting me adjust to him, but I wanted more. I needed more. I leaned down and kissed him hard, taking his bottom lip and biting down as his finger found my core. I moaned his name as I began to move at my own pace.

"Fuck me as you want to, Tristian."

He growled and picked up his pace, pounding into me with wild abandon. He removed his fingers and tightened his hands on my hips, leaving sweet bruises for me to see tomorrow. A reminder of what we did. He thrust hard into me and took me as if he owned every piece of me.

He took my nipple into his mouth. His tongue and teeth pulled, bit, and teased me until the point of pain.

"Trist!" I rolled my hips and met his thrusts match for match.

I looked over at Aden, who was leaning forward and digging his fingers into the armchair with his eyes on mine.

A wicked smile spread across his face as he mouthed, "Come."

A command I gladly took as I tightened around Tristian, then fell apart, screaming to the skies.

I dug my nails into Tristian's shoulders, and his skin broke, sending small rivers of blood flowing from his shoulders to his chest, creating the perfect pattern of lines intersecting his tattoos as he continued to fuck me. He quickened his pace before he slammed into me one more time.

"Oh god, Lil' Star!" he shouted before coming deep inside me.

He continued to fuck me roughly until he emptied himself completely. Small orgasms rolled through me in spasms until he stilled. Tristan fell to the bed bringing me with him, both of us slick with sweat and panting heavily, his arms around my waist.

"Fuck, I think I love you, Lexi."

I laughed it off, but I felt the same way, which scared me, because if I fell in love with all three of them in this same intense way, what would that mean? Would it be my demise, or would I have everything I always wanted? I looked up at him, exhausted, forcing my eyes to flutter closed. I kissed him softly to show him how he made me feel. I laid in bliss and found my magic completely full and satisfied.

I laid my head on his chest, whispering, "Watch," as I pushed magic into him, showing him my emotions, how happy he made me, how his laugh could bring me out of the darkest days, and how he truly cared about me, even from the beginning of all this. He was my sunshine. I needed him as much as I needed Aden and Bash.

When I pulled back from his chest, Tristian's eyes were glassy with tears. Sitting up, he pushed my hair off my face and kissed me once more, tenderly this time.

His head rested against mine, and he murmured, "That... was... even... better... Lil' Star."

I smiled at him, and he kissed the top of my head, pulling me close.

I turned my head to Aden, who stared at us with his head in his hands, a euphoric expression on his face as he smiled greedily at us.

"That was sweet, Lex, but it's my turn." He moved quickly, wrapping his hands around my waist and lifting me into the air with a chuckle.

Tristian and I let out a string of curses. "Damnit!" Tristian snarled.

"Aden!" I squeaked as he walked to the bathroom.

Once inside, he slammed the door shut and locked it.

He placed me on the counter, and I saw how hard he was.

"You gonna jerk off over me?" I teased.

His cocky grin grew as he tightened his hands around my waist, his fingers kneading into my hips.

"No, baby."

His tattoos moved as if they were alive. I reached out to touch the modern floral pattern that climbed up his neck. They framed his face, and I ran my fingers along the edge of his jaw. I admired not only his beauty, but the artwork that made him who he was, and how this beautiful man could be mine—knowing that he was always mine, even when I thought he hated me, even when I swore to the world I would destroy him. It seemed like centuries since I had that desire, and now? Now, my heart was full for each of my Devils.

A low growl escaped his lips. "You're playing with fire, baby."

I moved closer, skating my hand from his neck to his chest. His nipple rings glinted, and I gently pulled on one to get his reaction. A hiss escaped his mouth, and he moved back from me. He hooked two fingers into his pants and pushed them to the ground.

I shivered as I saw him ready for me. My sore muscles ached at the idea, but my body still responded, knowing full well I wanted him as much as he wanted me. I let a breathy moan escape. He moved slowly toward me, letting me take in all of him. And I did. From his perfect jawline to the curve of his shoulders, tapering down to the deep V above his hips, to the strength in his legs as he moved like he was a panther on the hunt and I was his prey. Our first time was spontaneous and quick. Now I planned on enjoying every minute of him.

"Aden." I moaned his name, my voice not sounding like my own.

His steel-colored eyes searched mine for an answer as he reached for me. He wrapped his hand around my neck, caressing my pulse and sending a delicious shiver racing through my body as I relaxed into his hand.

He grinned as if he knew he had already won. "Are you telling me you can't handle me? Are you not ready for me, baby?"

He leaned in and kissed my neck. His kisses were featherlight, but they ignited me all over.

"That's not what I said," I breathed out.

God, he felt good. I ran my fingers over his back as he moved me to the edge of the counter, spreading my legs to accommodate him. He kissed me hungrily, pushing me up against him, letting his length stroke me. I let a whimper out as my muscles reacted to him.

"Aden!" I gasped.

He smirked, his fingers running up and down my thigh until they

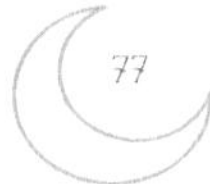

found my core. "Sore, baby?"

I nodded as his fingers softly stroked me. My hips lifted for more pressure, but he held me down with his other hand.

"Tristian fucked you hard. I saw how you fell into ecstasy over him and cried out as he hammered into you. It was the hottest thing I've ever seen, baby. You took him so well... I'll need to be gentle."

I moaned as his fingers entered me and found that perfect place. He began to pump faster as my cries escaped my lips. His lips came crashing into mine, swallowing my screams. I knew the house could hear us.

"Oh god." I clawed at Aden's shoulders and back, leaving a trail of scratches.

He kissed down to my neck, sucking on the spot where Bash had taken me, and tremors ran throughout my body. I felt Aden's smile against my neck, knowing he was thinking the same thing.

"Remember what my *frère* did to you?"

I groaned in pleasure and arched my back into his mouth as he continued the sweet torture.

"That's right, come on my fingers, baby."

I reached for him, moving my hand up and down his silky shaft and playing with his piercing. He gasped, pulling away from my neck. He gazed down at me as the lust in his eyes ignited.

"Two can play at this game, Charmante." I kissed his lips softly as I continued to run my hands up and down him.

He chuckled as he sped up his fingers, his thumb working my clit. "You'll be coming before me, baby. Then I'm going to turn you around and let you watch us come together."

It was almost painful, but I was so close to the edge. I took a deep breath to pull myself back, and my ache grew with need.

"You'll be the end of me," I moaned out.

"But what a way to go," he whispered into my lips as he deepened our kiss.

I was close and couldn't hold out much more. "Aden!" I whimpered.

He pulled back and arched a brow at me as his thumb rubbed harder and faster across my sensitive spot. "Yes, baby?" He taunted me as one quick flick of his finger had me falling into utter bliss.

I came hard, pulling him closer and biting down on his shoulder to stifle a scream. I had tears in my eyes as he slowly pulled out of me. He stepped back and took each tear into his mouth as they fell, moaning in delight.

"You taste so good."

My eyes were half closed as I sagged against the wall. He moved quickly, lifting and turning me to face the mirror. My knees wobbled, and I leaned on my elbows as he spread me wide and moved behind me. He wrapped his hands over my breasts to pull me up higher.

"Hold on tight, baby. I want to be gentle, but you drive me wild. I don't know if I can."

He lined himself up, slicking his length with my wetness.

I looked at him through the mirror, completely blissed out, and groaned his name, giving him all the permission he needed.

I bent forward and held on to the edge of the vanity as he entered me in one deep thrust. I arched back into him, and he began to move. He repeatedly hit the same sweet spot over and over again. Aden pulled me up against his chest, his hands over my breasts, squeezing gently. I wrapped my hand around his head as he kissed my neck. His fingers found my clit again, circling it slowly, pushing me to the edge again. He pulled away from me, and with his vampiric speed, he buried himself deep inside me. My entire body started to buzz with the sensation of his fingers and speed. It was like I was floating on air as he continued to deliver pleasure throughout my body. I panted his name and closed my eyes, leaning back on his shoulder to kiss him. His fingers left me as he took my chin and turned my head to the mirror.

"Open your eyes, Lexi. Look at us."

I opened my eyes. His intense steel eyes stared into mine.

Right when I was about to beg him to finish me, a deep growl

escaped him. "Come for me, baby."

My orgasm burst through, and I screamed his name as he fucked me hard and deep. He yelled my name and lost himself inside me, holding me against his chest. Our bodies glistened with sweat, and the smell of our arousal hung in the air. He kissed me sweetly as his fingers went back to circling my clit, sending small aftershocks over my entire body.

"That's my siren." He slowly removed himself from me, and I laughed as he kissed the back of my neck and down to my shoulders. "I knew you could handle more." He smirked as he held me up, gently stroking my back.

More? I wasn't sure how much more I could handle, but the thought of Bash walking in sent me moaning all over again.

"Aden," I breathed out in a pant.

He grabbed a towel and cleaned us up, and his eyebrow rose as he cradled me against him. "Don't tell me you need more. Should I go get Bash?" he murmured into my ear.

I shook my head, smiling at him through the mirror. "I don't know if I could handle more right now. I think two Devils are good enough for tonight. I need a shower." My voice sounded husky from all the screams.

"Let me." He turned the shower on, letting it warm up, and came back to me and held me in his arms.

Once the strength returned to my legs, I slowly made my way into the shower to clean the sweat off me. I knew I'd be sore for a few days, a reminder of my Devils. Aden followed in behind me, kissing my neck. We washed each other, laughing and sneaking quick kisses when we could. Aden was so easy to be with. He knew me so well. He knew my wants and needs, but I realized I didn't know him anymore. He wasn't the same friend I knew years ago. Now he carried a shadow around him that told me there was more to his story than he shared. I ran my fingers through his hair, pulling his face down to me.

"Why do I always see the sadness in your eyes, Aden? I don't remember it when we were kids. What changed so much that it stays there?"

His eyes suddenly turned hard, and he shut the water off. He stepped out of the shower and reached for our towels. I let him wrap mine around me, and he put his around his waist.

I realized I had overstepped by asking him something he wasn't ready to share. I took his hands in mine, intertwining our fingers, and he pulled me against him.

"It's okay. You don't have to tell me if you don't want to. I'm sorry I even brought it up." I placed a kiss on his cheek and moved to the mirror, picking up a comb to brush through my long hair. His silence was deafening. He looked like he was waging a battle within himself. "Really, Aden, you don't have to say anything."

He met my gaze in the mirror and moved my hair to the side to kiss my shoulder. "It's not that I don't want to tell you, baby. It's a memory I don't like to relive." He leaned in close, resting his chin gently on my shoulder, his eyes never leaving mine. "I discovered when I was sixteen that I wasn't a Charmante. My father is not my father. Mother had an affair, and they never told me, but my father pretty much cut me off from the family. Ethan told him to fuck off, but my mother didn't, and I haven't spoken to either of them in years. Ethan's wedding will be the first time I've been in a room with my parents for longer than an hour."

I turned around. "Is that why...?"

He nodded. "That's the reason I joined Morgan's coven. Morgan said the only way I could be in the coven was to be an enforcer, so that's what I became. I became hollow, filled with empty promises and pretty lies. I was trying to fill a hole that my own family made. If I didn't have Tristian, Bash, or Ethan, I would have put a gun in my mouth a long time ago." He straightened and turned me in his arms.

"Lexi, there's no excuse for what we did... for what I let them do to you. My head wasn't in a good space at the time. That night was right after my parents threw me out, when my father told me to leave the house and never return. We'll always regret that night for the rest of our lives." He kissed my temple, running his fingers down my spine. "Then, once we became the one thing all the covens feared, we began to think we were invincible, wreaking havoc and chaos in our wake and living for the fight every day. Then you came back into our lives, and it was like the smoke cleared, and we saw the sun again. We've lived in the dark for years, but you, Lexi, are our sun."

He lifted my chin, mimicking what I did to him in the shower. "I love you, Lexi. I have loved you with my whole heart for my whole life. You are everything to me and the thief who stole my black heart and brought it back to life."

Tears rolled down my cheek, and he wiped them away.

"Don't cry, baby, please don't cry for me. I don't deserve it."

I shook my head. "No," I argued, "you do, and I'm falling in love with you, too, Aden Charmante. I love you for who you are. I want it all. I will take the dark and the light every single day. Fuck your family, because family isn't just blood and bone. It's so much more. *We* are your family, and you aren't going anywhere, my dark knight." I pushed my lips against his, molding my body to him.

His kisses were soft and featherlight. He ran his fingertips down my face, and our foreheads met.

A knock on the door made us jump, and Bash's voice came through. "If you're done fucking, we need to talk."

I bit my lip. "Looks like we're in trouble."

Aden laughed. "Yeah, Dad seems upset."

I wrinkled my nose and cringed at Aden. "Let's not call him that."

I opened the door slowly to find one angry vampire glaring at me. Bash's eyes narrowed at the towel wrapped around my body. I tugged it closer, securing it in place.

"Yes?" I asked in an innocent voice, batting my eyelashes at him.

"Princess," he growled, opening the door wider to see Aden behind me in a towel as well.

I looked back, and Aden tried to hide a smile. I glared at him and turned back to Bash. He had no right to be angry, but it was rolling off him.

I crossed my arms, preparing for the fight with this stupid, jealous vampire. "Sebastian."

He looked to Aden and then back to me, and his eyes twinkled with a flash of mischief. The next thing I knew, he moved quickly to pick me up and throw me over his shoulder.

I yelped. "Put me down, you stupid caveman!" I pounded his back with my fist, but he either didn't notice or chose to ignore me. I called him a very colorful set of words.

"You smell like them!" he yelled as he swatted my butt playfully.

I stifled a moan from the sting of his palm. I was mentally telling myself not to get excited that this gorgeous man was carrying me away like some damn alphahole.

I wiggled in his arms, trying to get him to drop me, but his grasp just tightened around my legs.

"Damnit, put me down, Bash."

He swatted my ass again, and I let out a yelp, feeling the sting, knowing I'd have a handprint from him. He walked across the living room, where Tristian was waving at me like a damn princess and laughing.

"Traitor!" I yelled at Tristian.

All I heard was a burst of laughter coming from Tristian and Aden.

I flipped them off, and Tristian yelled, "Give her hell, *frère!*"

Bash moved to the bedroom, slamming the door closed with his foot. He gently set me down in my closet, his arms crossed and his face looking like he might murder me.

"What the hell, Sebastian?"

But he stood there with a stony expression.

I pursed my lips, looking around, holding onto my towel. "Soooo, do I get privacy to change or what?"

Bash walked into my space, and I had to lean my head back to look up at him.

"How sore are you, Princess? Did they both wear you out yet?" he snapped out.

I couldn't argue with him. I was thoroughly fucked but not just physically and mentally. My Devils were the thieves, and my heart was the prize.

Chapter Six

We stood in a silent standoff in my closet. He clenched his jaw, and his eyes flashed crimson. I crossed my arms, glaring right back at him. I blew out a slow breath, keeping my anger at bay as I reached out to sense his emotions. He was mad for sure, but I felt a sense of hurt and jealousy deep within him, too. Who would have thought the biggest, baddest vampire in all of Providence Village would have insecurities?

I dropped my arms and walked over to him, taking his face in my hands. "Sebastian Ryder, are you jealous of your brothers?"

He looked down at me, narrowing his eyes, and he huffed out, "No."

I bit my lip to stop from laughing, and a hint of a smile played on his lips. "So, what's up with the He-Man bullshit you pulled?" I let a chuckle escape my lips.

He rolled his eyes as he relaxed. "I'm not jealous of them but of your relationship with them, I guess." He ran a hand over his face and sat on my chair near my vanity.

"Sebastian, this doesn't work"—I raised a finger between us—

"unless you actually tell me how you feel and what's going on in your mind. I'm not a mind reader."

He laughed and leaned forward, looking at me. "I think that's supposed to be my line, Princess."

I smiled. "Well, I was never one for patriarchy bullshit." I shrugged as I moved to my dresser, pulling out underwear.

"You want to know, like, really know?"

I moved between his legs and pushed my fingers into his hair, lifting his head to me. "I wouldn't have asked if I didn't."

He closed his eyes, and his voice came out low and gravelly. "You still keep me at arm's length, and I know why. You forgave them, but deep down, I don't think you can ever truly forgive me for what I did to you."

His eyes opened, and I saw the pain in them. Bash didn't just break my heart, but I broke him too. My heart pounded as he spoke. I wanted to tell him he was wrong, but the truth was, I still had a fear of him doing the same thing to me again. To love me and leave me again. It was time for both of us to forgive each other, for all of us to move on from the past. That's where we would leave it, not only to heal, but to begin a new chapter where we could find each other all over again.

I leaned closer to him and kissed his lips softly. "Sebastian Ryder, what you did shattered me, but you also glued me back together. With each glance, each touch, each kiss, you fixed my heart. It might have cracks, but you're the reason why my heart is fixed now. I just need a little more time to feel confident I won't be wholly broken again. I promise to ensure you have all of me just as Aden and Tristian do. We're together to make better versions of each other, but we can't do that without honesty and love."

His eyes opened, and the green swirls lit up in them. "Take your time, Lexi. I'll wait until the last star in the sky fades if I have to."

I giggled as he pulled me onto his lap and held me close. "Until the last star, huh?"

He smiled and placed a soft kiss on my lips. "I'll wait forever for you, Princess. There is only you."

My heart beat harder at his declaration, and I kissed him deeper and slowly, enjoying the moment that belonged to us.

Sebastian Ryder might drive me crazy in every single way possible, but he always made me feel safe, and I knew it was time for me to give him my heart again. He pulled away, and my heart fluttered at the look he gave me.

"Get dressed, Princess. Hudson wants to meet with us about getting the keys. He thinks he knows someone who knows the location of the third key."

He kissed me one more time before helping me stand and walking out of the master bedroom.

I let out a breath I was holding on to. I was glad our conversation went the way it did and that we didn't take two steps backward. Now to try to catch a serial killer. The thought of everyone I had lost hit me hard, because grief was like that. It never truly went away. I let a few tears fall and then gathered myself back up and looked into the mirror, remembering what Daniels used to tell me when I was young.

"Tears don't solve the world's problems, kid."

I closed my eyes and wiped my tears away. "I miss you, Daniels, and I swear, I'll find out who did this."

I knew what I needed to do, and it was time I stepped up and acted like a badass coven leader.

I needed to focus more on finding out who killed him and Nyx and less on my heart and the men who had taken it. Okay, well, maybe try to do both.

I dressed in leather jeans and a low-cut tank, completing the outfit with a black motorcycle jacket and heeled biker boots. My long chestnut hair fell in loose waves around my face.

I was fixing my lipstick when Tristian came in wearing dark jeans and a black tee under a flannel jacket. His lips turned down into a frown, and I feared another mermaid might have been found dead.

"Hey, what's up? Did another mermaid...?"

He shook his head. "No." He sighed, running a hand through his hair. "No, it's just that... Aden and I heard everything you both said. We get where Bash is coming from."

I felt his hesitation about what he didn't want to say. The air left my lungs. "Tristian..."

He shook his head. "Lexi, you should stay here tonight. Let us talk to Hudson. Let us bond. Then we also won't have to worry about keeping you safe." He moved closer to me. "I think Bash needs this, and all three of us need to sit down and talk it out, *frère* to *frère*."

I swallowed hard, not wanting them to leave without me but understanding the reason for doing so. I moved to the door to follow him out. "I thought he couldn't leave?"

He smirked. "Hudson is his lawyer now, and he can leave to meet with his lawyer or coven business, so, loophole."

I pressed my lips together. "Discussing coven business without one of the covens' leaders?" I tried to joke, but it came out flat.

Tristian wrapped his arm around me, pulling me tight. "Lexi, we need this." His voice had a slight plea to it, and I understood, but I wasn't thrilled that they were running off, possibly toward danger. I just felt better when I could be with them.

"I get it, I do."

He kissed my temple. "Ella is coming over with Ethan."

Surprised, I turned to him. "So, babysitters?" I asked half-jokingly, pushing out of his arms, now getting pissed off. "So, you three can run off to go 'bond,' but I can't even stay here alone?"

Tristian looked defeated. "No, Lexi. Ella is coming over because you need someone besides us here. You need to spend time with her after almost losing her because of our lie. She almost lost her older brother, the one guy who cared for her. I think she might need you, too, and you need her, so stop acting like a brat."

"I'm not. I'm being a fucking angel as you three run off and exclude me from something I have every right to be a part of."

Tristian turned to me. I saw that I was pushing him, but I was sick of everyone thinking they knew what was right.

"See it from his point of view, Lexi? You run to Aden and me first at any sign of trouble. You feel safer with us than him, even though he has protected you since you were sixteen." I felt the tears fall, and he grasped my face, wiping them away quickly. "It wasn't until you almost lost him that you realized you truly cared for him. He always came last with you, when he always wanted to be your first." I opened my mouth, and he shook his head. "The only reason you don't run to him as you do to us is that you don't realize you love him. I don't think you ever really stopped loving him. Lexi, it's breaking him slowly, and I can't see him break again. I don't think he would come back from it. So, please, take care of his heart as he did yours."

I backed up slowly with each word, and by the end, my back was against the wall. I stared at a man I thought I knew—the one who always brought so much sunshine into my life. The truth of his words carried a storm of confusion through me as I sank to the ground and pulled my knees to my chest. I stared at the wall, my heart cracking at the truth.

Tristian knelt before me, pushing my hair away from my face. His voice was soft. "Ella will be here in five minutes. Come out to say goodbye if you want to. I promise we'll fill you in on everything when we return, Lil' Star. We all need space, okay? Our feelings for you haven't changed, and we'll always protect you, but you need to look at your relationship with Sebastian and us for everything to work. You both need to figure out what you want to do. Either jump into the deep with us or stay away. The choice is yours, and we'll respect it, but it's yours alone."

I looked up at him. "Okay," I whispered, because there were no other words I could say at the moment. My heart, though it may have been put back together, felt hollow. I could lose all of them.

He stood and turned to leave, not looking back at the door, clicking it shut. I clutched my knees as I heard Ella and Ethan walk in, Ella giggling at something Ethan said.

Her smile fell when she stepped into my room and saw me. "Oh shit... what did they do?"

I looked at her with tears brimming in my eyes. "Not them, me," I choked out.

She ran over to me and pulled me into a tight hug. "Hey, hey." She pushed my hair away from my face, which had fallen around me like a curtain. Her copper eyes searched my face with concern. "They're still here. I think they're waiting for you. Come on."

I looked at her. "They're waiting for me?" My voice sounded nothing like my own, full of uncertainty.

She nodded as she pulled me to my feet. "Hey." I looked up at her. "Remember, Roses don't cry. They make you bleed, so wipe your eyes and say goodbye."

I took a deep breath, pushing the tears away, and walked out to my Devils waiting for me. They were loading up on weapons, checking each gun, and strapping knives to themselves. I stood off to the side with my arms crossed around my midsection, holding on as if I was trying to hide the wound I so visibly wore now.

Aden wore leather pants, a gray sweatshirt, and his leather jacket. His eyes sparkled at the chance of danger, but he looked as worried as Ella did when he saw me.

He walked up and lifted my chin. "Hey, we'll be okay, baby. I'll be back in a few hours. Nothing to fear." He kissed my lips lightly.

Tristian looked down at the ground as he moved over to me. I saw the internal battle on his face. I walked to him, still keeping space between us but close enough that not everyone could hear.

"It's okay, Trist. I needed to hear it," I said in a murmur.

As the first tear threatened to fall, I quickly turned and wiped it away.

He stared at the tear that had fallen but moved to kiss my cheek softly. "I'll see you soon, Lil' Star."

Bash cleaned a gun before placing it in his leather holster. The

black pants and cream sweater made him look sleek—in a mob boss kind of way. He flung a long overcoat over his shoulders and was the last to double-check that his weapons were in place. I wanted to run to him, but my body stayed still. I didn't want him to know I was scared of falling for him all over again, that I was scared of what would happen if he left. I couldn't form the words I wanted to say to him. They seemed locked in my throat, dying for release.

I moved slowly to him as his eyes met mine. Leaning my head back, I cupped his face and whispered, "Promise you'll be careful."

He nodded and turned his head into my palm, laying a soft kiss on it. "I promise, Princess." The tear fell before I could catch it, and he wiped it away. "It's okay, Lexi."

"It's not," I said, and he kissed the tears from my cheeks and pulled away.

The sting of his kiss lingered on my cheeks. They turned and walked out the door, leaving me there but taking my heart with them.

I turned and walked back into my room, finding Dyna on my bed. I curled up next to her, pulling the ball of fur to my chest as I silently sobbed, feeling my heart ache for men I couldn't give my whole heart to. It felt like I was breaking into a million pieces.

It seemed like hours later when a soft knock sounded on the door.

"Come in." My throat was so dry, my answer barely came out.

Ethan poked his head in. "Hey, Lex, I have dinner."

I sat up in bed and pulled my knees up to my chest. "Thanks."

He set the plate down on the side table. "I made chicken, greens, and a bit of rice. I figured it hits all the main food groups." He sat on the edge of the bed, and I grabbed a fork and picked at my food. "Can I say something and you promise not to get mad?"

I looked up from my food. "Sure, I guess." Not sure if I could take any more truths today.

He let a small laugh escape. "I see how you look at each of them, Lexi, and I saw how you used to look at Bash when we were younger." I blushed at that. "It wasn't a secret that you liked him. Just like it wasn't a secret that he protected you from the covens for years. The only reason you were left alone was due to Bash and Daniels protecting you."

"So I've heard," I tried to joke, but my voice fell flat.

He moved closer to me, putting his hand on mine. "My point is, it's not the same now. You look at each of them like you look at the ocean. You see freedom within each of them."

Freedom was all I ever wanted for years, freedom from being the girl who lost her parents and the freedom just to be me. The tears started again, and I couldn't stop them.

Ethan pulled me closer, and I laid my head on his shoulder. "Lexi, look, our lives aren't simple. We're fae. We'll always have something or someone to overcome, but I know that if you have someone to share this life with, it'll be less lonely, and if you find that with them, don't let them go."

A small smile formed on my lips. "Kinda like how you found Ella?"

He smiled at the mention of her name. "Ella is my everything. She is my sun, moon, and stars. Without her, I don't exist. She is all-consuming."

I attempted a smile. "Sounds terrifying."

He laughed. "It is. Now come on, we let you mope enough. It's time to watch some cheesy rom-com movie. Ella has enough popcorn and candy to feed a small army."

I felt better after our talk. Yes, I was still confused about each of my Devils, but I hoped we would be okay. I stood and stretched, my fingers reaching for the ceiling.

He smiled. "Good talk?"

I chuckled. "Yes, but now I need more food and a comfort snack."

I took my plate and walked to the door with Ethan trailing behind me. I turned around, wrapped my arms around his waist, and whispered, "Thank you."

He hugged me back. "It's what I'm here for, that and being extremely good-looking."

His face screwed up into a serious model face that had me laughing.

"Whatever you want to believe, hoss." I left him, chuckling behind me as I walked into the living room to find Ella.

She was sitting on the couch, yelling at the TV. "Oh, come on! That is the most unrealistic thing I've ever seen. You could never get across the city like that in ten minutes! What utter bullsh—" She looked in my direction and jumped up. "Hey!" She wrapped her arms around me tightly, hugging me.

I suddenly couldn't breathe. "Hey, El... umm... can't... breathe... babes."

She jumped back and glared playfully. "I'm gonna dick punch my brother when he returns."

I shook my head. "It's not him. It's me and all my issues." I waved a hand around my head.

She frowned. "Okay, but I still wanna dick punch him."

I laughed. "Only if he really deserves it, okay?"

She huffed. "Fine."

I sat at the kitchen bar, eating a piece of chicken from my plate. As I focused on my food, I sensed Ella's shadow looming over me. I looked over at her and caught a look of worry on her face.

"Hey, Lexi, it's going to be okay. You know that, right?"

I nodded. "Yeah... sure." I looked out the window at the setting sun. "How long was I...?"

I looked up at a clock and saw it had been hours since they had left. It only felt like minutes.

Ella gave me a sad smile. "A few hours. Aden texted Ethan a while ago. They should be back within the hour."

I nodded, taking small bites of my food but not really tasting it. Back in an hour, what the hell was I going to do? What would I say to them?

After ten minutes of attempting to eat unsuccessfully, I gave up and made my way to the couch. Ella put on some ridiculous romantic comedy that made my heart sing.

Muffled voices came from outside, and the door clicked open. I closed my eyes as I gathered my strength and put on a brave face.

Aden strolled in first, followed by Bash and Tristian. Bash had a fresh bruise across his face, and Tristian looked pissed as hell. He stormed past us to his room and slammed the door. I jumped up from the couch, popcorn spilling around me.

"What the hell happened?" I looked at Aden, and a frown formed as his eyes landed on me.

"Tristian and Bash got into it," he said with a sigh, stripping off his jacket and weapons.

Ella looked at Bash. "Really? About...?"

I rushed to the freezer and got out an ice pack. I wrapped it in a towel while looking at Bash. "Sit." I pointed to the sofa.

Bash didn't say a word as he tossed his phone on the table and sat down with a sigh. I walked to stand in front of him and placed the ice pack on his face. He cringed at the cold.

"Big baby," I murmured.

He looked up at me. "I took the hit for you, Princess."

I raised my eyebrows. "Why?"

He cleared his throat, and his anger rolled out. "Because Tristian was blaming you for all of this shit."

Ethan cleared his throat. "Hey, Ella, come and look at Lexi's new bag."

Ella patted my hand and disappeared down the hall with Ethan.

I cleared my throat. "But isn't it, though? My fault? I mean, isn't all this because of my issues?"

He held up a hand to stop me. "Let me finish, Lexi. Yes, you have to work your shit out, but so do I. You're not the only one to blame. Not in this. I was trying to tell him that. He didn't take it very well. He punched me when I said we all needed to get our shit together. I deserved it, but he knows I'm right."

I stood still, looking at him. "Bash... I... it's not that I don't..."

He shook his head. "Not here, Princess, and not tonight."

He pressed the ice pack to his face and leaned back on the sofa, looking defeated by the night's events.

Ella walked out with Ethan in tow. "Kay, well, that's our cue to leave. Bye, Lex!" She wrapped her arms around me for a hug and did the same to Aden. "Oh, and big brother?"

He glanced her way, pulling the ice pack back. "Yes, little sister?"

She glared at him. "If she calls me crying anymore *or* I find my best friend crying in a closet again because of you three, I will dick punch all of you. Then hex you to have small dicks forever." Her eyes narrowed at both of them, and Aden backed away from her, covering himself.

I laughed silently, gave her a small wave, and mouthed, "Thank you."

Ethan gave a two-finger salute to each of the guys and guided her out before she carried out her threat.

The door closed behind them, and Aden looked between the two of us. "I'm going to go check on Tristian." He gave me a sad smile and moved toward the room they shared.

I looked down at Bash's green eyes, and he stared back at me. They held so much behind them.

"Screw it," I said and moved to straddle his lap, placing the ice pack against his cheek. "Stupid vampires," I muttered as I shook my head.

He pushed my hair behind my ear, studying my face. "You've been crying," he whispered, fingers running down my stained cheeks.

I stilled. "I have," I said in a low whisper.

"Because of me," he said, tracing the lines of dried tears.

I sat back on his thighs. "Because of everything, Bash, not just you. Tristian is right. I've been pushing you away for far too long. I ran to them when I needed help, but I keep punishing you, even after all these years." I swallowed hard. "I push you away because I'm scared of getting hurt again, that it would be the final crack that would completely break me. What scares me the most is to be completely broken." I knew he deserved the truth, so I gave it to him the best way I could. I pushed my fingers into his hair, and he leaned into my touch. "When I'm with all three of you, I'm whole. I feel something other than the fear and loneliness that has lived inside me for the last ten years. For my family, I have to put on a facade. Ella, Ethan, Jason, even Coco, they can't stand to see me broken. They don't want to see me weak."

He opened his mouth to say something, but I put a finger to his lips.

"Let me finish, please." I echoed what he said earlier. "You three made me realize I could be myself. I didn't have to put a shield up around you. You make my heart whole again. I can be my unapologetic self, and I can love you three the way I want because you let me be myself, which terrifies me."

His emerald-green eyes stared into my blue ones. "Lexi... I..."

I nod. "I know. You don't have to say it."

I bent and kissed his lips softly, a chaste kiss. I pulled away and stood, pulling him with me and walking outside. I grabbed a large beach towel and headed down the small winding path where rows of lavender blossomed and the hint of salt wafted through the air. We walked until we landed on the soft creamy sand that led right to the beach. I laid the towel out and sat, kicking off my shoes and looking up at him. His body language showed he was unsure if he should be there. I patted the spot next to me, and he shook his head and sat behind me, pulling me to his chest. We looked out over the ocean, watching the waves slowly drift in and out. Peace washed over me as the waves lapped at the sand.

Bash was quiet, and I listened to his breathing, finding myself in a peaceful trance.

"Tell me about tonight, Bash. What did Hudson say?" He hesitated for a moment. I nodded. "We can work on our relationship later, but right now, I need a distraction."

He took a deep breath. "Hudson did some research in the older grimoires that Trinity Coven has. There's a legend from the Ohlone tribes, who have been around for over ten thousand years. They lived on the land, hunting, fishing, and gathering alone before we were here. They're the reason we're allowed here." I closed my eyes, leaning farther into him, his warmth enveloping me as his deep voice continued. "The legend says a tribal princess once lost her way after her true love died in a war. Her own tribe caused the war out of their greed for power and magic. She turned on her tribe, killing many to avenge her true love. The tribe was one with the earth and searched for answers through Gaia, a goddess of Mother Earth who was worshiped throughout the tribes. Gaia's magic was remarkable. It could heal the sick, feed the hungry, and bring light into the dark. The chief and the leaders of the tribe prayed to Gaia, asking her to stop the destruction of the Ohlone people.

"Gaia and the Ohlone turned on the princess, cursing her with a life filled with darkness every day. She would relinquish the joy of the sun. The night would whisper her fears, food would taste rotten, and every drop of water she would drink would make her throat desire more. After months of torture, she finally called upon the chief to help end her misery. The chief said that in order to have Gaia favor her again, she must drink from the silver spring water that lay on an island surrounded by the sun, the moon, and the stars. The chief warned her that the island was full of danger and demons called wraiths, ready to destroy those who weren't worthy. The wraiths would take those who meant harm and devour their souls so they became one with the island, continuously feeding the island magic through the souls it had taken. Gaia told the princess that once she was on the island, a set of trials would take place. Within each element of the trial, a new trial would appear until all were completed. Only then would the princess's curse be lifted. She would be at peace and either stay on the earth or follow her love into the Veil. Some say she found the island and saved her soul. Others say she died trying to leave, screaming her lover's name to the stars as the wraiths devoured her. The story warns us from ever entering the island for fear of never returning."

Stunned, I sat up and turned to look at him. "That's really sad, Bash. I hope she found peace one day."

He hugged me closer. "It is, and I like to think she did. Hudson thinks the island is holding what we're looking for, but we don't know where the island is."

We sat for several minutes before I turned back to him again, with the realization hitting me in the face. "You mean to tell me not only do we have a creepy-ass island to go through but that we have evil-ass zombie things that will eat us?"

Bash laughed. "No, Princess, not zombies. Wraiths are a type of fae made of the wrong spellcasting. They're not just like the night. They *are* night. They live in the deep of the woods, and they feed on fear for power, so a 'creepy-ass island' is the perfect place for them to find victims." He looked down at me, tracing my jaw.

"Goddamn, that's terrifying."

Bash smirked. "Sounds like a challenge, which I love," he joked.

I rolled my eyes. "Okay, Mr. Big, Bad, and Scary." I leaned back into him again, turning to look up at him. "So, another adventure. After we get the key from the vault?"

He wrapped his arms around me and whispered into my neck, "Yeah, a journey into the cursed island. You brave enough, little siren?"

I smiled. "With my Devils? I fear nothing."

He kissed my head. "It's our duty to you."

I turned and caught his lips, whispering into our kiss, "I love you, Bash."

He smiled and pulled me closer. "I love you too, Princess."

His lips kept our kiss light and sweet, something just for us.

I pulled away and leaned my head back onto his chest, listening to his steady heartbeat. His hands laid on the small of my back, his fingers making little, lazy circles. We sat wrapped in each other's arms as we enjoyed the closeness of each other, something that had been stripped away from us for years.

Chapter Seven

We sat in silence for a while, watching the sun start to rise above the dark horizon. I looked back at the house and saw two shadows moving toward us. I knew it was my other Devils as they approached us. Aden's large frame came into view as he sat next to Bash, looking out at the horizon in silence with a pensive look, as if he was lost in his thoughts.

"Hey…" Tristian's voice came from behind us, holding sadness to it.

I turned to him. His hands were in his jeans, his shoulders were hunched over, and he looked defeated. He sat next to me on Bash's other side.

"Hi," I said sheepishly, giving him a coy smile.

We all sat in silence, watching the sun rise above the dark sky. The pink and orange rays peeked through the purple sky, and I knew this was where I wanted to be, with all of them around me.

I needed them just as they needed me. We were ashes of lost souls that found each other. Together, we were more than just ash. When we stood together, we rose from the depths of hell to become what we were supposed to be: the Devils and their siren.

I wrapped Bash's arms around me tighter, pulling his body heat to mine. I laced Aden's hand into mine and reached for Tristian's as he instinctively reached for me. Their hands warmed me from the inside and filled the cracks in my heart where the void had sat for so long.

"I'm sorry, Lil' Star."

I shook my head, my voice coming out shaky. "I needed to be told the truth."

He kissed my hand, tracing the lines of my palm. "I shouldn't have snapped. If I could take it back, I would. Your and Bash's relationship is your own. You two go as fast or as slow as you need."

Bash pulled me closer, and I pulled the others with me.

"No, Tristian, we're all four in this together. This isn't just my and Bash's relationship but also your *frère*'s too. It affects us all, so when I shut one of you out, I'm hurting all of you."

Tristian leaned in and kissed my lips lightly. "We're lucky to have you, Lil' Star."

Aden sighed dramatically and fell into my lap. "Finally! You three work your shit out." I playfully smacked his chest. He grunted with a smile. "Now that we're all made up, can we move on to the bigger issues?"

I rolled my eyes at him with a chuckle, and Tristian punched his arm, murmuring "idiot" under his breath.

I looked down at him with a tilt of my head. "Which issue do you want to talk about? The master plan of stealing from one of the most powerful fae in Providence Village?" I joked.

"Or trying to find a serial killer who kidnapped mermaids from our covens and now wants me to rot in jail if I don't stay away from Lexi?" Bash asked sarcastically.

Tristian leaned back on his elbows. "I got one. How about how your father is still probably helping said serial killer and possibly wants to kill his own son and his friends?" His voice darkened.

Our laughter died quickly, and we sat in silence, with a look of

dread crossing their expressions.

I cleared my throat. "That was supposed to be a joke."

Aden gave me a look. "It's hard to joke about it."

I kissed his head. "I found my parents murdered ten years ago. How do you think I handled most of the stress and grief?" I arched an eyebrow.

"Ridiculously bad jokes?" Bash asked from behind me with a chuckle.

I elbowed him in the stomach playfully. "If you don't laugh, you cry, so maybe try it, Vlad," I teased him. "Then maybe you wouldn't frown as much." I turned to him with my best impression of him.

"No, Princess, I don't do that." He stayed frozen with the exact expression I was trying to mimic.

I sighed and smoothed the little lines between his eyes. He glanced down at me, and his gaze softened.

"Princess, mocking me is going to get you punished. I can show you what torture really is," he whispered, promising me.

I blushed at the statement, because I could only imagine what domineering Bash was like in the bedroom. I wiggled slightly as I told my siren to calm herself down; we were still sore from yesterday, and this girl needed a break. I just wanted to have a moment with all three of them. A peaceful moment was a rarity, so I planned to soak this in as long as possible. A moment that was just ours.

It lasted about fifteen minutes until all of our phones went off.

Tristian's eyes narrowed. "That was security. They found another box."

Just like that, our moment was shattered. Dread sank into me as we stood.

We walked back from the beach to the patio area where the fire pit sat just as Sonny, the guard's captain, stood tall and wide with a grim look on his face.

"Boss." His deep voice addressed Bash. He nodded to Bash. "The box is heavy. Where do you want it?"

Bash pointed to the fire pit, and Sonny placed it on the table. Sonny stood back. "You want me to open it for you, sir?"

Bash whipped out a knife from only God knows where and flicked it open. "We got it, Sonny, thank you."

I held my breath as Tristian moved closer to me. Bash cut the top and opened the box. He took a deep breath and pulled out three ribbons with small red stone carvings, each one different, with a sun, a moon, and a star attached to the ribbons.

Aden pulled out a single black envelope with curling red letters on the front addressed to me.

"What does it say?" I asked in a low voice.

We all stared at the black envelope, preparing for whatever lay within it.

Aden slid the card out carefully and read it silently before his lips raised into a snarl that put us all on edge.

I moved quickly to his side and read the letter out loud. "Eeny meeny miny moe, which Devil has to go? The Wishmaker."

I wouldn't allow the fear to show on my face, though it ate away at my stomach, making me feel queasy. We knew the wreckage that came with The Wishmaker. So, I turned to an emotion I knew would help. Fighting hate with hate wasn't always the way to go, but when someone tried to hurt what was mine, I would let that anger show. I sneered as the hate and rage filled me.

"I'm going to enjoy bathing in their fucking blood," I hissed out.

Tristian wrapped his arms around me in an instant. "God, baby, it's hot when your bloodlust is in full swing." He smiled as I glared at him.

Bash carefully examined the charms, looking at each one with a critical eye, as if they would tell him the answers he was searching for.

"Why these symbols?" he murmured under his breath.

Bash might not know the why, but I did. They were mine, my everything, and I wouldn't let The Wishmaker hurt what I claimed.

"Because they know that you three are my everything. The sun is Tristian, the star is Aden, and the moon is you, Bash. In The Wishmaker's eyes, you're all my universe."

Bash's eyes softened as he pulled me to him. He rested his

hands on my hips as I gazed up at him. "Lexi, you are *our* universe, and they know that. They're playing a dangerous game and will eventually mess up."

I gave him a small smile, letting the feeling of reassurance set in. I pulled away and went to the box. "Yeah, well, let's hope it's sooner rather than later." I sighed and looked over to Aden, whose eyes were staring into the box in deep concentration. "What else is in the box?"

He lifted a cube that could only be described as ancient. It was about the size of a basketball. Its dark wood gleamed with fresh paint. Tiny engraved patterns ran throughout the box with a gold inlay of swirling waves.

Bash cursed, and Tristian frowned deeply. "What is that?"

Aden ground his teeth. "It's a damn Himitsu-Bako."

My eyes widened in surprise. I'd heard about the boxes before but had never seen one myself.

Tristian tilted his head to the side. "What the hell is a Himitsu-Bako?"

Bash ran his hands over his face in frustration. "It's a Japanese puzzle box, a mosaic puzzle with anywhere from seven to seventy-two moves. They want us to solve the puzzle."

I sank into a chair. "How?" I asked.

Tristian moved over to sit next to me, his eyes on Aden. "How the hell do you solve a puzzle without knowing where or how to start?" Bash's eyes stayed on the puzzle box, looking at it like it was a bomb. Aden moved to the package and peered inside. "There's another note here, but this one is addressed to Bash."

He pulled out another black note with Sebastian's name in the same elegant handwriting and handed it to him. I jumped up and rushed to Bash.

Looking at the letter, Bash ripped it open and read it out loud to all of us.

Dear Sebastian, did you enjoy my trick?
Well, here is another one to solve. Maybe this time,
you can save a life and find your own freedom.
Since I am feeling nice, I'll help you out with a clue;
look to the lightening sky to find the way to the depths
of the sea; if you divide yourself between the two,
you'll find the truth that you seek. WM.

I shook my head, rubbing my temples where a headache was forming. "It's nothing but mad ramblings."

Bash's phone buzzed. He looked down at his phone with a shout and slammed it into Aden's hands.

I jumped. "What is it?"

I looked at Aden, and he handed me Bash's phone. It was a photo of a girl with pale-blonde hair and light-blue eyes lying curled up on her side. You could tell she'd been beaten repeatedly from the bruising, and her eyes, which once were fiery with life, were now entirely dulled in defeat. Her blonde hair was matted and dirty.

"Is that...?" Tristian asked from behind me.

"Chella... yeah, it's one of the missing mermaids," I retorted.

Aden let out a string of curses, turning back to us. His eyes flickered a crimson flame, his teeth elongated, and his anger burned hot around us. "We have three days to solve this before he kills more of them—more mermaids—and then who knows who's next?" He growled and sat down with his head in his hands.

Tristian moved next to him, placing a hand on his shoulder. "We'll find them *frère*." Tristian glanced at Bash. "We have forty-eight hours before the robbery."

Aden slammed his hand on the firepit. "Fuck, we don't have time! What the hell are we going to do?" Aden ran his hands through his hair, messing up the perfectly styled look.

We all turned to look at Bash, who was stoic and glaring out at sea.

He turned to us, his arms crossed, and the alpha tone exuded from him. "Grayson, Hudson, and you three go to the robbery as planned."

Aden and Tristian looked like they were going to object, but I turned to Bash, smirking as an idea popped into my mind.

"The Wishmaker doesn't know we told Ella and Ethan everything. They can help you solve the puzzle."

He turned to me with an arched brow. "Look, that's sweet, but I don't need my little sister—"

I cut him off before he even got started with that older brother bullshit. "Don't be an asshat, Bash. First, Ella is insanely smart—smarter than you, for sure," I started ticking off on my fingers. His eyes widened in surprise, but I didn't miss the cocky smile playing on his lips. I continued. "*And* Ethan can hack into anything almost as well as Aden. He'll be all over this. Honestly, he'll probably like the challenge. Coco and Jason might even be able to help us. They both spent time in Japan before my parent's death. They might know how to help open the box."

He crossed his arms, defiance in his gaze. "No way, I'm not bringing them into our mess."

I held up my hands. "Look, they already know most everything, so it's not a surprise to them, and you can blame me if anything goes wrong. The more help we have that The Wishmaker doesn't know about, the better."

He didn't budge. Stubborn vampire. So, I decided to try another way that might appeal to him. I stood up and moved to him with purpose. My hair had been up, so I slowly took it down, and his eyes flared at the challenge. I walked with a sway to my hips and bit my lip as I leaned into him, resting my hand on his chest and standing on tiptoes to whisper softly into his ear, "Do this for me, Sebastian, and if shit hits the fan, I'll let you turn my ass red with your hand, like you've been wanting to do for years."

He groaned at the thought, and I moved back, my hand not leaving his chest. I found those gorgeous forest-green eyes staring back at my sapphire ones. "Bash, give Ella a chance. I didn't, and I truly regret it." I stepped back and returned to Aden and Tristian, who were trying to hide their smiles.

"Well done, Lil' Star," Tristian muttered next to me.

Bash was deep in thought as he likely ran through every possible scenario that could go wrong. When his shoulders dropped, I knew I had won.

He puffed out a breath and threw his hands. "Fine, but I swear, if anything happens to Ella…"

I smiled at his undying love for his sister. "I'll be right there with you. If anything happened to them, I couldn't live with it, but I know Ella and Ethan are the silent warriors we need. This is our chance to get one up on The Wishmaker."

He walked toward the group and bent down closer to me. "I'll make this ass red one day, Princess, don't mistake that." He kissed my head. "I hate it when you're right."

I shook my head and whispered, "No, you don't."

He kissed my head again. "No, I don't."

We called Ella and Ethan, filling them in on everything from the keys to the puzzle box. They were thrilled to help and agreed to come over tomorrow. Bash hung up when Ella started talking about the snack situation. As the day went on, we went into full planning mode, going over everything we had set up and trying to figure out the first clue.

It was late as I scanned over the blueprints one more time until someone came and booped my nose.

"Hey, Lex, dinner is here. Call it a day." Aden was eating noodles out of a takeout container with a pair of chopsticks. "I got you your favorite, a dragon roll."

I smirked, crossing my legs in the chair at the dining room table. "Now, how the hell would you know my favorite sushi? I didn't even like it when we were kids." I folded my arms, sitting up straighter in my chair.

A smile played on his lips. "Now, why would I share my secrets with you? Hmm?" He leaned down, his face mere inches from mine.

"I thought we didn't have secrets," I playfully snapped back.

"We all have secrets, baby." He carefully placed his takeout on the table away from the blueprints and cupped my face into his hands. "I don't keep anything from you that you don't already know. Maybe I leave out a few details, but let me keep a bit of mystery about me, Lex."

I stared at his face. He was so handsome, it was cruel, especially with his silvery eyes. I leaned forward and kissed him lightly.

"Fine, but only because I'm hungry and want sushi. Thank you, my dark knight."

He kissed me quickly, and with a laugh, he smirked at me. "Food first, as always with you, baby."

We sat around the kitchen eating and drinking wine when a buzzing came from my phone. I looked around the room to see it sitting on the couch across from me. I jumped up and raced for it.

With a mouth full of food, I picked it up. "Hello."

"Ah, good evening, sunshine!"

I laughed. "Hi, Aunt Coco. What's going on?"

She laughed. "Oh, nothing. I've been up since three a.m. perfecting my morning bun, but Jason distracted me, so."

I closed my eyes. "Coco, Jason is like an uncle to me. Please do not go into what he did to you on the kitchen counter again. I've walked in on it enough times to be scarred for the rest of my life."

She humphed at that statement. "Well, that man is so fine, I can't help myself. Speaking of fine men, I heard about Bash, and I'm glad he's out. How are the rest of you doing?"

I looked over at the men. They could hear everything, and I blushed. "Fine, they're good. What's up?"

"I was hoping you would tell me, young lady?"

I straightened up. "Uhhh, not much. Why?"

Coco huffed in irritation. "Morgan Ryder stopped by to visit the café today... Look, you know I know, so stop with this shit, Lexi Rose, and tell me what the hell is going on in Providence Village."

Shit, of course she knew about The Wishmaker. "Listen, Coco. There's something you should know."

She interrupted me before I could finish. "Yeah, like, how the hell does Bash get accused of murder, and you just conveniently forget to tell me?"

I swallowed hard and reached for my glass of wine. "Well, umm, we both kind of got arrested."

Coco let out a cry. "Buttery biscuits, Lexi Rose!"

I quickly continue. "*But* it's fine. Hudson James of Grayson's coven came and handled it. Bash had the Blood Moon's lawyer. We've been holed up at the house trying to figure out what to do next and to keep the covens safe."

It wasn't 100 percent the truth, but it wasn't a lie, either. We were trying to figure out how to get the keys from Morgan and find missing mermaids while proving that Bash was innocent and also stopping a drug from killing our people. One problem at a time, right? We can deal with the white lies later.

"Okay, so, when am I going to see you again?" Coco asked, concern lacing her voice.

I looked over to Bash, and he shrugged as he took a bite of his soba noodles. "Tomorrow morning, I can send Aden or Tristian with you. I need to handle coven issues anyways."

I smiled brightly and mouthed, "Thank you." He winked back at me.

"How about tomorrow? You wanna meet at the bakery?"

I heard the glee in her voice. "Perfect. Oh, now I have to make sure those morning buns are perfect."

I laughed. "Coco, you know they'll be out of this world."

"Uhh, Coco?! Is there supposed to be smoke coming from the oven?!" I heard Jason shout.

"Oh shit, I gotta go, babe. That's the morning buns! See you tomorrow! Love you." With a click, she was gone, and I let out a light laugh.

As I took a sip of wine, I turned to see three vampires staring at me like I was in trouble.

"What?" I sighed.

Tristian took a bite from his plate. "Should have told her, Lil' Star." He shrugged.

I looked between the three of them. "Do you all think that too?"

Aden cleared his voice. "Yeah, baby."

I swung my gaze to Bash. "Sebastian?"

He set his wine glass down, leaning forward with a smooth smile. "I think you need to ask why you *didn't* tell her, Lexi."

"Look, I know I should. I don't want to risk her safety."

Aden put his hand on mine. "Lex, I know you have this dread when it comes to telling someone you love what's going on, but Coco has a right to know."

I sighed. "I'll think about it."

I finished the last bit of my food before washing it down with the rich wine and raising my arms, stretching out like a cat. "I'm going to bed." I waved a hand, saying good night.

I knew Coco deserved to know the truth, but fear crept through me. What if I put her in danger? The fear of losing someone else I loved was terrifying when I had already lost everyone I had ever given a part of myself to. My parents, Daniels, and now Nyx, who was my friend and was only killed because of me.

I lay in bed with Dyna curled up on my side as I looked up at the cciling, sleep evading me.

The door creaked open as Tristian poked his head through it. "Can I come in, Lil' Star?"

A small smile formed on my lips. "Of course."

I made room for him to join me and moved to my side. He lay on his side to face me, and I rested my head on my arm.

"I know you know why Bash and Aden betrayed you all those years ago, but I don't think I ever told you why I did it."

My brows shot up. "I thought you did it because Morgan required it from you all."

He frowned. "Yeah, Morgan influenced us, but I had my reasons. My mother isn't my birth mother. She married my father when I was two. My birth mother was a high-ranking vampire in Blood Moon, and all she wanted was children, but given her ranking, she had to marry within her stature. One night, my mother attended the Full Moon dinner that the coven threw every month and met my father. They fell in love. The problem was that my father was already promised another coven leader. Your mother."

He brushed my hair behind my ear as I held my breath.

"My father went against coven wishes and married my mother. Silver Pearl was livid, saying my mother was a traitor to the covens and violated their law. Back then, apparently, only a few of the founding coven leaders' families wanted to keep the power structure high within the leaders. They didn't want lower power levels to mix."

I looked into his eyes and saw the pain he had hidden for many years. "But your dad is a powerful witch, isn't he?"

Tristian nodded. "He is, but my mother came from one of the most powerful vampire families, and her parents were... traditionalists, I guess, is the right word."

He rolled over, and I nuzzled into the crook of his arm, resting my head on his chest. His arm wrapped around me, pulling me closer as he continued his story.

"The covens sent their highest-ranking witches to capture her, to bring her in for her *traitorous ways*."

I swallowed hard and released a sharp breath. "Let me guess, my father and grandfather?"

He nodded. "They tracked her down and laid her out in the

ritual circle to kill her. My father rushed in and begged them to stop, telling them she was pregnant with his child. He explained that to kill a child who was brought into this world with love and want was against the sanctity of the covens." Tears hit my cheeks as Tristian looked down and quickly wiped them away. "Silver Pearl kept my mother as a prisoner until she was able to have the child."

I shook my head, not wanting to believe *my* coven would do such a thing. When my parents led the coven, they led it with kindness, compassion, and understanding. We didn't have these rules then. I knew that when my parents were young, they changed many of the rules. It was one of the reasons people saw our coven as the more progressive one.

"No. No, Tristian."

His eyes held mine. "There were complications with the birth, my father says. She had me, and once they handed me over to my father, she was already gone. My father found out years later that she made an Ame pact with your grandfather. Your father knew nothing about it."

His voice grew thick as his hands tightened, and I knew this pain. It was so hard to talk about someone you loved. Sometimes, tears were seen as a weakness, but when you talked about the people you loved, it wasn't a weakness. It was remembering who they were. For Tristian, this was all he had of his mother. Her greatest sacrifice was him, and I could only imagine how he felt about it.

"As soon as she had me, her soul was taken. She was gone before he even knew. Ame pacts are now outlawed. My father has been responsible for making sure it was never to be used again."

One man made all the difference in the world, and sometimes, a small change could lead to a bigger one, but I could see in Tristian's face he wanted to do more.

I turned and raised my hand over his cheek, his stubble grazing my fingers as he leaned into my touch.

"It affected my father for years, even after he married my

stepmother, who he deeply loved. But my father's heart broke that day, and something in his soul became cold. He hated the Silver Pearl Coven. He tolerated your father, but his hatred for the cruelty they showed grew, and it spilled into our house. So, Lil' Star, I felt like I had to hate you. I wanted to blame your family for every bad thing that happened to us, so when the chance came, I took it. I'm not proud of it, but I wanted you to hurt that night as I had for the first eighteen years of my life. It wasn't until after your parents' death that my father came clean about it all—my real mother, your parents, the coven's archaic way of punishments—but he gave me a letter, a letter from your mother to him, that she had written two days after my real mother's death. Your mother apologized for everything and swore an alliance of friendship until her last breath. My father never forgave your parents and raised me to hate the Silver Pearl and be loyal to Blood Moon, to Morgan."

I tilted my head at him and moved closer so our lips almost touched. "Tristian, I had no clue that…"

He kissed my forehead. "Shhh, Lil' Star. It's in the past, and I think we all have to forgive each other for the mistakes we've made, both past and present. We can't let our parents' hate for each other in the past become our future, and for what it's worth, Lexi, I am so damn sorry for it all."

I sat up and let the tears fall. "Tristian, we are not our parents. We can change the path laid out for us. We set our own way in the world. We'll learn from the mistakes that were made and set forth a new future."

He reached up, cupping my face and pulling me into a searing kiss. Our tongues danced with each other, and light caresses had us both out of breath. I laid my head on his chest and listened to his steady heartbeat. Tristian was my sun, always filled with light, but he still had dark days, and I planned to stay with him on those days.

Chapter Eight

The following day, I woke to a floofy white tail swatting my face.

"Dyna," I groaned. "Okay, off you go, you creature of chaos."

She squeaked a tiny meow as I gently pushed her off my chest. She promptly climbed over to Aden, who was asleep next to me, and snuggled into the crook of his arm that laid half haphazardly over his head.

I sat up and glanced around the room for my other two Devils, who were missing from our bed. The cool air hit my arms, and I pulled on one of Bash's hoodies to keep myself warm, leaving my legs bare.

I walked into the living room only to find it dark and silent, but a fresh pot of coffee was on, so they had to be here. I poured a cup for myself and took a sip of the smoky, bold flavor.

Noticing the patio door was slightly ajar, I walked toward it. Deep, masculine murmurs floated in from outside.

"Grayson says we might have an issue, that the keys might have more protection around them than we thought." Tristian's voice hinted at worry as I stepped out to see him and Bash sitting on the patio drinking coffee.

Bash's laptop was open, and he had his head down, typing away on his computer. Tristian looked up at me with a cocky smile. "Mornin', Lil' Star."

I scrunched my nose. "Too early to be that peppy, Trist. It's too damn early."

I plopped in the chair closest to Bash as he looked up and smirked at me. "I've been up since five a.m., Princess. This is midmorning for me."

He leaned over his laptop and kissed my lips lightly. The kiss was chaste, but it set my entire body on fire as the blush crept up my cheeks.

Tristian had his chin resting on his hand with a goofy smile. "You two are so cute. It's ridiculous. You know people are supposed to be scared of us, *frère*."

Bash pulled out a gun with one hand and aimed it at Tristian's head. Bash's smile was gone, and a menacing look replaced it as his fangs slid out to full length. Green eyes the color of acid peered at us. Deadly and dangerous, this was Providence Village's Prince Sebastian Ryder himself. This was the man I knew by reputation.

The one man who would not waste a second in destroying his enemy.

"That's so fucking hot," I murmured as my body reacted to his quick shift from his charming self to the villain of everyone's story.

Wait, did I have the hots for the villain? I shook myself from going down that wormhole.

I ran my fingers over my lips when his eyes turned to me. "Princess, do you have something to say?"

He moved his hand to my bare knee and crept his fingers up to my inner thigh. I looked over at Tristian.

I sucked in a breath, and Tristian's eyes sparkled with excitement, his smile still in place. "Oh... are we going to play this game?"

I looked over at him. "What game?"

Bash yawned lazily. "Oh, nothing, just a bit of payback for those two sneaking off with you."

I blushed and bit my lip. "Yeah, well, you were too busy being a bossy know-it-all."

Bash's fingers dipped low, circling slowly around the outside of my panties. "Wanna play chicken, Tristian?" he asked in a low voice.

"What are you...?"

Bash moved my panties to the side and sank a finger into me.

"Son of a—" I moaned as he slowly moved within me, his thumb finding my clit as he hooked his finger inside, hitting that perfect spot.

I dropped my mug on the table, almost spilling it. Tristian caught it from spilling over and set it to the side, his eyes never leaving Bash, who had a permanent cocky smile.

"Sit on my lap, Lexi," Bash demanded.

I moaned, "Screw you, Ryder."

He pumped faster, bringing me to the edge, his smile growing evil. "All in good time, baby, all in good time." He pulled his fingers out. "Now do what I say, Princess," he ordered me.

I gasped. "See...? So... bossy."

Tristian gave a masculine chuckle as Bash wrapped his arms around me and pulled me to his lap, my back flush against his chest.

He placed his knees on the inside of mine and then spread me out. The hoodie shifted with the movement, but he wrapped his arm around my waist and pulled the hoodie up more, exposing me completely to Tristian.

"Did you know you wore my hoodie?" I leaned back into him, feeling his arm tighten around me. "Usually, if you wear our clothes, it's Aden's or Tristian's, but you wore mine today."

I moaned as he kissed my neck, sucking lightly against my vein.

Tristian's copper eyes grew dark as he watched us, his smile gone as something more primal took over. Bash inserted two fingers inside me, pumping back and forth as I moaned incoherent thoughts.

My hips lifted to meet his hand.

"See, Princess, the thing is, you came out here looking fucking delicious and teasing me this morning, so we're going to have consequences."

His hand retreated from my pussy, and he slapped the inside of my thigh, not hard, but just enough to send a shiver of want through me.

"Fuck, Bash."

Tristian moved closer.

"How wet is she, *frère*?" Bash asked him.

"Soaked." Tristian licked his lips as he took in the view. "She's soaked."

Bash pushed two fingers back inside me, pumping at a speed that should have been illegal. Suddenly, he added a third.

"You want to come, Princess?"

I whimpered. "Yes, yes, please."

His fingers worked steadily, hitting that perfect spot. Bash looked over at Tristian and nodded as something passed between their eyes.

Tristian dropped to his knees and moved forward. He snaked his tongue out and took over, working his magic on my clit. He circled it slowly as Bash fucked me with his fingers.

An orgasm started bubbling up.

"Bash." I leaned my head to the side as Bash moaned.

His cock hardened beneath me as he moved to get the friction he needed. Tristian's tongue flicked my clit again, and I fell into utter bliss. Bash moved his lips to my neck as I gripped Tristian's head, pulling him where I needed him.

"Tristian." I gave him the permission he wasn't even asking for but knew he wanted.

Bash's fangs pierced my skin just a second before Tristian sank his fangs into my inner thigh. I came, screaming their names and gripping Tristian's hair as he moaned into my thigh, drinking me in.

Bash's fingers continued to pump in and out, and he had me coming around him one more time. I groaned softly, leaning against Bash as he healed my neck with a brush of his tongue. Tristian pulled away, his fangs dripping with blood as he licked his lips and kissed his way up my thigh.

He straightened while still on his knees and stole a kiss from my lips. "You taste like sweet sangria on a hot summer day, Lexi."

My eyes fluttered open, and Tristian's eyes were so full of emotion, I didn't have words to express them back. I kissed him again. Bash's fingers left me, and he pulled me back into another kiss. He was harder than before, and I wanted more. I liked what we had been denied for so long.

"Hey, guys, I just got a text from Grayson and Hudson that they'll be here in—" Aden stopped dead in his tracks, looking at the three of us, clearly about to take this thing to the next level. "Damnit, did I miss what I think I missed?"

I pulled away, laughing as Bash released my legs and pulled me to the side so I could curl into his lap. I laid my head on his shoulder and whispered, "Is it always like that?"

He looked down at me, and his eyes shone with a glint of laughter.

"No, Princess, that's just us. That's what we do to each other, and I swear, if Grayson weren't on his way, I would have you bent over this table, fucking you until you couldn't walk."

I licked his neck at that statement. "How fast can you—"

Aden was next to us in a flash. "Oh no, we have to see Coco, so get ready. No more moody vamp fucking for you this morning."

I sat up quickly, earning a curse from Bash as I leaped to the door. "*Shit*! I'm so freakin' late!"

Tristian laughed. "You can just blame it on me!"

I ran into the house and dressed quickly in tights and a crop top that said "Sirens do it better."

I met Aden at the car. He was leaning back in dark pants and a white button-down with the first few buttons open, his tattoos peeking out from the collar. He looked like he was ready for a photoshoot.

I shook my head. "You know you aren't supposed to be prettier than me, right?" I poked my finger into his hard chest.

He smiled at me. "No one's prettier than you, baby"—he leaned down to my ear and breathed out—"or tastes better than you. Don't think I didn't notice I didn't get an invite this morning."

I blushed as I nudged him aside to get into the car. "Let's go, Casanova."

He laughed as he entered the driver's side before sending us out the gates and heading downtown to Coco's Bakery.

Coco's Bakery was set in an old 1920s art deco building that had once been an upscale restaurant. Its bright white exterior gleamed in the sun with the striped seafoam-green awning welcoming its customers. The lights shone through the large open window, and I peered in as Coco set cupcakes in her display case. A sense of comfort surrounded me. Something about the café made me feel that way.

I had helped Coco paint the walls, I worked here in my teens and adulthood, and then, there was Coco herself. She had dropped everything for me after my parents died and was there for every important thing. She taught me how to cook, how to throw a punch, and how to find love again. Without her, I wasn't sure I'd be the person I was today. She and Daniels were the reason I was who I was, and I don't think I ever thanked them. Tears filled my eyes as I realized how much I needed to be here. How much I truly needed her even after all of these years.

I opened the door, and she raised her eyes to look at me. Relief passed over her expression as she rushed to me from behind the green counter, wrapping me in a tight hug. "Lexi, are you okay?"

I sniffled and hugged her closer. "Yeah, I'm okay, Aunt Coco."

She pulled back, looking at me. "You have sadness swimming in your eyes. What's going on?" My lip trembled, and the first tear threatened to fall. Her eyes widened as she looked back at Aden. "Aden Charmante, you better start explaining why my niece is about to burst into tears, young man. I swear, I will beat you with a wooden spoon if I have to."

I hiccuped a laugh. "He didn't do a damn thing, Coco. Back off. I just missed you, that's all."

Aden pulled me back and wiped my tears. "Let's sit down, baby."

Coco glanced between us and pointed. "Ummm, explain."

"Aunt Coco, can we get a coffee and maybe one of those morning buns? I promise I'll tell you everything."

She narrowed her eyes at me, considering her decision. "Fine, go sit." She waved us off.

We found a small round table near the back.

Coco brought us a pot of coffee and an assortment of pastries. "Here, drink and eat."

I poured a cup of coffee and grabbed the nearest morning bun, taking a bite out of the cinnamony goodness. "Coco, holy shit, these are insanely good. You're going to have a line out the door even more now."

She bounced in her seat. "I *know*!" She giddily laughed like it was the best thing she had ever heard. But then she turned to Aden and frowned. "Talk, Devil."

Aden sipped his coffee, the cup looking far too small for his large fingers. "I think it would be best if Lexi explains everything. Plus, you look like you want to stab me with a fork."

She huffed. "Please, like I would ruin my exquisite silverware on you, Charmante."

I took another sip of coffee and placed my cup down. "Okay, Coco, so it happened the night Daniels was killed…"

I started with the engagement party and told her about the missing mermaids, Nyx's death, and how The Wishmaker was behind it all. I didn't tell her everything—I left out all the sex with the guys—but she figured I was at least with the three of them. I also "forgot" the robbery for her protection—no need to have her and Jason as accomplices.

She sat still, taking everything in, and looked to Aden, who'd

stayed silent the entire time. "You love her?"

I blushed at the statement, and Aden nodded.

"I don't remember a time I didn't love her."

Coco turned back to me with a frown on her lips. "I know why you didn't tell me everything, Lexi, but what can Jason and I do to help? We're part of the Silver Pearl and have a right to protect our people, too."

I smiled because, of course, my wild aunt wouldn't back down from a fight to protect what she loved. "Actually, Jason might be able to help. Let me talk to the rest of the guys and see, but if we need help, I'll reach out. Coco, I couldn't bear it if anything happened to you too." My throat tightened as I choked back the tears. "You're all I have left."

She moved closer, pulling me into a hug. "Hey, listen, nothing will happen to me."

I held back the tears. I was exhausted from crying, and I wasn't going to start again.

She laid her cheek next to mine and whispered, "If and when I go, just know I'm always with you, Lexi."

I frowned. "I just don't want to forget you. I feel like I barely remember my parents sometimes. I can't remember their faces as I used to. I'm just worried I'll forget them both one day."

She pulled back and smiled gently. "They're always with us in some way. Just because someone is gone doesn't mean they're forgotten. Remembering who they were is the most important thing, and live for them every single day, Lexi. Don't let the bullshit destroy you. Make sure you remember that, don't let the politics, the danger, or even the men"—she smirked at Aden—"let you forget who you are and where you came from."

I smiled and pulled her in for one more hug. "Thank you, Aunt Coco. I needed that."

She murmured, "That's what I'm here for, and I want the dish later on the boys." She stood and winked before strutting away to the counter to help the line that was forming.

We sat in silence as we finished our coffee. I just wanted to bathe in Coco's comforting presence a bit longer.

Once the last drop of coffee was gone, Aden placed his hand on mine. "Let's go home."

I smiled down at the cup. *Home*. That was something that felt so lost to me for years. Now I realized home wasn't just one place; it could feel like many.

I looked toward Coco working behind the counter and smiled. "Yeah, let's head home."

We headed back to the house. I sighed out a breath of relief I had been holding on to since we arrived.

"Wasn't so bad, was it, baby?" Aden reached for my hand across the console, bringing it to his lips.

"No, I just want to keep her safe."

He nodded, keeping his eyes on the road. "You are. Letting her know what's going on keeps her safer than not."

I tilted my head, smiling at him. "You're wise beyond your years, Aden Charmante."

He laughed. "I don't know about that, baby."

He pulled up through the gates, and his relaxed posture stiffened.

"Aden? What is it?"

He held up a hand to silence me. "Something's not right. The charms Tristian put in place are down." He furrowed his eyebrows and cursed, and I followed his gaze. Two of our guards were slumped over on the ground. Sonny lay on his side, not moving, and fear trickled down my spine.

"Aden?"

He unbuckled his belt, reached over, and opened the glove box where a gun sat. "You know how to use this, right?"

I looked at him in shock.

"Baby, you know how to use a gun, right?" he asked firmly, placing the cold steel in my hand.

I wordlessly nodded as I gripped the gun, remembering what Daniels and Jason had taught me.

"Here are the bullets."

I took the box of bullets and checked whether the gun was loaded. It wasn't, so I added six rounds and put the safety on. I pointed the gun down as I opened the door and slid out of the car.

Aden walked to the first body on the ground and checked on them. He shook his head and walked to Sonny. Aden slid his fingers to his throat and pulled out his cell, calling 9-1-1.

I scanned the area, looking for anyone or anything in the trees. The sun was high in the sky, and something moved in the distance. I backed to Aden, keeping one eye on whatever caught my attention. I bent down next to him, his eyes following my movement with a frown.

In a quiet voice, I said, "I saw something in the woods." I nodded in the direction of the movement.

He squinted, looking at the trees. "Where the hell are Tristian and Bash?" he asked.

"Aden, you have super hearing, so freaking use it," I hissed at him.

He glanced at me. "Relax, Lexi."

He stood with his gun drawn at his side, closing his eyes and opening his senses to the forest behind us. I continued to search the trees for any danger that might be lurking in the thick redwood forest. Sonny's labored breathing rattled in my ears, so I crouched and took hold of his hand, where a piece of paper was crumbled up. I gently took it, opened it up, and growled at the note written inside.

Aden shot to my side, looking to the woods. "It's too quiet, Lexi, no animals, no rustling in the trees. I can't hear them nearby, but that doesn't mean they aren't here. One of us needs to stay with Sonny, and one should find Bash and Trist."

"I'll look for them." Before he could argue, I held up a hand. "Look, I'll be careful, and I'll be safer if I do find them versus you leaving me here alone to track them down yourself."

His eyes narrowed, and he finally nodded. "Go."

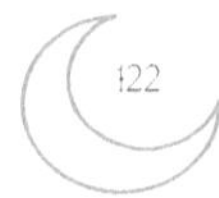

I put the gun's safety back on and put it in the back of my jeans. I shot off to the house, running as fast as possible, pumping my arms and forcing my legs to move. After I reached the porch, I pulled my gun out and wrenched the door open.

Only a dark room greeted me. Dyna was curled up on the couch, and when I entered, she opened one light-blue eye and immediately closed it again.

"Too busy napping to actually know any danger, huh?" I stroked her head as I passed and checked each room carefully.

I went to the back, only to hear the masculine laughs of two men coming from outside. Relief washed over me as I returned to the front of the house. I stepped out to the patio with my gun still clasped in my hand and pointed at the ground.

I made it around the path to the beach, where two surfboards sat in the sand. Bash and Tristian stood nearby, their chests bare and wet suits hanging from their hips. Tristian ran a towel through his hair to get the excess sand out, and Bash sat on the sand, leaning on his elbows and laughing at whatever Tristian had just said. I looked around warily for any signs of danger.

Fear lanced through me, knowing how easily they could have been killed out in the open. I closed my eyes, thanking the stars they were safe. To lose one of them would put an ache in my heart forever. I didn't know if I could recover if I lost any of them. I knew deep down that my heart would remain forever broken.

"Lexi?" Tristian's voice cut through my thoughts, and I opened my eyes. Concern creased his brows as he flicked his eyes to the gun in confusion. "Lil' Star, why do you have a gun?"

Bash sat up, his eyes wide. "Lexi?"

I swallowed hard and walked up to them, carefully handing them the note with the curly red script that Sonny had held.

A gift just for you, my darling Rose.

Bash read the note aloud, his eyes flashing red.

I whispered in a low voice, so only they could hear me, "Sonny's been shot, and the other guard is dead. The Wishmaker is here."

Chapter Nine

Tristian's mouth dropped open in surprise, and Bash pulled me to him. His hands wandered over my body, looking for injuries. I pushed his hands away but brought his face close to mine.

"I'm fine, but we need to get to Aden. He might be in danger. He called the police, so they're on the way. I thought... I thought..." My voice cracked at the end.

Bash pulled me closer as Tristian moved behind me. "It's okay, Lil' Star, we're okay." He kissed my cheek.

With glistening eyes, I looked up at Bash. "I thought I hated you all once. I thought I would dance on your graves the day you died. But now..." My voice tightened with the thought of losing any of them, my Devils. "Now, I don't think I'd survive if I lost any of you. If you guys exit this world, you better bring me with you. If not, know I'll be right behind you." As I spoke, Bash's eyes lit with a green blaze.

Bash opened his mouth to respond, but the wail of an approaching siren cut him off. "Let's get to Aden first, Princess. Can I carry you?"

I moved closer to him. "Of course."

He lifted me in a princess carry, and I wrapped my arms around his neck. What would typically be a romantic gesture was for practicality. A whoosh of air hit me as my stomach dropped with the shift of my body. I pulled myself closer to him and tightened my grip on his neck, closing my eyes. I was worried I'd throw up Coco's morning bun and coffee from earlier if I opened them. We halted in a smooth motion. It wasn't as sudden as I thought, but it was more like a graceful landing. I opened my eyes as Bash shifted and set me on my feet.

"Shit, this is bad," Bash said under his breath as he took in the scene.

EMTs were loading Sonny into an ambulance, and another covered the other guard with a white sheet.

Tristian took my hand. "Bash, was that one of Grayson's?" He indicated to the bag, and Bash nodded solemnly.

"He's gonna be pissed. We need to make sure he won't retaliate against us."

I huffed in agreement and scanned the crowd for Aden.

He wore a scowl as Agent Rengard, whose back was to us, pointed angrily at the dead guard. "Mr. Charmante, I will hold you for obstruction if you do not tell me where Ms. Rose, Mr. Cassium, and Mr. Ryder are!"

Aden raised his chin and looked over at us, a devilish smirk forming across his lips. "Agent Rengard, your detective skills are seriously inadequate if you can't locate three people. Now, if you must know the whereabouts of my girl and *mes frères*, I suggest you look behind you." He crossed his arms and nodded to us.

Agent Rengard twisted around. He seemed relieved at first, then turned his eyes to Bash. He clenched his jaw as he stomped toward us. "Explain." He pointed behind him.

Bash stood still, his shoulders back and his hands clenched to his sides. "We were surfing, didn't hear or see anything. What the hell do you want me to say?"

"Do you think I'm a damn idiot, Ryder? You weren't here, so you couldn't have possibly set this up? How about you, Cassium? Are you going to cover for your boss again, or are you going to let him keep from killing *again*?" He sputtered. "Maybe we can solve a cold case for once if you tell the truth, Ryder."

Bash snapped. "You think I fucking killed her parents!" He barked a laugh. "Wow, you really are a terrible FBI agent, aren't you? Tell me, Rengard, who the hell did you fuck to get that badge? How many dicks did you take up the ass to get that little sliver of metal? Stop playing stupid." His teeth snapped out, and his eyes turned crimson.

Rengard pulled forward, glaring at him. "You wanna play, little vampire, like how you love to play with the siren? Does he tell you he's in love with you, Lexi? Does he tell you he's sorry?" His eyes flicked to mine. "One day, he'll do the same thing again. They'll all break you again. They'll turn on you. Here's a bit of advice. Beware of the devil with the pretty face, Ms. Rose."

His words hit hard like punches to my stomach. Would they do the same thing to me? Would they leave me once this was over with? Was I just a pawn in this chess game? The underlying fear of what they did and that they might someday repeat it sank in, and I clenched my fist.

The air hissed as Bash's fist flew and landed against Rengard's cheek. Rengard stumbled back into Hyde, who had stood quietly to the side the entire time.

Aden and Tristian pulled Bash back. "Fuck you, you piece of shit sphinx. One of us has to do the hard work here to keep our covens safe while the rest of the FBI is off doing God knows what!"

Rengard snapped his head back to us. He snarled while wiping the blood trickling down his lip.

Hyde growled at us. "One word, boss, and I'll arrest his ass." He started to move toward Bash, taking out a baton.

Rengard spit blood out of his mouth and snarled and glared at us. "No, Officer Hyde. He gets one shot, that's it."

My eyes widened when Rengard turned to me. His eyes softened as he walked over to me and whispered, "Lexi, excuse me for the outburst. I... I find that I'm protective over you. Are you okay?"

"You mean because someone is trying to stalk and possibly kill me, and that same person is the one who killed my parents...? Yeah, I'm peachy keen about this all, especially the young man who died at my gates today," I bit out. "No, I'm not okay, and I would appreciate it if the FBI and the Providence Village Police could get their heads out of their asses and do *actual* police work instead of harassing my men and me!"

"Lexi, I know—"

I shook my head. "*No!* I'm tired of you blaming these three men for your mistakes. No one should have gotten through the charms placed on this gate, and no one should have been able to get past the guards, but somehow, they did. That means whoever killed this innocent man works for our inner circle. This is a betrayal of the trust and loyalty of the covens. Agent Rengard, if I can be honest, the lack of evidence and the fact you keep blaming my men means you have no clue who is doing this. Once you're done with your questions, leave and do not return until you have something better to tell me." His mouth was grim, set in a straight line, but he didn't say a word, so I continued. "I'll do what I see fit for my coven. If you come back here again blaming Bash, we're going to have issues. Good night, sir." I turned and walked away.

"Lexi!" Agent Rengard yelled.

I reluctantly turned around and glared at him. I shook my head. "These Devils—*my Devils*—may have pretty faces, Agent Rengard, but I'm the one you should be wary of. Remember, it's the siren's way to lure you to the ocean's depths and never return."

I sat on the porch steps, looking at the scene—the lights whirling colors around our heads, the quick movements of the EMTs rushing to get Sonny to the hospital.

A woman ran through the gates. She was tall with full hips and a beautiful warm glow to her skin. Her hair was up in a messy bun, as if she had just woken up. Her eyes were frantic, and they landed on Tristian.

She rushed over to him, and they embraced. He hugged her close, and a slight twinge of jealousy raced through me as Bash reached them, putting a hand on hers.

Aden came over and sat beside me. With his head low, a hushed whisper crossed his lips. "That's Isbel, Sonny's wife. I called her after I called the police." His shoulders fell as a deep sigh escaped his lips, and I felt ashamed of my jealousy.

I laid my head on his shoulder. "He's going to be okay, Aden. You saved his life," I whispered.

With tears streaming down her face, Isbel slid into the back of the ambulance with Sonny. Before the doors shut, she looked toward us and mouthed, "Thank you" to Aden. He raised a hand to her as an EMT pulled the doors closed, and they drove off. The reporter vans and newscasters tried to follow the ambulance while some stayed.

Their emotions were overwhelming with excitement, thrill, and intrigue, but none had grief, pain, or sorrow. A fae was dead, and all these people only saw the story. It was sickening but human. That was the thing with humans. If it didn't affect them personally, they usually didn't care, or they put up a facade. Aden shifted as he pulled me closer to him, and we watched people, medics, and others trickle out of the front yard.

Agent Rengard had his phone to his ear. An enraged look crossed his face when his eyes found mine. He stabbed at his cell phone, irately ending his call, and a snarl formed on his lips. He strode to his car, got in with a slam of the door, and sped away, leaving a trail of dust in his wake.

Tristian and Bash walked over to us. Bash had his phone to his ear. "Yeah, we'll see you soon." I lifted my head as he sat on my other side. "Grayson and Hudson are coming soon. We need to check the area where you saw something, Lexi."

I looked at his hand, and a bruise was forming already. "You good?"

He moved so he was in front of me. "Princess, I would punch a dozen more people to ensure you know I'm always on your side and will do whatever it takes to keep you safe. I'm not going anywhere. I would never hurt you again. I hope you believe me."

He laid a gentle kiss on my head, and I couldn't help smiling at the sweet gesture.

I nodded and stood. "Let's go."

We all stood and walked toward the wooded area that surrounded the north side of the house. I walked silently next to Tristian as Aden and Bash talked quietly behind us.

"You know he speaks the truth. We would... we would never hurt you again, Lil' Star."

I stepped closer and brushed his arm with mine. "I want to believe you three couldn't hurt me on purpose, but don't pretend you wouldn't do it for your coven. I would do it for my coven if I had to. Suppose I had to give you three up for the safety and well-being of my people. As much as my heart would shatter, it's my duty to my coven."

He didn't say a word, as he sensed the truth in my words. We walked along the edge where the ocean met the trees. I knew he felt the same, as his silence spoke volumes.

I scanned the woods as they hummed with life around me. The bees buzzed, birds sang in the trees, and the sun broke through the tops of the giant redwoods that sprung up around us. It lit up a small path through the moss that grew on the ground and gleamed against the sun's rays dancing on the forest floor.

Wildflowers scattered around the trees and the brush. Purple lupine and red, white, and yellow lilies peeked out of logs, rocks, and between growths of the forest.

I spotted a blue night witch nightshade. I made a note to come back and get some when I had the right equipment to store it. It was highly poisonous but was the main ingredient in many of our potions.

We kept hiking until Aden stepped through the brush and discovered the vantage point that revealed the house. "Lexi, we're close to where you pointed out that you saw movement. Everyone keep your eyes out for anything, and don't drop your guard, just in case they decide to attack again."

All three of them pulled out their guns as we searched. The forest got denser, and the sun was almost nonexistent through the redwood canopy. I scanned the floor but only saw pine needles, moss, and wild mushrooms.

I whispered next to Tristian, "I don't see anything." I sighed, looking around.

Tristian looked down at me. "Keep looking, Lil' Star. We'll find something soon."

Aden and Bash joined us. "Nothing," Bash said as he scanned the trees, expecting someone to jump out at us.

"I'm pretty sure they're long gone, *frère*," Tristian said, looking into the canopy of the trees.

I felt a twinge of magic and stopped in my tracks, narrowing my eyes and searching for it. "Something's here," I said barely above a whisper, and all three snapped their heads to me.

"Found something, baby?" Aden placed his hand on my lower back.

"Yeah, I can feel the magic. It's faint though, as if... it's under a disguisement spell."

I needed to concentrate to seek out the magic. Daniels had taught me the spell a few months ago. I only hoped my power wouldn't drain completely if I had to fight any danger. Witches had to practice weekly to be powerful, and I had been so deep into potions lately that I hadn't kept up with my weekly practices.

I found a spot near the trunk of a tree. Soft green moss grew around the ring, and I kneeled to the ground, pressing my fingers into the ground.

"Lexi, what are you doing?" Aden asked.

Aden looked concerned, but Tristian bumped his arm. "Shh, she needs to concentrate."

Bash stood in the distance, giving me room to focus. His intense gaze was on me while I felt the cold earth. I returned his look. He nodded for me to continue.

I gave him a small smile and blew out a breath. Closing my eyes, I concentrated on the feel of the magic around me. It was like a thick fog just sitting behind a veil. I had to pull at it slowly to feel the magic. A slight buzz ran through my fingertips as I cleared my mind and pushed into that feeling to see if I could seek out the spot.

I followed the slow movement of the magic, and it became thicker the closer I got to it. My fingers came up, and smoke slowly swirled between my palms. I focused on the spell and had it guide me to the spot.

A vision flashed in my mind. It showed a gloved hand slipping something into a log that sat behind a few fallen trees. The log was hollowed out and covered in snow-white flowers. I remembered Daniels called them fairy bells.

I opened my eyes and looked around until I spotted the log in the distance. Three very serious vampires stared at me, and I smiled with excitement as I stood up, brushing off my tights.

"Found it."

I turned and walked to the log as their feet shuffled through the woods.

"Did you see the power around her?" Tristian whispered behind me.

"You didn't think I could do it?" I asked with a frown.

Tristian held his hand up. "No, Lil' Star, it's not that. You pulled the magic around you."

"Only experienced witches can do that, and from what you've told us, you don't have the abilities to do that," Bash said from behind me. "We three are drawn to the more powerful fae, and we always thought it might be your siren that lures us in—even when you don't mean to—but I don't think that's it. I think it's a combination of both, Lexi. It's just you, and you're what makes us, us."

Heat crept into my cheeks at that proclamation. "I just did what felt right, like I was becoming one with my magic. It felt right." I stepped over a rock as we came to the log. I searched around the rock, not seeing anything.

"What are we looking for, baby?" Aden knelt to the ground, running his hand over the log, searching for the disguisement spell.

I wrinkled my nose, recalling the memory. "A gray glass bottle with a silver top. It has a red wax seal on top of it."

I saw a bundle of fairy bells hanging in a circle as if pointing out the bare spot on the log that moss had not touched yet.

"Here."

I traced the dampened wood and felt the thickness of the magic coat my fingers.

Tristian came over, his eyes wide. "I can feel it too."

I raised an eyebrow. "You sure you aren't part witch?"

He shook his head. "Nah, it feels too raw, like I'm not supposed to know it's there."

I bent down, pushing my magic as my hand fell through and hit bottom. Cool glass met my fingers, and I grasped it and pulled it out slowly.

"Got it." I smiled, showing the three of them the small bottle.

"You did, but the question is... what the hell is it?"

Chapter Ten

B ash gazed at the bottle like it might explode in my hands.

"Bash, I don't think it's dangerous." I sat on the log, examining the bottle.

"How do you know that, Princess?" He sat next to me as I turned the bottle around.

"Just a gut feeling."

The small vial felt ancient in my hands. Streaks of black ran on the inside, and the red wax was slightly cracking on the edges. I peered at the inside, seeing a dark-cinnamon liquid swirling around.

Bash stiffened. "What's that in the center?" He moved closer to get a look, his curiosity finally winning out.

The center of the bottle was hollowed out and held a black obsidian crystal. The crystal shined, despite its inky color.

"It looks like obsidian, which is used for protection," Tristian pointed out.

I noticed Aden from the corner of my eye. He was utterly still, his eyes pensive, as if he was trying to figure out what could be in the bottle and what trouble would come with taking it. I turned to him and gave him a slight smile.

"It can draw in the negative, transmute, and expel it again. If you use clear quartz, it can make balance around you." I must have looked shocked because he chuckled.

"How did you know that?" Aden's eyes tilted to me.

"How?" I raised a brow. "If you aren't a witch, you usually don't know these things." I shrugged.

Aden chuckled. "Morgan made us go through every single fae known. We know the strengths and weaknesses of most every fae." He tapped his chin. "Though some are trickier than others."

"I'm glad Morgan trained you three to know everything about all the witches in the covens. I'm lucky, because even with my lack of knowledge and training, Daniels drilled knowledge into me about every single type of fae in the covens. Hell, he even told me about the other covens across the country on the East Coast. We have bounds to the Celestial Flame Coven. He has—" I paused, noticing my mistake. "He *had* a good friend. Her name was Saoirse Kelly, and she had a daughter my age, Niamh. She had gone through something similar. She, too, lost someone she loved."

Bash took my hand and kissed it. "The past is the past. Like with us, we were fools then who wanted to be cruel, but now, *now*, you own our hearts. You're a true siren. You lured us without meaning to."

I smiled and kissed him softly. "Thank you."

His eyes lit up with desire, and I bit my lip when Tristian suddenly cursed, pulling out his phone and breaking our moment. "Grayson's here. We gotta go."

I stood and put the bottle in my pocket as we walked toward where we had come in.

Bash kept my hand in his, and Aden's finger brushed mine as we walked, sending little shocks throughout my body. We made our way down to the house and saw Grayson and Hudson sitting on the steps looking at us curiously as we walked toward them.

"They say Sonny is going to be okay," Grayson said to Bash as something silent passed between them.

Bash reached out and took his hand. "I'm sorry about Marcel. He was one hell of a wolf." A flash of regret passed through Bash's eyes, and my heart tugged at Grayson and his coven's loss.

Grayson's wall broke, and his grief from losing his longtime friend barreled into me. A vision flashed in my mind of Grayson as a teenager with a young skinny boy at his side. Marcel and Grayson weren't just coven members; Marcel was part of his pack, and the hit of losing a member was detrimental to him. They would feel this loss for a long time.

Grayson's jaw clenched, and he turned toward me. His eyes were yellowing as his wolf peeked out. He slammed his wall back up, blocking me out. "They said it was a long-range rifle and that they didn't stand a chance."

I walked to him and wrapped my arms around him in a hug. I knew how he felt. His pain was the same as when I found out about Nyx. "I'm sorry for your coven's loss, but know we'll find who did this to him."

Grayson held me close. I felt his wolf become at ease with the comfort of my hug. He inhaled deeply as I siphoned away some of his pain and grief. His grief was bitter like a lousy cup of coffee; it sat in my stomach, and I had a sickening feeling that I would throw up as I absorbed his anguish.

Grayson moved back slightly, loosening his grip on me. He gave me a small knowing smile as he whispered breathlessly into my ear, "Thank you, seductress."

I cleared my throat and turned my attention back to Bash, Aden, and Tristian. Their arms were crossed, and they sported a slight.

I rolled my eyes. Grayson looked between us with his usual playboy smile and let out a chuckle.

His deep Southern accent spoke to me quietly, "Didn't anyone tell you never to wander off into the woods? You never know what big bad is waiting for you, seductress."

He looked like he wouldn't have hesitated to take a bite out of me, and a shiver rippled through my body, but it wasn't pleasant. Grayson had a smoothness that no one else did. His wolf was strong, and with a dragon that lived within him, it made him casually dangerous.

"We can handle ourselves." I smirked back at him before I pushed away from him.

He let out a full belly laugh. "Oh, I don't doubt it for a second, Ms. Rose." He moved over to Hudson to put space between us. "You gonna tell us what you found or leave me in anticipation?"

I pulled out the small glass bottle. "Know anything about ancient witch potions?" I raised an eyebrow.

His smile dropped into a frown. "No, but I know someone who does. She just happens to be one of the oldest witches, but she's no coven witch, siren. She handles voodoo, mostly necromancy."

Necromancy was a raw form of dark magic, and with witches, it was all about balance. A witch had to be careful, or they could easily lose themselves in the dark magic, but if used correctly by balancing it with their own natural magic, it was a powerful tool. Using too much dark magic could corrupt the soul, and if used incorrectly, the spell would not only hurt the witch, it would hurt others around them. It was a balance that only a few witches could accomplish, and they had to be strong to control it.

My father told me horror stories of necromancers who had let the dark magic seep into them. It destroyed their souls and physically destroyed them, so they were nothing but hollow versions of themself and ashes.

Grayson must have noticed my shock. "She's not evil; not all necromancers are, *but* she is good at what she does. She's an ally you want to have since you're dealing with The Wishmaker's dark magic." He took the bottle from my hands. "Would you like to meet with her tonight?" He scrutinized the bottle as his eyes shifted to his wolf's amber color. "The etching on the side... it's in Creole."

I leaned over his arm and saw that part of the glass was worn and darker with smudges running along its side, but it had a slight bump. I ran my fingers along it.

"Damn, I can't make it out." I blew out a breath.

Grayson handed the bottle back to me. "We can ask Brigitte tonight."

Hudson, who had been silently on his phone, spoke up. "She'll meet us at the Ryder Estate in the graveyard by the mausoleum at midnight."

I had to bite down a laugh. The image of us walking through a graveyard to meet a voodoo queen sounded absolutely absurd, but that was the way of the fae. We did weird shit.

Aden threw an elbow playfully into my side. "Shh."

Hudson looked over at me, trying to hide his smile, explaining, "One of the most powerful times is midnight." He shrugged.

I nodded, clearing my throat. "That makes sense. So, there must be a reason you guys wanted to see us. Is it about what's going on tomorrow?"

Hudson moved closer, whispering, "I think we should go inside and speak where there aren't ears around." He nervously scanned the wooded area around us, as if trouble would pop out.

I followed his stare into the dark foliage that surrounded us. "Fair. Let's go inside." I stepped up to the porch as Hudson and Grayson followed my Devils and me inside.

I made my way to the kitchen to pull out six crystal tumblers and a bottle of whiskey. After pouring a large amount into each glass, I passed them out silently.

I raised my glass. "To Marcel and Sonny."

They echoed me, and we toasted to the two guards who risked their lives to stay true to the covens.

We sipped in silence, and Bash turned to Grayson. "The robbery."

Grayson nodded and motioned to the group. "I have a way in and a way out, but the way out is, well... it's going to be an issue."

He motioned us over to the dining room table, where the floor plans were laid out. Once we'd all gathered around, he pointed to a red circle in the center of the paper.

Hudson turned to me. "How much do you know of Celtic knots?"

I scrunched my nose, thinking about what I'd read in the grimoires. "Well, I know we use them for protection, strength, and even to balance our power. As for humans and their religions, I know they use them for so many different reasons. The covens use three interlocking arcs that form the knots. Many historians think it may date back to the fourth century, so we don't know if it came from the Romans or the Celts."

Hudson smiled widely. "You're correct, Lexi. Not that I didn't think you wouldn't have known. Here's another question for you." His smile grew. "Do you know what happens to be in the center of the vaults...?"

I groaned and pinched my nose. "Morgan had a witch put a damn protection spell on the vaults."

Grayson looked my way. "Bingo, seductress. We'll only have about thirty minutes down there before the witch who cast it is going to tell Morgan about the breach."

A stream of curses flew from everyone's mouths.

"What the hell are we going to do?"

Tristian leaned over the floor plan. "Which one is the most guarded safe? Morgan is smart, not cocky. He'll have extra men on that door."

Hudson pointed to the extended hallway. "Here. I've only been down with Kane a few times, but there are always three guards on this door."

Tristian set his drink down and glanced over to Bash and Aden, who nodded in silent agreement. "I know a spell that can take down the protection spell for about fifteen minutes. Will that give you enough time to steal the keys?"

Hudson rubbed the back of his neck. "If everything goes

perfectly, yeah."

Grayson spoke up in a low drawl. "Then it goes perfectly. You're the best damn thief in Providence Village. You got this."

Hudson let out a shaky breath. "I can do it." His eyes were set with determination.

"The problem isn't taking the spell down. It's who cast the spell. They'll know as soon as it breaks." Aden narrowed his eyes at the red circle, as if it would tell him the answer he was searching for.

"So, we know where to go and how we're going to break in, all while taking out a whole team of guards and stealing the keys, but we don't know what's protecting them in the vault itself. Then we have to get out in time, all while hoping the person who cast the spell doesn't tell Morgan. Yeah, that's gonna be a walk in the park," I sarcastically pointed out.

Aden huffed as he swished the amber liquid around. "I know who did the spell. I feel like an idiot for not thinking of it before."

I raised a brow. "Who?"

"Our favorite slimy little weasel." Aden smiled as he took a drink.

"Shit, it's Franklin." I groaned.

Grayson growled. "We're screwed."

Bash, who had stayed silent this whole time, finally spoke from the kitchen, where he was leaning against the counter. " I know how to keep him busy."

I jerked my head to him. "How?"

Bash gave me a half smile. "Let's just say Franklin doesn't just enjoy little sirens; he likes to dominate vampires too."

My eyes widened in surprise. "Oh…" Bash's smile was contagious, and I could tell he was going to leave chaos in his wake at the party. I chuckled. "Destroy him, my Devil." An evil smile formed on my lips.

Bash's grin turned dark. "Princess, I do love it when you get vengeful."

I walked toward him and rested my hand on his chest as I looked into his eyes. "Oh, you haven't seen vengeful yet, Sebastian Ryder.

No one tries to take what's mine."

He pulled me closer, letting me know how much he enjoyed me like this.

"Well, then, boys"—he looked down at me with a filthy smile when I cleared my throat—"and Princess. Let's steal from the King of the Blood Moon Coven and take down his sick weasel."

Chapter Eleven

Grayson and Hudson said their goodbyes and left, and Grayson sent a few wolves from Trinity to bring us ancient books on witchcraft. Tristian had a few allies of the Blood Moon bring us grimoires to search for the spell to break the protection spell.

We spent the rest of the day reading books and trying to find anything about the potion we found. I sat another stack of books down with a thump. The old books smelled of leather, wood, and vanilla. I began to open the first cover, which had a symbol of the moon phases with protection charms etched into the leather. I scanned the index for anything about breaking the spell, but so far, the books weren't full of valuable information.

I found about a dozen love spells, how to gain wealth, a few spells on sickness and warts, a charm against danger, and how to create small storms and fire in your hand.

I groaned, slamming a book shut. "Nothing about how to break a protection spell, damn it." I rubbed my eyes, praying the burn would leave.

I looked at the clock. It was close to the time we needed to leave. I pushed off from the table as Bash came up to me.

"Go get ready, Princess. We'll continue—"

All of a sudden, all our phones went off at once, the buzzing sound filling the room.

I reached mine, and a grainy video from our outside camera came up. I could see nothing but the driveway until Sonny and Marcel casually walked into the frame laughing, heading to the front gate. A pop rang out from the gun going off in the distance.

Marcel fell to his knees, and Sonny reached for him, shock written across his face. Then the realization hit him before he dragged Marcel back. He pulled his gun from his holster and began shooting in the direction the bullet came from.

The second pop was louder, and I watched it hit him in the shoulder. A few inches to the right, and it would have hit his heart. I didn't realize how close we were to having another casualty. He fell back, lying on his side. Sonny half-crawled himself and Marcel back to where we found them.

"He's lucky to be alive," I whispered to myself. Sonny escaped Death and his scythe today.

The video cut out to a wall of black stones with etchings along them. A figure in a black robe and a hood walked toward the camera. Their dark hood was pulled low so that you could see nothing beneath it.

A deep scrambled voice came out low from what I assumed was an altering spell that masked their normal voice, as it was unrecognizable. It sounded like a man but could be a woman, for what little we knew.

"You're playing a dangerous game, Ms. Rose. This is your last warning before I take something you love away. You did look lovely in the woods today. I only hope you can figure out your next move. This king has trapped his queen. Checkmate."

The video ended with a black screen and a red "WM" gleaming

back at me. The room was eerily quiet, and the air was thick with tension. I looked over to Bash. His hands were in fists, and his eyes were completely red.

"Bash," I whispered, and he turned to me, his face contorting with pain but not a physical pain. It was as if his heart was ripping in two. "Bash." I reached for him, but he shook his head.

"No! He doesn't get you, Princess."

I put my hand on his arm. "I'm not going anywhere, Sebastian."

He closed his eyes and breathed deeply. When he opened his eyes again, they had returned to the emerald green I loved.

I put my hand on his cheek. "I won't run from him, Sebastian. He can try to destroy my body and soul, but I'll fight him until I can't. He's arrogant right now. He thinks he's beaten us. What he doesn't know is that the king can only move one space at a time, but the queen... the queen can move wherever she wants, and that's what makes me dangerous."

His eyes searched mine. He gripped my neck, pulling me to him. "We are your dark knights, Princess. We will stand with you until our last breaths."

I felt Tristian and Aden behind me as they circled around me.

"Do with us as you will, Lil' Star. We aren't going anywhere." Tristian kissed my shoulder.

Aden moved in closer. "Your wish is our command, baby." He kissed my neck.

Bash leaned down, his lips dancing over mine. "We protect what's ours, and you are ours as much as we are yours."

I leaned into his lips, stealing the kiss I wanted. His mouth moved as one with mine as he teased me. The kiss was gentle and soft, as if I would break.

I pulled away. "I won't break, Bash."

He chuckled. "I know, Princess, but we have to go soon."

I looked at the clock. "Damn."

Tristian and Aden groaned and pulled away.

"Fun sucker," Tristian mumbled, flinging himself back on the couch.

Aden kissed my head and pushed me toward my room. "Go."

I moved away from them reluctantly.

"Fine, but someone owes me orgasms!" I playfully pouted as I walked to my room.

I pulled on a pair of ripped jeans, a gray turtleneck, and drew on my leather jacket, before I pulled my hair up in a high ponytail and applied deep-red lipstick.

"Putting your war paint on?"

I glanced at Tristian leaning on the doorway in leather pants and a gray shirt.

I rolled my eyes. "You would look as if you just stepped off the runway if not for the guns strapped to your side."

He chuckled as I walked to him. "Gorgeous and dangerous," he rumbled.

I booped his nose. "Who, me? Or are you talking about yourself?"

He bit his lip, and I swear my knees were suddenly weak.

"Both of us, Lil' Star. Ready to raise some hell?"

I grinned mischievously. "Always."

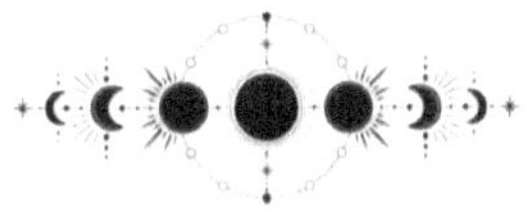

The drive to the Ryder's estate was quick.

"Kill the lights, Tristian. We don't want anyone to know we're here."

Tristian clicked the lights off, and the forest's foggy darkness surrounded us.

We slowly drove around to the back, avoiding any chance we might run into Morgan or his minions. Skinny trees surrounded the cemetery's iron gates, looming over us as if Death were calling my name. The cemetery had been around even before the estate.

Tristian slowed the car to a stop and turned it off. We got out of the car quietly and made our way through the gates that showed the cemetery's age. A few headstones lay on the ground, broken into pieces.

"Should we wait for Grayson and Hudson?" I pulled my arms around me, shivering from the cold night air—or was it from the cemetery?

Aden pulled me into his body, his warm heat instantly calming me. "I got a text from Hudson in the car. He said to meet him at the Ryder mausoleum."

Bash pointed to the left. "It's over there."

We walked in silence, our steps crunching against the grass. The white marble mausoleum came into view, standing tall in the middle of the cemetery. A set of crying angels were carved into the entrance, and an angel with black-onyx wings was perched on the top, its head tilted upward with its mouth open, screaming to the sky.

"Fuck, that's terrifying." Hudson's rich voice came from behind.

I jumped. "Shit! Oh hell, Hudson, please, for fuck's sake, make a sound next time."

Tristian put his arm around my shoulders, bumping into Aden. "Lil' Star, don't worry. We'll keep you safe from the big bad wolves."

I rolled my eyes at him and watched Hudson's figure walk through the fog, which became thicker with every step he took. The air chilled as the sounds of hollow steps came from in front of us.

Behind him, two figures walked side by side, and if I hadn't recognized the tall, broad-shouldered wolf-dragon, I would have peed my pants. I glanced at Hudson, who came to stand in front of me. Typically, Hudson was relaxed and calm, but now his posture was rigid, and his jaw was clenched as he stood in front of me. I poked him in the arm with my finger, and he looked at said finger.

"Would you call Grayson a wolon or dralf?"

Hudson's serious expression relaxed slightly, and a small smile formed. "Dralf?"

I smiled. "Dragon plus wolf equals dralf."

Tristian's arm was still around my shoulders, and he moved his hand to cup my mouth. "Lil' Star, normally, I love your antics, but this is not the time."

I nodded, and he removed his hand.

"Sorry," I mumbled.

"I'm not that horrible, am I, siren born of witches?" A deep French accent echoed through the night air.

Tristian stood straight, dipping his head and removing his arm from me.

"No, Madam Brigitte, I am here to seek advice from a great powerful woman like you and to only hope for your blessings."

Aden stepped up and pulled out a small bottle of wine, a small orange, and a tin of chocolates he had got earlier tonight. "Beautiful Brigitte, here are offerings from the Blood Moon Coven, the Silver Pearl Coven, and Trinity Coven." He placed the offerings on a memorial bench near the mausoleum.

"Aden Charmante and Tristian Cassium, two of the three Devils; tell me, where is your prince hiding?"

Bash stepped through the fog, holding out a hand. An elegant, ebony-toned hand inked with white tattoos clasped his. "Madam Brigitte." Her symbol and other standard protection charms marked her skin. Bash kissed the top of her hand. "Brigitte, thank you for seeing us this evening; your presence is a gift alone, but I came with another gift."

Brigitte smiled softly, her tattoos looking like they glowed from the night sky. "I do love gifts. Grayson, you can go next to your second."

Grayson looked grim but walked to us and stood next to Hudson.

Madam Brigitte was beautiful. She looked maybe thirty years old, but I knew she was much older than that. Stories about Brigitte were told when I was younger, and my father told me she never aged and that he had known her since he was a child himself. She had smooth skin and bright copper eyes. Her long chocolate hair tumbled to her waist. She wore a headdress made out of roses and skulls and a simple black dress.

She turned to me. "Ms. Rose, why, you are beautiful, aren't you? Tell me, what has your lover gotten you into?"

I cleared my throat, speaking carefully. "Thank you, Madam Brigitte. The legend of your beauty doesn't do you justice, but you got one thing wrong. I'm the one who got Sebastian into trouble."

Her eyes lit up with excitement. "Well, you know what they say about well-behaved women."

I arched an eyebrow. "What?"

"They seldom make history." She grinned at me, and I couldn't help but grin right back. "So, you found something in the woods, my dear Grayson said."

I looked over at Grayson. His eyes narrowed on the bench, his jaw stern as if he were being hurt.

"Is he okay?"

Brigitte looked back and shrugged. "Sometimes, walking along a necromancer has its struggles."

I narrowed my eyes at her and was about to ask her to explain when Tristian nudged me with his elbow, and Aden bent slightly, murmuring, "Stick to your questions, baby. We don't know what she'll want if we ask her more."

I looked from him to her and swallowed hard.

Her eyes sparkled with mischief, as if she dared me to ask more questions.

"My magic showed me this in the forest." I gently pulled out the tiny glass bottle and placed it in her palm.

Her magic trickled over my skin, and I had barely touched her. It was intense, like a barrier of wind trying to push through, and sometimes, strong magic could turn deadly. We would need to watch the priestess in the future.

"Ahh, it is old and powerful. I can feel it wanting to get out."

I concentrated on her words and felt the magic within the bottle.

It was chaotic, like a captured wild animal. "Are you saying that something or someone is in this bottle?"

Brigitte looked up at me, concern flashing through her eyes. "*Non*, but whatever it is, *mwne pa renmen*. It's *renesans lanmò*."

My eyes snapped to hers. "Rebirth of death?"

She gave me a knowing smile. "*Oui*, siren, *oui*. This is dark magic at its finest. The consequences of using it are grimmer than you know. With death, there is always a price."

She handed it to Bash. "Do not let them open the bottle." She pointed to Tristian. "The magic within this potion is strong, vampire." Brigitte turned to us. "Magic lives within you and can destroy you if you are not careful."

She turned to walk away, but I caught her arm, and the night around me darkened. Cold air blew on my skin, chilling me to the bone. My voice became fragile as her magic swept through me like a swirl of heat. The pain lanced through my whole body.

"Madam Brigitte, please, this could be the key to stopping the killings. I know this doesn't affect you yet, but if we let this dark magic spread, it will come after the city you love so much," I rasped out.

She turned her head back to me, her eyes completely white as she spoke in a strange voice. "The shadows of the night do not fear death. We welcome it, child."

Grayson was at her side in a minute. "Brigitte." His deep voice echoed through the graveyard. "Stay with us."

Brigitte's eyes returned to their copper beauty, and she blinked at Grayson with a smile. "Always bringing me back from the other side, Shenlong dragon, *mon amie*." They shared a moment before she turned back to me. "That potion is dangerous. Do not open it. Look at the side." She pointed out the word *lanmò*. "To hold this in your possession is dangerous. It can be deadly to anyone who uses it for good or bad." She gripped my arm tightly. "It will not help you with The Wishmaker. That is all I can tell you. You know where to find me if and when you need my help," she said to Bash.

She walked to Grayson, taking his arm. "Come, *loup-dragon*, take me home."

Grayson's eyes softened, and he kissed her hand. "Yes, Madam."

They walked away into the fog, disappearing from our sight.

"That was confusing, frustrating, and enchanting all at the same time." I sighed as I sagged into Aden, who wrapped his arms around me as he nuzzled my neck.

"That, baby, is voodoo."

Chapter Twelve

We returned to the house right before three in the morning and silently climbed into my bed, too drained from the night to even talk.

I think we all wanted to just lie in the comfort of each other. I lay between Bash and Aden. Tristian was on the other side of us. His soft snores were hypnotic, and we all were fast asleep in a dreamless land in no time.

The following day, I woke before any of my Devils. Dyna greeted me in the kitchen with a soft meow. I scooped her up in my arms, sipping coffee. I sat at the breakfast bar and stared at the box that held the *renesans lanmò*. "Rebirth of death."

I said to the empty room. "Why would anyone want to mess with such dark magic, Dyna?"

On our way home, the only thing Bash had said was, "You heard Madam Brigitte, Lexi, do not touch that damn potion. It could do more harm than good. Tristian, same goes for you, don't even think about it." Tristian opened his mouth to argue, but Bash held up a hand. "That's a goddamn order, *frère*," he growled out at us.

I slammed my mug down. "Ugh! This is bull. This could help us. Hell, this could be safer than using a necromancer." I ran my fingers through my hair. Anger settled in my stomach like a wound-up ball. I sat Dyna down as I stood. "I'm going for a swim."

I grabbed a towel and a suit as I silently snuck out through the back and down to the beach. It was early morning, and the fog was thick. The ocean waves were harsh today, large and rough, dangerous to anyone else but sirens or mermaids. I changed into my suit and dove into the frozen waves, where memories of my past came back to life.

It was right before my sixteenth birthday, the night before Ostara, and it was our coven's turn to throw the celebration. Ostara was one of my favorite celebrations. It signified a time to start over—new beginnings and the rebirth of the old.

Mom and Dad had put me in charge of the garden, and I was thrilled as I raced down the stairs, my long, flowy dress whipping out behind me. I jumped from the last two steps and landed with a stumble.

"Lexi!" A pair of hands gripped my arms.

I tilted my head up at Aden, his steel eyes staring back at me from behind a pair of glasses. "You okay?"

I grinned. "Never been better. It's Ostara!"

He laughed as he helped me stand.

Aden had been tall and skinny for as long as I'd known him, but recently, he had been hitting the gym and was gaining a bit of muscle. He was lean and nerdy, but he was growing into his own. He had this mysterious way about him, like I never knew what he was thinking.

"Did you get everything?"

He huffed a laugh. "Of course, you sent Ella and me out. She wasn't going to take no for an answer. It's kinda scary how she can make people do what she wants."

I laughed and smacked his arm. "She's a Ryder. What do you expect?"

As if we'd summoned her, Ella came in holding a tray of plants. "I got them all, Lexi!" Her sing-song voice and bright smile shone through the doorway.

My smile broke into a full laugh. "I can see that."

Ella, who was tiny but mighty, came in holding a flat of plants full of every color you could imagine. "Aden Charmante, get your ass in gear and grab a tree or something. We have Ostara to celebrate."

Aden murmured, "Damn bossy pants." But he saluted her and jogged out to the front of the house.

I turned to Ella. "Who did you con to help out tonight?"

Her face turned red, and she shrugged. "No one special. Aden, Tristian, Ethan, and Bash... oh, and a few of the guys suddenly were free when I told them you'd be here."

I rolled my eyes.

Over the summer, my straight stick figure had turned into curves. I was getting more attention from guys but didn't have time for them, not if I was going to be the leader of our coven. I needed to focus on my magic and studies.

"Ella, I don't have time for boys."

She rolled her eyes as she walked to the back of the house, where large French doors overlooked the back garden.

Mom and Dad had prepped the whole garden for Ostara. Bags of garden soil sat to the side near long tables for digging and repotting plants. Afterward, we would have a grand feast full of fruit, cheeses, meats, veggies, and the best damn desserts you've ever had. My Aunt Coco had flown them in from the French pastry chef she was interning for.

It would be the best night full of food, drinks, and dancing. You never knew what would happen during Ostara. It could get wild. I think that's why I loved it so much. A lot of the time, when you were the future of your coven, it could be a crushing feeling of utter failure if you weren't perfect, so it was freeing to be able to let loose.

"There are the guys," Ella breathed.

I turned around, and Tristian Cassium walked through the door with two big bags of soil on his shoulders. He had his white shirt tucked into his black pants, and his golden skin glistened in the sun. Even at seventeen, he was stunning. Girls flocked to him, but his beauty was out of this world. His tossed blond hair and copper eyes exuded mischief.

I had grown up with him, so I knew his goofy, playful side more than the suave attitude he used with other girls.

"Hey, Lil' Star." He winked at me. "Where do you want these?"

I smirked and pointed to the raised beds in the garden. "There. Where's the rest of your posse?" I looked behind him.

He jerked his head as he walked to the garden to place the soil down.

Aden and Ethan walked in carrying trees in each hand, arguing about something under their breaths. "No, dude, not gonna. We're just friends."

I waved. "Ethan, can you place those by the fountain?"

Aden glanced up. "You're as bad as her!" He nodded to Ella laughing.

I laughed. "You're to do my bidding tonight!"

Aden's face showed a hint of a blush. Aden Charmante and me? Could that be something? I shook the thought away. I turned back to Ella, who was staring at Ethan.

I nudged her with my elbow. "So, you gonna spill why you're looking at our friend's older brother with bedroom eyes?"

She blushed. "He asked me out."

My jaw dropped. "And?"

Ella pushed a lock of hair behind her ear. "*And* I said yes."

Grinning, I pulled her close and interlocked our arms. "That's great. Ethan is honestly one of the nicest guys I know. A true prince, he's handsome, kind, and charming. Unlike some other people I know."

I looked at the door as the air got thicker. In walked the Devil himself. Sebastian Ryder.

He had been off at some random private school on the East Coast. His green eyes found their way to my blue ones. It felt as if time stood still. His gaze was intense, and I could sense his eyes roaming over me, stopping at my curves as if he was drinking me in.

I cleared my throat as he approached us.

"Ella, where do you want these?" His eyes never left mine.

"Out on the tables. Hey, Lex, I'm going to help Aden. I'll be right back," she said in an absent-minded manner.

I cleared my throat. "So... how's school?"

Bash looked down at me. "You're asking me about school?" His laugh filled the room. Shaking his head, he handed over a row of plants. "Here, help carry a pallet, Princess. Let me show you how a real coven runs things," he said with a wink.

I rolled my eyes. Bash and I were always in competition with each other. We were the future leaders of our covens, so, yeah, I had to be better than him.

I grabbed a pallet and headed to the table to set out pots, tools, and soil.

"Listen, asshat, you know Silver Pearl always throws the best parties, mainly because we aren't stuck-up snobs."

He huffed at that. "There's nothing wrong with rules, Princess."

I rolled my eyes at him. "Well, generally speaking, but you have so many. Don't you ever wish you could... I dunno, be free from it all?"

He stopped loading and looked at me like he really saw me for the first time. "Always."

I just stared at him, frozen in place. It was the first time I realized that Sebastian Ryder and I had something in common. We wanted to be free without rules.

"Lexi!" Ella's voice broke through my train of thought.

I jerked in surprise, and the pot I was holding shattered with the movement. Dirt, roots, and leaves fell over me, and the sting of the pot cutting into my palm made me hiss in pain. "Ouch!"

Ella's face turned white with shock when she saw the blood. "Oh fuck, I'm sorry." She started to rush over to me.

I shook my head and waved her off. "It's fine. I'll go get cleaned up."

Before I turned to leave, I saw Bash with his fangs out as he watched the blood stream down my hand.

"Get your shit together, Sebastian," I whispered.

He snapped his eyes to mine, and his whole body relaxed. He cleared his throat. "Sorry. Go, Lexi, we'll clean this up."

I rushed upstairs to find my mom. She could clean the wound with her magic, and Dad could heal my hand.

The hallways were dark, with the only light streaming into the hallway from my father's open office door. I walked to my father's study and heard voices arguing.

"No, we can't. Do you know how dangerous it is?!" My father's voice boomed down the hall.

"He's right, you dickwad," Daniels said in a gravelly voice.

"Daniels, please treat him with respect," my mother's voice chimed.

"Yes, Daniels, let him finish," Morgan Ryder's smooth voice bit out.

A strange inhuman voice spoke. "If we had these ingredients, we could, as they say, free the chains that bind us to the human world."

I moved silently to the door's edge and saw my parents, Daniels, and Morgan surrounding a stranger darkened by shadows.

"It's wrong. It would hurt them. You don't know what would happen if they couldn't control it. You can't do it. It does more harm than good," my father's firm voice said.

"You're all idiots. I will rule the covens one day, and you shall all fall under me."

The shadow started standing, and I realized they were heading to the door. In a panic, I searched for an escape and saw a hall closet. I was rushing for the door when a hand grabbed mine. I looked up to find Bash staring at me. He placed a finger to my lips as he quickly opened the door and pulled me into a linen closet.

He put a hand over my mouth and breathed out, "Not a word, Princess."

I nodded, and he removed his hand as a scuttle came from across the hall.

"Please see it from our side… we've been friends for a long time… please see it from our side," my mother's voice begged.

"Never, Natalia. You and Alexander wouldn't understand. How could you?" the inhuman voice called out as it made its way down the stairs with determined steps.

"He's an idiot!" Daniels growled and hit the linen closet door, making me gasp and jump closer to Bash, who cursed as I stepped on his foot.

I covered my mouth with my hand and looked up at him in panic. His green eyes widened with shock.

He wrapped his arm around my waist and pulled me closer, moving my hand. "Trust me, Princess."

I breathed out, "I do."

Bash moved his face closer to mine so our lips were only a breath away from each other. He pushed his fingers into my hair, and I exhaled a shaky breath. It felt like my heart was in my throat, and time stood still as Bash leaned down and laid a light kiss against my lips.

I sighed and felt the heat from his lips. I gripped his shirt and pulled his body to mine, kissing him deeper. He groaned and picked me up. I wrapped my legs around his hips, and my dress bunched up between us.

"Fuck, Princess."

As he explored my mouth, I moaned into his kiss. I pulled his hair, wanting more, when the door swung open. My mother gasped, my father and Daniels cussed, and Morgan growled.

"That's enough, son," Morgan bit out.

Bash pulled back, and the flash of fear in his eyes made me

realize that being a Ryder might not be as cozy as he made it seem. He slid me down to my feet.

I ensured my dress was down before I turned and looked at my mother, mouthing, "Sorry."

Her eyes sparkled with laughter. "As if you never pulled me into closets at their age, Alexander." She elbowed my father.

He huffed. "Yeah, yeah, just don't do it again, not in my home."

He backed away and started to turn around but walked over to Bash instead. He leaned close to his ear, whispering, "Sebastian, if I see you even look at Lexi tonight, I swear to the stars I will curse you until the day you die."

I hid my face in my hands. "Daaaad."

Daniels's gruff voice added, "Make that two of us, *suceur de sang*."

I coughed. "Bloodsucker" was a harsh word to call Bash.

Morgan straightened and moved forward. "Now, now, no need for name-calling. I'm sure they know this isn't the perfect match." His eyes set firm on Bash's, and he cleared his throat. "It just happened. It won't happen again."

Bash's hand found mine behind his back and squeezed my fingers.

I looked over at Morgan. "Yeah. And we're just friends, nothing more to worry about."

I walked forward, removing my hand from his.

My mother gasped when she saw it. "Here." She rushed forward, cleaning away the blood and gunk with a wave of her fingers.

My father's voice cut in, "Well, downstairs, both of you." Before I could leave, my father gripped my hand. "Here."

He sent a healing light over my palm, and I gave him a warm smile. "Thanks, Dad."

He kissed my head and let me go.

"I'll be down to help with your dress," my mom called.

I walked to the stairs, and Bash's steps followed behind me.

"Good job, Princess," he whispered in my ear.

I dipped my head. "Yeah, thanks, you saved my ass back there..."

He stopped me by the arm and turned me toward him. "Lexi... was that your first kiss?"

I bit my lip and nodded, avoiding his gaze. "Yeah, what of it?"

He smirked and brushed my hair behind my ears. "Maybe I want all your firsts, Lexi Rose."

The memories faded as I gasped back into the present, water bubbles forming around my mouth. I propelled straight to the surface and swam as fast as I could to the shore. Once my feet touched the ocean floor, I broke through the waves and pushed my hair from my face. The wind was strong this morning, whipping around me as sand and the sea hit my legs. Back on solid ground, I grabbed the towel from where I had dropped it and pulled it around me. I jogged back to the house with the memories fresh in my mind. Bash was sitting at the table outside with a cup of coffee and a newspaper.

I came to a halt and bit my lip to keep from laughing. "You actually read the newspaper?"

He took a sip of coffee and smirked. "You should try it, Princess. Enjoy your swim?" He tilted his head, his eyes drinking in the ripples of water beading down my skin.

"You could say that. Do you remember the Ostara celebration the year my parents died?" I moved to sit next to him.

He folded the paper and set his cup down as if thinking about what to say. "How could I forget?" He ran his thumb under my lip. "I was your first kiss, and I'll never forget that I was the one to steal it from you."

I sighed and leaned into his touch. "I know you were, Bash." I gave him a small smile. "Did you hear what my parents were talking about when you found me?"

He shook his head. "No, I was distracted." He cleared his throat

and pulled his hand back.

I smirked, because he was undoubtedly distracting too. "Well, call Aden and Tristian out here. I got a story to tell you."

Bash called out to them, and Aden and Tristian stepped outside, looking slightly confused before sitting down.

I took a sip from Bash's coffee and shared the memory.

Their eyes morphed from curiosity to intrigue, and, finally, flashes of anger.

"I think The Wishmaker has been trying to push their plan for years now. This goes back to our parents." Bash growled, throwing the paper across the patio.

"Yeah, but think of it this way, Bash. We now can narrow our list of suspects."

Aden laughed. "What, to how many people knew our parents?"

I shook my head. "No. We know they were a strong ally of the covens; that takes our list from hundreds to less than fifty people. They had to be a part of the high coven orders—a trusted circle member of the covens, and that's not just anyone."

Tristian smiled.

Bash smirked. "Well, one problem at a time. Tonight, we need to focus on robbing my father blind." His smirk turned into an evil grin.

I had a feeling that Sebastian Ryder was excited to act on a bit of revenge against his own flesh and blood.

Chapter Thirteen

The rest of the afternoon went on slowly as the evening approached. We went over our plans again. We would have teams go in stages. Bash, Ethan, and Ella would attend the meeting to distract Morgan and Franklin. Tristian, Aden, Grayson, Hudson, and I would meet a few blocks from Anderson & Ryder. I was with Tristian and Hudson while Aden and Grayson were there to cause a diversion for the guards.

We would get in and out of the vault as fast as we could. All while trying not to be killed. So, yeah, you know, easy peasy. Not really.

As the sun set, we all got ready in silence, focusing on the mission ahead of us. I pulled my hair into a high ponytail and checked my reflection in the mirror. Dressed in black pants and a long-sleeved blacktop, I strapped knives to my thighs while a black holster with two Glocks sat snuggly on my hips. The finishing touch was the katana along my back, which Aden had gifted me. I wore dark makeup ringing my eyes so the blue looked like it glowed, and my lips were colored in a deep plum. "Yep, I look like I can do some damage."

The door opened, and Bash walked in wearing a navy pinstripe three-piece suit.

I whistled at him, eyeing him up and down. "You look handsome. Trying to impress someone tonight?" I batted my eyelashes at him.

He chuckled. "Not tonight, Princess."

His eyes searched mine, and I stilled. "What?"

He glanced down at the ground and then back at me. "Nothing, Lexi. You... you surprise me every day, that's all."

I stepped closer to him and ran my finger along his jaw. "It's been a long time, you and me."

He nodded. "It has."

I kissed his cheek. "Tonight, we get a piece of ourselves back from them. Tonight, we get some of our freedom."

He leaned down to softly kiss my lips and pulled back slowly.

"Promise me you'll be safe." I hooked my pinky up. "Pinky swear." He tilted his head as if I was being ridiculous. "Just do it, Sebastian."

He shook his head and wrapped his finger around mine. Then he cupped the back of my neck and lowered his head, bringing me against him. "Promise."

I smiled. "See, that's not so bad. Now let's go before the boys have a fit."

"Too late." Tristian and Aden leaned against the door. "Ella and Ethan are already at the estate to help keep The Weasel busy."

I backed away from Bash, zipping up my jacket. "Grayson and Hudson?"

Tristian smirked. "They're meeting us at the starting point." He glanced at his watch and then at the group. "Let's sync up first before we leave."

Aden placed a silver case down and handed out three tiny earplugs. We put them in our ears.

"So, do we get nicknames or call signs?"

They all looked over at me with an expression that could only be described as "what the fuck?"

"What? Look, we can call Aden Blue Steel, Tristian is 100 percent Sunshine, and Bash can be..."

Aden smirked. "Bash?"

Tristian grinned. "Snappy B? Grumpy Pants? Asshat...?"

I smiled back at Tristian.

"Bash the Ass?" Both of them laughed.

"Perfect!" I turned back to Bash, who had his arms crossed over his chest, shooting us a menacing frown.

"Seriously, Princess?"

I threw my hands up. "Okay, okay, Snappy B it is. Jeez."

He rolled his eyes before Aden smiled at me. "All done. We're synced up, baby." He leaned down and kissed my cheek. "You'll be careful."

It wasn't a demand, though, more of a promise.

I lifted my eyes to his. "As long as you are, too. My heart would break again if anything happened to you."

He smirked. "Baby, I'm steel. Nothing can hurt me."

Tristian smacked him across the back of the head.

"Ouch! Motherfucker! What the hell was that for?!"

Tristian folded his arms. "To prove you aren't made of steel, asshat."

I rolled my eyes at them. "Let's go before we all realize that this is the most idiotic plan we've ever come up with. Devils"—I checked my watch and smiled evilly—"let's go raise some hell."

Their grins spread across their faces, as if they were looking forward to their possible deaths.

I shook my head. "Boys are idiots."

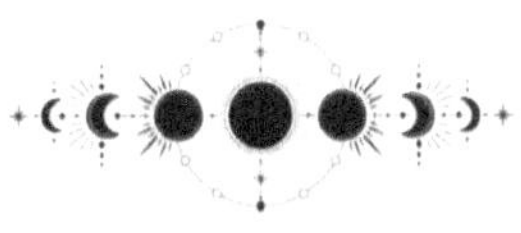

The alleyway was dark, covered in gray-looking muck, grim, and smelled like week-old trash that burned my nose every time I breathed in. The only light came from the full moon that was obscured by clouds, but it offered us enough light to see.

"Bash, Ella, and Ethan, we're in the alley waiting for Grayson and Hudson. How's the party?"

Ella's exasperation came through in a low whisper. "*Ugh*, it's so boring, and of course, I'm stuck sitting between my father and The Weasel."

I looked over at Tristian. "Uhhh, Ella, maybe don't say that too loud," he muttered.

She huffed. "Relax, Sunshine. I'm in the bathroom right now. Bash and Ethan are with them."

I snickered at the nickname for Tristian.

I heard her smack her lips and the sound of a sink running.

"Anywho! Holler if you need us. We'll be listening, so keep it clean! I do not need to hear you three going at it!"

I rolled my eyes. "That was one time," I hissed out.

"And I'm traumatized from it! Blondie out." And she went silent.

I looked over at Aden. "See, call signs," I pointed out.

He narrowed his eyes as if he was going to say something snarky, but a burst of deep laughter came from the darkness of the alleyway.

"Seductress... what would my call sign be?"

I looked behind Grayson to Hudson with a raised eyebrow. "Puff the Howling Dragon?"

Hudson snickered and covered his mouth with his hand.

"You'll pay for that one, seductress." Grayson was suddenly in front of me, his eyes sparkling with mischief.

"Looking forward to it, pup." I smirked as I arched an eyebrow.

"If you're done eye-fucking my girl, we can get on with this." Bash's smooth voice came through our earpieces.

My eyes widened in surprise. "Are you watching again, Sebastian?"

That statement got an eyebrow raise from Grayson.

"Princess, you like it when I watch, but unfortunately, I can only hear your humorous banter. I only assume Grayson is eyeing you like a shiny penny."

I looked at Grayson, whose eyes roamed over my body. "She's a treasure, Ryder. Be careful with her, or she might find out that dragons are better in bed than bloodsuckers."

I laughed. "I feel if Brigitte found out about this, she would bury you in the Louisiana swamp."

He stiffened at that comment and turned his eyes away.

There had to be more to that story. One day, I hoped to find out what our voodoo priestess had over the dragon-wolf.

"Let's stay focused, everyone. Bash, your father's looking for you." Ethan's voice broke through.

"Damn it. He's right." Bash's low voice came through. "Aden and Hudson, you two go knock down the electrical. Tristian, Grayson, and Lexi. Go get those damn keys, and for fuck's sake, don't get killed."

"Ahh, you do care about me, don't you, Bash? Tell me, if I died, would you be a wee bit sad about it?" Grayson grinned at me, mouthing, "He loves me!"

Bash growled. "I wouldn't say I would be crying, but I wouldn't dance on your grave."

Aden wrapped an arm around Hudson's neck. "Come on, let's go fuck shit up."

Hudson's soft laugh echoed as they walked down the alleyway.

"How are they going to get up there?"

Tristian came by my side. "Watch Aden, Lil' Star."

Grayson leaned against a wall. "It's pretty fucking cool." A smile played on his lips.

"Okay, now you have my interest." I eyed Aden, who strapped on a slim black backpack.

He waved to me as dark smoke emerged behind him and filled the space around us. When the smoke cleared, he was gone, and a low whistle came from above us. I looked up, and he was standing on the roof with bright red eyes and gleaming white teeth, smiling down at me.

"Now watch Hudson." Tristian grinned at me.

I turned to Hudson, who smirked as his eyes glowed. He dusted his hands off before running for the wall at full speed. Then he leaped while holding his hands out as a rush of air magic propelled him up to the roof with Aden.

My jaw dropped open. *Holy shit.* I gasped. "He's like a superhero... he's literally Superman," I whispered to Tristian, who was grinning.

"Cool, huh?"

I tilted my head at him. "What can you do?"

Tristian smirked. "You know I can do magic, Lil' Star, but I also have an excellent intuition, you could say."

I stopped and turned. "You have the sight?"

He shook his head. "No, but Grandmother did. I only know of one true seer right now. She's young, though, and highly protected by the Celestial Flame Coven."

Now I had a million questions. Celestial Flame was one of the East Coast covens. They were known for not only being super secretive about what they did as a coven, but most were CEOs, tech billionaires, models, actors, or Broadway legends. To say they were impressive was an understatement.

"Okay, I need to know more about that later. Let's go get these keys."

Tristian pushed me toward Grayson.

His arms were crossed, and his head was bowed. He looked as if he was asleep against the wall. I shook his arm, and his head popped up.

"Fire, that's what I have." He glared at us. "Scary fucking dragon fire, thanks for asking." He smiled at me sarcastically.

I pursed my lips, scrunching up my nose. "Yeah, kinda figured. Shall we, or are you going to nap some more?"

"Yeah, yeah, let's just get this over with," he said, as if he was bored already.

He straightened away from the wall, and the air shimmered around him. Grayson's features morphed as he cast a concealment spell on himself. His normal dark hair became deep red, his eyes pale blue, his nose broader than before, and freckles scattered across his cheeks.

"Impressive," I murmured, and he smirked.

"I can teach you one day, seductress."

I whispered, "Deal."

We walked toward the alley's entrance, staying close to the shadows. Grayson put a finger up for us to stop and rounded the corner of the front of the building. Looking bewildered, he glanced down at his phone and then up as if he was a lost puppy.

Two armed guards stood at the building's entrance. One was large with muscles, and the other was slender, like a jaguar. Both looked equally dangerous. Too bad they didn't know we were even more deadly. Tristian moved closer to me as we watched Grayson.

Grayson stumbled over to the guys as if he had been drinking.

"Hey, dude." His voice contained none of his Southern drawl but sounded more like a surfer from the cove. "Can you tell me where Addison Street is? I got this hot little pixie waiting for me."

The larger of the two guards grunted, "Love me a pixie. They taste like candy. Addison Street is about three blocks that way."

He pointed in the general direction, and Grayson whipped around and stumbled into the guard, who caught him.

"Whoa there, buddy, maybe you should get some coffee first."

"I'm in the mainframe. Aden, kill the lights." Hudson's voice broke through my ear. "Out in three... two... one."

The building lights blinked out, and the guards turned in surprise. Grayson made his move, and with a flick of his hand, the larger guard dropped to the ground.

The smaller one turned. "What the f—"

Grayson was on him in an instant, his reptile eyes turning to golden slits, and fear slid onto the guard's face when he realized he wasn't the only predator anymore.

To the guard's credit, he pulled his gun out and aimed, but Grayson was faster. He knocked the gun out of his hand and pulled him into a chokehold. The man was out in seconds.

We moved forward and helped Grayson zip-tie the guards and put them in the alley.

"Now that was impressive. Have you ever thought about joining MI6? Holsten, Grayson Holsten." I smirked, and he stood and tilted his head toward me.

He moved and opened his mouth.

Tristian interrupted whatever Grayson was going to say to me. "Guards down, good to go in."

"Good," Bash said. "Princess, you good?"

I blushed slightly. "I'm good, Bash."

His sigh was full of relief. "Aden and Hudson will meet you in the lobby."

Ethan's voice came through. "While Hudson was messing with the mainframe, I went into the system's back end and shut down the emergency security system. It's only shut down for twenty minutes. Then you guys have to book it out of there. Morgan has already been informed about the lights but thinks it's a power outage."

Aden's laugh came through. "Yeah, that's because I killed the surrounding blocks too, just in case. I didn't want Franklin snooping around."

"Good thinking, boy genius," I said, turning to the darkened building. "Okay, we're going in, Lil' Maid out."

Ethan's laugh echoed as we walked into the dark lobby.

I approached the gold-gilded elevator in the lobby's center. Hudson was next to me in a second, pulling out a small handle with a slim, flat metal blade sticking out of it.

"It's a drop key. This will open up any elevator," he answered before I could ask.

"You got that as, what, a gift?"

Hudson smirked. "Maybe."

He slid the flat blade into the seam where the doors met, and with a pop, he pushed them back. The elevator shaft was dark and empty with taut gray cables hanging down. The guys geared us up to go down the elevator.

"Ready?" Tristian asked as he helped me into my rope and harness.

I gazed down the shaft into nothingness. "That's a far drop."

Tristian smirked. "You'll be good."

I took a deep breath. "I'll be good."

"We're good to go," Aden said in a hushed voice.

Tristian smiled, leaned back in a low squat, and pushed out. He disappeared down the elevator shaft. Grayson and Hudson followed suit.

Aden rubbed my arm. "Let's do it together."

I smiled in relief. "Thank you."

We leaned to the edge, and I slowly pushed myself. I hung low in my harness, suspended in nothingness, the rope holding my weight.

I cautiously pulled myself down the system Aden had set up. I called it a complicated pulley system when he first explained what he would do to keep us safe, and he scoffed at me.

"It's more complicated than a pulley system, baby," he said as if I had insulted him.

I didn't dare look down. I focused on my hand placement and finding balance. I heard a soft thump.

"Blondie, Fierypup, and Moondust made it." Tristian's voice came from below us.

I let out a giggle.

"Lil' Maid and Man of Steel, coming in three... two... one."

My feet hit the hard cement, and Tristian's hands encompassed my waist to hold me steady.

"Glad you made it, Lil' Star." He kissed my temple.

A soft laugh escaped me. "Just don't make me do that again anytime soon." I unclipped myself and dropped the binding into

Tristian's hands as Aden came to our side with a rugged look.

"Power's still out. Once I give Ethan the word, we have twenty minutes."

"Then let us get in and out, *frère*." Tristian clapped his shoulder softly.

"Small problem with that." Hudson walked up to us. "When the power went out, the first thing that happened was a steel door slid in place over the threshold of the vault."

I let out a small string of curses and walked to the door. As he said, standing before me was a dark-gray steel door.

"There has to be a way in." I looked over to Grayson, hoping he knew what we could do.

He glared at the door as if it offended him before he glanced over at me. "A spell could work. Do you know any unlocking spells, or even one that could melt it?"

I smirked at him, getting an idea. "What about a fire so hot it can melt any metal?"

Grayson's frown faded into a wide grin. "Like dragon fire?"

I returned the smile. "Just like dragon fire."

Grayson's eyes shifted to golden slits, and his grin grew. "Anything you say, seductress. Let's watch it burn."

Chapter Fourteen

S tand back, Lexi." Hudson pulled me back to Tristian's waiting hands, and he wrapped me in his arms.

I craned around Hudson's giant frame to see Grayson standing in the middle of the door, his palms up as he took a deep breath. Fire sprang forth from his palms, and he placed them on the door. The glow danced under his hands as the fire grew. Bright flames licked against the steel as the heat began to bubble and melt it. A hole formed from the fire, slowly expanding and leaving a border of aqua and gold behind.

Grayson turned to me. His dragon eyes glowed with excitement. "Enjoying this, seductress?" A sinful smirk spread wide across his face.

Speechless, I shook my head. I walked toward him, but a tug on my arm stopped me. I turned to find Hudson holding me back.

"Be careful, Grayson has his wolf under control, but his dragon, it's a ferocious beast."

Concern clouded Hudson's eyes, and I patted his hand. "I trust him."

Hudson backed away and let go of my arm. He bobbed his head

toward Grayson. "Bring him back if you can, Lexi."

As I approached him, his hands were still on the door, his back hunched over, and he was panting.

"Grayson?"

He whipped his head to me.

I saw the fight in his eyes. "Come back to us, *mon ami.*"

He closed his eyes and slumped slightly. A deep shuddering breath escaped him, and he hung his head. When he looked up again, his eyes had returned to their dark-hazel color.

"Welcome back." I smiled and placed my hand on his. "That was impressive, Holsten."

He laughed. "I'm just a show pony, Ms. Rose, just a show pony."

I shook my head. "No, never a show pony. You're so much more. I wish you would see it."

"Get on with it." Bash's hiss came out, and I rolled my eyes.

"Way to kill a moment, asshat."

Grayson shrugged, but a slight blush colored his cheeks.

"My turn." I closed my eyes and flicked my wrist. "*L'eau vient a moi.*"

Water glided from my hands, and I focused on moving it over the melting metal, cooling it so we could walk through.

"Daniels taught me that when I was little. He wasn't surprised when I picked it up quickly."

Once I cooled down the giant hole, we all stepped through, entering a dark hallway. Grayson threw small fireballs into the air while Aden sped forward to me.

"I'm going to check for any guards first," he whispered.

He sped off suddenly, and I was getting dizzy watching him zip around.

He returned with a thumbs up, and we continued to the end of the hall, where a bright golden fence stood. Bright jeweled feathers escaped from the top of it. The three covens' symbols were carved into the center, forming a circle.

"This is the vault," I said, hooking my thumb to the fence.

"What makes you say that, Lil' Star?" Tristian teased. "Is it the golden fence, or is it the fact that Morgan is such a pompous prick that he put feathers made out of gemstones?"

I laughed. "Both."

"Bash, we're here. Everyone in position at the dinner?" I said into my earpiece.

"Yeah, we just got the sixth course, and Morgan is talking about his trip to France and how he bought the Château Margaux in 1787," Ella's voice came in mockingly.

I heard a laugh and groan come from both Ethan and Bash.

"Okay... anyways... Ethan, get ready. We need to be ready to go when I give you the count," I tell him.

"On it, Lil' Maid."

I smiled and looked at the gate, seeking out the protection spell placed around it. I let my hand float in the air and felt the pull as it sent a light tingle down my fingers.

"Got 'em, Ethan. Trist, we're up."

Tristian stepped up and took my hand as we chanted.

"Je t'appelle pour eclairer mon chemin et me montret ce que je cherche, ouvre les yeux et laissee-moi marcher dans la lumiere."

"I call on you to light my path and show me what I seek, open my eyes, and let me walk into the light."

The magic pulsed out of me, making contact with the gate. The magic barrier dissipated with a sizzle like when you put a fire out.

Aden walked forward and pushed the gate open with his foot. "It worked, fuck yes."

The tingles of magic still licked up and down my skin. It was the most euphoric high I had ever felt, like the sun was grazing my skin while I floated on the warm ocean water.

Magic with Tristian was just more. We had more power, were stronger when we were together, and it was very uncommon for two witches or fae from different covens to be stronger together than with their own.

"*Wow,*" Tristian gasped as he looked over at me, checking for injury as if his magic would hurt me.

"Wow indeed," I said, squeezing his hand with a grin. "Ethan, do it."

An evil snicker came from Ethan that I had never heard before. "You have twenty minutes, that's it." He reminded us. "Go *now!*" he yelled just before panicked screams from the party echoed in our ears.

"Remember to ask him what he did. I think I'm officially scared of my brother." Aden laughed as he picked me up and ran down the hall, only to enter a circular room with the covens' symbols carved in marble on the floor.

I ran the tips of my fingers along the smooth, tremendous walls. Each section had arches with an elemental sign over the arch: air, water, earth, and fire. Each hall was dark and cast in shadows.

"We can't all go together. We'll have to separate. Find the door, and meet back in the center so we can get the hell out of here."

"Aden and Hudson, you go down those two." Grayson pointed to the water and earth tunnel. "Tristian, take the air tunnel. Lexi and I will check the fire one," Grayson ordered.

Aden's and Tristian's growls echoed throughout. "Lexi stays with one of us."

I rolled my eyes. "Guys, we do not have time." I checked my watch. "Let's move," I said to Grayson as we headed to the fire arch, Aden's and Tristian's protests echoing behind me.

I stepped into the darkness, letting my eyes adjust.

"They're protective over you," Grayson whispered from behind me.

"Well, when you have a psychopath stalking you, threatening to kill you and your family..." I said numbly, focusing on the doors.

They were all different. Some looked like a typical vault, and others were decorated in gold, silver, and jewels.

"How are we going to tell where it is?" I asked in a panic. The fear of not finding the key finally kicked in.

"Feel the power of it. The key will be highly protected by a spell. Search for that barrier, Lexi. You can find it."

I closed my eyes and took a deep breath. I searched for the power that lived deep within me. A trickle of the energy from the spell tickled my senses. As I walked toward the energy it was expelling, the tingling got more substantial, pulling me to the end of the hall. A simple vault door stood in front of me.

"Here."

Grayson chuckled. "Of course. Morgan is so predictable, like someone watched *Raiders of the Lost Ark* too much."

I rolled my eyes and whispered, "He is a douche, isn't he?"

Ella's voice came through in a whisper. "Uhh, guys. Franklin knows someone is in the vaults. You're going to have company in about ten minutes. I'll distract him as much as I can, but hurry," she hissed.

"Wanna melt this too?" I asked hopefully, looking over at Grayson.

"No can do, seductress; it's not that kind of lock." He pointed to the phrase above the door.

A dark charcoal script was written over the arched door in French.

"To open what you seek, you must first look inside your heart and tell the truth from the start," I whispered.

"Of course it's a fucking riddle," Grayson grumbled. "Fucking pretentious ass."

I examined the arch. "So, I just have to tell it my truth, that it?" I turned to him. "You know you could tell your truth?"

Grayson shook his head. "Not my truth to be told, seductress. It has to come from a witch, and a witch I'm not."

I let a frustrated sigh escape, knowing time was ticking down. What truth did I have living within me that would open this damn door? My parents' death always felt like it was my fault somehow, and now, with The Wishmaker's confirmation, I knew that was true.

"I was responsible for my parents' death," I whispered.

I reached out to the cold steel and pushed. It didn't move, though. I pushed harder and sighed, resting my head against the door.

"Grayson, I don't know what it wants from me." I looked back at him.

His eyes held a pain that no one's should, and I knew my eyes were showing him the same.

He laid his hand on my shoulder. "Don't think about it, Lexi. It's not as deep as you think. Though I do believe you needed to say that. The truth is, darlin', you're not responsible for your parents', Daniels's, Nyx's, or Marcel's deaths."

I swallowed the tears that threatened to escape and inhaled deeply. "Try not to overcomplicate things." That's what he said.

I thought of the things that made me happy. The way Dyna was always there for me when I was sad. Jason, who would always come over when I had a problem around the house—because he could do it for free, so why pay someone? Coco, who always knew what to cook when you were upset. Ella and Ethan stood by my side even at the darkest times, believing in me no matter what I faced. My parents taught me my core morals, to stand up for myself and empathize with others. Daniels taught me daily, whether it was how to handle toxic plants or defend myself correctly. Last, the three men who stood by my side when my world came crashing down again. They each brought joy into my life every day. Even when we should hate each other, we overcame that and forgave each other. We forgave each other in our miserable times only to bring light and joy into each other's lives. That was my truth.

I lifted my head and squared my shoulders. "I forgive them, love them, and we are bound forever."

I held my breath as the locking mechanism dragged and clicked free. The door opened slightly. The room that should have been dark had one hanging light in the middle of the room, shining on a raised platform.

"Grayson, the key."

A marble pillar sat in the middle, and an antique key floated in midair above it, turning slowly in a lazy circle.

I started to walk into the room when I was pulled back.

"Ténèbres," hissed Grayson.

I looked down, seeing the black wisps inching closer to us.

"They sense our magic," Grayson cursed.

"Grayson, we don't have time."

"What do you suggest then?" he asked.

I examined every inch of the room. The ténèbres drifted in and out of the shadows, which were pitch black. The only thing they stayed away from was the key surrounded by light. I smiled, figuring it out.

"The ténèbres are only sticking to the shadows; they're afraid of light," I murmured to him.

His eyes glowed, and a venomous smile showed his bright-white teeth as a ball of fire flashed in his hands.

I held out my hand, concentrating as I said the spell, "*Faire briller la lumiere dans lobscurite.*"

A small glowing ball expanded in my palm, and my fingers tingled with the magic as it shone and shimmered against the firelight.

Grayson grinned at me. "Let's show them the light then and send these shadows of death back where they belong."

"Let's destroy them." I stared at the tentacles sneaking out, desperate for a taste of magic. If a bite was what they wanted, then I would ensure they suffered.

Chapter Fifteen

L et's see how these bastards like dragon fire," he snarled.

He threw his fireball into the middle of the shadows, and they shrieked back from the light. I focused on growing my ball of light to be the size of a basketball and hurled it into the middle of the trench where they gathered.

They moved back, as if the light itself had burned them. I moved farther into the room, getting another ball of light ready to blast if needed. Grayson had his fireball, and we walked together.

I felt the shadow more than I saw it as it hit Grayson's leg.

His knees hit the floor with a thud. "Damn it." I turned back to blast my light, but he shook his head. "No! Lexi, get the key!"

I hesitated, but his eyes were filled with determination. They wouldn't take the leader of Trinity Coven down so easily. I turned back and moved forward as I shot another ball. The light hit the shadow closest to me, and it screamed in pain as I reached the pillar.

I reached out to take the key from the column of light, and I felt the burn on my hand before I saw the red form on my skin. I gripped through the pain and grasped the key. The cold metal made me hiss as I pulled it to me. I turned to Grayson, and the shadows held him down as they surrounded him.

"No!" I screamed as his eyes burned in pain from the lack of air.

I didn't think. I launched as much light as I could into the room. The ball exploded into a million pieces and hit the group of shadows. They shrieked as they moved away from him. I watched in awe as they disintegrated from him. I ran to him and pulled him up with my good hand.

"We have to go, Grayson. I'm out of magic!" I stumbled, and we ran for the door.

I felt the shadows move quickly and slash at us, trying to prevent us from escaping.

Grayson flung fireballs at them as fast as possible, but the shadows were more than we could even imagine, and they seemed to be multiplying. The room became darker as they gained on our every step. I ran as hard as I could, my feet slapping against the floor. The door was so close, but something shot from the side. A dark, inky claw ripped at my stomach, slashing it open.

The pain was excruciating. I screamed as Grayson threw the door open and pushed me through. He slammed it behind him. I leaned against the wall, trying to catch my breath, but my breathing became heavy and stiff. Grayson picked me up in one swoop and ran down the hall with me tightly in his grasp. His voice seemed so far away, which was weird, because he was so close.

"Don't close your eyes, seductress! Stay with me."

He yelled out for Aden and Tristian, and I was shifted into someone's arms as they called my name. I tried to keep my eyes open, but they closed against my will.

"Lexi, baby. Look at me."

I forced my eyes open and saw Aden. He had ash on his face and looked like he was in his own battle.

"Today is not the day you leave me." His eyes held a pain I had

never seen before.

Hudson came next to him. "Ella... focus on how much time... ten minutes. Tristian, can you heal her?"

I turned my head, looking for my golden boy, and he was drenched in water, but the look on his face was deadly.

"Yes, I can. Ethan, keep Bash calm. Sorry, Lil' Star, but this is going to hurt."

His voice was grave. Gone was flirty Tristian. He moved to my side and focused on my stomach as he murmured a spell. A green light illuminated in his hands as he laid one on my stomach and the other over my heart.

Pain wasn't the word I would use. It was more than that. It was torturous. It felt like I was being burned from the inside out. My screams echoed through the hall, and suddenly, I felt light, like I was floating in cool water. I teetered in and out of consciousness with my eyes opening and closing.

A smooth voice cut through the haze. "Princess, come back to me, please. Lexi?"

Hmmm, that voice. I knew that voice, and it felt like home.

I gasped and sat up, looking around. "Sebastian?"

I heard a laugh that struggled to hold back a cry.

"I'm here, Princess. Tell me it worked."

My tears fell. "It worked."

His breath of relief made my heart skip a beat.

"Lexi, thank god you're okay," Ella said in comfort, then her tone quickly changed. "Fuck, Lexi, you scared the shit out of me, but you have another problem, babes. Morgan's guard just arrived at the building with that weasel," Ella whispered.

"Find a way out now," Bash's panicked voice echoed, and communication was killed between all of us.

Curses echoed around the room. I slowly stood and saw we were in the center of the vault. I started to walk but slipped on something. I glanced to the ground, where my blood pooled around me. I looked at Tristian, whose eyes were still hard.

"We don't have time, Tristian, we gotta find a way out." I squeezed his hand. I looked back to Aden. "There was a secret exit! Aden! Where is the exit?"

He looked over at me, shaking his head. "I don't know. I was never told."

I turned in a circle, this was a room with no exit or windows. I looked to the ceiling, which was vast and endless. There wasn't a way magic would work. I tried to use my earth magic, but I was so tapped out, I had hardly any power left.

"There has to be a way that a non-magical creature could escape," I muttered.

Each arch led to nowhere. I dropped to the ground and squinted at the carvings covering the floor. Each coven's symbol was placed at three points, all facing toward the center with shallow divots running together. I noticed my blood on the ground was flowing into the divots.

"It can't be that simple, can it?" I bent and placed my hand in the pool of blood.

"Lexi, what the..." Hudson's voice came out.

I walked over to the Blood Moon Coven symbol and smeared my blood on the emblem.

The ground trembled under me as the center dropped down, and a small set of stairs formed.

I gasped and pointed to the other symbols. "It's the symbols. Get to each one!"

Aden and Tristian stood on the Silver Pearl symbol.

"It has to be water," Aden said to Tristian. "They're mostly water fae."

Tristian shot a blast of water from his hands. The ground rumbled as the center dropped farther and more stairs formed.

Hudson growled. "The coven isn't going to like this," he grumbled to Grayson.

"It's the only way, brother."

Hudson's eyes shifted as he slammed his hands into a nearby door covered in jewels. He ripped out a shimmering stone.

Aden whispered, "Moonstone."

Grayson took it, threw it on the floor, and slammed his foot down, breaking it into pieces. Hudson stomped on it next, turning the stone into a puff of dust. A small whimper escaped his lips.

"What's...?" I asked.

Tristian moved to my side. "Moonstone, it's like how you feel about your tears, Lil' Star. The moonstone is considered a powerful gem to wolves who hold it. It can be used to heal a wolf or even hinder them from turning into their form. The moonstone is also Trinity Coven's symbol of peace and harmony. It has many meanings to them, but for a wolf to crush one is like having your tears stolen."

I shuddered, walked over to Hudson, and hugged him as he whimpered. "We need to move, Hudson."

The ground rocked underneath us, and a puff of dust came from the hole.

Grayson went first, and I followed behind him. I stepped onto the old stone steps and carefully made my way down. They were steep and narrow. I knew I'd tumble my way down with one wrong move, and I didn't want to hurt myself any more today.

"Here." Grayson grabbed my hand and led me down.

"Such a gentleman."

"If we get out of here, I'll show you how much of a gentleman I'm not," he purred.

"Like hell you will, dragon. Back off before I cut something more precious than your gold off." Aden's low, dangerous voice came from behind me.

We made it to the bottom of the stairs and entered a long stone hall with a single door at the end.

"Let's move. Lexi, have Tristian or Aden carry you," Hudson said, changing the subject.

Tristian lifted me without a second thought and zoomed past everyone.

Bash's voice came crackling through our earpieces. "Fuck, if you can hear me, everyone"—his voice sounded far away and echoed through the com—"Morgan just got a call. They found the vault and the circle. Get out of there now!" Bash's angry tone hissed into our ears just as a bullet whizzed by Tristian's head.

"Too late, *frère*. They're here, and they got guns." He smiled like a maniac.

I scoffed at him as we ran to dodge bullets, returning our own. "Of course you'd get off on this!"

Aden was by us in an instant, running backward while throwing knives at the guards. One pinned a guard's hand to a door, and another impaled another guard's thigh.

I looked back, and Grayson and Hudson were in what could only be called a brawl. Seven or eight guards surrounded them, and they both looked like they were having the time of their lives. Grayson threw a guard, and he landed at Franklin's feet. Franklin scanned the room with his beady eyes and scowled when he spotted me. He raised his hands, and ténèbres slid from them. Before they could reach us, I used the last bit of my magic that I could muster and sent him flying through the air using a simple air spell. He hit the wall so hard that I heard the crack echo off the hallway.

We were close to the door when Tristian was tackled to the ground, tumbling out of his arms and a guy who was twice his size wrapped his large hands around Tristian's neck, squeezing tightly.

"See if you can escape without your head, fang boy."

Tristian punched his sides repeatedly, but the guy was so big, he didn't budge. I looked over to call for the others, but they were all consumed with their own fights.

Franklin had sprung up and thrown out a hand, pinning Aden against the wall with green vines. Aden laughed and headbutted him.

"Aden!"

He looked up just as the little weasel kneed him in the stomach. I growled and moved to help him, but Aden looked more annoyed than hurt. He grasped the vines and ripped them in one swift motion. Then he caught Franklin by the throat and threw him. Franklin hit the ground with a yelp and scrambled to get up.

"You'll be sorry, Charmante!" He ran to the stairs and fled the fight, knowing he was beat.

I turned to Tristian, realizing I was completely out of magic. Panic started to flare through me, but my father's voice echoed through my mind. "*When your enemy has your back to the wall, don't lose hope; fight like an alley cat, and don't back down.*"

I jumped on a guard's back, and he jerked in surprise. I whipped out my knives and stabbed his side. He screamed in pain, and Tristian punched him so hard, we tumbled backward.

I braced myself for the fall, but a pair of hands caught me, and I was cradled in Aden's arms at the door. He set me down and stood back, kicking the door open.

"Okay, everyone who's not a guard, let's go!" he yelled.

Tristian was covered in blood—even more now—and he stalked toward us.

Hudson was behind him. He jerked his head. "Grayson said he's got the last one."

Grayson threw the last guard on top of a pile, jogging to me as if he had just won a game.

"Are they...?" I asked in horror.

"Dead? No, not all. I think we only killed like four or something, but they were trying to kill us, soooo?"

I smirked. "Eye for an eye?"

Aden walked through the door, and we followed him, emerging into an alleyway. I looked around, seeing the familiar downtown neighborhood in Providence Village.

"We're close to the car," I said in a low voice.

Our moves were quick and silent as we stuck to the shadows and crossed a few blocks to where our car sat near an abandoned building.

We were quiet as Aden drove us back to the house. I laid my head on Tristian's shoulder, and he wrapped me up in his lap, not wanting to let go. Hudson was texting someone quietly, and Grayson looked like he was asleep.

The key burned inside my jacket pocket. We got it. We pulled it off and got it.

I smiled, then laughed. "We did it. We got the key!"

Grayson grinned at me. "So, tell me, seductress, how does your first ever B and E make you feel?"

I returned his grin. "Like we just got a step up, finally."

Chapter Sixteen

By the time we made it to the house, our bodies were bruised, and I really wanted a shower. I was climbing the steps when Ella burst through my front door and looked at us. Her nose flared at the sight of muck and blood on us.

"You're alive."

It was more a fact than a question.

"You doubted me?" I asked, giving her a sad smile.

She cleared her throat, and her voice came out shaky. "After... we lost connection with you... and I thought... we all thought."

From the porch, I saw Bash's back. His head was down, and his shoulders were hunched over. Ethan bent and whispered next to him. His head snapped up, and his forest-green eyes burned into me.

I don't know how, but I was suddenly at my door, running through it and jumping into Bash's arms. Our mouths connected instantly, and we communicated everything we wanted to say as our lips moved frantically.

Our kisses deepened and slowed as I wrapped my legs around

his waist. His head rested against mine.

"I thought I lost you, Princess."

I shook my head. Staying in the warmth of his arms, I breathed him in as the magic that lived inside us poured into each other. His was scalding hot, like fire to the touch, and I ran my fingers down his arm, the cold of my magic sneaking into his. It felt like thousands of raindrops hitting my skin at once. I raised my head, and the worry in his eyes quickly washed away.

"We're okay, we got out just in time, but Bash, we got it."

His eyes widened in surprise, and I grinned. "We got the key."

He returned my grin. "Fuck yes, you did, Princess, fuck yes, you did."

I unwrapped myself from him and slid down, earning a small groan from him. I placed a soft kiss on his lips before laughing and walking to Ella. "I'm gross. I have mud and someone else's blood on me. I don't think…"

She wrapped me in her arms, pulling me close and holding me tight.

"Lexi, I thought you…" She sniffed, and I hugged her tighter.

"I didn't… almost… but I didn't."

She pulled back and looked at me. "And you tell me to stay out of trouble. Look at you committing crimes, punching people, stealing shit from the rich to give to the poor. You're a modern-day Robin Hood, babes." She laughed as tears streamed down her face.

I laughed. "Well, I prefer indoor plumbing. Speaking of which, I need a shower desperately."

Ella laughed as we walked back to my bedroom. I stopped and looked over at my Devils, who were in an embrace, laughing and joking. Grayson and Hudson stood to the side, quietly talking, and Grayson looked over at me.

I mouthed, "Thank you" to them. Hudson gave me a small smile and waved goodbye. Grayson's eyes were still on mine, and he nodded.

Bash walked up to Grayson, holding out his hand. "Thank you for taking care of her, Holsten."

He smirked and clasped Bash's offered hand. "She doesn't need that much help, Ryder. Your siren can take care of herself. You guys celebrate tonight. I'm going to go home to my coven, relax, and drink my sorrows away. Tomorrow, we'll talk."

"Tomorrow, *ami*, we talk to take down The Wishmaker," Bash said.

Grayson waved goodbye and walked out the door.

Ethan walked over with a bottle of champagne, smiling. "Let's celebrate!"

He opened the champagne with a pop, and bubbles fizzed over the top, spilling over his hand.

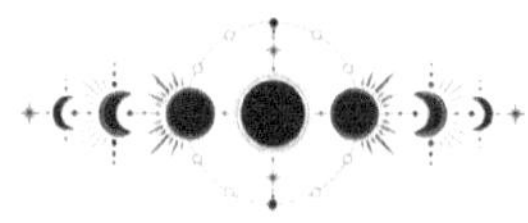

We continued to celebrate through the night. Ethan carried Ella off as she giggled in a drunken state. They snuck off to go to the beach to do God knows what. I was finally left alone with my three Devils.

I curled up on the couch in a pair of cotton shorts and a sweatshirt, snuggling against Aden. With his arm around me, he slowly brushed his fingers down my arm. His head was back, and his eyes were closed.

"Aden, are you asleep?"

He pulled me closer and mumbled incoherently.

Tristian laughed, and it turned into a yawn.

"Trist, go to bed."

He shook his head. "I'm good." He yawned again.

"Go to bed, *frère*," Bash said as he handed me a whiskey.

Tristian stood and stretched. "Not before I get a good-night kiss." He wiggled his eyebrows at me.

I rolled my eyes and downed the whiskey. Tristian started my way, so I put my glass on the table and went to stand, but he walked up to Bash and kissed him right on the lips! Bash's eyes went wide, and he pushed him away, playfully laughing.

"No, dude, just no, you aren't even half as pretty as our girl."

I crossed my arms and bit my lip. "Definitely not as cute."

Tristian grinned evilly at me and raced over, pulling me up and kissing me hard. He tasted like peppermint and whiskey. I moaned slightly, then he pulled away.

"Good night, Lil' Star. I have a meeting at the bar in the morning, or I'd entertain you until the sun comes up," he whispered, then disappeared into the bedroom.

"Tease!" I looked back at Aden, who had stretched out on the couch and was sleeping peacefully.

"Then there were two," Bash said in a quiet voice.

I felt his eyes on me and looked up at him. "Just us..."

The air shifted in the room. It became thicker. My eyes roamed over Bash. He was in black lounge pants and a thin Henley that clung to his muscles as he moved like a tiger hunting its prey.

"Princess, you seem nervous to be alone with me." He tilted his head to the side, his bright green eyes ablaze.

"I'm never nervous around you, Bash. Cautious is a better word to use," I said slowly, as if each word held a meaning of its own.

To put space between us, I moved to the kitchen, and I could feel him observing me.

I poured another glass of whiskey, taking a deep breath.

"Need to get drunk just to be with me?" He smirked.

"More like liquid courage, Bash."

He chuckled. "We've been alone before... many times, Lexi."

He used my real name, and it held so much more meaning than the nickname he used most of the time.

I placed the glass down and walked to him. "There is one thing I kept thinking about today. When I was hurt... I was so close to the fade, but your voice... your voice brought me back."

He opened his mouth to say something, but I shook my head. "Let me finish, please, because if I don't, then I'm scared I won't be able to say it again. I love you, Sebastian."

His eyes were so intense, it took a second for me to realize he was grabbing the back of my neck and pulling me close. His hands cradled my cheek.

"I am so in love with you, Lexi, that it hurts my soul every day. It kills me over and over again. I choose you, Lexi. Say you choose me too."

I wrapped my arms around his neck, and our lips collided. He nipped at my lips and teased them as he lifted the sweatshirt over my head, tossing it aside. The cool air hit my nipples, and I hissed as Bash kissed down my throat. I was lifted up, and I wrapped my legs around his waist, feeling his hard length against me. He kissed me again, this time softer, with meaning, and I pulled away.

"Bedroom, Sebastian."

He didn't say a word as he used his speed to get us to the bedroom and tossed me on the bed, climbing onto the mattress.

I sat up, moving his shirt and trailing kisses along his stomach. I traced each plane, memorizing him.

He let out a growl. "Princess..."

I quietly laughed as I dragged his shirt off. Making it a show, I lay back on the bed, arching my back and letting my hand skim over my stomach. He reached for my shorts and tugged them off. I was bare to him, and he could see how much I needed him.

"Come to me." I held my hand out as he removed his pants. I crawled farther up the bed, laying down against the soft sheets.

He traced my breasts and nipples with his fingers. His mouth followed his hand down to my stomach. He dipped his fingers down, teasing my folds, and I moaned his name. He smiled before bending forward and slowly licking me. I arched my back and gripped his hair.

"Fuck, Bash..."

He teased my clit with his tongue as he sank two fingers inside me. "Princess, you taste like heaven."

I couldn't speak. I just nodded and gasped.

He pulled a pillow over and lifted my hips as he moved back up my body. He never stopped touching me. His touches and kisses felt like ice and fire. It burned me to my core. I kissed him slowly, pouring every emotion I had into him. It was as if we were constantly battling to see who could bring the other more pleasure.

His eyes widened as he pulled back. "Lexi, you feel like a storm. God, I never want to quit you."

I pressed my hips up to show him how much I needed him. He sank into me in one fluid motion. My heart felt whole as we began to move with each other, each thrust hitting me where I needed him the most. I panted and brought him closer, kissing him with my arms wrapped around his neck. He groaned my name between our kisses.

I met his movements and wrapped my legs around his back. He sat back on his heels and pulled me up with him as he continued to fuck me relentlessly. He kissed me as enthusiastically as he fucked me, making me feel breathless from the sensations.

"Lexi, I feel every ounce of your pleasure. It's intoxicating."

I was so close when he thrust into me harder, and I felt it to my bones. As I orgasmed around him, he cursed the stars.

He moved slowly within me as another orgasm began to build. I raked my nails down his back, and his thrusts became erratic before I felt him spill inside me.

He tightened his arms and pressed his forehead to mine as he continued to move in and out, deep inside me. He rolled us over so he was lying on his back, pulling me on top of him. I lay catching my breath. He was still hard inside me, and I moaned because I needed more of him. I sat up and began to move slowly, rocking my hips against him.

"Bash," I groaned, and my breath came out in small gasps.

His fingers dug into my hips. "You look stunning riding my cock, Princess."

Thrusting hard into me, he sat up, taking one nipple in his mouth, moving faster.

I ran my fingers through his hair, our kisses hard and frantic as we moved with each other. His lips found my neck, and he let out a purr as he licked my pulse point.

I leaned my head to the side to give him better access.

"Are you going to come with me, Princess?"

I nodded and moved faster. He moved his finger between us, circling my clit, and I screamed his name as my orgasm captured me. Bash slid his fangs into me, taking my blood as he sent me to the stars.

I trembled and groaned, clinging to him. He wrapped his arms around me, and we fell back onto the bed. We lay like that for what seemed like hours. I slid off him, curling into his side. With his arm still around me, I laid my head over his heart and hooked my leg around his. We were perfectly wound around each other. His breath had finally slowed and calmed as ecstasy surrounded us.

I sat up, pushing his hair from his forehead, and he opened his eyes.

"I love you, Lexi Rose. I'll fight for you every day, do anything for you, even if it means my death, and if that ever happens, know I'll see you in the stars."

He kissed me so softly and tenderly that my eyes teared up.

I never thought in a million years that Bash and I would even be on speaking terms, but I found myself falling deeper in love with him and my Devils, even after everything that had happened between us.

Chapter Seventeen

The morning rays shone through the window, warming the room and making me snuggle closer to Bash, his arm instantly tightening around me.

Our legs were intertwined together. We fit like a perfect puzzle. As I stretched and felt the soreness from the night, I looked up at Bash as he slept. He looked younger in this state, less harsh in the morning light. He looked relaxed, like the world didn't darken our door daily. I ran my fingers along his jaw, capturing this memory and feeling of us in my mind forever.

I kissed his chest, and he smelled like the woods and me. His heart beat steadily beneath my hand.

He murmured, "Go back to sleep, Princess."

I laughed as I laid kisses on him, moving down slowly. He moaned, and his hands tightened around my waist. Feeling that he was already hard and ready for me, I stroked over his velvet softness, and he cursed.

"Insatiable siren, the night of fucking didn't satisfy you?" He looked down through hooded eyes.

I smirked as I took his tip in my mouth, tasting ourselves from last night.

He ran his hands through my hair. "Fuck, Princess."

I moved down his length until I felt him in the back of my throat. I pulled back, releasing him from my mouth, and kissed up his stomach.

"I'm making up for all the time we missed."

He propped up on his elbows, frowning. "I don't think I'll ever forgive myself for all those years lost."

I kissed and licked his neck as he brought his finger to my core and ran gently over my sensitive clit. "So damn wet already."

I moved to straddle him, and he turned me so my back was to his chest. My knees were on the outside of his, and he moved his legs farther apart to open me wider.

The door opened, and Aden walked into the room with a towel wrapped around his waist. "I thought I heard... Well, well, don't mind me." He crossed his arms and bit his lip as he saw me spread open on Bash.

Bash snickered evilly. "We won't."

He gripped my waist and slid me fully onto his cock. Once I was seated, he pinched my nipple. I gasped, and my eyes stayed on Aden. He leaned against the door, his gray eyes watching us move together intensely. Bash thrust hard into me.

"Fuck!" I arched back into Bash.

"Attention on the prize, Princess," Bash growled into my ear.

I reached up and wrapped my arms around Bash's neck and met each of his thrusts as our moans filled the room. Aden moved closer to us, his obvious arousal showing.

"Have you had her ass?" Bash asked in a deep voice that sounded rougher than usual.

"No, *frère*, I haven't." Aden had a mischievous smile.

"What are you waiting for then?"

I was about to object when Bash pulled out of me and kissed me roughly. "I get all your firsts."

The memories hit, and I moaned and kissed him back just as hard.

I pulled away breathlessly. "All my firsts."

He spun me to Aden, who pulled my chin up. "Tell me what you want, Lexi."

I moaned as Bash pushed me further, his fingers strumming me and coating his fingers with my arousal. He was gentle as he eased one finger into my back hole.

I bit my lip and whimpered. "I want you. I want both of you."

That was the permission Aden needed. He dropped his towel and pulled me into a kiss. He teased my nipples, pinching and pulling lightly. He kissed my neck, and as one hand played with my nipples, the other stroked my clit. Bash added a second finger, I sucked in a breath, and he chuckled. They both had me so close to the edge. Aden pulled his hand away.

"Not yet, baby. We haven't even begun."

Bash leaned close to my ear. "I have only two fingers in you, Princess. You'll need at least three before I take you."

I whimpered. "Please, I need to come."

Aden chuckled. "Dancing with the Devils comes at a cost, baby." He sucked on my neck and nipped at it, sending shivers all over.

Aden played with my clit, circling it slowly and teasing me, his fingers so close to where I needed them to be. Bash added a third finger, and I arched into him moaning, laying my head on his shoulder. Aden's mouth moved down, sending light kisses over the top of my breasts, teasing and nipping down my stomach. He removed his fingers, and I groaned at their retreat until his tongue replaced where his fingers had been. I screamed his name as Bash thrust his fingers.

"Good girl, taking it like this, taking it from your Devils."

I could only moan, my words coming out in pants and groans.

Bash and Aden both moved away, leaving me feeling empty. I

moved down to kiss Aden when Bash's hand smoothed over my ass. He slid his fingers through my core, pulling my wetness to my back. His fingers circled my tight hole.

"Ready, Princess?"

I breathed as his fingers found me ready for him.

"So... fucking... ready."

Aden smiled. "That's our girl."

Bash guided his head into me as Aden moved forward, his fingers finding my clit and circling it while kissing me.

Bash sat for a moment, letting me adjust. "So beautiful. Do you know what you do to us, Princess? I would fight heaven and hell for you. You bring the Devils to their knees. We are yours forever, Lexi."

He moved deeper in me until we were fully connected, and he slowly moved in and out until I was used to him. Bash's fingers circled my nipples, teasing them as he pulled me back against him, kissing my neck.

I closed my eyes, concentrating on Bash and the pleasure racing through my body.

"Lexi, look at me," Aden's voice growled out.

I fluttered my eyes open, and Aden's steel-colored eyes were on me just as he pulled his fingers back and lined up with my core. He moved into me with ease. I'm not sure what he saw, but his face was full of wonder as he pulled my hips down, both of them filling me up as new pleasures sent me into a sea of ecstasy.

"You are ours now, baby, and we are yours." Aden slammed into me.

Both of my Devils moved in sync, and I ran my hands over Bash's face, turning my head toward him as I pulled him down for a kiss while Aden gripped my hips. I had never felt this connection to anyone else in my entire life.

The faster they moved, the harder it was to hold back, and my orgasm crashed into me as the intensity had me screaming their names. Aden moved his hand down to my clit, dragging out my pleasure.

"Aden, please don't stop."

He let a masculine chuckle escape. "Never, baby."

He captured my lips and sent me to the edge again. Bash's thrusts picked up, slamming into me, and his grip on my hips tightened as I felt him frantically close to coming.

"Fuck, Lexi," he groaned and bit down softly on my neck, which was all I needed as I fell into pure bliss.

Bash followed, spilling into me. He fell back, pulling out of me as he rubbed my back.

"My turn," Aden said, taking his cue and lifting my legs over his shoulders as he moved within me with exquisite skill like a dancer.

I arched my back, and he sent me over the edge again.

"Hell! Lexi, so tight, baby."

He tried to hold out but leaned down as his orgasm hit him. Panting, he pulled out his cock and replaced it with his fingers as he pushed them into me.

"Come one more time for me, baby. Come for your Devils."

Bash sat up and kissed my neck, his hands sending shivers throughout my body. I fell into oblivion as I came around Aden's fingers one last time, gripping the sheets in my hands. Aden rolled to the side, pulling me with him. We lay in a haze of delicious euphoria, bathing in the afterglow of each other.

Aden cradled me between him and Bash. I nuzzled into the crook of his arm with Bash's warm body at my back. Bash traced feathery light circles down my side while trailing kisses over my shoulders to my neck and jaw.

"That's why they call you the Devils, right?" I panted as the orgasm rolled through my body.

"That's why the women call us Devils, Princess, but we earned that name through blood, sweat, and the destruction of our enemies," Bash whispered against my shoulder as he kissed my neck gently.

His hands wandered down my body again, and he grew hard against my back.

I rolled onto my back with a laugh, patting his arm. "Oh no, I'm

done. You guys have worn me out."

I sat up with shaky limbs as they both chuckled.

My phone rang, and I grabbed it off the stand. "Hey, Coco." I pulled the tangled sheet around me as if she was standing in the room.

"Hello, my darling girl. Bash talked to Jason last night at the party about the lovely gift you guys received."

I looked at Bash, confused as hell.

"Yeah, the lovely gift." Bash's head was down, and his finger sped over his phone as he sent a message.

Aden looked up and mouthed to me, "The puzzle box."

I mouthed a thank you. "Do you mean the Himitsu-Bako?"

Her laughter echoed through the phone. "Yes, well, after the eventful evening, Jason and I ordered Indian food and spent the rest of the night researching it. Then, after many, many, many espresso shots, I think we figured out a way to open it! So, gather your Devils and get over here for lunch. Oh, bring the box, and let's get this fucker open!"

I laughed and hung up. "We gotta go to Coco's. Let's go."

I started to stand as arms grabbed me, and I fell back.

"Hmmm, fine, baby, but I'll need you to make it up to me," Aden whispered.

"Wanna shower together?" I purred.

He smiled. "You soapy and naked? I am so down for that."

I laughed as I tried to stand on shaky legs.

"Oh no, baby, I got you."

I tried to wave him off, but my knees gave out, and Aden was there to catch me. He swept me into his arms easily, and I rolled my eyes. "Aden."

He kissed my temple. "Let me take care of you."

I blushed and kissed his cheek. "Thank you."

Aden looked over at Bash. "You coming, *frère*?"

Bash set his phone down, looking distracted.

"Who was that, Bash?" I asked as concern etched his face.

He looked up, his eyes roaming over my body in Aden's arms and going dark with lust, and shook his head. "Grayson, he talked to Brigitte. He thinks they have a solution for the potion to see what's in it. They want to meet tonight."

"Perfect. The more we know about what the hell is in there, the better." I closed my eyes with a groan.

We had so many problems facing us, and two more popped up once we had one figured out.

Bash stood, and my mouth dropped. I swear that man was made of marble.

He stalked toward us with a sinful smile. "No rest for the wicked, Princess. Now, let's get you cleaned up." His eyes gleamed with a look of wickedness in them.

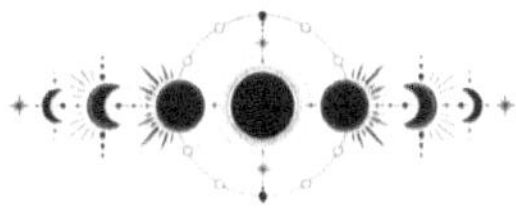

We met at the estate by early afternoon. I looked up at the large estate, thinking about how it had never physically changed in all the years I'd seen it, but it had changed so much on the inside. The people, the mood, it was still full of light and wonder, but a shadow resided over it, all because of The Wishmaker and their delusional dream of making fae the only superior race.

I walked into the long hallway as screams came from the kitchen. I looked at Aden, and we took off in a run. I pulled my blade from my thigh holster. Bash had insisted we were armed today just in case Morgan or Franklin tried to retaliate.

I passed through the large arches and looked around the kitchen. A pot of soup was boiling over, pots were thrown about, and a puff of flour was floating in the air. Coco was screaming hysterically on a chair with a tea towel in her hand, waving it around.

"I swear to the stars, Jason, if you do not find that vile creature of the night, I will curse your mother for the next ten years!"

Jason came around with a small shoe box and tilted his head. "Babe, that's a bit extreme, don't ya think? I got the little guy right here." Sweat gleamed across his forehead as he noticed us standing in the doorway looking confused. "Oh, hey, Lexi! Look, Coco, Lexi is here!"

Coco whipped her head around, and I pressed my lips together to stop a laugh from escaping. "Don't you dare laugh at me! You don't know the torture I've been through with that evil creature! Worse than the Lutin incident of 2015!"

Aden burst out laughing. "Ella told me about the time you found a helpless bunny rabbit and took it in, surprised when it turned out to be a Lutin looking for gold and treasure."

I giggled. "It took four huge bags of salt to get the bastard out of the house. What creature got in now, Coco?" I looked at the shoe box in Jason's hand.

Jason walked over to us with a mischievous grin and, in a deep voice, said, "Only the vilest kind of creatures. They sneak around in the dark, they can eat through even the toughest metals, and I heard once they even stole children's souls!" He cackled and lifted the lid. "It's the evil, villainous *mechante souris*!"

I laughed hysterically when he opened the lid and revealed a teeny tiny mouse sitting inside, nibbling on a piece of cheese slathered in peanut butter. He was the cutest thing ever, with big eyes and long whiskers.

"That is the most adorable little mouse I've ever seen," I scoffed with a laugh.

Bash walked to Coco and held a hand out to help her down. "I think it's safe to say the 'evil' mouse has been taken care of." He gave her a slight smile.

She took his hand but smacked him with the tea towel. "It ruined lunch." She huffed as she walked to her stove and stirred the soup.

"Tristian, can you check on the pies?" She pointed to the oven across the way.

"Ma'am, yes, ma'am." He saluted and walked over to the oven. As he carefully opened the door, a smell of cherry and apple escaped.

My stomach chose then to growl like an angry little man.

Jason looked over at my stomach, and his eyes widened with fear. "Coco... she's hungry, feed her now."

I crossed my arms, glaring at him. "I am not that bad."

"Yes, you are!" the whole room echoed.

I rolled my eyes and started cleaning as Aden set out plates, bowls, and silverware for us. Bash grabbed a rag and began to clean up any spills.

"Wow, she's got you three trained already. I'm impressed," Coco Rose said as my Devils worked on cleaning up the kitchen.

I shrugged. "I didn't do anything. This is all them."

"I took care of Ella and myself a lot when I was younger. Staff didn't work on the weekends." Bash tossed a few bits of trash away. "And I'm more scared of Coco than Lexi."

Aden tossed out, "Yeah, no one messes with Coco Rose. Not only is she a smoke show, but she's also one of the toughest women I know."

Tristian carefully placed the pies on the trivets.

"Smoke show, really?" Coco coyly smiled over her shoulder.

"Yeah, really, Tristian?" Jason crossed his arms and arched an eyebrow. "Wanna try that again, brah?" he mockingly asked.

"Dude... I mean, yeah, Coco is a beautiful woman and intelligent. I mean, you would totally have to be to run a business, and she is, like, the best cook in town... and I respect the crap out of her. Girl power!" he nervously mumbled.

A Devil scared of Jason Portions was a hilarious thing to witness.

I stood and crossed my arms, tilting my head slightly and looking at Tristian like he was a crazy person. "Ummm, Trist? The Spice Girls, really?"

He rushed to my side. "I got scared. Jason was giving me the evil eye, but don't knock the Spice Girls. They're awesome… I'm a total Mel B… which were you?"

I smiled and shook my head. "I always wanted to be Ginger, but I was a total Emma," I whispered.

"I got Posh," Bash said from across the room.

Every head snapped toward him.

"Umm, excuse me, Sebastian Ryder, did you just say you were Posh Spice?" My smile grew as he flushed.

"What? Ella made me do it… you try saying no to that blonde monster." He rolled his eyes.

"Anyway, lunch is ready, and while we eat, I can tell you about the time I ran into Prince Harry at the farmers' market one day… or at least I think it was Prince Harry." Coco walked past us to the breakfast nook off the kitchen.

We all sat down and began to eat the delicious pumpkin soup, roasted greens, and homemade bread and butter. Yeah, she was the best chef in this town.

Coco and I were chatting about Ella's wedding when Jason's voice cleared. "As much as I love Ella like the rest of us, let's talk about the box."

I smirked. "Too much talk of flowers, favors, and wedding gowns?"

He shook his head and laughed. "Lexi, I pretty much grew up with you and Coco. I can deal with the wedding stuff. Do you still want to marry that one pop star?"

I blushed, and every one of my Devils had a grin plastered across their faces.

"Not. A. Word." I pointed to each of them.

Tristian made a zip motion with his hand. "Not a word, Princess." But his voice held a hint of humor.

Aden looked up through his long lashes and smirked. "I bet I can guess who," he teased.

I sighed. "Look what you started." I looked pointedly at Jason.

"Bet Coco will tell us," Tristian stage whispered to the other two.

Jason put his soup down, clearing his voice. "The Himitsu... has seventeen moves that can only be done in the right sequence. The box will be tough to open. I don't think you can do it in time."

Bash put his silverware down carefully, and his eyes flashed red. "Jason... someone will die if we don't." His voice came out carefully and deadly.

"I know... that's why I said *you* couldn't open it... but Aden and I can," Jason adds. "The Wishmaker forgot one thing; it's not just you four they're going after, it's all of us, and I can't wait to kick their ass." His smile spread with a wild look in his eyes.

Bash's frown spread into a grin, and his eyes sparked with his magic as the lights flickered above us.

Chapter Eighteen

Aden and Jason set up a plan to meet and open the box tomorrow. We all said goodbye to them, and I gave Coco a more prolonged hug.

"I miss you," she whispered.

"I miss you too, Coco."

She patted my face gently. "Stay happy. I like this girl, Lexi."

I smiled and walked down the stairs to the car, where Jason was joking with the guys. I hugged him, and he said we'd talk soon.

We were in the car when Bash's phone rang. "Holsten."

I snapped my head to him, wondering what Grayson would want.

"The ritual will be done at midnight so he wants us to meet him at Trinity Coven. Brigitte will be there, so be on your best behavior, Princess."

I crossed my arms and glared at him. "I always behave."

That earned a burst of laughter from them, as they listed the many past incidents where I had not behaved.

"Whatever," I mumbled as we came close to the house.

Mrs. Wilson waved at me from the sidewalk.

I rolled down the window, and Bash cursed. "Lexi, we still have to be careful. Outside the gate, you could get hurt or fucking shot at."

I waved my hand in his face. "Shhhh, you're being rude."

He growled, grabbing my hand and yanking me forward. "Just do what you're told for once, Princess, or you'll pay for your misconduct," he purred.

I gulped. "Wanna expand on that, Ryder?" I leaned closer.

A knock on Bash's window had me arching my neck around to see Mrs. Wilson smiling at me, wiggling her eyebrows up and down.

"I told you," I mouthed.

I laughed and sat back as Bash rolled his window down. "Mrs. Wilson, how are you?" His smooth voice rolled off his tongue.

Mrs. Wilson blushed at him. "Mr. Ryder, you are looking much more relaxed out of cuffs. Lexi, I wanted to let you know an Agent Rengard came by looking for you today. He said something about a question he meant to ask you the other day... something about a key or a lock or something of the sort. Anywho, I told him you'd be back tomorrow."

I groaned internally but put on a smile. "Thank you, Mrs. Wilson! I appreciate you looking out for me."

She smirked. "We gotta watch out for each other, darling. I have to go. I have a new friend coming over tonight. He is incredible. You should see what he can do with his..."

The window slowly rolled up on her as Bash told Aden to go.

"That was more information than I ever wanted to know about Mrs. Wilson..." Tristian said in a horrified voice.

I looked back to ask him how he heard and noticed his window was down. "Ohhh, nooo." I gripped his hand. "You'll be okay, Trist."

"No, Lil' Star, I don't think I will."

Aden pulled the car up to the front porch, and we climbed out. Aden was laughing at Tristian when I looked up at the door. A shiny black envelope was attached to it. I stopped abruptly, and Aden ran into my back.

I heard the clicks of the safety being unlocked on three guns.

"Lexi, baby, stand behind me." Aden's voice was low, and he scanned the woods as he pulled me behind him.

I listened to him as Bash whispered into his phone. "Guards here in one minute." He took the envelope and unlocked the door carefully. "We'll have a guard stand point from now on."

Footsteps sounded behind us, and I turned to see Deke coming up the drive. His bright-blue mohawk was long gone. Instead, a shaved head made him look more menacing.

"Boss. Ms. Rose." He nodded to us.

"Check the perimeter, Deke, then stand at the front. One of us will watch the back windows," Bash firmly said.

Tristian was already inside, using his speed as he came to the door. "Clear. Lil' Star, inside now." His voice was strained.

"Inside, baby." Aden pushed me gently to the front door.

I walked into the living room and found Dyna curled up. I scooped her into my arms, kissing her head. A sweet meow escaped as she snuggled against me. We gathered around the kitchen counter as Bash placed the envelope down, glaring at the note.

"I hate these damn things," Tristian snarled.

I looked at Bash. "Do you need me to open it?" I placed Dyna down.

Bash's eyes flashed red as he picked up the envelope. "No."

An engraved card fell out, and Bash grabbed it before I could. His teeth immediately slid out. He slammed the letter down and stomped silently to the bar area, picking up four glasses and filling them to the brim. I looked over at Tristian and Aden, who picked the letter up and read it aloud.

My Lovely Rose,

Did you think I wouldn't know of your little adventures into the vault? My sweet Rose, I know all. All that precious blood spilled. Tell me, how did it feel to kill them? I can tell you that it was a rush to watch your darling mermaid breathe her last breath. She was scared in the end. She begged me to take her and not the littlest one. Stop searching for what cannot be found, and you'll keep those you love safe.

I am always watching. I have eyes everywhere. Three strikes now, my Rose. How will you be punished?

XXX
The Wishmaker

Aden handed me the letter, and I looked into his steel eyes. "I won't... they won't touch you, I swear. I'll do anything to keep you from going into that psycho's hands."

I took his hand. "I know you will, Aden."

I gave him a small smile and felt another hand grab my fingers. "We all would."

I looked at Bash. "That's what I'm afraid of," I whispered.

Bash pushed the drink toward me, and I sipped on it. "I need... change the topic. Let's try to focus on one problem at a time. "The potion? What does creating something like that mean for our covens?"

"Well, if in the wrong hands, it could bring back some seriously evil bastards." Aden sat as he opened a laptop. "I think Grayson is trying to recreate it where it doesn't have the lasting effects like trapping a fae's soul into a bottle. Either way, the potion is too dangerous to mess with. For now, I think Madam Brigitte should hold onto it."

"I agree. I think there's too much unknown about it. Brigitte said the price is high for many, so I have to wonder what you have to pay?"

Tristian came behind me and rested his chin on my shoulder. "Usually, with dark magic, it's always something the individual would never give up. That's why dark magic changes your soul. It marks it as its own."

Bash leaned closer. "We should tell Grayson to destroy it. It's not worth it."

I looked over at him. "What if it can help with The Wishmaker?"

Bash shook his head. "Princess, nothing is worth that. We'll find another way."

I slumped against Tristian. Why would someone use their soul for magic? There had to be a reason.

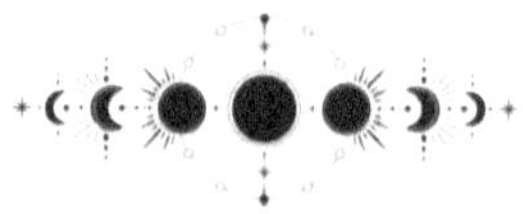

As the midnight hour approached, I dressed for the weather. I was pulling on black leather boots when Aden came in.

"Hey."

I glanced up and smiled. "Hey." I stood and took out my long camel coat. "I'm ready. I need to throw my coat on."

He leaned against the wall. "You're so beautiful, Lexi."

I looked over my shoulder. "Aden, are you okay?"

He shook his head. "I'm good, just have a feeling this potion could cause more trouble than we know." He came up behind me, helping me into my jacket.

"Always helping me dress, Mr. Charmante." I turned in his arms and looked up at him. "I love you, Aden."

He smirked. "I know. I love you too, baby."

He kissed me lightly. It was sweet, and it was ours.

"Get a hat. It's cold tonight." He pulled out a black beanie and placed it on my head. "Perfect." He stepped back and pretended to take a picture. "I want to remember you just like this."

I laughed. "You are too charming for your own good."

He held his hand out. "Ready, my lady."

We walked into the living room, seeing the others waiting. Bash was in dark jeans and a sweater, and Tristian had a long black coat over a pair of black jeans and a black sweater.

"Damn, Lil' Star, you look good enough to eat." He bit his knuckle, making me laugh.

"I am not your snack."

Bash's eyes flashed red. "Not yet, anyway."

I rolled my eyes. "Let's go, my Devils."

I swear, these men would be my undoing.

Chapter Nineteen

The drive to the Trinity Coven seemed faster than before. The dark trees bent to our will, and the foggy mist appeared to melt away. There was something about entering through their coven gates that made me feel at ease.

"I feel like Grayson is a friend, not just an ally, but can we trust him?" I looked over at Tristian, who was next to me.

He laid his hand on top of mine. "Before the vault? I would have said we should be cautious around him. After seeing him fight for you and my *frère*? I call him a friend and someone we want in our corner, Lil' Star." He intertwined our fingers.

We pulled through the gates to the cabin, if you could call it that. It was a massive three-story home with ivy and vines climbing to the sky. Aden stopped the car, and we stepped into the crisp night air. Beyond the house, a group gathered around with candles, flowers, rocks, and water bowls, creating a sacred circle for tonight's events.

Grayson's back was to us as we approached, and he was talking to a mysterious person cast in shadows. As if he knew we were there, he raised his hand in greeting. As he turned to us, we saw who he was talking to, someone I already knew. The drow who had tried to kidnap and kill me a few weeks ago stood among a group of soldiers.

Bash grunted. "The fucking Royal Prince of the Drows is here."

I looked over to the drows. Their prince stood in the middle. He was tall with broad shoulders and a tapered waist. His pale-blue eyes glinted in the night sky, and his dark hair moved like the wind. He was beautiful, not handsome. No, this man was gorgeous. Even with a scar running from his eye down to the top of his lips, he looked like marble with the way his skin glowed. It was as if art had come alive.

Grayson came up to me. "Lexi, I don't think I ever introduced you to Prince Kazimir Alarie."

He bowed his head to me. "Ms. Rose, it is a pleasure to see you again."

I bowed my head to him. "Under better circumstances this time, I hope?"

He smiled at me. "Much better. I have been working with Brigitte and her coven to figure out our dilemma, and as I stated when we first met, I am indebted to The Covens of Providence Village now. Grayson asked my men to help with protecting your circle."

Brigitte strolled up with a young girl with long dark hair braided to the side. "Anna, I know you want to help... you can watch, don't do any magic. You still don't have it under control."

Anna slumped her shoulders and agreed. She slung over to a group of witches and sat near the circle, helping them prepare.

"New witches." She shook her head as she joined our group. "She will be powerful one day, but you must learn to walk before you run, don't you, siren?"

I smiled gently at the name. For me, it sounded almost motherly. "It's true. I've set many things on fire practicing my magic."

She laughed and then turned toward Grayson, threading her arm through his. "You'll think on the request I asked?"

Grayson looked down with a frown at her as if it hurt him to speak. "I will speak to Hudson, Brig, but I don't think I'm ready."

She smiled sadly. "Not yet, wolf born of dragons, but you will be soon." Brigitte turned toward me. "We're almost ready to start the circle, and here, we will learn more about the potion and the sacrifice if one uses it. Without a spell, we are—"

A deep voice came from behind me. "We're fucked. Brig, don't put it lightly to her. She's a coven leader."

Brigitte sighed. "Yes, Griffin, I know."

A large man covered in tattoos broke through our group. Griffin was one of Brigitte's more powerful oungan. He was a powerful witch and had been with Brigitte for years. His rather expansive chest was covered in tattoos of ancient ruins and symbols as he stood beside Brigitte with a scowl, looking at my Devils.

Aden and Tristian icily glared at him, and Bash stood silently beside me, his eyes never leaving the group.

"You're quiet tonight, Ryder," Grayson said, looking a bit smug.

"Taking everything in, Holsten," Bash snapped back.

Grayson smirked, crossing his arms over his chest.

"Let us begin," Brigitte said to the formed crowd.

Witches were here tonight, as well as wolves, pixies, trolls, and even a vampire or two, who stood around to see what the excitement was all about.

"Brigitte?" I reached for her hand, and once our skin touched, it was as if I could see in her mind, and the darkness of the shadows that lured me in made me gasp as I stepped back.

She smiled sympathetically at me. "Careful, siren, the magic that lives in me is not for your pure soul."

"Sorry… I just wanted to ask if they know what the potion is. Will they say a word outside the circle?"

Brigitte shook her head. "We made everyone take a vow of secrecy. Even if they tried to talk about it, they couldn't. That is how the vow works. It can't be broken until death."

"Do we need to take the vow?" Aden said carefully.

"No, those in the inner circle will not take the vow, for they know the importance of the spell we are doing."

"Okay. Let's start then." I nodded to the circle.

I sat next to Brigitte in front of a bowl of water. Tristian sat on my other side as Bash and Aden stood behind us in a protective stance.

Brigitte knelt and pulled a dark shawl decorated with roses around her arms as she bent forward, whispering blessings. "A sacred circle in perfect love and trust protects me."

The crowd did the same and knelt to the ground. I followed suit and waited for the next phrase.

"I ask the loa to bless this circle so I may be protected during my magical working," I repeated and felt the pull to the water, and the magic rose up around me.

It flowed around my hands as I felt the energy work its way through the circle.

Brigitte sat up and smiled at the sky, lifting her hands. "The circle is cast, so bless it be." She looked over to me, and her eyes were glowing an eerie yellow. "Bring me the potion." Her voice dropped into a husky whisper.

Bash removed the box from his jacket pocket and handed it to Griffin, who carefully brought it to Brigitte.

"I feel the darkness in this magic, for those who use it will have to give up part of their soul to the darkness, a mark that only the strongest souls can survive. Is this something you still wish to know, siren?"

I swallowed hard and let out a breath. "Yes, I will pay your price."

Brigitte's smile turned sinister. "Hold your hand out."

I gave her my hand before she sliced a sharp knife across my palm, collecting my blood into a small bottle.

"Blood for truth. Magic always wants something in return, Lexi. Beware of what you are willing to give up. One day, this might not be the only blood you have to spill."

My palm stung as I cradled it in my lap. I pulled back and looked up at her glowing eyes. "I'm willing, Madam Brigitte, and I respect you and your magic. Let's find out the truth of what we want to know."

Brigitte looked at the potion, uncapped it, and poured it into a ceremonial bowl. "Air, come to me!"

A breeze hit my cheek, and Kazimir raised his hands and pushed the wind to Brigitte.

"Earth, crumble before me."

Griffin's hand came above the bowl, formed a flower from thin air, and dropped it inside.

"I call the ocean to me."

A tug pulled at my magic as I picked up the bowl of water, and I pushed my magic into it. The water swelled from within, and the ocean's salty air instantly hit me. I smiled as I raised my bowl to Brigitte's, letting the water fall slowly.

"Fire, I call upon you."

Grayson came to her side, and he formed a small fireball and placed it into the bowl. Brigitte smiled at Grayson.

She looked over the crowd. "The blood of the witch who wishes to know what is held inside." When she dropped the blood in, the potion smoked into a white cloud and turned into a golden glow. Brigitte leaned into the smoke, and her voice boomed over us. "*Vous detenez la vérité dans votre magie aidez-nous a trouvery une memoire du passe.*"

In the smoke, a dark figure formed and walked through the golden haze. "Those who want to know the truth will hear it from me." The soft, delicate voice was almost childlike, sending a shiver down my back.

Brigitte looked at me. "Ask, siren, what you need to know."

I looked up at the figure and spoke softly. "Your spell is the rebirth of death? Does this mean you can bring back the dead?"

The voice laughed with a high-pitched giggle. "No, daughter of Natalia and Alexander." The figure moved closer to me. "But I can show you what you want to know."

Bash growled. "Lexi does not—"

I cut him off. "Do it. I want to know what happened to Nyx."

Though shrouded in darkness, the figure looked up as a smile formed on its lips. "As you wish."

The figure swooped down, landing in front of me. A woman in her late teens was standing before us. Her long black hair hung loosely around her shoulders. She was dressed in a dark robe that covered most of her.

She smiled gently at me. "I am not going to hurt you, daughter of the ocean. You are one of us, but you will pay the price for this knowledge you are aware of."

I nodded. "Yes."

She reached out her hand, grabbed mine, and pressed it to her heart.

I was slammed into a vision of loud music and the smell of stale whiskey. When I reached a door, I threw it open and stumbled out into the dark. I slumped against the cold wall.

Holding my hand in front of me, I smiled. "Pretty." My husky voice came out, but it wasn't mine. It was Nyx's.

I turned to look into a puddle of water on the ground, and I saw pinpoint pupils staring back at me.

Footsteps approached.

"Nyx?"

I turned, and, seeing Bash, I smiled. "Wow, you're so pretty."

Bash rushed to my side and supported me. "Lexi has been looking for you everywhere. How? How did you escape?"

I laughed. "Oh, it was easy. I made friends with the local mice, and they freed me, but not before a pokey ouchy. Are we flying? It feels like I'm flying! Look at me!"

Bash wrapped his arms around my waist. "Nyx. You're high as hell. We aren't flying."

I saw his arms around me like the cage I was in. "No, no, no!" I tore at his arms. "I want to fly. Let me go. Let me fly! I won't be caged. I need to swim, I need to fly, maybe I should turn into foam, jump off a cliff, and become foam again. I miss the ocean so much." We cry out.

Bash let go of me and knelt in front of me.

"Nyx, think of your sister and friends, please. Where was The Wishmaker keeping you?"

I smiled at the thought of Viv, Cordy, and Chella. *I have to help them.* "It was whoosh and boom and loud, but we had water, fish swam up to my feet once, then he came, he's bad so bad, he's a bad man." I started to cry. "I just want to go home."

Bash held me. "I'll take you home. I'm going to go get water, do not move from this spot, okay?"

I nodded my head. "Okay, hurry. I feel the fire on my neck."

Then he was gone, and I was alone again, so alone, like the emptiness would never leave. My heart hurt, and I sobbed.

I lifted my head to the sky and saw him. A cloudy fog covered his face.

"Poor little mermaid, you thought you'd escape?"

I was wrenched from my spot and thrown to the ground with a loud thud.

How is he so strong? I thought.

His laugh filled my ears. It was high-pitched and hurt my ears.

"It has to end, and it's a pity, little one."

Vines wrapped around me and held me down.

A black dagger formed from the shadows in his hand, then the blade slid into my chest. It hurt. Burning formed around my heart as it spread throughout my body. It was an onyx blade, and the poison made its way through me. The pain wouldn't cease as it trickled to the tips of my fingers and down to my soul. The red pool of blood was warm as it slid from me.

My life slowly left my body. I felt heavy and laid my head to the side to look at the door. Bash would come back soon; I just needed to wait. I had to hold on. The world started to fade around me, my vision fading to dark as I fought to stay awake. My last thought was of my sister and family, wishing I could see them again.

"I love you, Viv, I love you," I breathed out.

Bash walked into the alley, and horror crossed his face when he was struck with a green flame. My tears fell, knowing he couldn't help me. They were too powerful. I felt light as I rolled onto my back. The last thing I saw was the moon and stars shining above me.

"Beautiful."

I screamed as I opened my eyes to the starry night sky. The grass was soft beneath me. The stars were not the ones of the alleyway. I was back at the Trinity Coven. My chest still hurt as I patted it to check for a stab wound. I was sick to my stomach and dizzy from the spell. A tear rolled down my face as I realized I had experienced Nyx's death. I experienced her death. I felt her thoughts and her last private moment. I sobbed as I sat up.

Bash was holding me. "Princess, it's me. I got you."

I looked up and saw a sea of concerned faces.

"I saw how she died," I sobbed. "I saw you and felt it all... Bash, I felt it all."

Aden knelt in front of me. He gently stroked my cheeks, wiping the tears away. "Baby, what did you see?"

Tristian stood behind him with concern etching his features.

"Her death. I saw how Nyx died."

Brigitte was there instantly with a glass of water. "Drink, siren. I know how the visions can be. This will make you feel better."

I took the water and looked at her with horror. "This is what you see all the time. Is that why you..."

She lifted her eyes to me, and they were cold. "It is what I am,

Siren of the Sea. My magic is dark, and it is not for the faint of heart."

"You should have told us, Brigitte," Aden snapped.

Griffin was in his face instantly. "How the hell would she know that your siren wouldn't be able to handle it, *moun sòt*?" he spat out.

Aden jumped up and pointed to him, his anger radiating off him. "Idiot? Fuck you. I swear, the Crescent Moon Coven is all about half fucking truths or lies," he growled.

"Keep insulting me, *vanpir*, and I'll show you what happens when you mess with us," he pushed back.

Aden's fangs snapped out, and his eyes turned red. "When it's about her safety, you better believe I will fight back!"

He pushed Griffin, who stumbled and came roaring back with a punch.

Aden's head snapped to the side as he laughed. "Oh, big mistake."

He wiped his lip and licked the blood. Aden pulled his sword out from his back. A glimmer of magic concealed in the blade rippled through the air, and the blade's steel gleamed under the moon as he swung it down in an arc.

Griffin lurched back, barely escaping the blade by inches. He formed a purple orb in each hand as he prepared to attack.

Tristian and Bash pulled Aden back, yelling at him to calm down, and Grayson and Prince Kazimir held onto Griffin's arms, murmuring to him in Creole.

Brigitte sat next to me, shaking her head, seemingly entertained by the commotion. "Men are fucking idiots."

I sipped my water. "I agree."

It was the way of the fae to not back down from a fight, but this was not the time nor the place for it.

"I'm putting a stop to this now," I said to Brigitte as she helped me stand slowly.

I gave her a small smile. "Thank you."

She returned my smile. "It takes a lot out of you. The fact you are standing, siren, shows me you are stronger than you seem." She looked over at Griffin. "He usually has to carry me out."

I glanced at the guys, who looked like they were on the verge of an attack. I cleared my throat. " Enough!" All three of them jerked their heads to me. "I think we have our answers." I moved to Bash. "You didn't kill her." His eyes closed like he needed to know the truth, and I was glad I could be the one to deliver it. "We knew you didn't, but we now know that you were framed for Nyx's murder. Whoever hit you with a spell made you forget everything. We're dealing with a powerful witch, concealment spells, memory spells, and killing."

Bash kissed my cheek. "Thank you, Princess."

Aden came over and gripped my shoulders. "Are you okay?"

I kissed his cheek. "Yes, but please don't kill anyone tonight, my dark knight. Plus, I have a feeling we'll need Brigitte again."

He smirked. "Okay, but I can't promise I won't beat the shit out of the witch doctor."

I laughed, but my chest stung in pain, and I clutched it. "Ouch."

Tristian was at my side, holding me. "You okay?"

I pulled up my shirt and saw a bruise blooming across my skin in the shape of the shadow's hand. "I'm fine."

He didn't look like he believed me but dropped it. "Did you see anyone?"

I thought back and shook my head. "No, just fog, but Nyx thought vines held her down, but it didn't feel like vines..." I looked to Brigitte. She smirked as if the answer was always there. "Could have been magic," I groaned. "Great. Speaking of magic, we should close the circle."

She nodded. "I will. You rest. The potion I think I'll keep for a bit. The shadow may need to speak more. I fear she may be a necromancer." She looked down at the potion, and sadness filled her voice. "Being trapped for however long in those shadows can change oneself. If I can free her and help her find peace..."

Grayson frowned and took her hand. "Brigitte, she should be set free."

She turned to him. "Yes, my dragon made of wolf. She deserves so much more than we can give her."

He bowed his head. "*Wi pretès mwen.*"

I didn't know much of the Creole they spoke, but I did understand that Grayson called Brigitte his priestess, and the love in his eyes that he had for the leader in front of me was plain to see.

Brigitte turned back to us. "Siren, take your men and go. We shall figure this out tomorrow when the sky is not so full of darkness."

I moved to walk, but my knees gave out. Just before I hit the ground, a rush of air scooped me up, and I was in Bash's arms.

"Bash, seriously, I can walk."

He shushed me. "Let me carry you, Lexi."

I sighed. "Fine."

We were walking away when Brigitte called my name. Bash turned, and she walked to me, her eyes on my chest where the handprint lay.

"Heed a warning, siren. You will have to give up something that you treasure for the shadow's gift tonight." Brigitte's voice was low, full of warning.

I looked back at Bash and knew that whatever it was, whatever I had to give up, meant that Bash could find peace of mind.

"It's a sacrifice I'm willing to make, Brigitte."

She tilted her head as her eyes turned solid white. "Sometimes, the price is more than your heart can handle."

"She's so fucking scary," Tristian murmured.

"Well, she is the Queen of Voodoo. What do you expect?" I said in a horrid whisper.

Chapter Twenty

The walk to the car was quick, and Bash gently placed me in the back. Tristian slid in on the other side and pulled me close against his body.

Bash growled, and Tristian held up his hand. "You carried her, and you"—he pointed to Aden—"fought for her. So, she gets my snuggles. It's only fair."

Aden grumbled, and Bash glared but eventually said, "Fine." Then he hopped into the front passenger seat.

I smirked and curled into Tristian's body. His warmth eased the cold that I couldn't seem to shake since I had awoken.

"Best snuggler of the group." I winked.

"Damn straight," he huffed out.

Aden turned the car on, and we sped away, leaving the wolves, witches, and drows behind.

I hid a laugh and closed my eyes. The soreness from the bruise started to settle in. I sat up and rubbed it softly but hissed when even that hurt. Tristian lifted my shirt and placed his palm over the handprint. A burst of light escaped his hand as he sent healing magic into me. The warm glow lessened the pain, and I turned to snuggle back into him, kissing his neck. His slight scruff grazed my face.

"Thank you." My eyes were on his lips.

"You're welcome, Lil' Star." He smiled at me, his eyes full of mischief. "Wanna play a game?"

I raised my eyebrow. "What kind of game?"

He licked his lips and moved closer, barely whispering in my ear. "To see if grumpy pants one or grumpy pants two notice you coming on my fingers." I gasped, but he licked my throat. "My lips." He kissed my ear. "My tongue. I only want to hear you come for me. You don't think I didn't hear you three earlier today, do you?" I shivered and moaned lightly. "Oh, and if you lose and they notice, then I get to punish you tonight when we get home."

Tristian dropped his phone on the ground near my feet and knelt to get it. His head was between my legs when his hand tickled my thighs to open more.

"Aden, turn up the music, please, and play something with rock." Tristian skated his fingers up my inner thigh.

Aden blared Def Leppard's "Pour Some Sugar On Me." It was loud enough to send vibrations throughout the car.

I sat up straight and widened my legs, looking down at Tristian with a smirk. He smiled, moving his hands to my tights. He gripped them tightly between his fingers and tore them slowly down the middle, making me squirm. My sweater, thankfully, was long enough to cover most of me, but if Bash turned his head, he would see everything.

Bash was engrossed in his phone, typing out messages with vampiric speed. Aden was drumming along with the song, eyes focused on the road.

Tristian moved his fingers to my core and began stroking slowly up and down, teasing me through my panties. I bit my lip to keep from moaning. When his lips brushed my inner thigh, I broke out into a shiver. He scraped his fangs along my thigh, sucking gently, so close to where I needed him.

I sucked in a breath, covering it with a cough. I intertwined my fingers into Tristian's hair and pulled him where I wanted him. I felt his smile as he rubbed against me roughly before sinking his fangs into my thigh. I stifled a scream, and he moved my thong to the side, sinking his fingers into me.

Tristian pulled back and straightened, his fingers still inside me. Their torturous movements had me lifting my hips, begging for more.

He leaned close and spoke low, "I'm going to be gentle now, but tonight, Lil' Star, you are mine, and I won't be gentle at all." He slowly circled my clit with his thumb.

I gasped, and Aden looked into the mirror and raised an eyebrow. "You good back there, Lexi?"

I nodded. "I'm fine, just sore… so sore." I faked a yawn, stretching my arms back and working my hips against Tristian's fingers as he pumped in and out of me.

His head popped up, and he sat back in his seat, his fingers still in me. I nearly growled at him when he moved me in one quick motion.

"Here, lay on me, Lil' Star," Tristian said.

I turned to him. "Cheater," I murmured.

He leaned over to my ear. "That's one, Lil' Star." He pinched my clit before removing his fingers and swinging my legs over his own. He smiled devilishly. "It's a long drive home. Just rest."

Bash let a light laugh out as he looked up from his phone. "Did someone keep you up last night, Princess, or was that from this morning?"

Before I could say anything, Bash's phone rang, distracting him.

"Hey, Tracy, what's up? That's weird. Yeah, go ahead and transfer him. Sullivan, how's life on the East Coast, man?" Bash continued his conversation as Tristian typed on his phone with one hand while the other was nestled near my thighs.

I leaned back against the door and rested my head against the window. The cold glass cooled my face. I rubbed my thighs together, trying to rid the ache between them.

Tristian slowly circled my ankle and traced lines up and down my legs, leaving behind a trail of goose bumps. His cocky smirk stayed on his face, and he moved closer, bending so his head was almost in my lap. As his hands moved up, I ran my fingers into his hair, and he lifted my sweater, kissing my stomach. He brought his fingers back to my core, rubbing me slowly and resuming the sweet torture.

He laughed as he whispered, "You're so wet already, Lil' Star. Do you want me to continue until you come all over my fingers?"

I nodded, unable to say anything without giving away what we were doing. He moved his fingers in and out while his thumb played with my clit. He smiled wickedly and moved to the center console between the front seats, looking like pop goes the weasel.

"Hey, Aden!" he chirped. "Where's that book you read the other day about ancient kung fu fighting styles and weaponry? Is it still in the back pocket?"

Aden glanced over at him and looked confused. "Uhh, yeah, it's there in the back pocket behind me. Why?"

Tristian shrugged. "Curious about it. Do you mind if I read a bit?"

His thumb never stopped playing with my clit. I was so close, I could scream.

"Trist," I growled, and he smirked back at me.

"Sure, *frère*," Aden said over me.

Tristian grinned evilly as he bent down to pick up the book, but instead of the book, he pulled me so I was sitting up and facing Aden and Bash. My sweater was in disarray, and my tights were ripped open from the front to my butt, the seat's cool leather against my bare skin. He pushed my knees apart and moved his head between my thighs to lick me from back to front.

I whispered, "Oh god," as I closed my eyes.

He mumbled against me, "So damn radiant, Lil' Star."

His deep voice sent a delicious hum through my core as I moaned in my throat.

"That's two, baby." His tongue continued to lick and suck my clit.

"Oh shit." I arched my back and whispered a string of curses under my breath.

Aden looked back again with a knowing look and smirked, shaking his head. "You two know you're not invisible, right?"

Bash looked back, and his eyes widened, but he continued to talk on the phone. "No, I'm here. It's all good, Sullivan." He licked his lips, and his green eyes, swirling with lust, never left mine.

Tristian pulled his head out and then smiled at me with glistening lips. "That's three, Lil' Star, and now Bash makes four."

That's all he said, then he ripped the rest of my tights off so I was entirely exposed to the car.

I let a moan escape. "Fine, you win, Tristian. Please just finish, or I swear... I will climb into Aden's lap and let him fuck me while he drives."

Aden gave a choking laugh. "Oh, please say no, Tristian. I'm hard as fuck right now." He adjusted the mirror to watch us.

Tristian smirked. "Don't worry, I got you, Lil' Star."

Bash cleared his throat and kept speaking to Sullivan. "Yes, you're correct. If you didn't provide the documents, it would be hard to obtain the offer."

I moaned loudly as he covered the phone and turned to me. "You come when I say, Princess."

Tristian dropped his head and savored me like a parched man searching for water. His fingers quickened inside me, which had my toes curling, and he swirled his tongue around my clit.

"Tristian, oh jeez, oh my... so close." I was panting.

Bash's eyes found mine. His voice came out in a growl as he quickly said into the phone, "Sullivan, I'm sorry to cut this short, but I'm walking into an important meeting."

He didn't even say goodbye. He clicked his phone shut, licking his lips and staring at me as I felt the high of the orgasm coming.

"Princess, come."

I dug my fingers into Tristian's hair, spurring him on. He pushed a third finger inside me and lifted my ass so I was on the edge of the seat, fully spread out in front of them. That was all it took for me to fall over the edge.

"Tristian, oh god, don't stop!"

I exploded into a sea of ecstasy. I was shaking from the orgasm, and he continued to draw out my pleasure. He pushed his thumb into my tight hole and pumped his fingers into my pussy in merciless movements. I screamed his name and kept saying it like a promise on my lips.

He sat up with a satisfied look as I panted, trying to catch my breath. I looked out the window and saw that the car had stopped. Bash and Aden were looking at me with fire in their eyes.

Bash growled, "Princess, you looked so good coming on that bastard's face."

He grabbed Tristian's fingers that had been inside me and slowly pulled them into his mouth, sucking the orgasm off them.

I groaned, and my eyes never left his as I licked my lips.

Bash opened his door and slammed it behind him.

Aden smirked at me. "Lex, that was fucking hot as hell." He hopped out of the car, stuck his head back in, and said, "Tell me, did you even notice that we went through a security checkpoint, or were you too caught up in Tristian's sweet tongue?" His eyes were alight with excitement.

I threw my middle finger up at him, and he laughed and walked over to where Bash was leaning against the porch, looking annoyed. He stared at the car with a wrinkled forehead and crossed arms, waiting for us to get out.

"Doesn't he know that can cause wrinkles?" I mumbled and noticed that my cheeks had turned bright red from embarrassment.

Tristian went to open his door when I stopped him. "Uhhh, Tristian? I need to cover up."

He smiled. "Need help, Lil' Star?"

I rolled my eyes. "You destroyed my clothes. This is payment. Give me something to cover up with."

He handed me his coat and helped me slide it on. I pulled the soft cashmere coat over my shoulders. It was enormous, but it smelled like Tristian, sunshine, and whiskey. I pushed up at the arms as I got out, my legs still wobbly from having Tristian's fingers and tongue on me.

I looked over to the gate to see two guards scanning the area for any potential threat of danger.

I hissed and turned to Tristian, giving him an icy glare. I poked his chest. "Did you know, asshat?" I crossed my arms.

Tristian smiled wildly. "Does it matter if I knew or not?" He leaned against the car door as he closed it.

My jaw dropped, and I closed my eyes, my anger not settling. "Yes, Tristian, it does."

His smile dropped, and he pushed off the car and walked toward me. He pushed a piece of hair behind my ear and cupped my cheek. "Baby, I put a silencer spell around us plus a concealment spell. Anyone who looked in or walked by would only see an empty back seat." He frowned down at me. "I'm a bit hurt. You think I would do that?"

I mirrored his frown, because he was right. A few months ago, he might have done that. But now? Now, they cared for me as much as I did for them. Our love for each other was growing wilder each day.

I uncrossed my arms and wrapped him in a hug. "Not anymore. I'm still getting used to trusting you three. I know you wouldn't do that to us."

His heart beat against my ear, the steady drum comforting me, knowing he was my safety.

I trusted all three of them. I needed to show them that now, and

I knew exactly where to start.

I lifted my head and kissed his cheek. "Actually, I have a favor to ask of you."

He perked up at that as his thumb made circles on my neck.

"Tristian... can... can you help me with my magic? After my parents died, I stopped my studies. I recently learned the basics again and some advanced magic, but..." I took a deep breath. "It's time for me to finally come into my magic and learn my limits, not just for my protection but for the coven's as well."

Tristian grinned at me. "Did my Lil' Star become the warrior for her coven?"

I chuckled. "Something like that."

His eyes sparkled with excitement. "Yeah, baby, I will. Now let's show the world why you don't fuck with witches."

I took his hand in mine, and we headed to the house where Aden and Bash waited.

I let go of Tristian and walked to Bash. Leaning into him, I tilted my head and lifted my hand to smooth the crinkle between his eyes.

"Are you mad at us?" I bit my lip as his eyes landed on me.

His face dropped, and he shook his head, cupping my neck and pulling me closer.

"Mad? No, Princess. I'm not mad. Horny? Fuck yes. That was hot as shit, but just because I'm happy to share you with my brothers doesn't mean I'm not jealous that I wasn't the one on my knees worshiping you."

He kissed me softly, his lips skating lightly over mine, and then he deepened the kiss, taking my breath away with his intensity.

Bash pulled away as two shadows came to our sides. Aden's hand replaced Bash's as he leaned me back and kissed me, his tongue sliding over my lips, teasing and welcoming.

They were all so different from each other, and Bash was right. We just made sense, like we were this imperfect puzzle that finally found its pieces to make it whole.

Aden pulled away and smiled sweetly at me, as if no one else was around. "Baby, we're all in this, the three of us. Oh, and Lex? We'll get Tristian back for his little stunt. Don't you worry." He wiggled his eyebrows up and down, making me laugh.

"*Ha*! Bring it, assholes," Tristian bellowed, making me jump and bump into him.

"No more punishments tonight. Even sirens need a break, you savages!"

I walked to the door, and they followed as I entered the house. I yawned and stretched as my stomach growled. "Okay, someone order pizza. I'll get the beer and candy. Then we're having a movie night!"

The guys laughed and agreed. The night was filled with greasy deliciousness, foamy beer, and laughter as we forgot the world for a few hours—a few hours that belonged only to my Devils and me.

Chapter Twenty-One

The following day, I woke up early and started to fix breakfast, humming along to early '90s boy bands. I sashayed my hips from side to side and sang into a spatula like I was on stage.

I flipped a pancake and turned to fix more coffee when I heard a car pull into the drive. "Who the fu…"

Bash entered the kitchen, stretching his arms as his shirt rode up his stomach, showing off his abs. His joggers, slung low on his hips, showed his perfect V-cut.

"Pancakes are burning, Princess," he pointed out, and I snapped out of my trance.

"Damn, stupid vampire, stupid abs," I mumbled.

He came up behind me and took my spatula.

"You expecting someone?" I popped a blueberry into my mouth.

"Nope," he said as he trashed my burned pancakes and started fresh ones.

I peeked out to see who it was, and Ethan's car was driving toward the house. "Did Ethan call you this morning?"

Bash looked over his shoulder. "Not that I know."

I pulled my phone out of my purse and saw five missed calls from Ethan and an angry text that said, "Call me now!"

"Oh, shit. Bash, check your phone."

He looked confused and pulled his from his pocket. "No calls…"

Aden ran in. "Ethan's coming, and he's pissed!"

My mouth dropped open. "Why?! What did you do?"

Aden turned to me with an arched eyebrow. "Not me, baby. You."

I swallowed hard and looked at Bash. "Wait, is Ella okay?"

Bash turned to me and threw the pan down. He headed to the door and swung it open. "She better be, or you're going to be an only child, Aden." He pointed to Aden, who was laughing.

"Yeah, my parents despise me and love him. You might want to rethink that strategy, *frère*."

We rushed outside just as Ethan slammed the car into park. He leaped out of the driver's side and ran to me.

"You…" He pointed at me, his eyes wild with anger. "You want to tell me what kind of place you're running here, Rose?!" Dark-red marks lined his arms, and his shirt had rips throughout.

I put my hands up in defense. "Whoa, Ethan, before you go psycho on me, tell me… is Ella okay? Is she hurt?"

He stopped before me and looked down in confusion. "What? No, why would you even think that?"

A shriek came from the other side of the car. "Omg, you sassy McSassypants! For goodness' sake, you'd think I tortured the poor thing. Dyna, will you stay still? Omg! Do not hiss at me. Young lady, wait until I tell your mother!"

I looked between Ethan and Ella, still confused. "What's going on? Why does Ella have Dyna?"

Ethan huffed and sounded a bit like a whiny Pegasus. "Aden texted us last night to see if we could watch Dyna after everything, just in case, and we did, but I swear to Lucifer, that cat is no cat. It's a demon! She is completely unreasonable. Look… look at me!" He extended his arms to show the deep cuts marring his skin.

I pressed my lips together, trying not to laugh. "Ummm, so you're saying Dyna did this?" I pointed to his arms and clothes.

"She did this to *all* my stuff! I saved my tux for the wedding, and Ella had to lock herself in the bathroom with her wedding dress. Her wedding dress!"

I let a laugh escape.

Ethan's eyes were wide, and a twitch began to form under one of them.

"Ethan, she's just a cat." I patted his arm as I walked past him.

Ella held out Dyna's cat carrier. "Here ya go!" She placed the carrier in my arms. "Look, she wasn't that bad, but man, she really doesn't like the carrier." She whispered as if Dyna could hear her.

"Nope, hates it, don't you, murdery floof?" I cooed to Dyna. A tiny angry meow escaped, and I laughed.

"Come on in, guys. I'll have Bash make his amazing cloud pancakes."

Ella's eyes glazed over for a second. "Okay." She grabbed Ethan's arms as he hissed in pain. "Oh, sorry, baby." She kissed his cheek.

He softened and brought her closer. "It's okay. I'd take a million more scratches as long as you're okay, my love."

Ella's smile grew, and the love in her eyes sparkled even more.

I smiled as I walked inside. "Come on, you lovebirds!"

Tristian was throwing a very black-looking pancake into the trash. "Lil' Star, you almost burned down the house. Thank the stars I was here." He smirked, and I hopped on the counter, kissing his cheek.

"Thank you. Bash is making the rest of the breakfast."

He smiled and moved between my legs. "Ohhh, so I get you all to myself then."

A throat cleared, and Ethan stood there with his arms crossed. "Bash is fixing all of us breakfast, dude."

Tristian pushed back and looked over to Ethan. "Spoilsport."

Bash moved to me and licked his lips. "Open up, Lexi."

He nudged my legs to open farther apart, and his fingers sent a shiver up my back. Then they were gone as he pulled open a small drawer where all my mixing spoons were.

I laughed and hit his shoulder. "Tease."

He smirked and kissed me sweetly. "Later." The promise left his lips.

"I'm holding you to that, Ryder."

He started to work on breakfast, and I turned to ask Ella and Ethan if they wanted coffee.

Her eyes were wide in surprise, and Ethan smiled like an idiot. "Go, Rose, nailing a Ryder. Welcome to the club," he said as Ella hit his stomach playfully.

"Shh." I felt myself redden, and I jumped down to grab a few mugs. "I'm gonna get everyone coffee."

I made coffee for the guys, as I knew how they liked it. Tristian liked a cappuccino with one raw sugar mixed in, Bash Americano with a splash of cream, and Aden wanted black coffee straight. I fixed Ella, Ethan, and me a cup as well.

"Let's head outside, Ella. Let the boys talk shop."

She took her coffee. "Let's go."

Bash looked up. "Don't be a brat, Ella."

Ethan smiled. "More like, don't you two wander off and get into trouble. They're notorious for doing it."

Ella huffed out, "I am not."

We all said at the same time, "New Year's Eve, 2018!"

She pulled me as she laughed.

We walked out to the small patio table and sat.

"You know, I knew you two always had something, but now that you finally realize it…" She paused to take a sip of coffee. "He's happy, Lexi, like, truly happy. It's nice." She held my hand and smiled.

"I am too." I sniffed, trying not to cry.

"I'm glad, Lexi, I'm glad you found them. It's not traditional by any means, but it works. It just makes sense when you see them with you."

I sipped my coffee and wiped a tear that had escaped.

She smacked her lips after taking a drink of her coffee. "So, last night, tell me all about it…"

I told her everything from the spell with Brigitte to Nyx's dying moments, the fight with Griffin, and even the back seat antics with minor details.

Ella's eyes went from surprise to shock. "How the hell are you going to handle those three?"

I laughed. "I tell you all about the witch craziness, and you're wondering how I'll handle the three vamps?" I hitched my thumb back at them.

"Well, you are a badass coven leader. I know you'll figure out who's behind all this. Plus, you have us, your Scooby gang."

I raised a brow. "Scooby gang?"

She grinned, as if it was an obvious conclusion. "Yep."

I shook my head. "I guess so. I'm glad I finally feel like the Silver Pearl Coven's leader. I have a purpose now. Speaking of which, Jason should be here soon, so let's check on the boys. Hopefully, they aren't full-on recon mode yet."

We headed back inside, seeing the guys gathered around the box, arguing about how to open it.

"We should just smash the damn thing," growled Bash.

Aden was carefully examining the box. "It could have a booby trap in it and ruin whatever the hell is inside, *frère*," he calmly said.

Tristian let a giggle out, and I came up behind him, whispering, "What's so funny?"

He jumped in fright and let out a yelp. "Damn it, Lil' Star, don't scare me like that."

I laughed. "I'm sorry, did I just scare one of the big bad Devils of Providence Village?"

He smirked and bent his head down to me. "Never." His eyes were alive with fire. "Just you wait. I'll get you back for that." He trailed his fingers down my throat and playfully snarled.

"As much as I love seeing you paw at my niece, can we focus, blondie?" Jason came from the hallway with a stack of books in his arms.

"Not your niece until you make Coco an honest woman." I smirked at him as I hugged him. "What do you have there?" I grabbed a few books on top of his stack. *The Art of Japanese Himitsu-Bako* and *The Key to Solving the Puzzle of Himitsu*. I smiled. "You went on a bender researching, didn't you?" I grinned.

"Coco had to drag me to bed around four in the morning." He returned my grin. "Aden." He nodded to him and walked over, setting the books down. "Let's do this." He put his glasses on, making him look so much older than he was.

Ella walked over. "I'm going to go do my recon. Ethan and I have dinner with Dad tonight. I'll let you know if we find anything interesting."

I smiled. "Girl's night soon, 'kay?"

She gave me a small smile. "I'll need one. I'm gonna be a married woman soon."

I laughed. "We have a few months."

She laughed. "Bye, big brother, don't be a pain in the ass."

She hugged him as Ethan clapped him on the back.

"I am not a pain in the ass," Bash grumbled.

Tristian, Aden, and I all answered, "Yes, you are."

Once Ella and Ethan left, we dug deep into research mode as Aden and Jason tried a million different ways to open the box.

"Can I see the box?" I asked Jason. He straightened and looked at me carefully. "I swear, I won't do anything stupid. I'm just trying to think like The Wishmaker."

Aden mumbled, "That's disturbing, baby."

Jason carefully handed me the box as Bash came closer to my side. He bent down with me to look at it. The box had seven different patterns on it. Some were lines. Some made flowers. Others were just geometric shapes.

"Maybe... these shapes make one whole shape."

Jason came to my other side, examining the box. His eyes roamed over it as he tried to figure out the puzzle. "When you move them, the lines make a pattern. Look." He moved his finger to the box and pushed two lines, and they clicked together.

"It forms a shape of a stem and leaves. Look," I said, pointing to inlays on the side of the flowers.

Jason's lips turned down as he concentrated on the next step. "What if it makes a rose?" He moved a panel to form the stem with the thorns sticking out.

I nodded. "Just like a rose."

I pushed a tile to the side, and it lined up perfectly, creating a petal. Another click sounded, and I grinned, looking over at Jason.

"You beautiful little genius." He smiled and clasped my shoulder, giving me a light squeeze.

Aden smirked. "One down, seventy-four more steps to go."

The minutes turned into hours as we worked tirelessly to open the box. The air grew thick with tension as Jason and Aden silently worked together to figure out each step. I sat with a notepad, writing down each step as Aden slowly moved a petal into the spot. I held my breath, praying we would hear the sound of a click. It didn't click, and I groaned into my hand.

"Damn it," I whispered as Jason and Aden restarted the puzzle box all over again, starting from memory as they tirelessly moved the pieces all over again.

Tristian stepped through the front door carrying a tray of coffees. "How's it going?" he said as he handed me my cup and moved to pass the rest out to the group.

I growled, "It's so fucked up that if you miss a step, it resets completely."

He leaned down to kiss my head. "That's why we write it all down, Lil' Star. Patience."

I sipped my cup of coffee, glaring at the setting sun. The Wish-maker made it almost impossible to open, and we all felt the clock ticking down.

"I did it!" Aden said as I heard a click.

I turned my head just as he lifted the lid, and a small pop came from the box. A stream of reddish smoke slowly floated up around us.

Bash yelled from across the room, "Hemlock!"

I gasped and threw up my hands, pushing out air magic to move Aden back. He hit the wall with a soft thud.

"Shit, baby," he said breathlessly.

Tristian flung out his magic to capture the smoke, sucking it into a ball of wind and holding it together. I walked over to Tristian and gave him my hand, letting my power move through him as we shared our power.

"We'll get it out of the house," I said in a low voice.

Wielding the magic together, Tristian contained the gas in a sphere while I used my air magic to maneuver it above our heads. We slowly and carefully moved outside.

"Dirty, dirty bastard doesn't play fair, does he?" I grumbled.

"He doesn't, baby, he doesn't," Tristian growled.

Bash followed us as we made our way outside through the back. He narrowed his eyes at the sphere as if his stare alone could destroy it.

"Where do you want to release it, Lexi?" Tristian asked, still looking for a place to release the poisonous gas safely.

The sound of the ocean hit my ears as the waves crashed against the shore. If we could throw the sphere far enough, it should dissipate over the ocean and not cause any damage when it hits the water.

"Let's release it over the ocean, far from shore."

We walked down to the beach, leading the red ball to the water's edge. Tristan and I shot it as far as possible so it dissipated into the air.

"It won't cause any damage, will it?" Bash asked.

Tristian shook his head. "Nah, once it's gone, it's gone. The first hit is the most dangerous. We should get back to Aden to make sure he didn't inhale any of it."

Jason was waiting for us at the end of the steps that led back to the house.

"Is Aden okay?" I could see the worry in his eyes.

"Aden's fine." He held up a hand. "But the box has the next clue."

He held a scroll of paper. The swirling red ink said:

Dear Devil, did you enjoy my trick?
Here is another riddle for you to solve,
and maybe you can save a life this time.

In the depths of the dark and the depraved,
you'll find a Madame to show you the way.
Are you ready to walk through the depths of hell
to see if you come out on top, or will I take another life?

A sacrifice must be made to save a life,
but are you willing to make it,
or will it divide you?

Don't forget the password is the only way in,
or you'll never see the light of day again.
Are you ready to go for a trip to the darkest places
of sin and immorality?

- WM.

"What the hell does this mean? A Madame?" I whispered to myself mostly.

Bash and Aden came out to join us. Bash handed me a card between his fingers. The card we found a few weeks ago. "It means we're going to Mort Noire, Princess."

Chapter Twenty-Two

We had to wait a few days to receive an invitation to Mort Noire. Bash had connections to get us invited through the Blood Moon elders.

In the meantime, Tristian and I reviewed different defensive spells and how to conjure objects out of the air. I had successfully gotten a seashell, but nothing more significant.

Tristian said, "Lil' Star, it'll come eventually. You have to be patient with your magic."

When I wasn't in a magic lesson with Trist, I would work out with Aden, who loved to have me spar with him. He kicked my ass almost every time, but I did land him flat on his butt the other day. I wasn't as lucky for the next few days.

Aden and I were walking back to the house from the beach when we found a wooden box with a white silk ribbon on our doorstep.

To say it was an ordeal was putting it lightly. Bash almost lost it, yelling at the new guard for fifteen minutes.

Tristian was seething mad, his eyes red with a vengeance as he eyed the new guard. "*Putain d'idiot.*"

I had to take Aden's knives away so he didn't get stabby. "We can't just kill every guard," I chastised him.

Bash was busy threatening the guard's family and friends. I started to head over when Aden stepped in front of me.

"I got it, baby." He walked over to him to calm him down. "*Frère,* I was with her. Nothing would have gotten her when one of us was with her."

I was never alone anymore. We all agreed that one of them always stayed by my side. I understood, but I would have liked some "me" time.

I sighed, walking past the three vampires arguing to some degree with each other or someone else. With the box in my hand, I pulled the ribbon off and slowly opened the lid. A gold invitation engraved in black ink sat on a bed of red rose petals.

"Is that real gold?" Aden looked over my shoulder.

I nodded, reading the front of the invitation. "It's a bit over-the-top, isn't it?" I huffed out as I pulled out the heavy invitation from its box.

A picture of a black death moth with flowers for wings in a crescent moon sat on the top of the invitation, and the glimmering black ink glistened in the sun.

Dear Ms. Rose and her Devils,

Your presence is requested for a night of debauchery.
Saturday - midnight.
A car will be waiting for you at this address:
408 Beaumont Lane.
Black tie only,
and a concealment spell is required for the entire night.

Sincerely, Maître Noir

The invitation was heavy in my hands as I looked over my shoulder, seeing each of my Devils glaring at me.

Bash stomped to me, taking the invitation from my hand. "Princess," he seethed out. "Do. Not. Ever. Do. That. Again."

I crossed my arms and glared right back. "Listen, asshat! You. Do. Not. Tell. Me. What. To. Do."

He crowded my face, and a snarl escaped his lips. "You are the most spoiled brat I've ever met! You could have been hurt, Lexi! You didn't know what was in there!"

I poked his chest with my finger. "Listen here, buster. I never asked you to protect me. You're always there, breathing down my neck. I can't stand it. So what if I opened the damn box? First, it wasn't anything harmful."

He threw his hands in the air. "You didn't know that, Lexi!" He stomped away before returning to me. "You didn't think of the consequence of opening it. It's not just your life, Lexi! It's ours too, and we are both bound to the *covens*. We don't need another fucking leader dead! And I can't watch you die…" His green eyes found my blue ones.

I took in a sharp breath and held back the tears, letting my anger take control. We stood there glaring at each other, and I shoved the invitation into his hands. "Just read the damn invitation, Sebastian. Then one of you can explain what the hell we're walking into."

I walked to the loungers and sat, crossing my legs, turning my back to them. I looked over my shoulder at Aden and Tristian, who still looked pissed as hell but moved closer to Bash, each one reading the invitation, as if it told them something different.

"Overbearing asshats," I mumbled as I typed out an angry text to Ella, telling her that I needed the girl's night sooner rather than later.

Lexi: Your brother is a dick.

Ella: *You're just now realizing this?*

Lexi: They all freaked over an invitation.

Ella: *Yeah, I'm gonna need more than that, babes.*

Lexi: We got another box, they thought it was
       The Wishmaker, but it was an invite to
       Mort Noire.

Ella: *I mean, I see their point, Lex.*

Lexi: Ella! You're supposed to be on my side!

Ella: *I am, but I see it from their side too. So, what did
       the invitation say?*

Lexi: The usual, a night of debauchery yadda,
       yadda, yadda.

Ella: *Uhhh, you aren't going, are you?*

Lexi: That's the plan, or it's mine. It's an opportunity
       to save the rest of them. I need to bring
       them home.

Ella: *I know we do… be careful. I've heard stories, and
       not just the kinky kind, the kind that end up with
       people dead, Lex. Keep the guys close, even if they
       are driving you nuts with the overprotectiveness.*

Lexi: I promise. No funny business.

I set my phone down and pinched the bridge of my nose before
I felt someone sit next to me.

"Hey." Aden's voice was low.

I looked up and gave him a sad smile. "Hi."

He pulled my legs over his lap. "We just want you safe, Lexi."

I fiddled with the hem of my sweatshirt. "I know, it's just… it's
been a lot."

He sighed and closed his steel-gray eyes, tilting his head to the sky.
"I don't know much about Mort Noire, but it isn't just any club. It's

been around since the early 1900s, and how to enter the club has always been a secret. By the '20s, it was a speakeasy where most local covens did business. It wasn't until the '30s that it became what we know today, full of the best-kept secrets in the covens and a place where you could live out your darkest, deepest, sickest fantasy. The Madames are not normal fae. They are so much more. They all play into dark arts and let it consume the club. We won't be ourselves. Our darkest and carnal selves will want to come out to play."

I opened my mouth to say something, but he stopped me with a hand. "I don't say this to scare you. I say this to tell you what to expect. We won't be fully able to protect you, baby. Are you sure you want to do this?"

His eyes turned to me, and I took his hands in mine. "I have never asked you three to protect me, Aden."

I moved to his lap, looking down at his handsome face and tracing each plane with my eyes. As he studied me, I pushed back the hair that had fallen into his face.

"I accept your protection because it makes me feel safe, but I never asked for it." He winced as if I had hit him. "I don't mean for that to be ungrateful or cruel. It's not that. I'm trying to explain this to you without us screaming at each other." I took his hand in mine. "I have to do this. I have to try anything to help find them. They need to come home, Aden. If not for the coven, for Nyx." I choked out the last few words.

He cupped my face. "I will always protect you, baby, as long as I have air to breathe. I will die before you're hurt, but I know you need to do this—not just for the coven or even Nyx. You have to do this for yourself." He kissed my forehead, and I stayed there curled up in his arms, feeling his warmth and not letting the fear of the unknown sink into my heart.

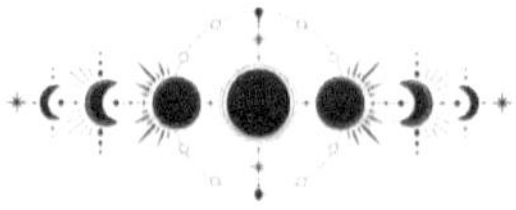

The weekend came quickly, and soon, it was time for us to leave for the club. I wore a cream silk dress with high slits on each side of my legs. It was designed to be sexy, but for me, it was for practicality. I needed to be able to pull my onyx knife out, worst-case scenario, or run like hell. My hair was down in loose waves as I finished the last-minute touches on my makeup. I pulled my grimoire close, studying the concealment spells Tristian and I had gone over the last week.

"Princess?"

I glanced toward the doorway where Bash stood in his all-black suit with a red pocket square peeking out, folded into a shell shape.

He had been very distant the last few days. I wasn't much better, trying to avoid him since our fight. He was busy with meetings and getting everything ready, but he slid into my bed every night and lay next to me. I was usually in Tristian's or Aden's arms, but Bash was always on my other side every morning.

"I'm almost ready," I said in a steady voice, praying it didn't break.

Too many times, I'd found myself in a closet, crying over our fight, though I would never let him hear or see it. My heart felt like it was slowly breaking with his distance.

He nodded. "Okay. You have your concealment all set?"

I brushed my nose with a setting powder. "Yeah, I'll do Aden's, and Tristian said he has yours all set."

He frowned at that. "If that's what you want."

I turned to him, leaning back against my counter. I crossed my arms over my stomach. "I don't want any of this, Sebastian."

He leaned his shoulder into the doorframe and sighed. "Me neither." His eyes narrowed on the dress. "I like that dress..."

He stalked into the room and placed his hand on my waist, mov-

ing slowly up my rib cage. It was the first time he'd touched me since our fight, and it felt like fire and ice running over me. My breath was slow and steady as his eyes met mine.

"These slits are quite handy." His other hand pulled my leg up.

I gasped as he pulled me close, his nose brushing mine.

"I'm sorry, Princess," he whispered, and I leaned into him.

"I am too. You were right. I should have been careful."

He shook his head. "No, I need to let you still have a life. I know this whole mess isn't what you wanted. I know you didn't want us to live with you invading your space."

I wrapped my arms around his neck and tilted my head back. "I wouldn't have it any other way, but maybe a girl's night or some alone time would be nice."

He smiled. "I think we can do that."

He kissed me slowly, lifting me onto the counter, and his hands ran up my thighs. I moaned as he pulled my thighs apart, pushing himself into my space.

"Very handy indeed." He inched his fingers to the apex of my thighs. Finding me naked underneath, he pulled back in shock. "Nothing underneath, huh, Princess?"

I moaned breathlessly. "It left lines. We couldn't have that."

He moved his lips to my neck, laying featherlight kisses across my skin. "No, we couldn't have that."

A throat cleared, and Bash jumped back.

"As much as we love seeing you two make up, we have somewhere to be." Tristian's voice came from behind us, sounding amused as he stood to the side in a sharp black jacket and an open collar.

He was holding his phone out, looking like he was taking a video.

"Tristian, were you recording us?"

He smiled innocently. "No, Lil' Star, that would be wrong." His eyes twinkled with wickedness.

I tilted my head to the side, crossing my arms. "Uh-huh."

His shoulders slumped over. "I'll delete it."

Bash cleared his throat. "We need to get going."

Tristian pouted as his fingers moved over his phone. "Fine."

Bash walked up to him and wrapped his arm around his neck. "Ask next time, asshat. I would love to see her every damn expression when she's coming…"

Glaring at Bash, I tossed a makeup sponge at the back of his head that bounced off perfectly. "Hey! Maybe, just maybe, I don't want to be filmed. Did you stupid bloodsuckers ever think about that?"

They turned, and I walked out to Aden, grabbing his arm. "You're my favorite right now."

His black suit with a vest sat perfectly against his skin. He ran his tattooed hands up my arms as he smiled down at me. "You have favorites?"

"I do." I batted my eyelashes at him.

He bent to my ear, whispering, "I'd rather you be mad at me. It makes the sex better." He purred.

I threw my arms in the air. "You three are ridiculous."

Tristian strolled in with a smirk plastered on his face.

I turned to him. "Ready to put on the concealment spell?"

"Yep, and you're going to love mine." He wiggled his eyebrows up and down.

Bash brought over my grimoire, and I opened the book to the Glamour a Vior spell. I pulled down my magic supply box that Tristian had set aside earlier for me. I set out a mirror, and around it, I gently laid out a jade stone, water from the petals of a rose garden, a small red candle, and the air from the top of the mountains that lay behind us.

Tristian came beside me. "That's perfect, Lil' Star. Shall we begin?"

I looked up at him, and pride was shining in his eyes. "I have a good teacher. I'm going to do Bash, okay?"

He smirked. "I figured that much. No worries, I got the dark knight."

I kissed his cheek and turned back to the guys. "Bash." I held out my hand as he approached me. "Ready?"

He nodded and repeated, "Ready."

I lit the candle and recited the words I memorized earlier today. "*Chachez mon apparence a ceux qui veulent me faire du mal et gardez-moi fidele a qui je suis. Changez mes cheveux mon visage et mes yeux pour ceux qui veulent que je me cache.*"

A ball of water appeared in my hand, floating just above my palm. Bash leaned down, and I placed the water over his face. It glimmered, and his entire face shifted. His dark hair turned to a dirty blond, his green eyes morphed to a piercing blue, and his jaw became square with a short dark beard adorning his chin. He was still handsome, but he wasn't my Sebastian.

I smiled and turned to Tristian and Aden, who had already performed the spell.

"*Wow*, dude, you look like Captain America." Tristian's normal playful voice was more profound and rougher. Long gone was the blond hair. Now he had dark, wavy, shoulder-length hair, deep-set chocolate eyes, and a straight nose.

"You look like a desert prince, *frère*." Bash's deep voice boomed with a laugh.

I laughed and stepped toward Aden, who was hidden behind Tristian. "Aden, let me see." He turned, and I was in shock. "You… Aden, that's something new."

Crystal-blue eyes set in a sleek chiseled face with a straight nose and Cupid's-bow lips stared down at me.

"Nice ink." I smirked at him.

Tattoos ran up his neck, and an upside-down cross sat under his eye. He looked deadly and delicious.

His shocking bright-white teeth gave me a sinister smile. "The better to eat you, my dear."

I ran my hand over his and across his face, tracing the tattoo over his brow and the upside-down cross on the corner of his eye.

"You all look great, but I like the real you more."

Aden took my hand and laid a kiss on my palm. "We're still here,

baby, different skin, that's all."

Tristian tugged me. "Lexi, we need to go. Go ahead." He pushed me lightly to the circle.

I stepped up to the mirror to perform the ritual and held the ball of water to my face. It was cold as it hit my skin, and the magic tingled as it took over. I ran my hands over my face to my hair and continued until I opened my eyes. I still felt like myself, but I could feel the subtle changes taking over.

I finally got the courage and looked at myself in the mirror. A gasp escaped because my normally dark chestnut hair was now bright pink and turquoise blue with soft curls. My eyes were the brightest aquamarine I had ever seen, my nose was thinner with a sapphire piercing, and my lips were fuller than I imagined.

"It's like I got plastic surgery; I feel like myself, but I'm not." My voice was higher, not shrill, but higher than normal. It had more of a melody to it.

I ran my fingertips over my lips. Bash came up behind me, wrapping me in his arms. "I like my Princess more than this version," he said as he played with a strand of pink hair.

I turned in his arms and smiled up at him. "Don't want me to change, huh?"

He shook his head. "Never. Let's go."

Chapter Twenty-Three

The ride over was quiet. I kept looking at each of them, forgetting they had changed. It was surreal and strange. Their mannerisms were still there. Tristian slightly smirked at his jokes, Aden's fingers drummed along to the music like always, and Bash still stared intensely.

"You know, I heard he has a chest tattoo." I poked at Bash.

"You want me to get ink?"

I smirked. "I wouldn't hate it."

He chuckled. "What kind of ink?"

I tapped my chin. "My face? Or Dyna's face."

This led to a discussion about which tattoo would be the most ridiculous for Bash to get.

"How about Dyna saying 'Fluff you'?" I laughed as the tension we'd been holding onto diffused.

Aden slowed the car down in a small suburb outside Providence Village. The little box houses sat in a row, all similar but with slight differences.

"We're here." He killed the lights, and we waited.

A few minutes later, a thick fog filled the street as a set of car lights shone on us, flashing twice.

"I guess that's us."

As we climbed out, my stomach twisted with nerves.

Bash was next to me, and his hand found mine. "Hell hath no fury like a siren scorned. Let's show them who they're messing with."

The door opened, and a young girl stepped out of the car, her white hair in a braid. She was wearing a Victorian choker, her eyes were solid black with white pinpricks, and her dress was so tight, you could see every inch of her body.

"I'm Corvina, your guide to Mort Noire. Please sit."

Her eerie voice elicited goose bumps on my arms.

I gripped Bash's hand tighter. He squeezed back, and we all slid into the limo.

"Interesting choice of concealment." She looked from my dress to my brightly colored hair. "Not that it matters, but most do something... more ominous."

I cleared my throat. "I didn't choose it. My magic did."

Her lips lifted. "Hmm, interesting....I like this one." She placed a finger on Aden's temple. "Can I taste him?"

I snatched her wrist and pulled her to me. "Mine." My sharp fangs slid out, and I snarled at her. "They are mine. You do not touch."

Her face turned to stone, then she laughed maniacally. "I like you."

She turned and knocked twice on the window that separated us from the driver, and we were off into the night.

Our windows were blacked out, so we couldn't see where we were going.

"Champagne?" She turned with a flute, handing it out to me.

"No, thank you." I looked at the glass, unsure of what was in it.

"I didn't poison it, if that's what you're thinking." She sighed. "That's not my style. I prefer a slow death, and poison is just too fast." A sadness surrounded her voice, as if she was upset that it didn't last long enough.

I looked at Aden, and his eyes were wide in surprise, and he mouthed, "Psycho."

Tristian, who was usually full of conversation, was quiet, and I kicked his foot with mine. He lifted his head and gave me a slight smile.

"First time?" She looked at Tristian and me.

"Yes," he said, not wanting to continue the conversation.

She tilted her head and hummed softly. "Hmmm." She pointed to Tristian. "You'll find it fascinating." She gestured to Bash. "You. Keep your cool. It'll save your life. Don't try to be a hero." She turned to Aden. "Don't let the crows crowd you." Then she turned to me, taking my hands in hers. They felt like ice, and it burned. Her black eyes were now entirely white. "When the light flickers, use your magic, or one of them will be lost."

She let go of me, and I took my hands back, the cold lingering on them as if I had just stuck my hand into a bucket of ice water.

"You have La Vue? You're a seer?" I had only met a few people with true sight. Tristian said he had strong intuitions, but to have true sight was the sign of a powerful witch.

She slumped back, her head tilting back. "It's painful." The car stopped, and she sprang up. "We're here. Come, we must make haste."

I looked over at the guys with concern. They turned to each other and shrugged.

We got out and entered an alleyway surrounded by tall brick buildings. We were in the city's financial district, I could tell by the buildings, but that's about all I could figure out.

Corvina walked faster and mumbled, "The pixies could at least clean up after themselves. It would be helpful." She lifted her head and looked down the alley, then back out again. "Hmm, yes, yes, I know the spot's right about... *here*!"

She pulled a curved claw from somewhere in her dress and carved a triangle with a circle in the middle.

"Is that...?" I pointed to the claw.

She smiled. "Yep, 100 percent ancient green dragon claw. Ain't she a beauty?"

With a flick of her wrist, the stone shifted, creating an arch overhead, and a door appeared shrouded in shadows.

"Dark magic," Tristian hissed.

A rich voice that sounded like a snake hissed out, "Password."

Bash walked up and spoke, "Hemlock Falls."

The shadows fell, and a thin man in his late fifties stood before us. He had thinning hair, and a twisted smile formed on his lips when he looked up with eyes darker than chocolate.

"Welcome to Mort Noire. I am Laurent, your gracious host for the evening. Maître Noir welcomes all who wish to enter."

We stepped through, and I turned back to see Corvina bowing to us. "I shall retire for the evening. It was pleasant. Let us do it again soon."

I waved goodbye in confusion.

"Strange girl," Tristian said next to me.

Laurent held his hands out to usher us into the club. He glided down the bright white hallway. His feet looked as if they weren't touching the ground. My stomach told me to run from this man, to run far away, but for my coven and all the covens, I stayed and got ready to face the demons that awaited us inside.

"Mort Noire is a place for your one true self to escape, to dive into the carnal pleasures your heart truly desires." He spun in a grand gesture and looked back at us. "To truly escape the outside world rules and to live by a set of your own!" He swirled back around, running his fingers down the wall like some unhinged vaudeville heckler.

I looked at the hallway walls. They were shaped like spheres, but when I looked closer, I saw they were lined with skulls and bones. The white of the bone was almost blinding in contrast to the inky darkness we just came from. As we passed, I looked at a skull and saw two sharp canines protruding from its upper mouth.

I swallowed a gasp and turned to Bash, gripping his hand and finding comfort in his strength.

"They're all fae of some type," I pointed out to him in a neutral voice, not letting the fear sink in as I wanted it to.

Some were small, like pixies; a row of dragon heads lined the wall, and even a large wolf skull sat among them. It was as if they silently watched us, judging our every move.

"This isn't what I expected," I said to Aden out of the corner of my mouth.

"Is it better or worse?" Aden tried to say jokingly, but it came out more in anger.

"Worse…"

Laurent turned around to face us with a sinister smile on his face. "Fascinating, isn't it?" He gestured to the skulls. "We keep our enemies as a warning to others that Mort Noire is not for the weak or judgmental. Here, you can be your 100 percent authentic self!" He dramatically opened a pair of double doors that appeared out of nowhere. "Welcome to Mort Noire." His eyes sparkled with delight, as if we knew nothing of the hideous acts that awaited us.

A soft drum of music buzzed throughout the club. The interior was three stories tall and draped with ebony silks hanging from the ceiling. Amber and violet tapestries lined the circular walls.

"It's circular to create a never-ending feeling… every fantasy you want is here. Tell me, will you indulge in those tonight?" Laurent's voice dropped to a whisper as he pressed into me. "I, for one, would love to play out one of mine on you, my beautiful unicorn." His eyes lingered on my hair before he moved aside, clasping his hands together, and a slimy smile returned. "Enjoy a night of depravity."

He started to walk away but turned and held up a finger. "Before I depart, I believe the Maître will want to see you later. She finds you all very… interesting."

A sickening feeling formed in my stomach as it took every ounce of my being to stop myself from running away from this parasitic man. He smiled as if he knew more than he should and backed away like a creepy butler.

Once he left us, I turned to my Devils and snarled, "He gives me the icks; do not let him touch me."

Tristian narrowed in on me, his eyes tight, as he tried to control his rage.

"You okay?" I took his hand, pulling him closer, wanting all my Devils near.

"Yeah, it's just so…"

I raised an eyebrow. "Lecherous?"

"Yeah, that keeps it simple." He smirked. "Well, I can't say I blame him for hitting on you. You smell like the heavens, Lil' Star."

"Where should we start?" I looked over the balcony and saw a multitude of bars and stages surrounding each level.

Some had girls dancing in cages with glitter covering them. Others had girls in nothing but lingerie and black wings, spinning in the air as if they were flying. I looked down to the center, where a massive raised dance floor had poles on each side and a sea of humans and fae moving to the music.

I saw beds, couches, and tables laid out for anyone to engage in different sexual acts. My lips parted when I saw one girl bent over a sofa with a guy behind her, one in her mouth, and a girl on her knees servicing her.

"See something you like, Princess?" Bash's voice was rougher and more resounding, coming from behind me.

Aden moved closer, breathing into my neck. "I don't think she's ready for such deprivation, *frère*."

Shivers raced through my body, and a pair of hands ran up my sides lightly. "I think our Lil' Star can handle it—maybe not in public… yet, but behind our doors. I think she's been thinking about it."

The image rushing through my mind of all three of them doing whatever they wanted to my body made me dizzy and overwhelmed with my lust for my Devils. My fingers tightened around the railing as my Devils moved closer.

Aden laid gentle kisses on my neck. Sebastian was at my back, his arm wrapped around my stomach, his fingers caressing the silk dress. I could feel how exciting he found the little show.

Tristian pulled up a chair and sat down. His hand skated through the slit on the side and wrapped around my thigh, hugging me to him. "Will you watch them, Lil' Star? Will you dream it's you?" His fingers caressed my thigh.

I leaned my head back onto Bash's shoulder and lifted my head. He gave me a knowing smile.

"Kiss me." I pleaded with him, needing his lips on mine.

He bent his head, his lips hovering above mine.

"Bash." A hushed whimper escaped.

He closed the space and kissed me slowly, taking his time. His hands gripped my hair, and he pulled me to his back, holding me in place as we deepened the kiss. Aden's hands skimmed over my breast, and I let a moan escape as Bash swallowed it.

Tristian traced his fingers up my inner thigh, finding nothing separating me from his hand. "Fuck, Lil' Star." He moved his mouth to my outer thigh and whispered kisses across my skin.

Bash's fangs slid out, and I licked them, slicing my tongue. Bash growled, pulling me closer, our kisses becoming frantic.

He pulled back, and his eyes turned red as he kissed down my neck. "*La faire jouir.*"

I groaned as Tristian shifted and pulled me wider.

"Trist..."

He smirked. "Don't worry, Lil' Star, no one gets to see you but us. You're ours." His fangs scraped my inner thigh.

Aden's mouth was on my wrist. He snaked his tongue out, and when I looked down, his fangs were gleaming in the lights hanging above us.

"Just let it escape, Lex," Aden said as he kissed my pressure point.

Bash moved to my ear, whispering, "Three... two... one."

I started to ask why they were counting down when Tristian,

Aden, and Bash sank their fangs into me all at once.

I gasped at the pain, then euphoric pleasure danced along my skin as my Devils fed from me. Blood ran down my chest, and I moaned. I wrapped my fingers into Aden's hair, pulling him back. My lips parted as a purple haze took over, and I let my siren out.

"Your eyes are so fucking hot when they turn like that, Lex."

I pulled Aden into a kiss, tasting my blood on his tongue. This was perfect. This was what I wanted for us—to be as one. I could feel each of them separately and all at once. The high was fantastic. Aden's kisses became frantic as he moved to my breast.

"Aden, Bash, Tristian..."

Bash stole a kiss, and images of keys, mermaids, and pixie dust rushed through my mind. We were supposed to be doing something important, but I only felt the lust of my Devils, and it overtook me.

"The keys, Lexi." Nyx's voice cut through my mind, and I gasped.

I pulled back and touched Tristian's cheek, and he looked up as he stood. He moved his fingers to my core and groaned, feeling how wet I was for him.

"Tristian..."

He smiled, his eyes glazed over, caught up in the magic that felt so good. He bent his head to the top of my breast, leaving a string of kisses across it.

"Something's not right..." I moaned as I pressed more into Bash's mouth.

Tristian moved back and looked at me. I saw the confusion in his eyes as the realization hit him.

He snapped his head to Bash and hissed, "Sebastian Ryder, get the fuck off our girl."

Bash looked up. His eyes were red as they shifted with anger.

"The magic's messing with us."

Bash's eyes faded to their grassy-green color, and he took a deep breath. "Fucking hell."

He pulled Aden away from me. "Get it together, *frère*."

Aden snapped at Bash, "She's not just yours!"

I grabbed Aden's collar and pulled him to me. "Aden Charmante, snap out of it *now*!"

Aden's hardened face relaxed, and he shuddered, looking at my wrist in horror. "Lexi, I... I am so sorry. Are you okay, baby?" He grumbled as he examined the mess he had made on me.

"Here." Tristian laid his hand on my wrist.

A warm, gentle glow healed my wrist, and then he did the same to my neck and thigh.

Aden laid a kiss on my wrist. "How can you forgive us for this, Lexi? We could have killed you."

I tilted my head to the side. "Aden, this wasn't you three. How can I blame you for that? Magic is powerful. Even the best witch can be overpowered by it. If we could all control ourselves, then we wouldn't have witches who use dark magic."

His eyes stared into mine, as if he was weighing my words. "You're too good for us, my siren." His fingers skimmed my cheek.

I noticed a crowd had formed around us, and I flushed.

"We need to move now." Bash grabbed my wrist, pulling me gently through the crowd.

"Bash, where are you going?"

As Bash pushed through the crowd, he stumbled into someone's back. A throat cleared, and Laurent turned to face us with a tray of colorful drinks. Tiny bubbles created fog that wafted over the rim of the glasses.

"Maître Noir requests your company. Please follow me." He turned as three large fae came up to our sides and began to move us through the crowd.

"I guess we don't have a choice," Tristian murmured.

Chapter Twenty-Four

We followed Laurent to a small roped-off area that said VIP. It had a few chairs, a couch, and a low table. Behind the sofa, a rainbow of deep-colored fabric was gathered together, making small pleats along the wall. They all met in the middle of the wall, creating a Gothic burst of color around us. Above the couch, two golden Victorian candles hung on each side, with an incandescent flame twinkling in the dark. It looked as if a thousand fairies were dancing in the glass of the candle's flame.

Laurent walked behind the couch and whispered into the light. It flickered out as he turned, and the fabric fell to the side with a swish, revealing a door.

"Right this way."

We walked into a large hallway with black arches reaching high to the ceiling. A plush carpet met our feet as we walked down the hall to a pair of dark oak double doors.

One of the larger fae moved ahead and opened the doors that led into what looked like an office. It was huge, with a fireplace and a bed. A door off the side opened, and a gorgeous woman stepped out. Her skin was white as snow, and her jet-black hair lay silky straight. Her double-breasted dress sat off her shoulders as she walked with the confidence of a queen.

She curled her deep-red lips into a smile when she saw us. "The three Devils and their angel. Though those are not very good disguises, I'm afraid. See, everyone knows that something is going on with you three." She reached a small bar and began to make a drink. "But the concealment spell is excellent. Ms. Rose, you will be a powerful witch one day."

I ground my teeth. "Half witch." I bit out.

"If you know who we are, why the big show?" Bash said from beside me.

She smirked as she stirred her drink. "Mr. Ryder, I, for one, needed to make sure you were the Prince and Princess of the covens. Plus, you are all quite beautiful to look at. Let me give you a proper introduction." She bowed her head and dipped into a curtsy. "Emmeranne Noir at your service. Maître of Mort Noire." She lifted her head with a twisted smile and raised her drink, taking a sip. "Shall we sit?" She gestured to a small sitting area. "I believe Vina told me we were destined to meet one day. Though I don't know what I can do for you."

I sat in a large armchair as my Devils surrounded me.

She let out a low husky laugh. "You have these men wrapped around your little siren finger, don't you?" She looked at me with a glint of jealousy in her eyes.

I held her gaze and carefully constructed my following words. "I don't think they're wrapped around my finger, and we share a bond, a love that is way beyond mere lust and fascination."

She set her drink down and crossed her legs. Leaning forward slightly, she crossed one arm over her chest and rested her head on her hand. "You're attached to each of them. Would you not give one up for the evening? The Prince, The Soldier, or The Light?" She looked pointedly at Bash, Aden, and then finally Tristian. "Which would you choose if you had to only pick one?"

I didn't answer, because the truth was there was no way in hell I would be able to pick one of them. They were mine in every sense of the word.

I gripped the armchair as my fingers elongated into sharp claws. I clenched my jaw and tried to control myself, my magic desperate to escape as the haze washed over my eyes. When I opened them, I knew they had changed.

Her eyes widened. "You shouldn't be able to do that." She tapped her chin. "I fear you may be stronger than you know, Ms. Rose, which is dangerous in the position you hold," she pointed out.

I cleared my throat, and my words came out low and dangerous. "The Wishmaker..."

She straightened, and I sensed the fear lying deep within her, but her face gave away nothing. "What of them?" She took a sip of her drink.

"Do you know who they are?"

She smiled sarcastically. "Why would I?"

Bash scoffed. "You know every deep dark thing that passes through these walls, Emmeranne. Tell us if you know who's behind this mess we've been cleaning up for weeks."

She looked back to Laurent. "Laurent, my love, bring me the box that was delivered a few days ago."

The pale-skinned butler bowed his head and left.

We sat silently until he walked back a few minutes later with a small box in his hand.

He bowed to Emmeranne. "Mistress."

She reached out and grasped the box with her thin, skeleton-like fingers. "I found this one night on my bed. A note said to give it to the Prince and Princess when they came, but I want something for it."

I sighed. "Of course you do. What do you want, Emmeranne?"

She looked over at Bash, her eyes lingering on him momentarily.

"I want the Prince for a night."

I hissed as my claws ripped into the armchair. "Not a chance in hell."

She smiled. "Not into sharing, I see? 'Tis a shame." She caressed the box with one finger. "A kiss then? One kiss from each of your Devils."

The air left my lungs, and my stomach twisted. "I'll give you anything but them. Money, jewels, a promise not to tell the FBI what horrors happen inside these walls." I glared at her.

She snarled at me, and her hair moved on its own. But it wasn't hair at all. Hundreds of small snakes slithered on her head. *Gorgon.* I smiled because she had a disadvantage. Vanity. If we appeased her vanity, she would be more inclined to help us.

"Threats do not work on me, little girl. It's best you remember that I am not your enemy."

She straightened as her hair turned back into the silk sheet it was. I removed my claws, and they turned back into my small hands.

I lifted a hand, realizing I needed to play this chess game with her. "Forgive me, Emmeranne. I fear even a kiss from you would bewitch them."

She smiled dreamily. "Yes, I have been told many times that my beauty can leave a man in physical pain, and I enjoy seeing them writhe in their torment." Her eyes flashed bright green as her gaze landed on Bash.

He winced in pain as he was slashed across his stomach. Blood trickled down to the floor, and her smile grew.

My eyes widened, and I clenched my jaw. "If you touch him again, I will show you what a true siren can do, *la pute.*"

She laughed. "Whore? I haven't been one in years—no need for name-calling. I'm just proving a point. That should have had him on his knees crawling over to me, yet he stayed by your side." She stood and walked over to us. "I don't care for The Wishmaker. The drug is destroying my elite clientele. They are a danger to many of my ongoing operations. It's a problem. So, if you're willing to make this little problem of ours disappear, why should I stand in your way?"

She laid the slim box on my lap and whispered closely, "Remember who helped you in the end, and I will contact you in the future on how you can repay me. Be prepared to pay the price, though." She stood and walked to the desk, quickly picking up a pen and writing on a pad of paper. "Laurent can show you the way out, unless you want to enjoy the club more. A private showing room, maybe?" She arched one perfectly sculpted brow.

I stood. "I think we've seen enough." I cleared my throat. "Goodbye, Emmeranne. I hope we don't see each other soon."

Her eyes flashed with excitement. "Oh, but my dear siren, that is what makes this so fun. You don't know who is your friend or foe." A wicked laugh escaped as we turned to leave.

Suddenly, Laurent was there to usher us out, damn creeper.

"Oh, Lexi." She stood and walked to me, gripping my arm, and I was suddenly pulled into a vision.

We were still in her office, but it was just us. I looked around in shock.

She inclined her head. "You aren't the only one with tricks, little one. I am older than I look, my dear, practically immortal. There is one thing that will help to find these missing mermaids you are so desperate to find."

I looked at her in confusion. "What?"

She smiled. "I make it my business to know what is happening in this town."

I considered for a second and decided she deserved the truth. "If your people went missing, wouldn't you do anything to find them?"

She regarded me for a moment. "Depends on the people. Some are better off dead, don't you agree?"

I shook my head. "These girls have done nothing to deserve what is happening to them. They are being beaten and tortured. They were taken away by a madman when they have done nothing but belong to my coven. No one deserves that, Emmeranne."

She laughed. "You say that now in all your righteousness, but one day, you might have to make a very different decision."

I cleared my throat. "One day, maybe, but now is not that day. What do you know?"

She shook her head. "Not me, Corvina."

Corvina walked through the door and smiled sweetly. "Hi! Wow, you are beautiful. I mean, I liked the unicorn hair from before, but this is very much you." She waved a hand over me.

I looked over to the mirror, and seeing my concealment was gone, I panicked.

Emmeranne held up a hand. "In my visions, your concealment won't hold. No worries, Lexi, you will be returned safely once Corvina has shared her vision. As I said before, I am not your enemy."

Corvina walked over to Emmeranne. "My sister is right, you know." She held my hands. "We aren't your enemy. I think one day we might even be friends."

I smiled in disbelief. "I'm not sure, Corvina, but I'll always be here to help you if you need me."

Her eyes glazed over, and she smiled. "Yes, one day we will be friends. Oh! The exciting adventures we will have…" She giggled.

I pulled my hands away from hers. "Corvina, can you see what my future holds?"

She held up a hand. "No, I can't. It could change, and that's not how life works. It's not set in stone. I don't know how it will end or how it will begin. I get snippets. It's from the middle. The beginning and the end of moments are completely up to you, Lexi, though I am very good at the stock market." She looked at her sister sadly, pouting. "I have seen my sister's death many times, but her choices are her own. I'm not a guardian of life, Lexi."

I nodded in understanding. Our moments on this earth were not only up to us. Things changed, and we made different decisions that put us on the path we led.

"What is it that you came to tell me, Corvina?"

She gave me a hazy smile. "To find what you seek, look to the sky and to the sea where the stars meet. You'll find a hallow where only the purest can drink from the vines of truth. To see if you are worthy to sleep. In your dreams, you will find the answers that your heart that only you truly seeks."

I groaned. "You can't just tell me an address, can you?"

Corvina laughed as if it was the funniest thing she had ever heard. "What, no, silly girl. Sometimes it is clear, but most of the time, it's just a glimpse. Plus, the flowers told me this one, and they speak in riddles." She shrugged as if it was totally normal to talk to flowers.

I was back in the room, laying on my back, as my Devils bent over and stared down at me with concerned looks. Laurent and Emmeranne were in deep conversation, and they glanced at me.

"Welcome back, Siren of the Sea," Emmeranne said.

"Hey." I sat up, and Aden scooped me up in his arms.

"You scared us, Lex."

I explained that Corvina needed to speak to me alone.

"I hope it was worth it," he growled.

Laurent smiled. "Please, this way to exit."

I pushed at Aden's shoulder. "Aden, put me down."

He reluctantly set me on the ground.

Laurent was at my side. "This way, madam." He turned to a door, waved his hand over the knob, and led us to a dark alleyway—not the same one we entered through. "I thought a subtle exit would be needed," he explained as we entered the cold night.

I looked back at Aden. His eyes widened at me as my Devil returned to his normal self. The concealment spell was gone, and we returned to our forms.

"Ms. Rose, are you sure I can't sway you to allow me to entertain you tonight?" Laurent licked his lips. "I can show you things you've never seen before."

Bash barked out a sinister laugh. "You could try to take her, but I promise, Laurent, it would end with your head on a pike."

Remembering Corvina's warning from earlier, I elbowed Bash. "The warning," I murmured.

Bash looked down at me in acknowledgment. "He needs to watch his next words, then."

Laurent grinned like a madman. "The Devils at their finest, it's a shame, really. You three could have been such good adversaries." He sighed as he turned and stepped farther into the dark alley, and we followed him.

Tristian looked to the sky just as clouds moved away from the moon, casting a soft glow around us. With the light from the moonbeams, I saw we were at a dead end. There was no way out except through the way we came, which had disappeared into the wall.

"Bash, it's a trap!" I screamed.

I was dragged back by my hair, my body held against Laurent as he drew a sharp blade to my throat. "Don't do anything stupid, Mr. Ryder."

Bash snarled, "I'll enjoy killing you, Laurent."

I held still and begged Bash with my eyes not to be a hero.

Aden's lips pulled back in rage. "Let her go now before I rip your heart out of your chest." His fangs peeked out, and his eyes shifted to the red of his kind.

Tristian was eerily calm, his eyes glazed over, and he appeared to be in some sort of trance, but the tension in his shoulders let me know he was anxious about what would happen next.

"Remember what Corvina said," I said in a steady voice.

Laurent's cold laugh filled the alleyway. "That freak? *Ha*! Emmeranne only babies her. I can't wait for the day I get to slice the little harlot's throat. She's not pure like me. She is just like you, a little half blood. One day, The Wishmaker will see that all you monstrosities are sent back to where you belong."

He flicked his wrist, and a fluttering sound came from the darkness. Suddenly, Aden was covered in what looked like black crows, but they were made of shadows.

I gasped. "Ténèbres!"

I screamed as they started to peck at Aden and Bash. The

shadow-like crows beat their wings against them and clawed at their faces.

Laurent let out a menacing laugh. His grip on the knife loosened, and I slammed my elbow into his stomach, causing him to drop the knife and bend forward. I spun around and threw my knee into his face. He wrenched back, cursing my name.

"Don't let them crowd you, Aden!" I screamed, remembering Corvina's warnings.

Aden pulled his blades from his back, and they glinted in the moonlight as he ripped through the shadows. A hand gripped my ankle, and I turned to see Laurent's bloody face as he pulled me. I kicked out, but his fingernails dug into my skin, drawing blood that flowed down my foot.

I called on my power and shifted; my claws came out and slashed at his face. A spray of blood arched in the air as he screamed in pain.

"You stupid little girl, I can't wait to see you beg for mercy. The Wishmaker has plans for you."

He croaked as I kicked him again.

I turned to see Tristian still in a trance-like state.

"Tristian! Remember who you are!"

He turned his head in confusion and looked over at Bash and Aden, who were battling the ténèbres. Then Tristian snapped out of the trance, looking frantically between the guys and me, like he didn't know who to help first.

"Go save them!"

A warrior's scream escaped in rage as he ran to his brothers.

Laurent had stumbled to his feet, and the deadly curved knife was in his hand as he lunged for me. I jumped out of the way, barely evading Laurent's attack. Before he could come at me again, I formed a fireball in my hand and threw it at him. It slammed into him, and he fell to the ground, rolling to extinguish the flames.

"Lexi!" Bash called for me, and I turned to see them overpowered by the shadows.

I ran over, yelling, "Get down!"

All three flattened themselves to the ground as I formed a ball of light to shoot at the ténèbres.

"Go back to wherever you came from, hell demons," I snarled.

The light hit the shadows, its beams so bright, I had to shield my eyes, and the shadows shrank back with a scream.

Aden, Bash, and Tristian stood covered in mud, gunk, and sweat from the fight.

"Is he dead?" Aden looked over at Laurent's body.

"I don't think so," I said as we walked over to him.

Bash kicked him to his back, and he let out a yelp from the pain.

"You messed with the wrong coven, Laurent." Bash smiled sinisterly down at him.

"You should have thought twice, Lauri Boy, but you didn't think, did you?" Tristian crouched and held his shoulders down, causing him to whimper. "Because now you have to deal with us..."

Aden pulled my onyx knife from my sheath. "We don't show mercy to those who try to hurt our family." He took the knife and slammed it into his chest.

I bent near his ear. "Now, how does it feel to be broken by my Devils?"

The light in his eyes faded into nothingness as he stilled. His chest heaved one last time, and blood fell from the corner of his mouth.

"He was working for The Wishmaker?" Emmeranne's voice came from behind us.

We jumped and saw her staring at the heap of what was Laurent.

"He tried to kill us."

She nodded. "I knew him for three hundred years." She sighed. "He was my right-hand man, and the little imp betrayed me for The Wishmaker." Her eyes looked as if the betrayal hurt her more than his death.

"Emmeranne, we don't want a war with you," Bash said steadily, "but he tried to kill my family, and I will not let it stand."

She shook her head. "Go. Take your Devils and go. Please never return, Ms. Rose, unless you are invited."

She dismissed us and waved a hand, the brick wall opening with the gesture. A limo waited to take us back to the tiny quiet houses. Their inhabitants would never know what nightmares lurked in the night as they all slept peacefully.

Chapter Twenty-Five

Once we were safe in the car, I wondered how it got so messy so fast. I tried to scrub the dried blood off my hands, holding back a slight shake. We did get the riddle, so we were one step closer to finding my coven members and destroying The Wishmaker.

The question that hung in the back of my mind was, at what cost? Was this my life now? Full of blood, death, and uncertainty? My body slumped as the adrenaline wore off from the fight.

My eyes started to flutter shut as I relaxed more, sinking into my seat. I had lost my shoes as soon as I got in, my legs curled against me, and my head lay on Aden's chest. His arm was safely around me.

Tristian was driving, and Bash sat next to him, his head leaning back and his eyes pinching in pain.

I reached my arm over to his shoulder. "Are you hurt?"

He turned his head to me. "I can wait 'til we get home."

I shook my head. "No, Sebastian, show me now."

He lifted his shirt without a word, revealing three angry slashes across his abdomen. They were slowly healing, and for a vampire, that was rare.

"The crows... I think they had some type of poison in their claws," he explained before I could ask.

I cursed and placed my hand on his side.

"Lexi, you're drained..."

I glared at him. "Shhh." Bash snapped his mouth shut. "Good boy."

I focused on healing him as a warm light shone from my palm. I pulled my hand back, and the lines were a light-pink scar.

"Damn it," I whispered to myself.

Bash pushed my hair behind my ear. "Princess, I'll be healed by morning, don't worry." He brushed his fingers over my cheek. "Thank you."

He kissed my forehead and pressed his against mine. We stayed that way for a moment, and I kissed his lips and cheeks.

"We're okay, Lexi."

I nodded, not realizing I was crying.

I wasn't crying because I was scared for myself but because I was scared for them. "I had a moment, just one brief second, I thought what would happen if I lost you three, and I felt it, Bash. I felt my heart shatter."

He held my face, then pulled me onto his lap. He whispered sweet words in my ear and rubbed my back in deep, slow circles. "We're here, Princess. We're okay."

A warm hand gripped my leg, his thumb caressing up and down. "Lil' Star, we would claw through hell to get back to you; we're not indestructible, but we're pretty damn close."

Aden leaned between the gap in the front seats and moved closer, taking each of my hands. "Lexi, baby, we can't promise forever, because none of us can—your parents and Daniels are proof of that—but they did teach us one thing. We live each and every day with a purpose, and, Lexi Rose, you are our purpose." He kissed each hand.

I looked at each of my Devils, and my heart felt full. A heart that was once broken was now being slowly filled with new memories of love.

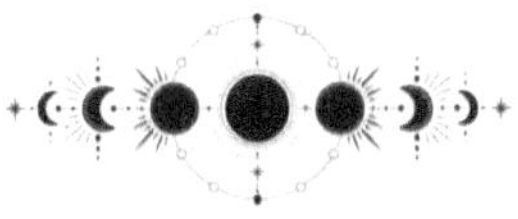

After a shower to clean the muck off me, I climbed into my comfiest pj's and fell into bed with my Devils. My dreams were filled with shadows, doubt, and a hooded figure holding a glimmering gold bottle of pixie dust.

The next morning, I climbed out of bed and got a cup of coffee to watch the sunrise. I had been sitting outside with a blanket wrapped around me when I felt the lounger dip, and Aden's warm body joined mine.

He was bare-chested, just his tattoos on display, in a pair of navy joggers that left nothing to the imagination. His glasses rested on his face. With a steaming cup of coffee in his hand, he raised the cup to his lips, the steam fogging his glasses for a moment. I smiled at him. He was so beautiful, it hurt. My best friend, my lover, and the one person who knew my soul.

"Aden, I love you."

He looked down at me. "I know." He didn't say it smugly, but as if it was an obvious answer. He kissed my head. "I know, because I've loved you my whole life, Lexi. Ever since I was eight years old, I've always had a look in my eyes when I see you, and last night in the car, I saw that same look in yours."

I snuggled closer to him, kissing his chest lightly. We stayed that way until the sun rose slowly over the ocean, its orange rays meeting the inky-purple night sky. He played with my hair, running his fingers through it.

I traced small circles along his stomach, laying a kiss now and

then. It was so peaceful—something we hadn't had in so long.

"My mom and I would come out and sit on the beach every now and then. She would have tea, and I would have hot cocoa. It was our secret. No one knew about it. That's why I chose this house." I pointed to a small spot on the beach. "That was our spot."

He smiled down at me. "You surprise me every day, baby. Can it be our spot now?"

I looked up into his steel-gray eyes and nodded. "It's our spot now, all of ours."

He kissed me softly, and we looked back out to the ocean, basking in the quiet.

Bash stepped outside, finding us cuddled up, and he tapped my nose. "Princess, Tristian and I are going for a quick run."

I gave him a quick kiss, and Tristian slapped my ass as he left. "Bye, Lil' Star, don't do anything I wouldn't." He winked at me as he ran off to catch up with Bash.

My phone dinged as a text came through.

> **Unknown:** *Hi!!!!!! Good morning, starshine! It's Corvina! I hope the laughs lasted all night!*
>
> **Lexi:** I wouldn't say it was full of laughs, but hi, Corvina, it's good to hear from you.
>
> **Corvina:** *Oh right, yeah, and Poor Laurent was killed in the Prime of LIME! Oh well, he was a creeper anyway. SOOOOOOOOOOOO this morning, in my early dreams, a little mermaid swam up to me in the sky (I didn't know you could fly!)*
>
> **Lexi:** Umm, I'm a siren.

Corvina: *Right! Emmer just told me you aren't a mermaid… ah, you'll never get to walk where the people are or have a best friend who's a crab! How sad!*

Lexi: Sadly, no. Corvina, are you okay?

Corvina: *What? You are a weird one. I am perfectly imperfect. Anywho, okay, so the mermaid handed me a shell, and inside the shell was the message I gave you yesterday, but it was different.*

Lexi: How was it different?

Corvina: *She said to look through the glass to see clearly, and repeated the riddle. "To find wHat you sEeK, look to thE skY and to the Sea Where the stars meet. You'll fInd a haLLow where only the pureSt cAn drink from the VinEs of trUth. To See if you are worthy to sleep. In your dreams, you will find the Answers that your heart that onLy you truLy seeks."*

Lexi: That's exactly what you told me last night, Corvina.

Corvina: *Oh, look at that, it is, haha! But remember, like an old man once said, "It's not always what it seems." Or maybe that was a cat… Anyway, good luck, and we will talk soon, but not before. Oh, and avoid the right side of the house today, whatever that means.*

I looked up from my phone, and the confusion must have been written across my face.

Aden looked over at me. "What's up?"

I shook my head. "Corvina... she's... you know I like her, don't get me wrong, but she is a bit..."

I was trying to search for the proper word, because I saw that her heart was in the right place, but her mind, well, I guess if you saw flashes of the future, it would be a little hard to tell the difference too. I held my phone out as he read through our text thread.

"She is either totally a genius, baby, or she is mad as a hatter." He placed the phone next to me with a cup of coffee.

I moaned as I put my head in my hands. "Can we go back to bed? I promise to make it worth your time."

I tilted my head and batted my eyelashes at him, and he chuckled. "Baby, I, for one, would love to do that, but Bash texted saying Grayson is stopping by today. My guess is he heard about last night and wants to check in." I let another groan out. "One problem at a time." He patted my back. "No time to mope about it. Come on, Lex."

I pouted. "Damn it."

He kissed me hard and quickly. "I promise, once we figure this shit out, I'll take you back to the bedroom and make you forget your own name."

I smiled. "Deal!"

We headed inside, and I told Aden I was going to shower and change. By the time I pulled one of the guy's old sweatshirts over a pair of leggings, he was all set up and typing away on his computer. A large whiteboard was behind him. I leaned against the counter next to him.

He pulled me in closer and laid a kiss on my shoulder. "You smell like me."

I smirked. "Is this yours?"

He shook his head. "Nope, that's Tristian's, but the body wash is, and on your skin, it is positively intoxicating." He gripped my hips, pulling me to him.

I pinched his ear. "Focus. Remember, orgasms later." I smirked, knowing I still affected him after all these years.

A knock sounded at the door. I walked over and opened it to see Grayson standing with a somber look on his face.

My smile dropped into a frown. "What happened?"

Grayson held out a box. "Found it when I was walking up." He stepped inside. "It doesn't seem to be dangerous, I checked it quickly, but do you want to open it inside or outside to be safe?"

I sighed. "Let's check it inside. Aden, we got another one."

I heard a chair slam back against a wall, and he sped over to me, pulling me slightly behind him and taking the box from Grayson.

"Lexi, stay back." He held a hand up before taking a knife from his pocket, then sliced the lid open.

I waited as the anticipation killed me. "What is it, Aden?"

He hissed, "Motherfucker!"

Grayson and I ran to Aden, who was walking away and kicking the ground.

Grayson looked into the box with a perplexed look on his face. "Uhhh, seductress? You wanna explain to a poor old country boy what the hell this is?"

I peered into the box, preparing myself for whatever horror lay inside. A black coil sat wound up, and at first, it looked like a snake, but it wasn't moving. When I looked closer, it was a whip.

"What... the..." I reached for it, but my hand was yanked back.

"Lexi, let me," Grayson's rough voice said. He lifted the whip, and his eyes widened with a smile. "Kinky."

I rolled my eyes. "They're fucking with us. If they were at Mort Noire, they would know nothing like that happened. We had con-cealment spells on too."

I checked the box again, and a white silk scarf with a deep-red bow tied around it sat in the middle. A dark-red streak soaked across the silk, and I knew it wasn't a design choice.

"Blood," Aden said as he walked over to us.

I pulled the edge of the ribbon, and it fell away and opened as if magic was behind it. Staring up at us were two eyeballs. I yelped and jumped back with my hand over my mouth, almost falling. Grayson steadied me as he let out a string of curses.

Aden looked back to me and then to the eyes.

"Aden, don't tell me…"

Aden looked over at me. "The Wishmaker has claimed another victim."

Grayson looked down. "I know those eyes."

I looked at him in confusion. "How?"

"Emmeranne and Laurent are part of the Trinity Coven, Lexi. Laurent is the only one with those colored eyes that dark." He bent and picked up a simple white linen paper with one line. "I'm always watching, sweet Rose. WM."

Chapter Twenty-Six

I stared down at the two dead eyes in shock as Aden and Grayson argued about what to do. I snapped out of it, looking around and noticing we were on the right side of the house.

I remembered Corvina's warning. "Aden, we need to get inside! Corvina's—"

His head snapped like he heard something that our ears couldn't.

He sped to me and picked me up. As he ran, he turned his head back, yelling, "Holsten, get the box, or you'll end up dead!"

Grayson didn't waste a second as he darted to sweep the box up with one hand.

Aden and Grayson ran to the door. Aden ran full at full vampiric speed before a boom echoed through the yard. A bullet hit the spot where the box had sat, barely missing Grayson.

Aden threw the door open as we sped in, and Grayson was right behind us, slamming the door shut.

Grayson walked to the dining room table and placed the box down. "Fuck, Charon is going to hate this."

My mouth dropped open. "Charon? As in the ferryman for *Hades*?!"

Grayson smirked. "Hades has been dead for a long time, seductress. However, he would have loved you. Charon is just a *faucheuse*—a reaper. One of many, actually." He shrugged as if we should all know that bit of random information.

Aden glared at me. "*Focus*, you two!" He whipped out his phone and called for the guards to double up and send someone to the door to stand by. Next, he sent a text with such speed that it made me dizzy.

"Aden! Bash and Trist—"

He looked up. "Already told them, baby. Bash, Tristian, and some of the guards are in the forest looking now for the idiot who thinks we're so stupid that we aren't going to hunt them," he huffed out.

Grayson laughed. "They didn't even use a silencer." He paused and rolled his eyes, making him look about ten years younger. "They wanted us to know they were there."

I closed my eyes, remembering the note. I opened them quickly, went to the box, and pulled out the paper carefully, trying not to look at or touch the eyeballs.

"I'm always watching, my sweet Rose," I said to Aden. "Have the guards check for any cameras in the forest."

Aden jumped into action, making phone calls and pulling his computer out. "I'm checking our cameras now to see if I can catch a glance of the shooter."

"Grayson and I will look over the riddle. Join us when you're done."

I walked to the whiteboard and wrote the riddle out. "Tell me more about Charon. I thought the Greek gods were a myth made up by humans?"

Grayson smiled. "Well, I guess it's somewhat true. They weren't these powerful immortal beings. They were fae." He shrugged as he pulled out a few books, flipping through the pages. "Charon isn't really on friendly terms with me but isn't my enemy. We're just competing with each other. He mostly stays on the East Coast these days, though." Grayson smirked. "Bonus is that it pisses him off when a seer screws his plans up." He laughed. "Corvina would put him on his ass."

I finished writing the riddle, and we sat back to look at it.

"Okay, so let's begin."

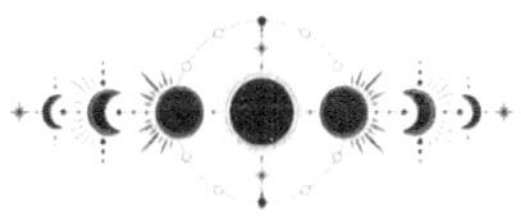

A few hours went by before Tristian and Bash walked through the door. Bash kissed my head, and Tristian hugged me tightly.

"Did you find anything?"

They shook their heads. "Nothing yet, but the guards are going to go over every single inch of the forest tonight," Bash said as he pulled water out for Tristian and himself.

"The bullet we found was a blank." Tristian tossed it in the air and caught it.

I sat up. "So, it was a warning?"

Grayson looked at the bullet. "It's silver. Not that it would hurt us, but someone is making a point for sure." He turned to Bash. "Bash, look, I don't want to tell you how to run things, but I think you gotta bring the FBI into this."

Bash's eyes flashed red. "I'll call him."

He made the call and walked outside to the back to talk to the FBI agent who hated him.

I watched Bash from the window. He was standing perfectly still, but the tension in how he held the phone gave away his anger.

He stormed back in and narrowed his eyes at Grayson. "He'll come by tomorrow. You three almost getting shot isn't a top priority, apparently."

I pulled his hand, and he came to me. I brought my hand to his face and smoothed down his furrow. "We don't need the FBI, not when we have us."

Bash nodded. His fingers were skimming the books near me. "Any luck with the riddle?"

I shook my head. "Nope, nothing in these books speaks of where the sky and the sea meet."

Bash smirked. "You may be thinking too metaphorically, Princess. The Wishmaker likes to make us think, but usually, the answer is right in front of our faces."

"Like, literally? The sky and the sea meet the horizon?" I jumped up and rushed to the bookcase. "Dad had a book on the California coast and Providence Village in particular. He always had one map out on his desk. He said the clue to the treasure lies out here... but what if it was a *key*?"

I found the old map tucked between a few books I had taken from his office at the estate. I unfolded it onto the counter as the others gathered around me.

Its pages were yellowing, and the corners curled in with torn edges. This map was unique because it showed the constellations in the sky. On the back, it showed the levels of the ocean.

Bash looked over my shoulder. "May I, Princess?"

I nodded to him.

He moved next to me, scanning the map, and ran his fingers gently over the bottom. "I think if we take this end..." He reached for the folds of the map that ran along the bottom and folded them together, bringing it up to where the sea met the stars. The folds formed a new picture; it was an island with jagged rocks jutting around it.

I gasped, "Bash." I pointed to the island. "Do you know where it is?"

Aden cursed, and so did Tristian. I turned to them, and Grayson's face looked grim.

"It's Crows Hallow," he said in a gruff voice.

I must have looked confused because Aden walked to me, explaining, "Crows Hallow is said to be the home of nightmares. The ténèbres look like fluffy bunnies compared to what's on that island. It's something dark and demented. We can't go there because we most likely wouldn't survive."

I slumped in my chair. "But the riddle…"

Tristian spoke up, "She has a point. What if you drink the water and pass its test? You would be worthy of the knowledge."

Bash glared at him. "We aren't risking her."

Tristian shook his head. "I'm not saying we are, *frère*."

I crossed my arms and glared at them.

Grayson muttered "uh-oh" as he leaned back, crossing his arms.

I stood. "No, you do not get to say what I can and cannot do. If you three go, I am going with you."

Bash swung around toward me. "Lexi—"

I held up my hand. "Sebastian, could it work?"

He sighed, running a hand down his face. "Maybe… I don't know… maybe Corvina knows more. Maybe we can ask her." He glared down at the map.

Grayson looked up from his book. "Lexi, let me see what Corvina sent you."

I tossed my phone to him. "Sure, but most of it's nonsense."

He looked down and shook his head. "Clever girl, she is."

I raced over to his side. "What?"

He smirked. "Look."

"To find wHat you sEeK, look to thE skY and to the Sea Where the stars meet. You'll fInd a haLLow where only the pureSt cAn drink from the VinEs of trUth. To See if you are worthy to sleep. In your dreams, you will find the Answers that your heart that onLy you truLy seeks."

"Do you see it?" he said.

"You mean the weird way she types? Yeah, I see it, Grayson. I don't know if she's all there. I'm glad Aden fixed the typos."

He laughed. "You've lost your damn mind."

I huffed.

He grinned. "Seductress, it's a code. Look." He grabbed the marker, walked to the whiteboard, and wrote out the code:

THE KEYS WILL SAVE US ALL.

I repeated what he wrote and turned to my Devils, all standing with their arms crossed, looking menacing. "We have to go."

Aden's eyes closed as if it was the worst thing I could say. Tristian's face dropped into a concerned frown, and Bash was stone-cold still.

"Grayson, give us a minute with our girl." His voice was deep and held a tone only a true ruler would have.

Grayson patted my shoulder. "I'll be right outside. I gotta fill Hudson in anyways."

I gave him a wary smile.

The door clicked shut, and I turned to him. "Sebastian—"

He held up a hand. "I'll talk first, Lexi, then you can have your say, but I want you to listen."

I uncrossed my arms and sat at the counter across from him. "We're negotiating again... which you haven't stood by, by the way," I pointed out.

"We've been busy, Lil' Star." Tristian pointed back at me.

"Fine, talk." I waved to him to continue.

He looked down as he leaned forward on his elbows and spoke in a rough, dry voice.

"The Island is what Aden said it is. It is a pure nightmare, but it is also so enchanted that it could give us an advantage. I don't know if we'll make it out of this, Princess. One or all of us might and probably will die. We will be pushed to our limits, both physically and mentally. I don't know if you'd come back the same. Your heart would be stained black. Your soul would be cracked. Tell me, are you willing to risk all that for our lives? Because that's the thing, Lexi.

It's not just your life anymore. It's our life now. If one of us doesn't return... how much will it break you?"

When he lifted his eyes, they were deep red, and his fangs were completely elongated. He looked like the Devil himself, and that's when I knew.

I knew in my gut that these men would not just go into battle for me but were willing to die for me, and I was ready to follow them. I let my fangs slide out, and my eyes went blurry until I blinked and a haze of violet clouded my vision.

"It will take a hell of a lot more to kill my Devils and their siren. Whatever is on that island doesn't know what we have in store for them."

Bash smiled evilly at me, and I looked to Aden and Tristian, who looked stoic. "Boys, it's time to go cause a bit of mayhem. Let's go catch us a nightmare."

Chapter Twenty-Seven

Grayson walked in smiling at me. "I'm not going to say I wasn't listening, but I was listening."

I gave him a teasing grin. "Not even gonna try to deny it, huh?"

He smirked. "Nope. Besides, you'll need my help. Brigitte knows much about Crows Hallow. She'll know what to do."

I inclined my head to the side. "You know, one day, you'll have to tell me more about that situation."

I swear, a blush rose to his cheeks.

"Maybe one day I will, seductress. Maybe one day I will." He looked down, trying to hide a smile.

Bash walked in between us. "As cute as that little love story is, Grayson, I think we need Brigitte and Corvina to help. Is there a way we can get them here?"

Grayson gave Bash a dull look. "Corvina, yes, she's part of the Trinity. She'll come if I ask, but Brigitte is another story." He gave me a pointed look. "She likes you, Lexi. She says she sees a lot of power within you, and that is rare for a voodoo priestess to acknowledge;

they're usually the most powerful one in the room."

It was my turn to blush. "Tell her thank you."

He was typing a message out. "Tell her yourself." He flashed his phone to me, showing me the text he had just sent to Brigitte.

She typed a simple "yes."

He moved to the door. "Name the time and place, Ryder, they'll be there. I gotta go, but Hudson said to call him if you need anything." He shook Bash's hand and turned to me, wrapping me in a tight hug. "Stay strong, seductress, and keep those Devils in line."

I tightened my hold on him. Grayson was becoming a faithful ally, but more than that, he was becoming a friend, and the more we had, the better off we were against The Wishmaker.

His phone buzzed, and he pulled away to answer it. A small hushed voice came through the phone, and he hung up.

"Corvina says it has to be after the wedding bells?" He arched an eyebrow. "Which one proposed?"

I choked on air. "*What*?! None! No one... what the hell is she...?"

Tristian patted my shoulder. "I think she means Ella, Lil' Star."

I looked back at Aden and Bash, who were trying to hold in their laughter.

"Oh, yeah. That wedding."

Shaking his head, Aden went back to the open book on his lap while Bash walked to the kitchen and poured another cup of coffee. "After the wedding, we head to Crows Hallow."

Grayson looked almost giddy. "Scared the shit outta ya, didn't I?" I glared at him. "See ya later, seductress."

He waved goodbye to the rest and left me in a complicated storm. I opened my mouth to explain.

Bash smiled and sipped his coffee. "No need to worry, Princess. None of us are ready for that."

I walked over to Tristian and sat next to him. "Wanna be my research buddy?"

He gave me a cocky grin. "Kinky, I like it."

I slapped his arm playfully. "You know what I mean."

He licked his lips as his cocky grin faded, and his voice came out deeper. "I do, Lil' Star, but it doesn't change the fact I only think dirty thoughts around you."

I rolled my eyes. "Let's get to work. Maybe later you can act out those dirty thoughts."

I walked to my small collection of books that I had collected over the years from around Providence Village about the history of our city. I set a stack down with a thump. "I guess we should start here." I patted the books and pulled a few down, opening them up.

Their pages had started to yellow around the edge from age, and the paper was soft and velvety. I wrote down a few notes here and there, mainly if anyone mentioned the island by name. One thing I did find was from a water witch's journal that Daniels gave me. She called the island *L'île de Mort*—Island of Death. She said the island was small but surrounded by death at every turn, and she wasn't wrong. The jagged rocks were miles tall with a gloom about them, the fog was a thick blanket of white, and visibility was nonexistent. Add in the dark magic that kept the island protected and could distort your way, and there was no way anyone would survive that. I scanned the maps that showed the island and copied any possible routes we could take to get there safely. So far, one way was not as dangerous as the others.

I sighed. "It looks like we might have two ways in." I tapped the map leaning closer to see if I was missing anything. "This way is the lesser of the evils, I think. It has a small opening that could get a small boat in, but nothing more, and that's if the island itself doesn't kill us."

Tristian frowned, staring down at the map. "You act as if you think the island is alive."

I shrugged. "It is." His brows rose. "In theory," I said, "if dark magic has inhabited the island, then it's alive."

My phone started ringing. It was Hudson, which was weird.

"Hey, Hudson, Grayson just left. What's up?"

He sounded winded with panic. "Lexi, Agent Rengard, Hyde, and some guy in a suit are on their way to your house now. Hide anything to do with the investigation, and I mean it. Hide it well!" He hung up swiftly.

I looked at Tristian with wide eyes. All three moved so fast that it was a blur. "Damn vampiric hearing," I murmured as I pushed the map and books into the shelf.

"The whiteboard!" I yelled and ran over to pull it into Tristian and Aden's room. I grabbed the eraser and put it on the board.

Aden stopped suddenly. "Wait!" He took out his phone and took a picture. "Go!"

I erased it all. "Aden, they could take our phones. Easy."

His fingers moved quickly over the phone. "Done. Uploaded to a secure doc and deleted from the phone."

Just as we were getting the last of our notes, a booming knock came on the door. "Ms. Rose, it's Agent Rengard of the FBI. Open the door now!" His angry voice echoed through the house.

"Hold on, Rengard!" Aden yelled to the door as he gathered the last of the books. "Distract him!" he hissed as he sped off.

Tristian took off his shirt and whipped me around.

"What the hell, Trist?" He pulled my sweatshirt off so I was only in my crop top and leggings. "What are you doing?" I hissed.

"Just do what I say," he ordered. "Get on the floor and start to plank."

I glared at him. "Ugh, Fine." I lay on the ground and lifted myself into a plank.

It was awful. My stomach immediately started shaking. My arms and legs were strong enough, but the constant tightening of my abs made me want to barf.

"Go open the damn door," I ground out between my teeth.

Bash opened the door. "Agent Rengard, Officer Hyde, and Agent Acheron. What a pleasant surprise." His voice was laced with sarcasm. "Acheron, it's been years. How are you? Do you still have that tape of me from graduation night?"

A low laugh sounded from the door. "Ryder, nice to see you too, but this is business."

Bash smiled. His eyes were tight, hiding his tension. "Of course, maybe at a later time."

Bash moved back as Agent Rengard walked in as if he owned the place.

"Exercising, Ms. Rose?" He looked down at me, suspicion all over his face.

"Gotta stay strong. When someone is trying to kill you," I grunted out. "Tristian…"

He smiled down at me. "Oh, sorry, Lil' Star. You're all done."

I sat on my knees, glaring up at him. "Asshat," I muttered.

Hyde stood at the door looking like a pissed off badger. Next to him was a handsome younger guy with light-brown hair and hazel eyes. His suit was crisp and clean with elegant lines, and a high-end watch adorned his wrist.

Agent Rengard cleared his throat. "Ms. Rose, you know Officer Hyde, and this is Agent Cillian Acheron."

I raised an eyebrow at the last name. "Acheron?"

He gave me a crooked smile. "I know… I think my ancestors had a weird sense of humor. Ms. Rose, I'd like you to answer a few questions about Laurent Forrest and what happened at Mort Noire yesterday."

I moved to stand, and Tristian was there with his hand. I smirked as he pulled me to stand. "We were there, but we had concealment spells on us."

He nodded. "Yes, but we have a few witnesses who saw you leave. The Providence Village's Devils and the Princess are quite recognizable now. Are you aware that you're in every news article of late?"

I shrugged. "I don't keep track of the gossip column." I walked to Agent Acheron and held out my hand. "My father always taught me it was polite to shake someone's hand during the first meeting."

He eyed my hand with suspicion. "Are you not a siren?"

I smiled sweetly. "I am. You don't think I would use my gifts on you, do you? I, for one, am quite offended."

He narrowed his eyes, examining me, then reached out to take my hand.

"Pleasure to meet you, Ms. Rose, finally. Bash used to talk about you in school."

I looked at Bash, grinning. "You used to talk about me?"

His glare told me enough. "Every now and then," he grumbled out.

"Or when you were a bottle or two in." Acheron winked.

"We're here to ask questions about last night, Agent," Rengard said.

I waved a hand for them to sit at the dining room table, and we all moved to take a seat around it.

"Where's Charmante?" Hyde asked Bash, his arms crossed over his chest.

"He's around here somewhere," Bash said in a bored tone. "Let's just start."

Agent Acheron pulled out a small notebook and pen, looking over at me. "Ms. Rose, why were you at Mort Noire?"

A flush spread across my cheeks as I remembered what had happened. God, it felt good having all three of them where I wanted them. I cleared my throat, and instead of lying, I decided to stay as close to the truth as possible.

"I was there because we got invited," I said with a simple shrug.

Rengard huffed, and Hyde growled lowly.

"We want to know what happened to Laurent. If I'm being honest, he wasn't a good man. The world's probably better off without him, but it was still a murder we have to investigate," Cillian said.

I looked over to Bash and then to Tristian as Aden walked into the room.

"I'll tell you what happened." He moved smoothly and pulled a chair out to sit on it backward. "I got us the invite. We wanted to go to a place that wouldn't... judge us."

"So, you're saying that...?"

I bit my lip as the embarrassment hit me hard.

"We are hers, and she is ours," Bash said in a dangerously low tone. "That is all you need to know, Cillian."

Cillian smirked. "Of course, many fae are in a poly relationship, nothing to be ashamed of."

My eyes snapped to him, and I saw a glint of laughter. I opened my gift slowly and crept it over him. Cillian was human, but the lust that came off him told me there was something more.

I leaned forward. "Look, Laurent met us at the door, showed us through, then left. We went on with our night, and Laurent was out there seeing us out when we were trying to leave."

Tristian leaned back in a stretch. "Then, when we got outside, Laurent asked if Lexi would 'entertain' him." He glared at Cillian. "As I'm sure you can guess, we didn't take that very well. He pulled a knife out on Lexi, threatening us to do what he wanted."

Rengard's eyes widened in anger, and he muttered a curse. "Why the hell didn't you call me before today?!"

I held up my hand. "Rengard, as much as I respect you, what would you have done? Laurent was determined to kill me and what is mine. He used dark magic to hurt Sebastian, and it was only by pure luck we didn't get hurt more than we did. I had to heal him with the little magic I had left, and you're sitting here judging us. *That* is the reason we didn't call you."

A hand squeezed my arm, and Aden looked at me. "Calm yourself, baby. Your eyes went all sireny."

I stared into his steel eyes and nodded. "Agent Rengard, I apologize. I'm just tired of people trying to kill me." I wrapped my arms around myself, calming down. I quickly glanced at Aden, then looked over at Cillian. "I grabbed Laurent's knife in the fight and stabbed him in the chest," I said.

Hyde growled, "She just admitted to killing him. Why are we not arresting her?"

Cillian raised a hand to stop him from going on. "Did Laurent say anything to you before he was stabbed, Lexi?"

I nodded. "He admitted to being part of The Wishmaker's cult."

Agent Rengard moved forward on his elbows. "Did he say anything else?"

I shook my head, swallowing hard. "No, all I know is that Laurent was determined to kill me. It was him or me, so I chose survival, not just for myself but for my coven too."

Cillian looked up from his notes. "Anything else?"

I shook my head. "We got out quickly and left as soon as it happened."

Rengard looked over at Bash. "Mr. Ryder, are you okay, or do we need to get a witch in here?"

Bash looked surprised. "I'm good, Agent Rengard. So nice of you to finally ask." His voice dripped with sarcasm.

"Is that all?" I asked Cillian.

"Do you know Corvina or Emmeranne Noir?"

I glanced at him. "I do. Corvina was our escort to Mort Noire. A bit weird but sweet. Emmeranne, I only met that night. We had a brief conversation." Which wasn't a total lie.

"Care to tell me what you talked about?"

I blinked. "Coven business and... The Wishmaker. She wanted to know... if we knew anything about who he was."

Cillian stared at me as if he didn't believe me but nodded. Hyde and Rengard were glaring at us.

"She's lying," Hyde grunted out.

I held up my hands. "Hand to God." It was probably good that I didn't believe in any higher power, or I might have been struck down right then and there.

"Okay, I think that's it, unless Agent Rengard has anything for you. As for Laurent, I'm sure we can *all* agree it was self-defense, though get a lawyer just in case."

We stood, and Cillian held out his hand. I took it and was hit with so many emotions at once that I stumbled back—happiness, love, laughter, pain, anger, and loneliness was the last. Humans could feel so many emotions at once. I was grateful I was only half witch. I'm not sure how I'd manage it daily.

"Goodbye, Agent Acheron. Don't take any offense, but I hope I never have to see you again."

He laughed. "Well, maybe one day, Ms. Rose, when it isn't so complicated." He waved to Bash. "Ryder, good to see you. I wish it were under better circumstances, though." He looked over at Aden and Tristian and nodded his head. "Boys." He turned and left with Hyde on his heels.

Rengard came up to me, his hands in fists, and he took a deep breath. "Lexi... please call me if anything comes up with The Wishmaker. I do want you safe." He sounded mournful as he walked past.

I watched all three men walk to the car they came in, and the one thing I wanted to scream was: You're supposed to keep us safe, you should keep us safe, but it was me and my Devils who had to do the work! We had to be the nightmares that made you scared at night!

Well, fine, if they wanted me to be the monster of the night, then I'd be the biggest, baddest monster they'd seen. To keep our city safe from an even bigger demon that lay dormant until the time to attack was ready.

Chapter Twenty-Eight

The days seeped into weeks as a quiet storm built. It was calm around the house as we got into a routine with each other. I discovered that Bash ran daily, and they all worked out for hours. I sometimes joined, but three hours of a workout was too much for me.

Tristian and I studied more magic by visiting the estate and gathering different plants and spells to bring back. So far, I could control my fire magic more, and my air magic was getting as strong as my water magic. Earth was a whole other story. I couldn't get something to stay alive longer than a day. It usually died right on the spot. To say I was frustrated was an understatement.

Aden had gone into full-research mode. He had taken over the entire dining room. A massive monitor was set up with security, and we had maps upon maps laid out to find our way. It wasn't getting onto the island that was tricky, but getting back seemed impossible, which is why Tristian and I were working to build our magic. If we needed an escape, we needed to combine our magic to get us all out of there safely.

I had my grimoire open on the counter and a small pot. I was bent over the book, reading the spell. It was supposed to create a path of light to mark our way throughout the island. I gently muddled juniper and poppy together with other ingredients.

A booming knock shook the house, and I jumped, spilling my coffee all over my lap. "Shit, shit, shit!"

I opened the door, and Grayson and Hudson stood there with looks of despair on their faces.

We usually saw them at least once a week lately. Grayson was in talks with Brigitte and Corvina about their help on the island. Corvina called or texted me every day at three to either tell me some ominous tale or talk about the latest book she was reading. This week's book was about two friends who had known each other their entire lives, then one day, they fell in love and broke each other's hearts. It reminded me of a sad-girl country song.

"Grayson, I didn't think you were coming over today. The guys are working out what... Wait, why do you look like someone just took a puppy away from you?"

His frown was deep, and his eyes looked red, as if he hadn't slept for days. I reached out to him. "Grayson?"

I looked to Hudson for something, but he shook his head.

"I got a present yesterday... from The Wishmaker," Grayson hissed out.

My eyes widened at his response. "What did he send you?" My voice came out in a low breath.

"Five of my people's heads," he growled out. His wolf took hold of his eyes and turned yellow. "*My* people!" He hit his chest. "*My people* do not belong in this fucking war!"

My heart ached for him. His emotions overflowed into me. His anger licked at me like an open flame, but his anguish hurt the most. It was like a slow rip spreading across your entire body.

I swallowed hard and took a deep breath, trying to use a calm, soothing voice to shield him from his pain. "Grayson, I am so sorry this happened to you. Let's go inside." I moved out of the way for them to come in.

Grayson looked up at me. His control over his beast was diminishing. He would shift soon if we couldn't calm him down. Hudson whimpered, his pain knocking into me. I laid a palm on him as I opened up my power to take some of his pain away.

Hudson sighed and laid his hand on mine. "Thank you, Lexi."

I looked up at him with a frown. "It's the least I can do."

Grayson was pacing back and forth. "I don't... I want to help, but what about my coven? Lexi, these were someone's people—mothers, fathers, sons, daughters, friends—and they were *my* people. I'm supposed to protect them, and I let them down."

I held out my hand to him, and he looked at it as he took it. I gently pulled him into the house. Hudson shut the door behind him.

The aching in my chest grew as his emotions rolled off him. "Grayson, you did not do this to your people. The Wishmaker did this to your people. He, she, or whoever they are... is out for vengeance against us, against the covens. We can't let them win."

Hudson came up to him and clamped his hand on his shoulder. "Look at this like a coven leader. What would you do as a coven leader to get your revenge?"

Grayson's eyes flashed frightfully to the eerie yellow of his wolf. "I know what *I* would do, Lexi. I would burn them to the ground, and I would destroy everything and everyone they ever loved." He sighed and ran a hand over his face to his hair, hanging his head. "But as a coven leader?" he said, looking back at me. "I'll wait. I'll plan, and I'll gather the information I need to keep my coven safe and strike without them knowing that I was the one behind it."

I smiled. "Then do both, Grayson. Think about it, plan it, and when the perfect timing strikes, burn it."

Hudson looked over at me, and his eyes widened. "What?"

I turned to him. "I said burn it to the ground, but plan it and wait for the moment to hit, and when it does, Grayson, watch their ashes fall from the sky. Show The Wishmaker what happens when you mess with the Trinity Coven."

Hudson smirked. "Now that's how a true leader of the coven thinks."

He knelt and bowed his head to me, a gesture among the wolves that showed respect to an alpha.

Grayson stared at me for a brief moment, then shook his head. His Southern drawl came out. "You're right, Lexi. Damn it! You're right. We'll wait, we'll make a plan, and I'll destroy The Wishmaker's life as much as he is trying to destroy ours." He looked at me, and his eyes were set in determination, and I knew my decision was reflected in my eyes as well.

Hudson stood and came to our sides. "We'll make The Wishmaker pay for his crimes, all of them. Lexi, we did come here to give you something." He dug around in his side bag. "Brigitte said to only use this when the darkest time is among us. When all hope is lost." He held up a hand. "Her words, not mine."

I smiled. "She is quite theatrical, isn't she?"

Grayson groaned, his head in his hands. "You don't even have a clue."

Hudson handed over a glass bottle full of red liquid. A raw string was tightly twined around the tall neck with the seal of a small skull covered in black wax.

"Ominous, isn't it?" I mumbled as I looked over the potion.

"She said this is the watered-down version of what we opened the other night. She said you'd know when to use it, but heed her warnings. This potion is voodoo magic, Lexi. It is darker than yours. It should only be used in special circumstances."

I looked at Grayson and could see questions sitting behind his eyes. "What?"

He looked at the potion, then back to me. "Cut the innocent act, Lexi. It doesn't look good on you, and tell me everything, and I mean everything. What does this have to do with The Wishmaker?"

I walked to the fridge and pulled out three beers. I popped the tops and set one in front of both Hudson and Grayson.

I pulled myself onto the countertop, nodding to the bar stools in front of them. "Sit, and I'll tell you everything, but it doesn't leave here, and I want a *promesse entre amis*—a promise between us three—that no one breathes a word to anyone out of this circle."

Hudson's eyes widened. "Not even your Devils?"

I shook my head. "They know most of it. I forgave them, but it would hurt them more if they knew everything."

Grayson picked up his beer and took a swig. "*Je jure de garder tes secrets jusqu'à mon dernier jour.*"

I smiled at him. "Until the day you die?"

He shrugged. "I thought it was dramatic enough. Isn't that how most witches are?"

I busted out a laugh. "We are a pretty dramatic bunch."

Hudson rolled his eyes, but a smile hinted at his lips. "Fine, I swear to keep your secrets until my dying day."

I hopped off the counter and walked over to them, and we clinked our bottles together. "So it is said, so it is done."

Nothing special happened, but it felt like the air around us shifted into something more, like all three of us would always be linked together.

I started at the beginning and told Grayson and Hudson everything. From my secret relationship with Bash to the night my heart was destroyed in more ways than one, to Daniels's death and the start of the letters, and finally, to meeting them. To their credit, Hudson and Grayson were quiet the entire time.

When I finished, I placed my now-empty beer bottle down and cleared my throat. "So... that's it."

Grayson's hazel eyes held a look of sorrow I knew he had felt before. He nodded his head, his hand resting on his chin. I looked to Hudson, who had a grim look on his face. He reached out and pulled me into a hug.

"Hudson, it's okay," I rasped out.

My throat tightened, and he shook his head. "No, Lexi, it's okay to not be okay." His gruff voice held an edge of pain.

I pulled away and placed my hands in his. "I know it's okay to not be okay, but I have the strength now that I didn't then. I see how my power is growing, and I plan on using that power to help not just my coven but all of our covens. The Wishmaker wants to destroy all fae? Then he will have to fight me for it."

Hudson brought my hands up for a kiss. "I know you'll make him pay, Lexi, but it doesn't mean you have to do it alone."

Grayson looked over at me. "She's not alone, Hudson. She has us." He smirked, wiping his face with his hand. "The Wishmaker might start a damn war, but he won't win it."

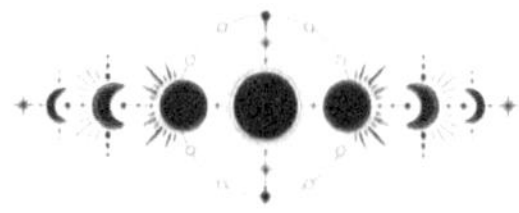

I walked Grayson and Hudson out, waving bye and telling them we would fill them in on anything we found. As they drove away, Tristian pulled up, his face pinched as he talked stiffly into the phone.

He stepped out of the car dressed in slacks and a white button-down shirt. His tattoos peeked from the collar, and his rolled sleeves revealed the twisted ink on his arms. I heard the tail end of his conversation.

"I know what has to be done. Tell the vendor it'll be finished soon, but I'm not giving up any of the properties. No, that's a nonstarter. I keep her. It means more to me than what he wants from me." He looked up at me. "I have to go. My girl just walked out."

He slid his phone into his pocket. "Lil' Star."

I raised an eyebrow. "What was that about?"

He smirked, kissed my lips softly, and whispered, "Nothing, just one of the bars giving me issues. It'll all figure itself out."

I pulled away. "Uh-huh. I don't believe you."

He pulled me into him. "Can see through my bullshit?"

I smiled as I tilted my head back to look at him. "Always."

He laughed. "Ouch, Lexi. Okay, okay. You know Cillian?"

I arched an eyebrow. "The FBI agent?"

He nodded. "That one. Well, he's an investor in one of the new bars, and let's just say he's causing issues with my investment."

I sighed and put my head on his chest. "This is getting messy."

He pulled me back. "Baby, messy isn't even going to cover it. We're rollin' in the deep shit of it all."

I looked up at this man I once hated and realized that I loved him wholeheartedly. Tristian was like the sun, but I needed the dark. I needed that haunting hour. I needed the pain because, without it, I don't think I'd be as strong. The strength you got from the pain meant something. You had to go through darkness to be able to survive, but the light would always find you home.

CHAPTER TWENTY-NINE

I sat on the couch as I rolled the potion between my hands. Tristian sat in a chair across from me, his hands steepled at his chin and a pinched expression between his eyes.

"Lil' Star... are you crazy?! Messing with voodoo is beyond dangerous." He groaned. "Fuck, this is bad. Did he explain what the hell it is?"

I shrugged. " I don't even think Grayson knows what this potion is. All we got was Brigitte's vague explanation."

"Fucking voodoo queens and their bullshit," he mumbled.

The front door opened, and Bash and Aden walked in. Aden threw his shirt off, and his abs glistened with sweat from the gym. I watched as he moved slowly toward me, and my throat went dry.

He bent down to me, his lips inches from mine. "Lex, like what you see, baby?" He placed a kiss on my cheek. "You can help me shower if you want." A glint in his eyes said he had no intention of getting clean.

I pushed him back gently. "That would be an ideal situation."

Bash hopped over the sofa, gently landing next to me like a cat.

"What if we both showered together with you?"

He laid soft kisses on my shoulder, making his way up my neck. Fuck, why did these three light my soul on fire? I moaned, not wanting this feeling to end, and I looked over at Tristian.

His eyes twinkled with fire as a cocky smirk played at his lips. "Need help, Lil' Star?"

I shook my head and pulled away. "Grayson stopped by. He received a present from The Wishmaker." Bash snapped back. "Five of his coven members' heads in a box."

Bash growled, and Aden stilled. "How is he?"

I shook my head. "How do you think? He's grieving, mad, yelling, angry. He blames us."

All three of them started shouting, but I held up my hand. "*Guys!*" They stopped and turned to me. "Before you get all defensive, I handled it."

Bash crossed his arms and arched a brow. "Grayson is laid back, but when it comes to his coven, he's vicious."

I shrugged. "I told him to use that anger to get his vengeance. He and Hudson swore an alliance to us."

Bash straightened and smirked. "What do you mean? He wasn't our ally to begin with?"

I took a deep breath, unsure how much of Grayson's story I should tell, but I knew they wouldn't say anything beyond our circle. "His sister was killed. By pixie dust."

That got their attention.

"What?" Tristian sat up with a frown.

"She was killed a few years ago, and he's been secretly searching for who was behind it. Now that we know The Wishmaker is behind pixie dust, Grayson wants vengeance." All three of their brows were furrowed. "I don't blame him. I know what wanting vengeance feels like..." I trailed off, looking over each of them.

Bash stalked slowly toward me. "Do you still want vengeance, Princess?"

I looked over at him, pressing my lips together. "Yes, and no," I said lowly. "Sometimes, I wish you three knew the pain, the actual physical pain I went through, and there are times when I want to act on that vengeance, I won't lie. But that's the difference between forgiving and choosing not to. I am *choosing* to forgive each of you. I know that you're all sorry for what happened in the past. Each of you has told me so, but it doesn't always change the fact that I've had ten years of anger built up for you three. It doesn't just go away. I hope you all understand that..." The pain they caused didn't leave. It would never leave, but it was in the past, and I chose to look toward the future. I looked beyond them to the ceiling, and suddenly, the need for air and to think alone was overwhelming. "I think I need some time alone. Excuse me."

Their faces were all drawn in a frown. "Lexi..."

I looked over at Aden, who looked at me as if I would slip away. "I'll be back. I need the ocean and to get my head straight."

I walked through the door and down to the beach. I walked along the shore until the house was nothing but a tiny dot, and I found a small tide pool with smooth, shiny rocks sticking out of the clear deep-blue water. I slipped my shoes off and walked on the rocks until I found one that was perfectly smooth and sat down, letting the cold seep into me. It felt refreshing, as if the water could wash away the pain.

I dangled my feet in the cold water, and I wasn't sure how long I sat there, but the sun had gone down when I heard footsteps.

"If you want me to go, I will, Princess, but I needed to ensure you were okay. I saw the hurt in your eyes, and we were the cause of it."

I looked over my shoulder to Bash, giving him a small smile. "Come on, Prince, you can sit, but let's not talk yet."

He nodded at me. "Okay."

He moved slowly and steadily through the rocks until he reached where I was. He sat next to me, his thigh up against mine. We sat there for a while, just watching the ocean waves coming and going.

As I watched a few crabs move about, my fingers played with the water.

"It's not that I want to act on my vengeance, Sebastian, but it's hard to forget a feeling I've had for years. It's like you three came busting back into my life so suddenly, and it's been chaotic. My life was forever changed when I lost Daniels, and my heart still breaks every day not seeing him. He was my family, my parents and him. And now he's gone. The pain doesn't just go away because you're here now."

He looked down at his hands, looking like a younger version of himself, like the teenager I once knew.

"You broke my heart that night, Sebastian. You shattered it into a million pieces, and I would have been okay, but my parent's death was a blow to my soul, so hard that I don't think I'll fully heal from it. I don't think I'm supposed to. I'm trying to shape myself into something more."

"Princess, you don't owe us any explanation. I take all the blame for how we behaved. I'll take any punishment you see fit, because I won't stop loving you. I won't lose you again, Lexi, not when I've found you again."

His hand found mine, winding our fingers together. He brought it up to his lips, laying a soft kiss against it. This man, who was once my worst enemy, had stolen my heart, and I knew I would have to fight myself every day to choose forgiveness, but that was what made the difference between good and evil. I preferred to forgive them and not live in the hate anymore.

I looked back at the beach that led to the house, not wanting to go back just yet but knowing the others would be worried.

"We should get back," I whispered as I laid my head against his shoulder.

He looked down and kissed my temple. "Let's stay a little bit longer," he murmured.

So, we sat there, a girl and a boy who were once sworn enemies, full of hatred for each other, finally coming together to find peace within ourselves and in each other.

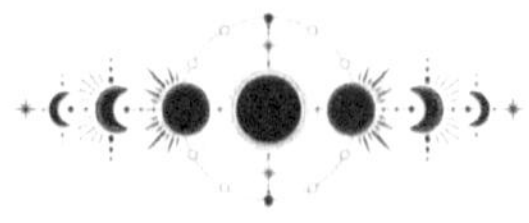

We were walking back hand in hand when Tristian came out to greet us. "Better, Lil' Star?"

I nodded. "Much, thank you."

He looked to Bash. "Did he behave?"

Bash rolled his eyes. "She's safest with me, between the three of us."

A smile spread across my face. "I think you're the most dangerous." I bit my lip, and Bash's fangs slid out, his eyes going red.

"Oh, yeah? Tell me something, Princess. How fast can you run?"

I yelped and moved behind Tristian, shielding myself from the vampire who tried to grab me. "You have to fight Trist first. The winner gets a kiss!"

Tristian turned to me, his smile turning dirty. "Do we get to pick the spot?"

I yelped and backed up, running into Aden.

"Ohhhh, I wanna play. Think you can escape us, baby?"

I laughed, moved to the fire pit, and threw a pillow at his face. "If I go into the ocean, you're screwed," I mocked.

Aden leaped for me, and he missed me by a fraction of an inch. "Don't you dare, Lex!"

I jumped over the chair and dashed to the pool. I pulled my clothes off, throwing them at the guys. My shirt hit Tristian in the face, and he ran into the loungers, falling forward, only to be saved by his vampire instincts as he rolled into the ground.

I laughed as I was about to dive into the pool when someone hit me from the side, wrapping his arms around me and twisting me so his back hit the water. I shifted to my sparkling scales, and my long nails popped out, my pearlescent skin shimmering in the afternoon sun. I blew bubbles out of my mouth to see Aden swimming quickly to me. I smiled as tiny bubbles escaped his lips. I swam to him and ran my finger down his face. He pulled me close and kissed me under the water as the surface rippled above us. His tongue pushed at mine, and I wrapped my arms around his neck, pulling him closer.

With my full powers exposed, his emotions spilled into me. Lust, joy, and love were on the surface, but I felt his hurt too. I wanted to take it all away. I wished there was a way to, but I pushed my emotions into him. I felt the comfort, joy, and love for him in each kiss, in each hug, in each way he moved me to be better, and in how I pushed him to be better. We were equals in our love. It wasn't perfect, and it was complex, but that was what love was. You had to fight for it every day. My Devils. I knew we would fight for it every day we breathed.

We came to the surface laughing, and Tristian was glaring at us. "What? Aden won."

He pouted. "Damn lounger ruined everything."

I pulled myself out of the pool, shifting from my siren form. "Get me a towel, and I'll give you a kiss, too."

At that, he perked up and jogged to the stand. After he pulled out a towel, he grabbed my hand to help me up and wrapped a soft, fluffy white-and-blue striped towel around me.

"What about me?" Aden looked up from the pool.

Tristian pointed at him. "Figure it out, *frère*. You won, but that doesn't mean I'm happy about it."

I looked around. "Where's Bash?"

Tristian cleared his throat. "Morgan."

That one word sent anger seething through me. "What does he want now?"

Bash walked from the side of the house. "That's easy, Princess. We've been invited to the Blood Moon Coven's Full Moon ritual dinner party this weekend."

My eyes widened. No other covens were ever invited into the Full Moon ritual. For Morgan to ask me to the dinner was either a gesture to work together or a trap.

I couldn't help feeling it was the latter. "Well… okay, I guess we're going to a dinner."

Bash's emotions spilled over, and I felt his worry. I moved to him, looking into his eyes, which held a sense of uncertainty.

"Princess," he growled out.

"Yes?" I replied in a husky voice.

He wrapped his hand into my hair and pulled me closer to him, pulling my head back until I looked up into his forest-green eyes. "I won't let them destroy us." His eyes were set in a green blaze, and I smiled as my Devil showed his true colors.

"I know."

He leaned down and stole a kiss from my lips, setting my entire being on fire. I moved my hands to his chest. He moaned and bit my lip hard until I felt a sting of pain. His moans deepened, and I felt our powers intertwine. His shields being completely down sent my siren into a frenzy as she fed off his emotions. It was like the ultimate high. The world disappeared for a moment, and it was just us. Our magics swirled through each other, his warm power of the Blood Moon and my cool power of the Silver Pearl.

I heard a distant noise and pulled away. Seeing Aden, I turned for a kiss, but he shook his head.

"Lexi," he mouthed and blinked. "Lexi? Can you hear me?"

I looked at him in confusion. "Of course I can."

His eyes widened. "You and Bash have been that way for over ten minutes. It was weird, like, somehow, you both shared magic as witches do." He looked between the two of us. "I don't know what the hell it was, but you're the only witch, Lexi. Bash doesn't hold any power of the witches."

I looked over to Bash. Tristian had his hands clasped to his shoulders as Bash swayed, his eyes glazed over.

I gasped in horror. "Is he okay?" I started to move over to him.

Aden wrapped his arms around my stomach and pulled me to

him. "He's fine, baby, just a bit under your spell. Tristian is taking care of him."

Tristian helped Bash move to the lounger, and we walked over to him.

My stomach was in knots, fearing I might have hurt one of my Devils. "Tristian?"

He looked up at me, his eyes softening when he saw me. "You, Lil' Star, are so strong, my powerful *sorciere*."

A blush snuck up my cheeks as I sat next to Bash. His head was in his hands, his breathing deep.

"Sebastian?" I touched his shoulder gently, and he turned his head and gave me a lazy smile. "Princess, that was... Wow, I don't think I've ever felt power like that. She might be little, but she is mighty."

I brushed his hair out of his face. "I'm glad you're okay."

He kissed my palm. "Always."

Aden's phone rang from the lounger where it sat, and he stepped inside to answer it as we sat while Bash gained his strength back.

"It was crazy, Tristian. I've had power emerge before, but it was like turning it up to a hundred with Bash. It was the biggest high I've ever felt. I never wanted it to stop."

Tristian's hand hovered over my arm. "I still feel it, Lexi. It's like a magnet. It's exhilarating."

Aden walked out, and his face looked like he was about to murder someone. "I'll tell her! Don't yell at me. I'm on it. No... No... *No!* I will not!"

He looked down in disbelief at the phone. "She hung up on me..." He looked at me. "*You!*"

I pointed to myself innocently. "Me?"

He huffed as he stomped over and leaned over me. "Go get dressed. We're going out. Dress nicely. It's a club," he grumbled.

I held up my hand and pushed him back. "Explain more, and don't ever just send me demands without an explanation." I raised an eyebrow in question.

"Lexi... Ella is picking us up in a half hour to go club hopping for her bachelorette party," he groaned out.

I grinned. "We're going to a male strip club, aren't we?"

Aden flopped down on a lounger. "Yeah, we are. Not that it's wrong by any means, I just know I'm gonna be babysitting both of you in your drunken states."

My grin widened, and I laughed as I looked over to Tristian and Bash. "You guys going to be okay?"

Tristian nodded. "Go have fun, Lil' Star."

Bash smirked. "Just return to us."

I giddily stood and walked to the door. "I dunno. A dancer named Henry might steal me away." I winked.

Chapter Thirty

I checked myself in the mirror. The sparkliest purple shoes I'd ever seen popped against my black leather pants and black corset bodysuit. My long brown hair was curled and flowed down my back. I opted for dark-purple lips, and I lined my eyes in black. I looked like a sexy assassin, which was precisely what I was going for.

I pulled out a small clutch and added my phone, ID, lipstick, and a few other essentials. When I walked into the living room and heard a whistle, I turned to see Tristian.

"Looking like a million dollars, Lil' Star." His boyish smile splayed across his face as he took a sip of dark-amber liquid.

"Bash? Is he...?"

He pointed to the other bedroom, and I walked back to the door, quietly closing it behind me. As I reached the doorway, he was propped up in bed with his laptop out and his phone to his ear.

He looked at me, and his eyes darkened. "Listen, Anderson. We'll meet tomorrow to discuss this. Yeah, we're planning it after the wedding. Good night."

He hung up, his eyes never leaving me. They wandered along my body.

"I came to say goodbye." I walked to his side, sitting next to him.

"Hmmm." He licked his lips, eyes scanning my face. "You're beautiful, my powerful siren." He set the laptop on the side table and pulled me into his lap. He ran his nose over mine. "You look stunning, Princess." I blushed as his fingers gently traced the bodice of the corset. "This... will be mine later tonight. Let the dancer get you excited, but know that it will be my name you'll scream tonight." He paused. "Maybe all three of us will get you tonight."

The idea made me moan, and I wasn't sure how I could handle all of them, but the thought excited me more than it scared me.

"Lex!"

I groaned. "Shh, maybe he won't find me yet."

Bash laughed. "Just want a few minutes alone?"

I moved to straddle him and felt him hard against my center. He tilted his hips up and pulled me down for a light kiss.

"I wouldn't want to mess up that pretty lipstick yet." He grinned against my mouth as I kissed him deeper.

"Fuck the lipstick, Bash." I ground against him, and he let out a heavy moan.

"Princess." He pulled back. "As much as I want this"—he smirked—"and I do, Ella is counting on you being there for her tonight."

I sighed. "I know." I moved off him. "I'm holding you to your promise, Sebastian Ryder."

I walked to the door, stopping to check my lipstick in the mirror. Not a smudge out of place. No smear is the key.

I opened the door to Aden, who wore a black button-down with rolled sleeves. His tattooed knuckles read "Blood" on his right and "Water" on his left. Tight black jeans and boots finished his outfit, and I smirked because he looked three seconds away from keeping us home.

"Going to a funeral?"

He took in my outfit and then my face, and he smirked. "He didn't fuck you yet, good."

I rolled my eyes. "Don't be an ass."

He held up his hands, his grin still in place. "I'm not, but don't forget one thing, Lex." I walked past him, and he yelled, "Vampiric hearing!"

I flipped him off as he trailed after me laughing until he was gasping.

I kissed Tristian quickly as he said, "Be a good girl tonight, and enjoy Belladonna!"

I looked over at him, confused. "I thought we were going to a club."

Aden jogged up to us. "We are. We're pregaming at Belladonna."

I knew Ella well enough that I should have known we would be pregaming. "Right, she knows we aren't twenty-one, right?"

Tristian laughed. "Have fun, you two, and get her home by midnight!"

I turned around and smiled at him. "I'm not a pumpkin!"

He laughed. "No, you're my Lil' Star. Let Aden have some fun, yeah?"

I nodded. "On it!"

We quickly made our way to the bar. I had never been, mainly because I knew who owned it then. I didn't step into any of their owned businesses if I could have helped it back then. The dark oak doors were closed, and a line of fae and humans stood outside, forming a line to get in, a dark-green velvet rope keeping them from entering. Aden pushed us to the front of the line, nodding to a security guard.

"Boss," he said and let us pass.

A few of the humans grumbled, but I noticed all the fae were perfectly still, some even bowing their heads in respect of the Devil who walked among them.

I was expecting some modern plush lounge, but no, it was dark academia with an old Hollywood twist. It was the opposite of what I thought my light and bright Tristian would do.

I smiled wildly. "It's gorgeous."

Aden chuckled. "Yeah, Tristian did an amazing job, with the help of us, of course."

I turned to him. "Wait, do you all three own this place?"

He shrugged. "A small portion. Tristian owns most of it, then Bash and I have a small part."

He led us through the bar. It was dark, but not like Mort Noire, with lights in all the right places. Mirrors were placed strategically so a soft glow floated around the room. We passed a small dance floor that only a few people were on, but the other side of the bar was a lounge with dark leather tufted couches. Chandeliers hung low from the ceilings, and quiet conversations from the couch abruptly stopped as Aden walked in with me on his arm.

A blonde with a horse face snarled, "I heard it's true, she's with all of them."

The skinny redhead next to her stared dreamily. "That's her? Wow, Aden could do so much better. I mean, I'm prettier. She probably bespelled them."

I laughed and tugged on Aden's hand. "One second." I turned toward them and walked over to the girls with Aden behind me. "Hi!" I said brightly, a smile plastered to my face.

The blonde looked shocked, and the redhead was staring steadily at me. "Hello." She took a sip of her drink, as if she was bothered that I had interrupted her.

"Sorry, I couldn't help but overhear. You're prettier than me, that's true, and I'm with them, but it's not because I spelled them." My smile was sweetly still in place. I leaned forward and whispered in the girl's ear, "It's because not only do I know what each of them needs, I'm what they want, not some frigid manic pixie who doesn't know how to please a Devil." I stood and turned back to the blonde. "So, it was nice to meet you. I hope I never have to see either one of you again." I took Aden's hand and pulled him close. "Let's find Ella."

He smirked. "Of course, baby." He kissed my cheek softly, looking over to the girls.

As we walked through the bar, Aden laughed out loud. "Lexi, I swear, you are so possessive over us."

I raised a brow. "I remember you threatening Grayson with a knife."

We went to a set of green ropes, and Aden signaled for someone to open them. A younger man with the biggest arms I had ever seen clasped the rope and dropped it for us.

"Boss," he mumbled.

"Hey, kid. How are classes?"

He smiled. "Good. I got a few more to go before I get my degree."

Aden smiled. "Good job, kid."

He smiled back and bowed his head. "Have a good night, boss. Ms. Rose, lovely to see you this evening."

I smiled and walked with Aden as I spotted Ella, a few of her friends from the engagement party, and Cassandra.

"Oh, fuck." Aden narrowed his eyes. "What the hell is she doing here?" he growled.

Ella jumped up and ran to me. "Hey! Umm, so before you freak out, Cassandra came with Chanel." Ella pointed to a girl with dark hair and eyes like a cat. "She didn't know you'd be here."

I blinked at her and smiled. "It's fine as long as she doesn't start shit. Because we know how it will end."

I walked over to the group. Aden was quiet as he walked to the bar to get us drinks. I sat next to Ella as she introduced the girls to me again.

Cassandra leaned forward with a plastic smile in place. "Lexi, I know we've had our issues, but tonight is about Ella."

I crossed my legs and smiled. "You're right, Cassandra. It's Ella's night, and she doesn't need any drama." I turned my back to her as I saw Aden walking over with our drinks. He handed me a vodka soda. "Thank you," I said to him with a small smile.

He sat next to me, putting his arm over my shoulders. I sipped my drink and looked over at Cassandra. She was wearing a black pantsuit with a diamond-encrusted bra peeking out. She leaned forward, her breasts practically spilling from her bra.

"Aden," she purred and then pouted. "Nothing for me?"

He looked over at her with a bored expression. "No."

She looked startled but huffed a mumble and leaned over to her friend.

He turned back to his drink, took a sip, and leaned into me, whispering, "Do you think Ella would notice if I took you to the back for a bit?" He wolfishly smiled at me.

"Oh, and, pray tell, what will you do to me?"

He smiled as if I had taken the bait. "Well, I'll start by exploring this corset more." His fingers played over the swell of my breasts. "Then..." His hand slipped between my thighs, and he leaned close. "Then I would lean you back on Tristian's desk and eat your sweet pussy like it was a goddamn man's dying wish." My face flushed, and he continued. "Then I would fuck you until you couldn't remember your name." He licked my neck, sending shivers down my body, and I saw the fire working behind his eyes.

"Aden..."

A throat cleared, and I saw Ella looking at us. "Wanna stop pawing at my girl, Aden? Lexi, let's dance. I talked to the DJ, and he said he'll play our favorites."

He held up his hands. "She's all yours. Just don't go far, baby," he said as he scanned the room, looking for any potential danger.

I stood, finished my drink in a gulp, and set the glass down. I took Ella's hand and smiled. "Let's do this."

She squealed, and we walked over to the dance floor as Beyoncé came on. We started moving to the music, and more people joined us.

The music changed to Britney, and we busted out our dance moves. Ella and I were laughing at each other when a group of guys came up to us.

"You girls look like you're having fun," a deep, gruff voice said from behind me.

I turned around, and a man well over six feet tall in jeans and a flannel shirt looked us over like he was ready to find his nightly prey. My stomach twisted when I saw him.

I smiled politely. "Yeah, we are! Just girls only tonight."

He grinned a toothy smile at me and moved into my space. "Oh, but I saw you earlier, girl. You were all over some emo-looking tattooed boy. Let a real man show you a good time."

I pushed him back. "No thanks, and that boy is more of a Devil if you ask me." I smirked with a raised eyebrow.

Ella and I smiled at each other, knowing this creep needed to be taught a lesson.

"But it's not him you should worry about." I dropped my shield, letting my power wash over him, and his eyes widened.

"Fucking fae."

I smiled and let my eyes turn as the haze of lavender washed over me.

Ella's head rested on my shoulder, and she smirked. "I'm hungry." She smiled, and the guy jumped back.

"Not worth it." He held up his hands and walked away to his friends at the bar, murmuring something as they all jerked their heads over to us.

We waved at them, and they turned quickly from us as Ella and I burst into giggles.

She breathlessly gasped out, "Did you see them scurry away? Ahhh, I kinda feel bad."

She straightened her dress, and I shook my head. "Ella, when you get creeps like Mr. Creepy back there, you say 'fuck being nice,' because I don't think he wanted to get to know you. More like he would have kept you tied up in the middle of nowhere."

She huffed out a breath of air. "You're right. It's not like he's some angel going around granting wishes."

"You good, baby?" Aden asked as he walked over to me.

I smiled as Ella pushed me to Aden, and I turned to her and started to object.

"Go. We'll leave in twenty minutes for the real fun." She wiggled her eyebrows.

I laughed and walked up to him. "Dance with me."

I pulled his arm as a fast pop song came on, and we moved to the music together. Aden's hands were on my waist, and my arms were on his shoulders.

"This is nice," I said in his ear over the loud music.

"I feel like you needed a night of normalcy," he whispered in mine.

I pulled back and realized he was right. I needed this; I needed a night of not worrying about anything. I pulled him down and kissed him with all my might.

"So, the office?" I wiggled my eyebrows, and he grinned, sweeping me up in his arms and speeding to the back.

He nodded to a bodyguard, and they led us into a dark hallway behind the bar area. A few doors lined the hallway, and then a solid wood door with stars carved into it was at the end of the hall staring at us.

I grinned. "Lil' Star?"

I looked at Aden, and he rolled his eyes as he set me down. "*Bâtard* has it everywhere, baby. You have to look for them." He pulled me into him, pushing me to look up at him. "As much as I love my *frère*, I don't want you thinking about anything but me right now."

He pulled a key out of his pocket, and the door clicked open as he gently pulled me into a massive room. My jaw dropped in surprise, as I'd expected something similar to the bar, but it was lighter with light bamboo wood and gray walls, making the office appear more prominent. A sitting area with a comfy cream-colored couch was to the side with sizable deep-forest-green and dark-gray pillows thrown upon two oversized chairs, and a small kitchenette sat to the back with a fridge and a sink. A green lamp, a few pens, and a stack of papers lay scattered on a long stainless steel desk. The office perfectly mixed all three of my Devils, but it screamed Tristian.

"Baby, wanna remind me what I was going to do first?" he breathed out as he stalked over to me.

"I believe it was my corset."

He grinned and lifted me by my ass, kissing me hard. He ground

against me, sending a delicious shiver down my spine. I gasped as I felt the desk hit the back of my legs as he sat me down. I moaned from the cold of the desk and the heat of Aden's hands as he ran his hands up my side and gently cupped my breasts.

He pulled away from me. "What's your name?"

I laughed at his promise from earlier. "Fuck you. It's Lexi."

He laughed as he shoved the papers and pens aside and pushed me back. I lay on my back as he knelt and slowly removed my shoes. His fingers ran up my leg, leaving a trail of goose bumps behind.

"Aden..."

He smirked. "Shhh." He continued running his hand up to my core. "How wet are you, baby?"

I groaned. "So much."

He sat up and unbuttoned my pants, pulling them off gently. The cold from the desk made me gasp as he pulled me to the edge. He ran his mouth up my thigh and pushed the fabric of my panties into me.

"Oh, fuck." I wrapped a hand around his hair, the softness of his strands brushing against my thigh.

"Not yet, baby. What's your name?" he teased as he pushed his finger harder against my clit, and I whimpered.

"Please... Lexi."

He smirked. "I guess I have more work then."

Aden pushed my thong to the side and licked my center as I gasped for him. He continued to torture me and my clit with his tongue as he pumped his fingers into me. He devoured me until he left me gasping his name. I arched my back for more contact.

I put a hand over my mouth to keep from screaming as I pulled his hair tight in my hand. He continued the pace until I fell over the edge, calling his name repeatedly. He looked up, and I pulled him to me, kissing him frantically and pulling his clothes off in a rush. I undid his belt, and he kicked his clothes off.

"Name!" he snarled as he pulled away.

I smirked, biting my lip. "Lexi."

I reached for him, ran my hands over his silky shaft, and gently pulled him to me. His eyes were molten gray, and he moved quickly, pulling my leg up and sliding into me quickly. I moaned as I lifted my hips to meet him. He bent down to me, capturing my lips.

"We'll have to be quick," I breathed out as I felt him right where I needed him to be.

He gave me a smile that made him look more devious than I had ever known.

He bent to kiss me as he thrusted into me. I wrapped my arms around his neck, trailing kisses along his jaw and neck. As he quickly moved in and out, pleasure rippled throughout my body. I kissed him hungrily, his head against mine as we became one.

"I love you, Lexi."

I kissed him. "I love you, Aden."

I looked into his eyes as he fucked me harder. I screamed his name as he watched me fall into oblivion, following right behind me. He laid me back on the desk as a sheen of sweat coated our bodies. He rolled to lie next to me and turned his head to me.

I met his eyes. "Hmmm..."

He smiled. "Name?"

I laughed and felt the soreness sinking into my bones. It wasn't a painful type of soreness. It was the kind of pain that was the best.

I closed my eyes in a dreamy state of bliss. "I'm not sure I can answer that yet." I moaned and sat up, looking around at the mess we had created. "Trist is going to kill us!"

Aden kissed my shoulder. "He'll be fuming that he missed it, but he won't give a shit about the mess. I say we leave it so he knows." He wiggled his eyebrows.

I hit his chest and kissed him quickly on the lips.

A buzz came from his pants in the pile of clothes on the floor, and he strutted over to them, pulling the phone out.

"Ella, everything okay?" I heard her yell my name, and he paled. "Okay, okay, calm down, you tiny pixie! I will. *Ella*, no need for name-calling! Yes, yes, we'll be there shortly." He hung up. "God, she scares me."

I laughed as I pulled on my clothes. "That's probably a good thing. She's mad because we snuck away?"

He smirked and came up to me, still completely naked. "Yeah, but I can handle her."

I was pulling on my corset top when he swept me into a kiss. "But I wouldn't have changed a second of it."

I giggled like a schoolgirl. "Prince Charming, huh?"

He grinned evilly. "Nah, I'm more like the villain who kidnaps the princess."

I laughed and pulled out of his hold, putting my shoes on and grabbing my bag. "Are you going to get dressed?" I said as I looked down at my phone, seeing ten texts and four calls from Ella. "Aden, we gotta go." I looked over at him, and he walked to me, fully dressed. I shook my head. "Never mind."

He smiled. "Vampiric speed." He ran a thumb along my lips.

"How bad is it?"

He shook his head. "You look beautiful."

I rolled my eyes and ran to a mirror hanging by the entryway. I tried to smudge my eye makeup and clean up my lips quickly.

I sighed. "Well, it is what it is. Let's go."

We walked into the bar, and Ella was by the door, arms crossed and a grin on her lips. "Finally, you two."

Cassandra glared at us, and I crossed my arms. "Something wrong?"

Ella shook her head. "No, just those creepy guys again."

The guys from earlier glared at our group as we turned to leave. "I have a feeling that won't end well." I nodded to Aden.

He looked over and smirked. "Ahh, but a good brawl sounds fun."

I laughed at him. "Well, it's a good thing the club is just down the road."

Ella grinned at Aden. "Come on, Devil, do your sworn duty. Lead the way."

He laughed and led us outside.

Ella wrapped her arm in mine and squealed, " Let's go see half-naked men!" I laughed with her, and she looked over at me and whispered loudly, "Oh, and Lexi, you have a pencil in your hair." She gave me a knowing look.

A hand plucked the pencil from my hair, and I turned to see Aden smirking. "Must not have gotten all the pencils, oops."

I rolled my eyes and continued walking with Ella. "Let's go."

"Your lipstick's smudged, too," she teased in a sing-song way.

We walked a few blocks to the club with Aden leading the way. The club, Over the Rainbow, was a two-story dark-red brick building with a giant poster advertising the main star of the evening.

We were almost to the door when Cassandra took my arm, pulling me back, and she asked in a whisper, "Shoot, I forgot my phone back at the bar. I wouldn't normally ask, but I'm worried those guys from earlier will do something. Can you come with me, Lexi, please?"

I was genuinely surprised she would even ask me, but she might want to make amends. "Sure, hold on, let's tell Ella." I called her name, and she turned to me with a questioning look as she looked at Cassandra's arm hooked to mine. "Hey, Cassandra and I have to go back to get her phone from the club. You good with the girls and Aden?"

She looked at Cassandra for a minute, then nodded. "Yeah, we'll be fine. Hurry, you don't wanna miss the fun." She grinned and danced with her shoulders.

We laughed and waved goodbye as we turned back.

We walked in silence for a few minutes when Cassandra blurted out, "I don't know what to say, Lexi, but thank you."

I shrugged. "It's not like I'm saving the world, just walking back with you to get your phone." I looked over at her as she frowned.

"Well, I mean, after everything. I just... I'd like us to be friends. Bash is the future leader of our coven. We all know that, but now... Well, anyways, now I see he's truly found his match."

Her voice sounded off.

I looked up, and the guy from earlier was walking straight to us with a sneer across his face, holding up a phone.

"Miss me already? You dropped this earlier, Red." He tossed the phone to Cassandra, who stumbled to catch it.

"Might want to run, Lexi!" She laughed demonically, her eyes glowing a solid eerie green as her gorgon form emerged.

Her long red hair turned into black hissing snakes, and her skin shifted into a dark gray. I had never seen a gorgon in its complete form. Now I knew why most people feared them. She was one of the most frightening things I had ever seen, but this siren wasn't going to wait around to see what would happen if Cassandra and Mr. Creepy caught her. So, instead of fighting, I did the next best thing. I ran.

I ran harder than ever before, because sometimes, you have to get to an even playing ground. I looked back, and he was gaining on me. I turned a corner and ran right into the center of town. It was late in the evening, so only a few people stumbled around, getting to the next bar for that last drink. I spotted the vast fountain that sat in the middle of town. It was a three-tier fountain that held a glowing globe of fire. Smiling, I ran and stepped in, the water splashing up my legs. I let my fingers skim across the surface and formed a ball of water on my right hand and a flame on my left, using the natural elements that surrounded me. If he wanted a fight, then I'd come at him with all my power.

He barreled down the street, his heavy feet stomping along the way.

His body slowed when he saw me standing in the water, and he grinned sinisterly at me. "You thought I was human, didn't you, Ms. Rose?" His eyes flicked to his hand, and a twisted vine exploded from his palm as it made its way to me.

"You're an earth witch." I cursed.

He shrugged. "The Wishmaker told me to tell you, 'Hello, my Rose.'"

How had I not noticed his magic earlier? It was obvious now, but I was betting he had a shielding spell around him to keep others from sensing his magic.

"You can tell The Wishmaker to go to hell," I hissed out.

I pulled back my hand full of fire and threw a fireball at him, which he dodged easily with a side step.

"The element of surprise always works best, didn't your dead parents teach you that?"

I snarled at him. Bringing up my parents only added to my anger. Screw this guy. He was dead meat. I formed another one in my hand.

"You gonna get out of the water?" he taunted.

I glared at him. "Why don't you come on in and see for yourself?"

His eyes twinkled. "Well, I guess I'll just have to pull you out myself."

The vine sped to me and wrapped around my left wrist. The fire in my palm flared with power and burned through the vine quickly before its thorns dug into my wrist. Another vine came at me, and I took a running jump to the edge and rolled onto my shoulder, landing on the ground with a hard thud. The pain in my shoulder burned, but I somehow rolled to my feet, springing up.

Mr. Creepy ran at me. I formed a water ball and threw it at him. It hit him right in the face. He gasped for air as the water formed around his mouth. Bubbles slowly escaped as his screams became silent. My anger grew into an intense storm as I saw him shrink down. He was one of the people who wanted to harm all three of our covens, to harm my friends and those I loved. He had to pay. He had to go. I let the darkness loose that had lived in my heart for so long, and it kept repeating over and over again, seeing all the awful things The Wishmaker and his cult had done. They killed my family, my mentor who knew me better than anyone else, and then a friend. My innocent friend, who got caught up in this mess only because she knew me.

My grief screamed its revenge into the night air, cursing the stars for allowing them to put these cracks of pain into my heart. I reached into myself, accessing a darkness that lived in each of us, and I willed the water to move in and out of his mouth. It didn't take long before he realized I wouldn't stop. His eyes widened with fear and the knowledge that he would die tonight. He started to struggle more, and his face went ashen as his eyes fluttered shut.

So close, I thought, but then movement sped toward me, and Aden was at my side.

"Lexi, don't! You don't want to kill him. He's not worth it." I looked over at him and saw the concern across his face. "Baby, please stop."

I shook my head and dropped my power.

Mr. Creepy fell to the ground and gasped as he coughed up water. His relief washed over me, and then his anger swooped across his face. "You fucking cunt," he rasped out.

Aden snapped his head to him and growled. His eyes turned red, and his fangs snapped out. "What did you call her?!" He stormed over and lifted the guy by his shirt.

The guy gasped but fought by throwing punches into Aden's sides. Aden didn't seem to notice the assault, and he didn't waste a moment before slamming his mouth against his throat. I saw the fight fall from Aden's victim as he fell still.

"Aden," I said one word. It was a statement, not a command, but his back flinched.

He pulled back from the guy's neck and dropped him to the ground. As he turned around, blood fell from his mouth. In the light, he looked like a beautiful demon.

"Bash will want to talk to him. I want to talk to him and keep him alive."

He smirked. "Yes ma'am."

I looked down at my hands. They were scraped up, and I had a few cuts on my legs. I knew I would be black and blue for days, but what horrified me was that I went somewhere so dark, terrifying, and powerful, yet I loved the feeling of it. I relished the sense of the power rushing through my blood. That was dark magic. It could corrupt so easily.

Chapter Thirty-One

A den walked to an open umbrella and pulled out a curved knife to cut the rope that held it up. He strolled like a panther circling its prey back to the large man crumpled on the ground. Reaching down, he started to tie him up with one hand while his phone was in the other.

"Hey, we ran into a snag. Can you send Hudson?" Hudson? Why would Aden call Hudson to help? "No, some earth witch tried to attack Lexi. She's fine. You know our girl doesn't take shit lying down—a couple of scrapes and bruises. Bash, calm down! *Frère*, she's fine. Jesus, you don't have to... Okay, I'll see you soon."

He sighed and hung up. Once he finished tying the guy's hands, he walked over to me. "Lexi... baby, put the ball of fire away?"

I looked down at my hands. A fireball was still alight in my palm. I extinguished it and looked from Aden to the guy tied on the ground. My anger was still there, my heart pounding against my chest, but the realization that I almost killed this man hit me. Laurent was in self-defense, but this was out of revenge. Though there may be a fine line, I knew I almost crossed it.

"I almost killed him," I whispered.

Thoughts swirled through my mind. If I could kill so easily, didn't that make me just as much of a monster as The Wishmaker? I turned to Aden with wide eyes, tears pricking behind my lids.

Aden straightened his back, moving closer to me. "But you didn't, and that matters, Lexi."

I looked to the sky and sighed, my shoulders slumping, finally letting myself come down from the fight.

I turned my head toward him. "But I wanted to... I wanted to see his blood run red in the streets. What makes me different from The Wishmaker, Aden? I've killed people. I've hurt people. What makes me less of a monster than them?"

Aden placed his hands on my shoulders, forcing me to look at his face. "You killed Laurent and the guard in defense. They would have killed you without a thought. What makes you different? That's what you're asking?"

I nodded, looking up at those steel-gray eyes that always gave me comfort, those steel eyes that always knew how to calm my storm.

"This, Lexi." He placed a hand on my chest, over my heart. "Your heart, it's not black. You care, love, and live each day, as if you're grateful to be here. That's the difference."

The adrenaline left my body, and the tears I tried to hold back filled my eyes.

Aden cursed and pulled me into his chest. "You're safe. You were amazing, baby."

I heard a car pull up and stop quickly. I looked up to see Bash and Tristian jogging over to us.

"Keep me away from him, Tristian, or I'm going to rip his motherfucking heart out." He sneered down at the witch, spitting on him. "Fucking useless witch."

Bash walked over to us while Tristian easily lifted the guy and threw him in the back of the trunk with a whistle. He looked me over for any injuries. "Aden... is she?"

Aden shook his head. "Hurt physically? No. Emotionally, that's a different story."

Bash's face dropped, and he brushed my hair from my eyes. "Lexi?" I turned to him, and his face softened. "Hey, Princess."

It took me a few tries, but my voice came out in a soft, "Hi."

Tristian joined us and looked at me. "Grayson is coming with Hudson, and Agent Rengard is on his way. A few humans saw the whole fight. Tristian is going to cause a distraction so we can interrogate him. We wouldn't want to let the humans see what is going on."

I looked around the town square. "Coco's Bakery is nearby. I have a key. Bash, Cassandra... oh god, what about Ella?!" I pulled back from Aden. "Go! Go to her! What if she's hurt?"

Aden shook his head. "Ethan's with her and the girls. Everyone is safe."

Bash turned me to him. "Coco and Jason are safe too. We called when we were on our way. Princess, we promised to protect you, which extends to those you love. I'll do my damnedest to ensure they don't get hurt by The Wishmaker."

Relief rushed through my blood. "Okay. Let's go."

We got into the car and drove to Coco's Bakery. It was completely dark inside, and I dug my key out to open the door. I flipped on a few lights as we walked through the café and to the back, where the alarm sat. I pressed in my code. I always had the code since I would often help Coco in the bakery—never with the actual baking, because no one was as good as Coco was, but with setting up.

"I'll make coffee," Tristian said as he pulled out cups and ground espresso for us.

Soon, we were all sitting around a table drinking coffee and eating pastries in silence. A soft knock made our heads jerk up, and we saw Hudson and Grayson at the door. Bash stood and let them in. Their faces were sad as they greeted each other. Hudson came over and sat next to me.

"Hey."

I smiled. "Hi, Hudson."

He looked down sheepishly. "You okay?"

I sipped my coffee. "I guess, just tired of people trying to kill me."

He smirked. "Welcome to the covens."

Grayson came over and looked me over. "You hurt anywhere else?"

I shook my head. "A few cuts and scrapes."

He nodded and handed me a bottle with a glowing green potion inside. "Courtesy of your favorite voodoo priestess."

I smiled and took the bottle. "I'm supposed to drink this?"

He nodded. "It'll heal your cuts as long as you're not seriously hurt."

I opened the bottle, and it smelled like peppermint and sandalwood. I brought it to my lips and drank it down. It tasted earthy with a minty twist.

"I feel like someone just put the AC on." I shivered as my cuts began to close up. "So, you were just casually with Brigitte?" I asked with a knowing smile.

He turned on his 100-watt smile and laughed. "I don't ask you about your love life, do I?" He sat next to me. "I was. She was helping me deal with what happened." He cleared his throat, but pain still laced his words.

"Grayson, I'll help you any way I can."

"I know. Anyways, we were going over what we found when they were discovered. It was weird because, at first, I thought it was just theatrics."

I looked to Bash, who furrowed his brow and narrowed his eyes, looking like a million questions had just popped into his mind. "Grayson, what are you saying?"

He pulled his phone out and opened a picture of the boxes lined up in a straight row. Each box was tied with a giant bow and had a large black feather sticking out. "I won't show you the gory details, but this is how they came, lined up perfectly with a bow and a feather attached."

I patted his arm. "I'm sorry, Grayson."

He zoomed in on the bow and feather. "The feather. Do you know what kind of feather that is, seductress?"

I shrugged. "I mean, a black feather could be from anything—raven, grackle, or a magpie. Hell, even a crow has—"

He pointed to the photo. "A standard American crow, one that, in particular, lives on an island just beyond the horizon."

My mouth dropped open as Bash whispered harshly, "Crows Hallow."

Aden and Tristian stilled beyond silence. It was scary. I saw my Devils' minds whirling through what Grayson told us.

"He's on the island." I smiled. "Bash, he's on the island." I laughed. "The Wishmaker slipped."

Grayson's grin widened. "He did, and Brigitte gave me a gift." He pulled out a small bag.

I took it and opened it to see the contents inside.

In the bag was salt, thyme, a rune, basil, and mint with a long white candle. I knew this spell because it was one of the first that Daniels ever taught me.

"Thanks, old man." I smiled and closed my eyes, tilting my head back. "Thank you." I laid each object out. "Tristian, bring me some hot water, please."

He nodded and walked to the back.

Bash stepped closer to me. "Am I right, and this is a truth spell, Princess?"

I nodded. "Might wanna bring Mr. Creepy back in so we can question him and finally figure out how to get on the island and who The Wishmaker is."

Aden and Hudson volunteered to bring him in as I cast my circle, lighting the candle and adding the herbs into the warm water. The liquid turned a pale yellow. I poured it into a tea cup and let it cool.

Mr. Creepy walked in next to Aden, and Hudson brought a chair for him to sit in.

Aden pushed him into the chair and hissed, "Not a fucking word until she says so."

I crossed my arms and glared. "I'll give you one chance… What's your name?"

Bash huffed. "We don't need to know his name."

Grayson grunted. "For once, I agree with The Lost Boys."

Tristian bit his lip, trying not to laugh, which made me smile, but I made sure it wasn't sugary. It was full of vengeance. I let my eyes shift over into their lavender haze. "It's rude not to tell someone your name, Sebastian. I should know the name of the man who tried to kill me. He owes me that."

"You heard her." Aden smacked the back of Mr. Creepy's head.

"Fuck! Fine, crazy vampires. My name is Linden, you stupid siren slut."

Tristian threw a punch into his stomach. "Hey, that's not nice."

I pulled up a chair, swung it around, and straddled it. "We'll have to do this the hard way, I see. Hudson, please serve the tea."

Hudson stood and brought a pot of tea and cups out for us. "My pleasure. I'll keep watch outside." He walked to the door and stood in the shadows of the storefront.

I poured the tea. "As you can see, one was already filled. That's yours," I pointed out. "See, that's a special tea, but you know that, don't you, being a witch? *And* you know from the scent alone that it's a truth potion. One sip, and you're going to be spilling your entire truth out to us, but you know that, *don't* you?" I set the tea down and passed out everyone's cup but Linden's. "And I mean everything. We'll know every single dirty little secret you've ever had, so you should choose your next words carefully before I have one of my Devils force-feed you this tea." I sipped my tea. "Hmmm, jasmine, my favorite." I sat down again and gave him a small smile. "So, Lin, what's it going to be?" I let my fangs slide out as my smile grew. Lin looked like he was staring at Death itself. I sat patiently, waiting to sip my tea. "What does The Wishmaker want with us?"

He huffed out a laugh, like I should have known the answer all along. "I serve a master worthy of more than you, siren whore! We'll get what we want. We are everywhere. The Wishmaker will have his reckoning one day, by ridding our society of the lesser and weaker magics and embracing the shadows that all live within us. When that day comes, and it will, little witch, then victory will be ours!"

He was still bound by the ropes as he struggled against them, but they were so tight, they didn't budge.

"Okay. Devils?" I felt Bash at my back, and Aden and Tristian held Mr. Grumpy down.

Grayson stepped up. "I know I'm not your Devil, seductress, but…"

I inclined my head toward him. "Go for it."

Grayson picked up the teacup and moved to him.

Lin struggled and attempted to close his mouth as Bash squeezed his jaw open. He screamed and tried to buck up, but Aden's and Tristian's weights pressing him down kept him in place. He was massive in size, and it was like they were trying to hold down a bear.

Once Bash had his jaw open, Grayson didn't hesitate. He poured the liquid down his throat, slapping his hand over his mouth, and Bash closed his nose as Lin swallowed down the potion.

"Let him go. The potion will kick in soon."

They all let him go as Lin's whole body reacted to the tonic, and he slumped down in his chair.

I bent down to him so we were eye to eye. "Lin?" He grunted. "Tell me something true."

He lifted his head and glared at me as he tried to keep his mouth shut, but his words spilled out, as if it was painful to keep them locked up. "When I was five, I stole candy from the store. I cheated on my senior exam to get into college. I cheated on my wife with her best friend and her husband. I've been using dark magic for years now to gain power," he sobbed.

"Are the mermaids being held on Crows Hallow?" Grayson growled out.

Lin jerked his head back and screamed, "Ahh, you will not get me, you devil! I must not spill the secrets of the Makers. See, we are the ones who are not seen but always heard. The mermaids, they are just a tool to us. They hang from the sky. Their tears fall upon us as we collect them."

He kept talking nonsense and in circles. I decided to try a different approach. "Lin," I said softly, his eyes wild, searching mine.

"You, beautiful siren, can't save them, but you know that, don't you? The Wishmaker won't allow it."

I nodded, as if I was agreeing with him. "But I have to try. Wouldn't you?"

I let my power flow, and I took away his fear. His fear left a bitter taste on my tongue as I lowered myself closer to him.

"How do we get onto the island?" I asked in a soft voice.

He sighed as if my voice was the only thing that could comfort him. "You must take a boat to the cave and find the ruby skull to enter, but you have to send a message to the stars by the light of your hand to ask for what you seek," he breathed out as tears fell down his face.

"Who is The Wishmaker?" Bash asked.

Lin looked at him, and his face was ashen. "They are one and all. They are dark and light. They are not human or fae. We do not know their face or voice. They are everywhere and everything! The star protects them. Fear motivates them."

I looked to Bash. "It's nothing but a ramble."

He crossed his arms. "The Wishmaker must have cast a curse on the members to conceal their identity."

"We aren't asking the right questions," Tristian said.

Aden nodded. "We should think outside the box."

Grayson grunted in agreement. "Lin, who is The Wishmaker, a female?"

He shook his head violently. "I cannot say."

I sighed. "Male?"

He babbled nonsense, and tears streamed down his face. "They

are the same and neither. I know they are more than just powerful. They have the blessing of the shiny gold stars. Where the eagles fly so high in the sky, take a look in a book. It's a unicorn!"

I looked at Bash and Grayson with concern.

"We might not be able to get anything, Princess." Bash turned and pulled a gun from his back and checked it carefully.

I stood. "No, Bash! We can't kill him, and we certainly are not killing him in Coco's Bakery, for God's sake. Put the fucking gun away. We'll find a way."

He swung around to me. "Find a way!? Lexi, all I've been doing is trying to find a way to keep you safe, to keep our covens safe. He tried to kill you! The Wishmaker tried to kill you *again*. Let me protect you!"

The terror in his eyes explained it all. Losing me would break him, it would break my Devils.

"There has to be another way, Sebastian." I placed my hand on his.

"Wait. Isn't there a spell where you can see memories? It might just be a flash, but what if..." Tristian walked over toward me, and I knew where he was going with his thought.

"What if we see The Wishmaker or get more information on the kidnapped mermaids?" I smiled back.

"Exactly." He grinned.

I walked over to Lin, and he was looking between the four of us, mumbling something about pixies playing bunt the leprechauns. "Lin, as a witch, you could show me your memories. You won't be telling me the truth if you show them to me. No harm, no foul."

His gaze softened, looking defeated, but I sensed relief wash through his mind. "I'm tired. I just wanted the world to be sunshine and rainbows, but it's on fire, and I'm so angry."

I nodded. "I know. Aden, untie his hands."

Aden cut his hands free, and I reached for them. "Tristian, you know the spell?"

Tristian nodded. "Yeah, I do."

He knelt next to me, and Grayson came over to us. "Here, let me form a circle of protection first."

He sprinkled salt around me and chanted the words under his breath. He flicked a match to light a white candle. The power pushed slowly into me like a whisper across my skin.

"Repeat my words," Tristian said as he clasped my shoulder.

"Take us back from which we came to find what we seek—a time and place where the memories speak. Show us what was once lost now is found. Tell us the memories that you keep."

I repeated his words and closed my eyes, thrown into a memory of Lin's.

We were in a cave of some type. The floor was wet, and moss softened the rock that Lin knelt on. Darkness encased us, and a circle was set with four candles at the directional points—water, air, fire, and earth. Lin knelt at the circle, chanting a protection spell. Figures in white robes entered the room and began to chant the spell as well. Then one person entered with a girl in chains. I gasped because it was Nyx. Her hair was dirty, and she wore a sheath dress. Bruises bloomed across her skin, and ribs and hip bones stuck out from her thin body.

"Bring her to the center," a voice called from behind.

She struggled and screamed for help, but everyone ignored her. Two people in robes picked her up and dropped her in the middle of the circle.

"Calm yourself, my dear. We're just here for the gift you grace us with."

She snarled at the figure, her eyes changing to an aquamarine color with a slit of black for her pupil. "You can cut me, beat me, try to destroy me, but I am a Silver Pearl fae, and I will not let you take what I do not give freely!"

The person who had spoken from behind swept around the circle. They were in a black robe that looked as if it was made up of smoke with the way it moved. You couldn't see their face behind the darkened hood, but glowing yellow eyes looked back at me. *This is The Wishmaker*, I thought as I viewed them through Lin's eyes. This was the fae who had been haunting me for years.

His ethereal voice hissed, "My dear, you think you are in charge? No, no, you aren't. You will give me those tears, or I will take them from you."

She struggled against her chains, and I smiled, knowing she wouldn't ever stop fighting; my friend never gave up. I only wished I could have saved her in the end.

"If you don't want to help willingly," the voice said in a long pause, "then we can make you help. *Mon numero de sorciere*, bring in the sister. Maybe seeing her younger sister being tortured will help things move along. I have a few giants dying to see how damaged they can make her. She is so pretty, you know."

Nyx screamed, "No! I'll do it. Don't touch her! She's just a kid."

I couldn't see the smile behind The Wishmaker's hood, but I could feel it. He waved his arms, and he entered the circle as if he were floating on air. He kicked her hard, and she landed on her hands and knees. A whimper escaped her, but she didn't let her fear show. He held a small bowl under her face and brushed her hair behind her ears.

The gesture was more disturbing than comforting as he whispered, "Now, that wasn't so hard."

She glared at Lin, looked over her shoulder, and spat out, "Go to hell."

He laughed. "No, but you will, you abomination. Now, this will hurt."

The Wishmaker pulled out an onyx blade, one of the deadliest blades to the fae. A stab wouldn't just kill you. If you were lucky enough to survive, it could corrupt your soul. He sliced a thin line down her arm and moved quickly to the other side as she screamed in pain, and the tears fell from her face and landed in the bowl. She yanked her chains back, stood to make a run for it, and pushed one of the white-robed men down, their hood falling back and revealing white-blond hair I would have known from anywhere. Franklin.

I ground my teeth as pure chaos played out. People yelled and screamed to kill her. Lin went to stand when I was sucked back into the bakery with more clarity about what happened to Nyx and what The Wishmaker truly was doing to our covens.

"It's a cave of some type that they perform the ritual in. It was damp, so water freely flowed through it."

Bash helped me stand as I swayed, my magic wholly depleted.

"And The Wishmaker?" Grayson asked.

"All I saw were yellow eyes, not like your wolf's, but he is some fae. I don't know which kind, though."

I turned to Lin. "Thank you, Lin."

He smiled at me wistfully. "Did I help? Did I do something right for the first time?"

I gave him a sad smile. "Yeah, you did."

He grinned before a red dot appeared over his heart, and I screamed for everyone to move.

Iron-clad arms hauled me to their chest as they pulled me away quickly, and a shot rang out. Glass shattered, and a bullet hit Lin in the chest. He slumped forward, sliding down his chair. Blood seeped through his shirt and down to the ground. I looked to the window, and a shadow with a dark hood raced across the rooftops, jumping from one to another.

I was in such a state of shock. *He killed again. When will he stop?* But I knew that answer. Not until I was dead too.

Chapter Thirty-Two

Hudson came rushing into the bakery, gun drawn, his eyes scanning the scene before him. A dead man was slumped over in a chair, and I lay on the floor with a two-hundred-plus-pound wolf-dragon on top of me.

"Everyone okay?" Hudson asked.

"Yeah," I gasped out. "Grayson, can you get off me? I can't breathe." I tried to push him, but damn, that wolf-dragon was heavy.

"Sorry, seductress."

He pushed off the ground, and I sat up.

Bash rushed to me, cupping my face in his hands. "You good?" His voice held a severe tone, but his eyes said something different.

"I'm good."

He shook his head, pulling me to him. "I couldn't get to you fast enough." He looked over at Grayson. "Thank you, *frère*."

Grayson stiffened at the word "brother."

I smiled at him and loudly whispered, "I think he likes you."

Grayson smirked, dusting off his pants. "Can't let another coven leader die, especially one as hot as you." He winked.

"Always flirting." Hudson grunted and then turned to his leader, checking over him. "Don't get your stupid dragon ass killed. I'm not dealing with the redcaps if you die." He bumped his shoulder into Grayson, who laughed.

Aden came to me and helped me up.

"Agent Rengard and Cillian are here." Tristian said, staring out of the shattered window.

We jumped into action and quickly gathered up the potion contents. I tossed a candle to Aden, who, thanks to his vampiric speed, handed the bag over to Grayson. He placed it inside his jacket. I looked for the teapot and cups, but just as I started to panic to find them, Hudson walked from the kitchen and gave me a wink.

I brushed away a few pieces of glass when the two FBI agents came strolling in. Cillian looked like a boy awaiting an adventure, like everything in the bakery was fascinating. He picked up a few of the books Coco had laid out on the table for people to look through, flipping through them and huffing out a laugh before looking at the crime scene. He was in jeans and a sweater, with a casual smile. The things that made him dangerous were the guns holstered to his hips and the twinkle of trouble glinting in his eyes.

Agent Rengard followed behind, and his anger rolled off him in waves as he stormed in. "Ms. Rose, why am I not surprised? Of course it's you." He was red in the face, his suit downright messy with his tie askew, as if he was woken in the middle of the night. "*You*! It's always you!" He pointed to me, fuming as he walked over to me.

"Me?" My mouth dropped open in shock.

Bash stepped in front of him. "Agent Rengard, check yourself before you come in here screaming at Lexi."

Aden pulled me protectively behind his back as I peeked around him.

Rengard glared at me. "Can't stay out of trouble, can you?" He looked around, his hands on his hips, surveying the scene before him.

This man, who was supposed to be protecting, supposed to be

finding The Wishmaker, was now blaming me for everything when he wasn't even close to solving the murder of Daniels, not to mention my parents' deaths. Okay, that was it. Now I was pissed—the damn audacity of this man.

I shook Aden's hands off and walked next to Bash. "Me?! You! Tell me one thing, Agent Rengard," I spat his name out like a curse. "Tell me, have you found Nyx's killer? Daniels's? How about the last five victims The Wishmaker has sent us? Here is the million-dollar question, what about the murder of my parents? Huh? Tell me, how fucking close are you to finding out who this serial killer is?" I turned to Cillian. "Shall I explain what happened, or are you here to arrest me now?" I raised my voice to ensure Rengard didn't miss a single word. "Or can I tell you how I was chased and almost killed *again*?!"

Cillian covered his mouth with his hand, casually pulled a chair out, and sat down, his leg crossed over a knee. "No, love, explain away." He gestured for me to sit across from him.

"At least one of you has some goddamn brains," I muttered as I sat down.

Cillian looked at me with amusement. "I like you, Lexi. That fire in you is what the covens finally need. Before we start, can I get tea and maybe one of Coco's pastries?" he said in an amused voice.

I couldn't help but give him a small smile. "Sure. Wait, first, Trist?"

I searched for him, and he came out the side door. "Yes, Lil' Star?"

I smirked at the nickname. "Can you call Coco and let her know what happened tonight?"

Tristian laughed as he pulled out his phone. "She'll be so mad that she missed the fun."

I looked at him with a question. "Fun?"

He shrugged. "Yeah, Coco's badass."

I shook my head, trying to imagine Coco doing anything but baking in a cute pink apron, but I knew she was one of the most talented witches in our coven. I just never imagined her other than the Coco I knew.

Hudson came out from the kitchen. "Tea's up." He set down a fresh pot of tea and cups with a little stand of crumpets. "It's passion fruit; I thought it would balance well with the lemon zest in the crumpets."

Agent Rengard looked between everyone, as if he had just walked into a mental hospital. "What the hell is wrong with all of you?"

We all stopped, and Grayson muttered "so many things" from behind me. I had to sip my tea to keep from laughing.

He huffed, picked up the tea and crumpets, and walked to the kitchen. "Do you not see that this is a fucking crime scene? If you're going to question her, Agent, go to the damn kitchen!" he yelled back at us.

Aden leaned against the wall with a bored expression, his eyes closed. "He does have a point, even if he isn't the brightest crayon in the box." Opening one eye, he looked at him as Rengard stopped and glared at him.

Then Rengard stomped to the back like a child getting their favorite toy taken away.

"Someone's grumpy," I whispered to Cillian.

"Yeah, he's not getting much sleep and hasn't been to the office in a while. I think he's drinking. It happens sometimes."

We followed him to the back, and I sat on the stainless island in the middle of the bright white kitchen.

Cillian poured a cup of tea and took a sip. "Damn, she's outstanding, isn't she?"

I smiled at the mention of Coco. She was the best of the best for a reason. "Grows the leaves herself, or I guess Daniels did…" I tried not to think about how much I missed that old bastard.

My heart tugged in pain, thinking about how he wasn't here anymore and what I would give to have him back. To have them all back. My grief flooded my heart, and my cracks broke a little more.

Taking a bite out of a crumpet, Cillian wiped his mouth and looked at me. "Ms. Rose, please explain to us what happened tonight."

I sipped my tea and looked over to Rengard. He was staring at me with such intensity. His anger radiated off him and hit me like a fiery blast. It was almost choking how much anger he had in him.

I sighed, looking over at him. "Agent Rengard, have a cup of tea, please, I can feel your anger, and it's making it hard to focus."

He closed his eyes, took a deep breath, and pulled a stool out to sit down. Hudson poured him a cup of tea, plated a small cookie, and slid it his way.

"Are you here to represent her? If you were a witness, you can't," Rengard huffed out to Hudson.

Hudson raised his hand. "I know the law, Agent." He smiled, and a wicked spark crossed his face. "I heard the shot while I was out for a stroll and came running to discover what happened when I saw my coven leader on the ground. I came in to see if he was okay. As I'm his second, it's my duty to protect him."

Cillian saw through the bullshit, but Rengard glared at him and then looked at me. "Start from the beginning, Ms. Rose. Don't leave anything out."

I let the story unfold, leaving out the office sex, me almost killing Lin, and the potion we served to get the truth about The Wishmaker. Cillian looked at me with uncertainty as if he detected my bullshit.

"The salt circle around the victim?" Cillian asked.

"We needed to ensure he was secure and wouldn't try to kill me again." I took a bite of the cookie casually.

An hour passed as the rest of the units came and started to clean up the scene, taking pictures and evidence into consideration. I hoped we got everything, and as fast as my Devils were, I was sure this wasn't their first crime scene.

"Aden tied him up as we waited for you to come. I asked him why he wanted me dead, and then I saw the red dot. Next thing I knew, I was being pulled away, and he was dead."

Jason and Coco came through the back door just as I finished the story. She rushed to me and threw her arms around me, asking if I was okay, her eyes full of tears.

"I'm fine, Coco."

She sniffled as Jason wrapped an arm around her.

"She's okay, Coco." He looked at me. "Are you hurt?"

I shook my head. "I was healed." I left it simple. I didn't need to explain that the Voodoo Priestess of New Orleans was a friend and ally to the covens.

Coco held onto my hand, and she glared at Rengard. "Where was her protection? She would have been dead if it wasn't for the coven leaders and their men. Is that what you want, Rengard, my entire family dead?!"

Jason soothed her, hugging her closer to him. "She has a point, Cillian." He looked over to the young agent.

"She does." He stood, brushing his hands together. "I'll be in contact if I have any more questions, but Ms. Rose." Rengard huffed. "This is strike two. I don't want to see you in a situation like this again. Are we clear?"

"That's the understatement of the year. I don't want to be in life-and-death situations on a daily, Rengard. Ever think of that?"

He grunted in agreement and signaled for the rest of them to follow.

Before Cillian exited through the doors, he stopped, looking over at Tristian. "Cassium... a word, please." He pointed to the outside.

Tristian, leaning against the wall with the rest of my Devils, moved silently, walking with Cillian outside.

Coco sighed, looking at the damage.

I stood, turning to Coco. "Coco, I'll pay for everything."

She waved her hand. "I'm glad you're okay, but I want the truth. Tomorrow, you and your Devils come and tell us everything. Agreed?"

I frowned. "You want to know everything?"

She gave me a small smile. "Not all the gory details, but, yeah, Lexi, I need to know everything." She looked over at me, and a sly smile formed around her lips. "You're getting stronger in magic, aren't you?"

I couldn't help but smile back. "Seems like it might run in the family or something."

She grinned. "It sure does." She kissed my temple. "Get home, my dear."

I walked to Grayson and Hudson. "Thank you for everything." I hugged them both.

"We'll speak soon," he said, and they left.

I walked to Aden, who was in his mind, and Bash looked pissed off.

"Let's get Trist and go home. I want to be with my Devils tonight."

Bash laughed as he pushed off the wall. "Let's go home, Princess, for tomorrow, we face the true devil."

I raised an eyebrow.

"My father."

Chapter Thirty-Three

In the morning, we all stayed in bed drinking coffee and lazing around like a bunch of cats. Dyna was thrilled and would take turns jumping from one of us to another.

I stretched and looked over at the clock. "Coco is expecting us. We should get going."

Groans came from all three of my Devils.

"Just a little longer, Lil' Star." Tristian pulled me to his chest, and a laugh escaped.

"No way, Coco will be pissed if we don't show up, and I'm not dealing with the wrath of that redhead."

Aden laughed. "Remember the time when Jason spilled red wine over her vintage apron? I don't think I have ever seen someone throw a pastry so fast."

I smiled. "Jason had a bruise on his head for a week. Those rolls were deadly!"

My phone buzzed, and I smiled as I answered it. "Hey, Coco, we were just about to get ready."

I heard an oven ding in the background. "Perfect, you good with a Southern classic, biscuits and gravy?"

I sat up straighter. "With flour gravy?"

I could almost hear her smile. "Only way to make it. Don't offend me."

I laughed. "Perfect, we'll be there in forty-five minutes."

"Good, see you soon." She paused for a second. "And Lexi?"

I moved to the edge of the bed. "Yeah?"

She cleared her throat. "Never mind, we'll talk when you're here. Bye, darling."

"See you soon, Coco." I hung up and looked down at my phone, feeling a strange, anxious pit growing in my stomach.

"Hey, Princess?"

I turned to Bash, shaking my head. "Hey," I said softly.

"We lost you there for a second. Everything okay?"

I shook my head. "Yeah, just have a feeling that Coco wants to talk to me about something."

Bash kissed my temple. "Whatever it is, we'll handle it together."

I gave him a small smile. "Okay."

I quickly changed into leggings and an oversized sweatshirt shirt that said "Cadogan House" and braided my long hair.

I walked into the living room and picked up Dyna, snuggling her sweet face against mine. "Missy prissy, you be good, okay?"

She gave me a tiny meow and rubbed her face against me.

"I fed her earlier." Aden hopped over the couch, landing softly next to me.

Dyna jumped down and strolled over to the kitchen, leaving us alone.

"Do I need to put a bell on you? You are so damn quiet." I smirked.

"Seen but never heard. Besides, I like to people-watch." His smile turned dirty. "As you remember."

I bit my lip, remembering how he watched Tristian and me. A blush rose to my cheeks. "You aren't the only Devil who likes to watch."

He leaned closer. His breath skated across my cheek, and he whispered in my ear, "Oh, yeah... Did you stare into Tristian's eyes as you came?"

I swallowed deeply, and my voice came out husky. "Bash watched us in the library."

Aden's fingers trailed up my thighs. "Did you like that, baby? While both of us were on our knees worshiping you? Did you like how he stood over you and commanded you to come on my tongue and Tristian's fingers?"

I arched into him and met his steel-colored eyes with my blues. "I relished in it."

He groaned, his head against mine. "Baby."

A throat cleared, and we both jumped back as Bash and Tristian stood, arms crossed over their chests.

Tristian had a smile, and Bash arched his eyebrow.

"Please tell me we get to have group sex. Please tell me we get group sex!" Tristian's eyes lit up with excitement.

I laughed and pushed Aden back. "Food first, group sex later!"

I was not going to feel ashamed by them or the fact that each of them turned me on more than I knew.

"She didn't say no!" Tristian yelled as I opened the door and walked to the car.

"Last one to the car has to drive!" I took off in a head start and made it to the car just in time, as they all used their vampiric speed to meet me.

"I guess Tristian has to drive," Aden said as he threw him the keys.

"Let's go, driver, chop, chop!" I slid into the back, waiting for Aden, but Bash slid next to me and put his arm around me.

"Princess."

I looked up at him through my lashes. "Yes?"

He smiled and pulled me closer. Tristian pouted as we drove to Coco's but cheered up when I told him she was probably fixing a feast for us.

We walked through the front doors, and the smell of bacon filled the morning air.

"Mmmm, bacon." I sighed as my stomach growled.

Coco came in laughing. "Are they not feeding you?" She glowered at all three of them.

"They are. I didn't get to eat anything yet."

She wrapped me in a hug. "Come on, let's feed you, and then we can talk about everything."

I groaned. "Do I at least get a mimosa?"

She laughed. "Jason is already prepping them."

Jason smiled and walked over to me with a mimosa in hand.

"Thank you, sir."

He playfully bowed. "Whatever the Silver Pearl leader wants, the Silver Pearl leader gets."

I rolled my eyes.

He walked away but turned around quickly. "Actually... Lexi, can we talk in private?"

I tilted my head in question and walked over to him. "Uhh, sure."

He looked between me and Coco and nodded. "Great, let's go."

I told the guys I'd be back, and we headed up the stairs to my father's office, which I guess was now Jason and Coco's. They hadn't changed much about the house, and the scent of old books hit my nose when we entered the room. It brought back memories of sitting in here with my father, reading by the fire and talking about anything and everything. The memories stung, and my heart ached.

"There are so many things I wish I could have said to him," I said, running my fingers over the books. "I want to yell at him for not telling me anything. I want to be mad at him. I want to cry in his arms and beg him not to leave me. I want him to tell me it's going to be okay." I sniffed. "Childish dreams." I shook my head. "Sorry."

Jason gave me a small smile. "You know your father was a courageous man, kind and smart, but that doesn't mean he was perfect, Lexi. I think we sometimes put our parents on this pedestal, but they're just like you and me. We all have flaws, and we all make mistakes. His and your mother's mistake just cost them their lives."

I wiped a tear and shook my head. "What did you want to talk about?"

He cleared his throat and looked nervous. "Well, since you are Coco's only family, I just... damn it, let me just show you."

He walked to the desk, opened a drawer, and pulled out a red box. My eyes widened as Jason opened it up. The most beautiful ring with starburst clusters of diamonds, rubies, and sapphires sat on a black cushion.

"Jason..."

He rubbed the back of his neck. "I figured she could finally make me an honest man."

I laughed and ran to him, hugging him. "You're gonna propose to Coco!" I sang out.

"Shhh, yeah, in a few days. I have a plan. Wanna help me set it up?" His eyes twinkled with excitement.

"Of course! What do you need?"

He jumped in, talking about what he wanted to do, and we started planning everything.

A quiet knock came from the door, and Tristian came in. "Breakfast is ready. Everything good?"

I nodded in excitement and ran to him. "I'll tell you later when we don't have wandering ears around us." I quickly kissed his lips and took the stairs two at a time.

I reached the kitchen, schooling my emotions as Ethan and Ella walked in. Ella looked worse for wear, and Ethan whistled in his happy, not-a-care-in-the-world way.

"Ells, you a little hungover?"

She moaned and laid her head on the counter. "Can you heal me?"

I shook my head. "I'm drained, but I can fix Coco's famous hangover smoothie."

She groaned. "Fine."

Ethan came over to me.

"Did she have fun?"

He nodded. "Yeah, she did."

I smiled. "Good."

I filled the blender with coconut water, ginger, kefir, and orange juice. I hit blend, and Ella covered her ears.

"No, no, no," she mumbled.

I poured the concoction into a glass and handed it to her. "Drink up, babes."

While Ella nursed her hangover, I met Coco in the dining room, where she was setting the table up. "Need help?"

She smiled at me. "Sure."

I gathered the plates and laid them out. "Last night was…"

Coco tilted her head. "Nuts? Crazy? Intense? Pick an adjective, Lexi. They all fit."

I flicked a piece of dust off the table. "Scary?" I looked over at her, and her smile fell.

"Yeah, scary, but you handled yourself?"

I nodded. "I did, but, Coco, I felt this darkness, this blackened hardness that crept in and buried so deep that I don't know if I'll be able to stop it."

She walked over to me and grabbed my shoulders. "Lexi Rose, we all have a darkness that lives in us. What we do in those minutes makes us who we are. You can see the darkness, but do not live in it."

I fiddled with the silverware. "What if I liked it, though? I liked that utter depth of unknown and power. It was exhilarating, the rush I got knowing I held this witch's life in my hands for a moment and the fact I knew that I could end it. It didn't feel right, but I was so angry, Coco. I'm so angry."

She wrapped me in a hug. "You have every fucking right to be angry, Lexi," she choked out. "Every fucking right."

I bit my cheek so hard to avoid the tears that the taste of blood filled my mouth. I cleared my throat. "Extra place setting?"

She sighed. "Anderson called. He's joining us. He wants to know."

I sighed. "He wanted to know what we found."

She gave me a sad smile. "Yeah. He needs to know."

I placed the napkins down slowly. "He does, but I'm still unsure what his endgame is."

Coco smirked. "No one does, Lexi. Those men who sit up in their tower looking down on us nobodies? We will never know what they want unless Anderson is willing to tell us."

She shared a look with me that said "be careful." A ding from the kitchen broke us apart as we gathered the food and everyone to sit. As if he was called, Anderson walked in and talked to Bash and Ethan.

We all took our seats and broke bread, laughing and smiling. It wasn't until afterward, when we were sitting outside, that Anderson approached me. "Ms. Rose."

I looked up at him from my chair. "Anderson, I think you can call me Lexi if you want me to call you Kane."

He laughed and sat next to me, looking over at my Devils. "They're something, aren't they? Feared by so many, but not you."

I shrugged. "I think when you grow up with them, you don't fear them, but I did once. They nearly destroyed me."

He sat straighter in his seat. "Be careful, Lexi, playing with fire like that. You'll get burned."

I laughed. "That's where you're wrong, Kane. I'm their fire, and they wield it. You came here for a reason. What information are you searching for?"

He cleared his throat. "To the point?"

I looked over at him. "To the point, Kane."

"The Wishmaker? Did you find anything?"

I looked over him, not knowing if I could trust him. So far, Kane had never steered us wrong, but I was still wary of him. "We think we found the place where the last key is and possibly the kidnapped mermaids. As for who The Wishmaker is? Your guess is as good as ours. The only person who was able to show me anything was killed."

He sighed. "I don't want to push you, but—"

I tensed up. "I know it's a matter of life-and-death." I stood. "If that's all, I want to enjoy the rest of my afternoon before succumbing to the bullshit of Morgan Ryder."

He laughed at me. "We all have to play a part tonight, Lexi, and yours is to be the dutiful leader of the Silver Pearl Coven. I'll see you tonight." He nodded to me as he left.

Oh god, how was tonight going to go? Were we walking into our bloodbath, or was this just a chess game of power? Only one way to find out.

Chapter Thirty-Four

As the afternoon wore on, the mimosas kept flowing. Wanting to forget about all the drama and The Wishmaker, I danced. Coco, Ella, and I danced to the best music from different '90s boy bands. I was singing loudly to "Bye Bye Bye" when a pair of hands gripped my waist and threw me over a couple of shoulders.

"Heeeeeeyyyyyy! I was just gettin' started. This is soooooooo rude!"

Someone chuckled. "Sorry, Lil' Star, Bashy boy said to get you so we can sober up."

I huffed as I bounced on Tristian's shoulder. His butt was in my direct eyesight. His perfectly shaped butt.

"Tristian, you have the best butt. It's like two moons. Boom, boom, boom."

Someone came up to us, and I tried to look, but the world spun. "Oh nooooooo."

A pair of hands cupped my cheeks. They were calm and soothing as a pair of gray eyes came into view.

"So pretty," I said as I looked into those eyes.

A masculine laugh escaped. "You too, baby, you too. Are you going to be sick?"

I shook my head. "No, but I would like to get down."

Aden smirked. "Fair."

I was placed on my feet as I steadied myself. "That was fast. Where is Sebastian Ryder?"

Aden raised a brow. "Umm there." He pointed to the car where Bash was trying to cover a smile.

"Seb... Bash... ain! Ry... der!" I walked up to him, leaning back to look at him. "You're tall... why are you so tall?"

He tried not to laugh at me, and he kissed my cheek. "Let's go, Princess. I promise you can use me as a pillow."

I gave him a dreamy smile. "A nap sounds good."

"Might do you good." He smirked at me.

I laughed. "I do what I want, Ryder." I hiccuped. "Oh, no!" I whispered to him. "That's bad."

He opened the door and helped me into the car. "Let's get you home, Princess. We can't show up drunk to my father's tonight."

I sighed. "I needed this."

Aden looked at me from the driver's side. "You did, Lex, you did."

I smiled, Bash slid in, and I laid on his chest.

"Thank you," I whispered.

"For what?" he asked.

"Everything."

I closed my eyes for a second, and then someone called my name.

"Lexi, Princess, we're home."

I opened an eye and groaned as the headache crept in. "Home sweet home. I want a shower." I sighed.

Tristian was opening my door and helping me out as he murmured, "It's like teaching Bambi how to walk."

He picked me up and carried me into the house, where Dyna greeted us with protest meows. Aden picked her up and soothed her as he petted her white floof.

"Lexi, do you want to sleep or shower first?" he asked.

"Shower." I pointed to the room.

We walked in, and Bash started the shower.

"I can stand, Trist."

He set me down gently, and I pulled my clothes off and took my hair out of its braid. As soon as I stepped into the shower, I groaned when the hot water hit my skin. Tristian came in behind me and wrapped his arms around my waist.

"Tristian... I'm not really in a sexy mood."

He laughed. "I know, but I can heal your hangover."

I turned to him, sobering up, because if he had his magic, that meant he must have filled up. "You drank from someone?"

He pushed my hair back. "I did, but don't worry. It isn't like you think it is." I nodded, feeling hurt but knowing I shouldn't, because a vampire had to feed. "Coco had someone bring us bags. Not the best way to feed, but they were fresh. We have to be strong for tonight. We don't know what Morgan has planned." His copper eyes hardened, and I saw the beast within him.

He pushed his magic into me, and the alcohol's effects faded. My head still hurt, but nothing a few pills couldn't cure. Once we were done showering, Tristian dressed as Aden read a book on the bed.

I sat in a towel, and Bash brought in a sandwich. "Food. Eat."

He looked yummy in his dark jeans and tight shirt. I gripped his shirt and pulled him down, kissing him softly.

"Thank you, and I will. But I really should repay you for your kindness."

He smirked. "Oh yeah, Princess, and, pray tell, what will you do?"

I pushed him back as I stood and dropped my towel. "I can think of a few ways to make it up to you three."

They all turned to me, and I bit my lip, looking up through my lashes.

"Lil' Star, are you serious?" Tristian's voice was rough as he stood frozen.

I blushed. "I want all three of you."

I walked to Bash, his eyes holding an intense stare. I moved closer, but his hands stopped me at my hips.

"We've never shared before." He looked to Tristian and Aden as if they were having a silent conversation.

Aden ran his thumb over his lip. "We haven't, not all three of us, but, *frère*, I don't think that matters all that much to you. You need to be sure, Lexi. Because if we break this, we won't go back."

I looked to Aden, held my hand out to him, and then did the same with Tristian, pulling them both to us. I looked at Bash. "I want us to be together. Together, we're stronger."

That was all the answer Bash needed as he captured my mouth with his own. His shoulders bumped into Tristian's and Aden's, and I put each hand on a chest. My heart was beating frantically as I was pulled away, and Aden's lips found mine. Tristian's hands moved slowly down my body, tracing each curve until he gripped my hips, drawing me back into him.

I felt every inch of him against me, and I moaned. I pulled away and tilted my head to Tristian as he came down and kissed me.

"Why am I the only one naked?"

Tristian laughed. "I can fix that, Lil' Star." He whipped his shirt off.

I reached for Aden and pulled his shirt off while Bash followed suit. I returned to Bash and kissed him again. I felt like I couldn't move fast enough as I pulled at his belt and unbuttoned his jeans, reaching through to finally grip him through his boxers.

He groaned. "Fuck, Princess, your damn hands feel like heaven."

I licked my lip, kissing his neck. "I would rather you take me to hell than heaven, Sebastian. Hell is more fun," I whispered against his cheeks.

I got three masculine laughs from them as they came in closer, damn vampiric hearing. Tristian pulled me to the bed. His fingers traced my nipples, and I arched up as he took one of my breasts into his mouth.

Aden came to my side and whispered, "Are you ready, baby?"

I moaned as I felt myself grow wetter with each kiss.

As if he could read my mind, he looked to Bash. "How wet is she, *frère*?"

Bash spread my legs and slid his fingers to my heat. "So fucking soaked. You're ready for us, aren't you, Princess?"

I nodded as Bash pushed a finger inside me. I moaned his name as Tristian continued to drive me to the edge, taking his time and exploring every part of my body he could reach.

Aden smiled. "That's my girl. Look at you taking it so well, baby."

"Aden, I need you." I writhed my body, wanting to feel all of them.

He smirked. "I'm here." He kissed my neck and moved slowly down my body, tingles spreading in his wake.

Bash moved to the side for Aden, his fingers still pumping in and out of me. "No going back, Princess," he said as Aden's lips found my clit, and I screamed for each of them.

Tristian swallowed my screams as Aden and Bash drew out my pleasure with their fingers and tongue. The pressure built up, starting low, and I exploded, the high of my orgasm hitting me so hard, I saw stars.

I smiled at Tristian. "My turn." I sat up and pushed him back. I hovered over him as I kissed down his perfect tan body, making sure I didn't miss a single spot. When I reached his cock, I gently took his tip into my mouth. A hand caressed my back, and I looked over my shoulder to see Bash licking his lips, I moved to my knees farther back and arched my back to give him better access.

Tristian gently wrapped his hands in my hair as I slowly moved down his length, taking him all the way into my mouth.

"For the love of the moon, you do that so damn well, Lil' Star."

I felt Bash ease his way into me, but I didn't want soft, I needed him now. I pushed back and sank into him as he cursed me and began to move his hips into me. Tristian began to move steadily as I took him to the back of my throat. Aden was by my side, and his fingers found my clit again. I gasped, feeling as if my nerves were on fire.

"I could worship you like this forever, baby. The look on your face. Fuck, Lexi, I love you," Aden breathed out as I closed my eyes, feeling each of my Devils.

Bash pounded into me relentlessly, filling me up as Aden worked my clit. The sensations were almost too much.

"Fuck! Fuck! Fuck!" Tristian moaned as he pushed me down completely, hitting the back of my throat. Then his orgasm filled my mouth, and I swallowed it down.

He held me there for a moment before pulling out, and then Bash lifted me, holding me against him.

Aden moved in front of me, kissing my lips suddenly while continuing to stroke me with his fingers.

"Aden."

Bash groaned, and Aden pulled back with a laugh. "Are you ready, baby?"

I moaned, needing both of them. "I want to feel you both."

He kissed me again as Bash pulled out of me, and I groaned. I missed the feeling of him inside me. I reached back for Bash again, only getting a laugh from him.

Aden wrapped his hand into my hair. "Baby, behave."

I looked into his steel eyes, and he sank into me in one swift motion. "Fuck!"

He gave me a dark chuckle as he moved steadily in and out of me. Bash was at my back, spreading my ass apart.

I knew what he wanted, and a breathless groan escaped. "Yessss."

He sank a finger inside my tight hole, moving slowly in and out. As I loosened for him, he added another finger. Aden began to fuck me harder, and Tristian had one hand on my nipples and the other skating to my clit.

"That's it, Lil' Star, let him in."

I was so close to the edge; I felt myself building up from the high of the last orgasm.

I groaned as Bash's dick slid over my ass. I couldn't help but

moan as each of my Devils sent me into ecstasy. Aden slowed as Bash pushed in, and the feeling of both of them had me whimpering.

Tristian continued to circle my clit and pull my nipples gently. "Good girl, look at you taking him so well."

When Bash was entirely inside me, he and Aden began to move with each other, their pace and rhythm in sync.

"Can you handle Tristian too, baby?" Aden moaned into my ear.

I nodded and smiled as he moved faster, and I fell into orgasm after orgasm as he cursed and called out my name as he came inside me. He slowly pulled out, and as soon as he was done, Bash began to pump faster into me, and I could feel he was close. Tristian moved to where Aden was underneath me and slid me onto his dick. I moaned as he slowly pushed up into me while Bash pushed me down. They moved in tandem, so I constantly felt one of them. I was already getting closer again. I gasped out as Tristian smirked and pounded harder into me, Bash matching his pace. Aden pulled my face to him and kissed me hard, biting and nibbling my lips. I was breathless as he pulled away, only to move farther up me.

"Take all of us at once, Lexi. Let us show you what pleasure we can bring to you."

I opened my mouth and sucked at his tip, tasting our arousal.

He threw his head back and cupped my cheek. "Just perfection," he purred out as he pushed farther until he hit the back of my throat.

I couldn't really move, so he started to fuck my face with slow motions. My throat contracted as I tried to swallow him down, which only caused all of them to groan.

"So fucking tight, Lil' Star," Tristian panted.

"Fuck, Princess, Lexi!" Bash's cock thickened as he pounded deep inside me.

Tristian took his cue from Bash and fervently upped his speed, hitting me right in the perfect spot.

Aden grasped my head as he slammed into me, moving me with him. "*Baise-Moi jusqu'aux etoiles*," he gasped.

He spilled down my throat and fell to my side, taking my hand in his and bringing it up to kiss across my knuckles.

"Princess," Bash growled, "you took both of their cocks so well."

I moaned as he lifted me back against him and squeezed my throat, slightly cutting off my scream. He slammed into me as he possessed each and every part of my body and soul. This was how Sebastian Ryder loved, as if it was a burning fire, hot and intense. This was us—we were the fire. It was dizzying, and I loved every minute of it. He reached down and found my clit, circling it a few times while he sank deeper inside me. A shot of pleasure raced through me as I fell over and over again. Bash tightened his arms around me and stilled as he came with me.

He pulled out and rolled to the side as Tristian smiled dangerously.

"To the stars, *frère*."

He slammed me into him, dragging my orgasm out as he fucked me hard. Waves of pleasure incessantly crashed through me. He nipped at my neck and sucked hard as he came deep within me, falling back against the bed and pulling me to his chest. He held me there momentarily, both of us trying to catch our breaths.

"We are definitely doing that again," he panted.

We laughed, and I rolled off, sandwiched between Aden and him.

Aden wrapped an arm around me, pulling me against him. "At least two more times."

I laughed again and lifted a hand to smack him playfully, but it just fell. I reached for Bash, and his fingers found me. I opened my eyes to see his green ones. They held something I had never seen before. True happiness. In that moment, I knew this: this was his family, and I knew I would do anything to protect it from anyone.

Chapter Thirty-Five

The following day, I woke with an ungodly amount of soreness from the night before. Like my Devils promised me, I remembered the way their hands felt on me, their kisses, and all the dirty things we did in between.

I climbed out of bed as the three of them slumbered. I grabbed a shirt and pulled it over my head before finding a pair of leggings. After fixing myself a cup of coffee, I went outside and down to the beach. I walked to the spot I had shared with my mother, letting the water wash over my feet. Once I found the perfect place, I sat on the cold sand, watching the sun rise above the horizon.

Crows Hallow was sitting in the distance, and the island's silhouette taunted me. Ella's wedding was next week. I just prayed that The Wishmaker didn't do anything drastic to the mermaids.

My stomach twisted, and I wished that my parents or Daniels were here to guide me. I knew I was growing into my role as the leader of Silver Pearl, but it would be a lie if I said I didn't doubt myself still. I held my hand over the sand, using air magic to move it slowly in a small whirlwind of sand and shells. I concentrated on slowing the movement. I lifted my other hand to add tiny ocean water droplets to the center.

My tears fell into the tiny tornado as the stress of our world sat on my shoulders. "How did you do this, Mom, Dad… Daniels? How did you deal with all of this? Goddess, I miss you three so damn much," I said to the ocean, as if they were able to hear me.

As I dropped my hands, the sand, shells, and tears fell into a neat mound beside me. I knew what they would say. Daniels would say, "Suck it up, kid, and figure it out." My mother would have held me and told me, "Do what your heart and mind say to do. You can't go wrong trusting your heart and mind." My father would have smiled sadly at me and told me, "We are the witches of the Silver Pearl. It is our duty and gift to protect what is ours, and that's what we would do."

The brush moved behind me, and I leaped to my feet, a ball of fire in my hand.

Tristian walked out with his hands held up. "Don't fire, Lil' Star."

I extinguished the flame quickly. "You might not want to sneak up on a witch who's already on edge."

He walked to me and laughed. "Well, I called your name, but you were in your world."

I sat back down, pulling him with me. He wrapped an arm around me and drew me closer. His skin was warm, and I laid my head on his shoulder.

"Do you want to talk about what's on your mind?"

I snorted. "You want me to list out everything that's wrong?"

His grip tightened. "I don't like to see you in pain. It hurts." He rubbed his chest in a small circle, as if it would eliminate the pain.

I looked into his eyes, and the copper swirled with his pain. "Tristian? Are you an empath?"

He shrugged. "I don't know if I would call it that, but I can feel pain,

happiness, passion, and fear in others. It's like a fog around them, but with you, the closer we've gotten, the more I feel your emotions."

I looked at him with wonder. "An empathic vampire, that's rare. Can you shut it off?"

He took a deep breath and blew it out before turning to look out at the ocean. "I did for ten years."

I swallowed a gasp. "Trist…"

He shook his head. "I don't want to talk about the pain and agony I have locked away, and I won't let it out again. I will tell you this: I went on a spree. Whenever Morgan gave us an assignment, I relished in the hunt and the kill. The blood that coats my soul will never come out." His hand gripped mine, and he brought it up to lay a kiss on the back of it. "It wasn't until our friend pulled me aside one day and told me to get my shit together and suck it up. 'Life sucks, kid, and sometimes, you fuck up. Life is made for you to fuck up, but don't stop living because you can't deal with it.'"

I laughed as fresh tears fell. "Let me guess, Daniels?"

He nodded. "Yeah, the old man was wise, and I miss him too. You know he never stopped talking about you? I liked that I got a sneak peek into your life even though you hated us."

"I did hate you three for years. I blamed you for everything, but I now know that my revenge shouldn't have been directed at you but at The Wishmaker. Though you three still have some payback coming. Don't think I'll let you off so easily."

He smirked. "Bring it on, Lil' Star. I'll take your punishment any day of the week."

I laughed. "What should I do to you then, Tristian?"

He smirked. "Torture is always a good source of retribution, but you already did that for ten years." He kissed my forehead. "Whatever you decide, it'll be worth it as long as you're still mine at the end of the day."

I smiled and moved closer to him. "Did Bash send you out here?"

He pulled back. "No, but we should go back, big day and all."

I groaned. "The dinner. Do we have to go?" I whined.

He laughed. "Unfortunately, I don't think we can get out of this, being that it is a dinner for the leaders of the covens and the future of fae." He stood, pulling me to my feet.

"Fine, but I want a burger and milkshake afterward. You know Morgan's only going to serve fancy food that tastes awful."

Tristian laughed as we walked back.

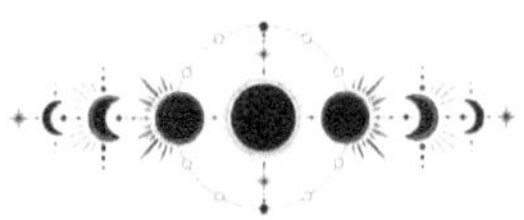

The evening came faster than I cared. I slid on a long-sleeved black dress with a cutout that reached just above my butt, and my hair fell in a straight cascade down my back. I finished my eyeliner, making it so sharp it could kill a man, slid my feet into silver shoes, and clasped the ankle strap. I stood and looked in the mirror. I didn't look like myself. I looked fierce and like a coven leader should.

I strolled into the living room, and all three of my Devils, in dark suits, turned and stopped. Tristian's mouth dropped open, and Aden smiled as he bit his lip. Bash's eyes were ablaze, and his fangs slid out.

"You look like a murderous dream, Princess." His voice was low, sexy, and dangerous. His words sent a shiver through me.

"Baby..."

I held up a hand, looking at Aden. "You are not destroying this dress; we don't have time."

Aden laughed. "I wasn't going to say that, Lexi, but if we did have time..." He shook his head. "You look unbelievable, baby. A true leader of Silver Pearl." He walked to me and kissed the crook of my neck. "Later, that dress will be on the floor, and I'll be between your legs."

I bit my lip and moved away, putting space between us and

walking to Tristian.

"You, behave," I said pointedly.

He grabbed his chest. "Man, I had a dirty joke and everything."

I laughed and nudged him. "Save it for later. I have a feeling we'll all need it after tonight."

We arrived quickly at the Ryder Estate. The iron gates closed behind us, and I had a pit in my stomach that tonight would not end well. I slid my onyx blade into its thigh holster, feeling more secure having it at my side. The estate was fully decked out with valet drivers to take the car. We walked up the estate's towering steps into Bash's childhood home.

Tristian shook his head. "Dude, I still can't believe you grew up here. It's like a museum."

Bash laughed. "As a child, it was amazing, like a new adventure every day, but as a teenager and adult, it's stifling, like it'll bury you alive with all the dark secrets that live between the walls."

I put my arm through his. "We're here now."

He looked down at me and ran a finger across my cheek. "That you are, Princess. Are you going to fight my demons away tonight?"

I smiled at him. "I got a blade and everything to destroy whatever or whoever tries to touch what is mine."

The door opened, and a butler who looked to be one hundred ushered us through until we were in the backyard, where a dozen white outdoor couches were placed. People were milling about chatting with drinks in hand. Some of the faces I knew from my coven and friends of my parents. Hudson, Grayson, and Brigitte sat on a couch, talking. Morgan and a group of men were laughing as they smoked cigars.

Franklin stood to the side, his eyes on me and a sneer on his lips. I glared back when Bash placed my arm in his. Aden moved to my other side as Tristian stood at my back.

"What are you doing?" I whispered to Bash as the butler cleared his throat and lifted a finger just below his chin.

Magic spilled from his finger as his voice amplified throughout the estate. "Master Sebastian Ryder, Ms. Lexi Rose, the Silver Pearl Coven's leader, and her consorts, Mr. Tristian Cassium and Mr. Aden Charmante."

I suppressed a groan as we descended the steps into the crowd. Morgan walked to us, his face set in a pleasant smile, but I knew he was anything but.

"Son, Lexi, boys. Thank you for coming tonight. I know it's important to our covens to show a united front."

I placed a smile on my face and slid my arm out from Bash's and into Morgan's. "Yes, I know. Silver Pearl wants to keep our alliance with the Blood Moon equal. We are here to help in any way we can." I smirked to Bash and arched an eyebrow.

He came to my side, whispering, "Let the games begin, Princess."

Morgan placed a hand on mine as we walked and greeted other coven members and fae from different parts of the world.

"Let me introduce you to my board members." He led me to a group of men because, of course, it was all men on the board. "Gentlemen, you knew Ms. Rose's father, Alexander, our good friend and fallen fae."

A grumble of sentiments escaped their mouths, and I kept my smile in place.

"Gentlemen, I know my father would be so grateful for those kind words."

Bash stepped in and shook hands with each man, talking to each one as if he had known them his entire life. He walked to his father, leaned in, and asked, "If I can borrow Lexi for a moment, I see a few people who are dying to meet her."

Morgan looked over at me and waved a dismissive hand. I guess I served his purpose. It took all the energy in the world not to roll my eyes and keep my face neutral.

As we began to walk away, a large man with a round face and a slimy smile approached me. Slowly licking his lips, he leaned to

Bash, speaking as if I wasn't there. "She's beautiful, Ryder. Does she entertain you and your men, or does she…"

I bit my cheek, and Tristian and Aden closed in.

Bash, who was still gripping the man's hand, smiled sadistically. "I'm afraid not, Anwir."

He leaned closer to him and whispered in his ear. The man's face whitened, and sweat trickled down his face as Bash slowly spoke to him. I couldn't hear what he said, but the more Bash whispered into his ear, the more the man began to sweat.

"Do you understand me?" Bash's eyes flashed red, and as he squeezed the man's palm, his fear trickled out.

All the while, I kept my smile in place.

I heard the crack in his fingers as Bash broke each of them in his grasp.

"Sebastian, I think you made your point," Kane's deep voice came to the circle.

Bash let go of the man's hand. "Anwir, it's always a pleasure to speak to you."

He ran off, holding his hand to his chest, and Bash turned to Kane, smiling.

"Careful, Sebastian. Anwir is a collector; if he sees something he wants, he will collect on it."

I turned my attention from the large man scurrying away and back to our circle. "A collector of what?"

"This and that, but he likes special types of fae and people too. See, Anwir is old, Lexi, and he likes to collect unique items, from a cursed box to a gold-horned Pegasus, and unfortunately for you, my dear, you are one of those unique things he would want."

I scrunched up my nose. "Men are disgusting."

Kane sipped his drink. "Yes, most of us are." He glanced at me. "Are you well?"

I nodded. "I am."

Tristian and Aden were at my side instantly, ever cautious of anyone else around us, even Kane. Aden handed me a glass of champagne. I smiled in appreciation as Tristian kept his hand resting on my back.

"Anderson, what do you want?" Aden asked in a bored voice.

Kane held up a hand. "Find me later. We can discuss this once curious ears aren't near. Enjoy the night, Lexi, and keep your wits about you. You're surrounded by some of the most powerful fae."

I raised my glass in a toast. "Thank you for the advice. We'll find you later." I turned to the guys. "What's with the cold act?"

Aden took a drink from his glass and looked down at me. "We're the Devils, baby, and here"—he pointed around us—"we act so no one sees our weakness. If you act cold, then for these people, you earn respect. It's all a facade. No one here is perfect," he said, taking another deep swig of his champagne.

"Let's go find Ella and Ethan," Tristian said as we walked around, stopping to talk to a few fae. Some were friendly, and others were colder than us.

We found Ella and Ethan speaking to Aden and Ethan's parents.

"Great," Aden muttered. "Come on, baby, it's time to meet the Charmantes."

Tristian grinned. "Are you going to punch your dad again, Ad?"

My mouth dropped open. "What?" I turned to Tristian, whose smile spread.

"Oh, yeah, last dinner party, Aden's father went off on him for not taking over the business and planning all of his time with the worthless task of being a Devil. Apparently, he's just not as perfect as golden boy Ethan over there."

I laughed. "Ethan is far from perfect." I turned to Aden, pulling him close to me. "You shouldn't let them compare you to him."

He smirked. "You worried about me, baby?"

I shook my head. "Never." I leaned in and kissed him softly. "We already have the sharks circling us. Let's dive in."

He pulled back, a streak of red on his lips, making him look like

a demon ready for revenge.

I started to wipe it away, but he grabbed my hand. "Leave it. Let them know who owns me."

Chapter Thirty-Six

As we walked over to Aden's family, I looked up to one of the balconies and saw Agent Rengard and Cillian casually talking with earpieces in their ears and scanning the crowd. Cillian saw me and gave me a small wave. Rengard looked down at me, and a frown clouded his features.

"What are they doing here?" I asked Bash.

He looked over to Cillian and Rengard and bobbed his head in acknowledgment. "Father received a death threat a few weeks ago. It's common, but since The Wishmaker is taking a stance against the covens, Cillian thought it would be best if they came here just in case anything went down."

I looked around the party filled with the most powerful fae of Providence Village and wondered if they knew what danger lurked around them.

Ella saw us and waved us over. I had never actually met the Charmantes in person. I had only heard about them through my parents, Daniels, and Coco. Aden and Ethan grew up with Nanny more than their parents. We walked over, and Aden cleared his throat.

His mother turned to us with a smile, her blonde hair in a perfect chiffon bun and her wrap dress fitting her perfectly. She looked ideally put together. Her smile never faltered until she looked at Aden. Her expression softened, and her eyes looked more alive than before.

"Darling." She moved to him, kissing his cheek. "Good to see you, my dear. You look so handsome."

She turned to me, and Aden smirked down at me. "Lexi Rose, may I introduce you to my mother, Helena Charmante." He gave her a small smile, and she reached for me.

"Lexi Rose, why do you look just like your mother? It is a pleasure to meet you. I hope my Aden is behaving."

I took her hand and smiled. "He is."

She gave me a light squeeze. "Good."

She turned to Tristian and Bash. "Boys. Staying out of trouble?"

Tristian laughed and kissed her hand dramatically. "You know we aren't, Helena."

She giggled and pulled her hand back. "Sebastian, how are things with the new bar?"

Bash smiled. "Great, the whiskey bar is booming, and of course, our restaurants are always popular."

A gruff voice came from behind Helena, and I saw her jump slightly, her smile returning to the plastered version it was before. A handsome man in a smart suit stood behind her, his hair white as snow and a scruff of beard on his face. The same gray of Aden's eyes stared at me.

"The Silver Pearl's leader... Lexi Rose, it's a pleasure to meet you finally." He took my hand into his, his grip firm. "I'm not sure why Aden has been keeping you hidden. We thought he was making you up." He huffed as he drank from a deep-amber glass.

I pulled my hand back and wrapped it through Aden's arm. "No, we've wanted to keep us private. You know how the gossip can spread." I smiled and looked up at Aden with the doe eyes I could imagine. "We haven't wanted to leave the house much anyway."

I let the blush rush to my cheeks. Usually, I wouldn't showboat like this, but I was good at it. Years of growing up with coven members, you learn to play their game quickly. It was all a chess game for people like the Charmantes. Who can they help, and who can help them?

"Well, yes, young love can do that. Don't you remember how we were once, Richard?" Helena hit his tie with her clutch.

He chuckled. "I do. So how are things, son?"

Aden cleared his throat. "Fine, the new restaurant systems are in place, and I figured out the coding for the online reservation system."

Bash, Aden, and his father talked shop for a few minutes while Tristian chatted with Helena.

I slipped over to Ella and Ethan and hugged them. "Ethan, your parents don't seem that scary."

He choked on his drink. "Just wait. This is the way of the Charmantes. It's all an act."

Ella handed him a napkin and snagged us two drinks. She passed me one and walked over to Ethan. "Babe, we're going to take a lap and talk. I'll be back before we're called for dinner."

She kissed his cheek, and he pulled her closer sweetly. "Have fun. Don't tell her too much." He laughed.

She kissed him again and motioned for me to follow her. We headed down the lawn, close to the cemetery.

"You two are so adorable, you know that?" I pointed out as I took a sip of the champagne.

She smiled. "He really is the best." I laughed, and she sighed. "God, I hate these parties."

I moved closer. "I can't say I blame you, but my life will be filled with these." It was my turn to sigh now.

Ella took a sip. "So, has Aden ever told you about his father?"

I shook my head. "No, he only says he's an ass." I left it at that because I knew Aden hated his father, but I never wanted to push him to tell me the *why* of it.

Ella moved us along the edge of the cemetery, and the party became quiet background noise. "I only witnessed it once on a trip when I was seventeen. We had snuck out to go to this beach party, all three of us, and got caught coming back in. Richard scoffed at Ethan and me, telling us to go to bed. So, we did, but I had left my phone downstairs. When I snuck down to get it, Aden was leaning over a table with red welts on his back. His father said he deserved it, that he was supposed to be the responsible one, and that it was his God-given duty to protect the family name." Her voice started to crack.

I pulled her into a hug. "Ella, don't cry. Please, he's okay."

She sniffled. "I was so scared, I ran upstairs and woke Ethan. He bolted downstairs and pulled his father off Aden. He said it was his idea, and his father's entire attitude changed. He dropped the belt and pulled Ethan into a hug. I helped Aden clean up and made him sleep in the room with us." I saw a bench up ahead, and we sat as her tears fell. "I was so scared for Aden for so many years, Lexi. You hated him, you hated him so much, and they deserved it, they did, but I couldn't just leave him, Lexi. I couldn't let him be in the hands of his father. So, I invited Aden to more places with us. To get him away from his father. When he turned eighteen, he moved out, and the relief we felt..." She wiped a tear. "Aden got his freedom, something he never had, Lexi."

Tears fell from my eyes as well, and we cried in each other's arms for our best friend whose life wasn't filled with joys and riches but with demons and nightmares.

We sat there for a while, and I wiped my tears. "We should go back."

Ella nodded as we stood. A gong went off in the distance.

I rolled my eyes. "I guess that means dinner is served."

Ella smirked. "Let the bloodbath begin." She laughed as we made our way to the ominous estate that sat above us.

I looked back at the graveyard, thinking, *Lucky bastards.*

Just as we reached the top, someone yelled my name. I turned, and Corvina was running to us in a silver flowing gown, her hair down and wild around her. She looked like a water sprite the way she laughed, running full out.

Emmeranne was right behind her in a deep-navy silk dress. "Corvina! Get back here!"

Corvina turned back to Emmeranne and waved her off. "I'll be fine, sister." She stopped right before Ella and me.

I smiled. "Corvina, you could have just walked over to us. We would have waited for you."

She smoothed out her dress and murmured about the imps and how they kept stealing her flowers.

Ella looked over to me and mouthed, "Is she crazy?"

I shook my head. No. Corvina might be many things, but she was far from crazy.

"Lexi, I'm so glad I saw you!" She reached for a hug, and I wrapped my arms around her. "Did you figure out what the thing we talked about was about?"

I took her arm, and we began to walk to the house again. "You don't have to speak in code. Ella knows."

Corvina looked over at her and examined her with pursed lips. "Hmmm, yep, you aren't full of the twisty mist of clouds. You're safe."

Ella's eyes widened as she tried not to laugh. "Thank you, Corvina."

I tapped Corvina's arm and lowered my voice just in case. "I think we did figure it out. We're stuck on how to get onto the island, though."

Corvina sighed dramatically. "Oh yes, the way." She closed her eyes, and her magic washed over her. She opened them, and they were glazed over. "It will only be by the stars and the sea to guide you through, but beware of the X-shaped trees and the red in the sky. Those will only lead you down a path of destruction and dismay." Her eyes closed, and she took a deep breath. She opened them again. "Did I say anything helpful?"

"You did. Thank you, Corvina."

She sighed in relief. "Oh good, sometimes it just comes out as complete and utter nonsense. Oh, look, Cassandra's here. She's looking like a strumpet puppet today. Beware of the soup, that one spills its secrets."

I followed her gaze and saw Cassandra standing near Franklin and Morgan, a drink in hand. Her red dress was so revealing that it left nothing to the imagination.

"She sure does like attention, doesn't she?" I growled out. "Bitch has it coming to her."

Ella tensed up and gripped my arm. "Lexi, I know what she did, but not here. Play it smart. She'll get what's coming to her. We'll make sure of it."

I turned to Ella, her bright-blue eyes glaring at the redhead. "You're right, Ella. We'll make sure she gets her retribution."

Corvina laughed. "Oh, you two are simply the keenest."

I found myself liking Corvina even more than before. I looked back and saw that Emmeranne was a few feet away from us and looked utterly miserable to be there.

"Do you need to go to your sister?" I pointed to Emmeranne.

Corvina frowned. "Sister's heart hurts. Her gentleman caller was killed a few days ago. Grayson found his head."

My heart broke for her. I knew if I lost one of my Devils, I would burn the world to bring them back.

"Please give her our condolences and tell her that The Wishmaker will pay for his crimes." I looked back at Emmeranne, and she lifted a hand to her chest, bowing her head to me. I returned the gesture.

Corvina turned away from us. "'Til we meet again, Lexi. I must go. Sister awaits!" She hurried off, bumping into people as she made her way to her sister.

We walked up the steps, and just as the patio flattened out, I came face-to-face with my Devils, Ethan by their side.

Ella bit her lip. "Ethan."

He walked to her and pulled her close. "You were gone too long, my ash girl."

He pecked her nose as she giggled, then swept her into a dip and kissed her deeply.

She hit his chest and laughed. "Ethan!"

He set her up on her feet, and she waved. "See you inside." Ella winked as they walked away.

"Then there was one." Bash smirked as he offered me his hand.

I took it and pulled him close. "What's a girl gotta do to get that kind of greeting?" I grinned.

"You want a grand gesture, Princess?"

I leaned into him. "It might be nice," I teased.

Morgan appeared in front of the crowd, and a confident smirk adorned his mouth, as if he was the most important person in the room. "Friends, guests, and leaders of the covens, welcome to the Blood Moon Coven's Full Moon Fest. Please enjoy the festivities of the evening, and let us eat, drink, and be fae!"

The crowd cheered and began to move into the mansion's massive doors.

Bash turned to me and grinned. "If my Princess wants a grand gesture, then she'll get one, but you'll have to wait." He kissed my temple. "These things take time to plan."

Tristian and Aden joined us with glasses of champagne in their hands, looking down and smiling softly. "Ready, Lil' Star?" Tristian offered his arm.

I sighed. "No, but let's get this over with. What's the worst that could happen, right?"

Chapter Thirty-Seven

Aden strolled next to us. "She did not say what I think she did. Did she?" he groaned.

"Afraid so, *frère*." Tristian smiled.

Bash laughed. "Cursing us already, Princess?"

"If you always think negatively, you'll only ever receive it in return."

Three growls escaped them, and I walked toward the doors, leaving my Devils to trail behind me.

I walked into the large entry that always gave me the feeling of a tacky modern Dracula. It was cheesy with its darkness and gloom. The Prince of Darkness would not approve of Morgan's horrible taste.

"You look lovely tonight, my Rose," a snarky voice from behind me said.

I turned and gave Franklin a closed smile. He wore an all-white suit, looking like the slimy rat he was.

"Hi, Franklin, and don't you look dreadful." I walked closer to him, lowering my voice. "Tell me, does Morgan know you're working with The Wishmaker?"

He snarled at me. "Stupid blood slut, you know nothing," he spat out.

I laughed, and a few people turned our way. I gripped his arm tightly. He tried to pull it free, but I kept it locked within my grasp.

We continued to walk to the dining room. I pulled him close, a smile still on my lips. "You know, at first, I thought it was Morgan. I mean, it adds up." I waved a hand around the room. "He would want power, control, and money. But you see, you forgot one thing: Morgan is old school and wants to take the glory of it all. He wants his face in the papers. The TV interviews. He wants people to know his name, to love him, and to see him as a savior. That's not what The Wishmaker wants, though."

Franklin stiffened, and his eyes scanned the room.

"Don't worry, Franky. The Devils aren't who you have to worry about tonight. It's me. Deliver this to your boss. Their reckoning is coming soon, and I will have them begging for death when it does. They took everything from me, and I plan to take it back and more." I shoved his arm away, sending him stumbling into a nearby wall as I walked to the dining room.

Bash was by my side instantly, and his eyes said he wasn't happy. "You shouldn't have approached him without us, Lexi."

I looked over my shoulder at him. "I'm a big girl, Sebastian. Franklin is sending a message to The Wishmaker. Let him be unsettled for a few weeks until we destroy him."

Bash guided me into the dining room. Long tables were covered in black tablecloths with dark roses, centerpieces, and candles lined down the middle. Gold plates with deep-red napkins were set at each place, and a white card with our names swirling in gold stared up at me.

"Is he always this over-the-top?"

Bash laughed. "You have no idea."

He pulled my seat out, and I took it. As he settled in his chair, our legs brushed against each other, and he looked over in amusement.

He leaned close to my ear. "Princess, Franklin is dangerous. We know he's killed before. If you want to talk to The Weasel again, at least have one of us with you."

I moved back from him, scanning his eyes to see if a joke was there somewhere. "You don't think I can handle it?" I retorted. I knew I sounded childish, but I thought I had paid my dues. "Sebastian, I can speak to whoever I want. I took care of myself before you came along. You need to trust me."

His eyes flared in anger. "I do, Lexi. I don't want to see you die like your parents."

I bit my lips together to keep from screaming at him, but he saw in my eyes how much he was infuriating me. "You're not the only strong one here, Sebastian Ryder, and you can kindly fuck right off, asshat," I huffed out and looked around the table.

Aden and Tristian were near us and looked our way. I shook my head at them too. "They think the same, don't they?"

Bash placed his napkin in his lap. "Yes."

I stood. "Fine."

Bash grabbed my wrist, pulled me into my seat, and hissed into my ear, "Sit down now, Lexi. You're a leader of a coven, so act that way, for fuck's sake. Yell at us later, but tonight, we have to put on a show." His anger lapped at my wrist.

I pushed it away when another hand landed on my shoulder. It felt like a warm night, and I turned to see Grayson. "Grayson, I haven't seen you much tonight."

He sat next to me, grabbing a drink from a passing tray, and downed it in one gulp. "Had a problem I needed to solve."

My eyes widened when he gestured for another drink.

"So, did you solve it?"

A waiter magically appeared with another drink for him. He took a long sip. "No, but you could help." He smirked.

I smiled, because I was game for anything to distract me from thinking about my Devils right now. "I'm in. Will it piss off Bash too?"

I looked over to Bash, who was in conversation with a group of fae.

He chuckled. "Fuck yes, it will, seductress."

I grinned evilly. "Even better."

He pulled my chair closer to him and wrapped an arm around my shoulders, leaning his head toward me. "Want to know how to make a voodoo priestess jealous?"

I raised my eyebrows. "Brigitte? Oh hell no, Grayson, I'm not screwing with her."

He laughed, his breath tickling my neck. "She won't come at you, but it will help me get my point across."

I looked into his eyes for a moment. "Fine."

He leaned closer, his lips near my neck, and I bit my lip to hide a smile. He started to sing a song under his breath, and I laughed.

"Are you singing 'Witchcraft'?"

His lips skated over my ear as his deep voice sang softly. I got goose bumps across my arms. Grayson was handsome, but I never thought of him as any more than a friend. I just hoped he felt the same way.

"Is she looking?" he asked.

I tilted my head closer and scanned the table, finding almost everyone staring at us. Brigitte's dark eyes connected with mine, and they sparkled. A tilt of her mouth told me she knew what he was doing.

"Yes, and she knows your game."

"If you would take your seat, the dinner will begin shortly," Morgan said. "If you'll excuse me, I have important business to attend to, but I'll be back. Please eat, drink, and enjoy the entertainment!"

Music flowed around us as a ballerina entered with a man, and they began to dance, telling a story about a man trying to rescue his love from the underworld. It was beautifully tragic watching them move so gracefully. So many emotions flew across the room, and I felt like I was hit with the feelings of twenty people.

I stiffened and quickly threw up a shield. Grayson pulled back as we watched, and his hand found mine under the table. He lifted it out and kissed the back of it.

"Seductress, has anyone told you that you look ravishing tonight?"

Three low growls echoed around us, and I looked to my Devils, who all looked like they were about to go on a murderous rage.

I smiled at them. *Serves you right, asshats.* "No, they haven't. Thank you, it's nice to feel appreciated." I heard a huff from Bash behind me as Aden cursed under his breath.

Dinner was served, and Grayson carried on a flirty conversation with slight touches. I batted my lashes and laughed at his jokes. My Devils grew more agitated with each contact or laugh. On the other hand, Brigitte only noticed a few and carried her conversation on at her table.

"Ms. Rose, I have a question for you." A voice cut across the table.

We both turned to see Franklin glaring at me.

I glanced at Franklin, who was sitting near the center of the table. I did my best not to glare at him. "Yes, Franklin?"

He leaned forward on his elbows. "How many coven leaders and their seconds are you screwing? At least the rest of the Blood Moon has standards. You are nothing but a coven slut."

I smiled. "Is that how you attack? By insulting me and calling me a slut? I'm a siren. We tend to have a lot of sex and enjoy it. You would know that if you could even get it up."

He turned red. "You best know whose house you're in tonight, Ms. Rose," he spat out.

I looked to Bash to see if he or any of my Devils would say anything, and they sat in silence, letting me handle Franklin with smug smiles on their faces. They now knew that I could handle Franklin and his weasliness.

"And you need to understand that I don't give a shit anymore. What else do I have to lose? Now, excuse me, and give my regards to the host." I dropped my napkin and beelined out of the dining room.

I walked quickly upstairs, the dark handrail guiding my way. I needed to get out of there for a minute to breathe, and Ella's room was the perfect place.

I heard two voices coming from one of the many rooms along the hall, so I slowed my steps so I wouldn't disturb whoever was talking. Light spilled from a door that was partially open, and the voices became clearer as I approached. Ella's room was just a bit farther down the hall; I tried to pass the door without being noticed.

"Is it all here?" Morgan's deep voice traveled down the hall. "Pixie dust? What did you find?" A muffled voice responded, but I couldn't hear it clearly. I stepped toward the door when Morgan boomed, "We can always get more! Ask the crew to see if we can get more tears, and let him know if he fails, then I will take his fucking head and display it to the entire coven so they know what it means to betray me."

A clacking of heels clambered over, and a female voice became clearer as I peered through the door. Morgan's back was turned to me, hiding whoever he was speaking to. A hand reached out, and she purred, "It's all here, Master. You are so stressed out. Let me help with that."

Morgan turned, and I swallowed a gasp as I saw Cassandra sink to her knees. "That's my good little slut. You do like to take Ryder cock, don't you?" Morgan growled out at the sound of a zipper being undone.

Oh hell no, I am not waiting to see this, I thought. I turned quickly, but not before I heard Morgan's groan of pleasure. I put a hand on my stomach. *Do not throw up, Lexi. Don't throw up.* I walked away as quickly and quietly as possible. *Fuck,* I think I was wrong about Morgan. Maybe, just maybe, Morgan was The Wishmaker.

I quickly walked down the stairs, only to find all three of the Devils waiting for me.

"Lexi..." Aden started, but I put up a hand.

"We can fight later. Come on." I moved to the doors and left. I waited until they shouted for me to stop, but only when we were halfway to the cemetery. "I think Morgan is The Wishmaker."

They all stopped.

Bash narrowed his eyes. "Explain, Princess."

I turned to my Devils and tried to purge the image of Cassandra and Morgan from my head. "I was going to Ella's room to just breathe for a minute when I overheard your father." I looked at Bash pointedly. "He and Cassandra were talking about pixie dust and how they needed more. She called him 'Master'. The same way Lin called The Wishmaker 'Master'. I think... I think he *is* The Wishmaker."

All eyes landed on Bash, watching him process what I just said.

Tristian turned to me. "I get why you think that, Lil' Star. I do. But Morgan—though he showboats his power... I don't think he's the type. Cassandra is too stupid to help run an organization like The Wishmaker's."

Aden ran a hand through his hair. "Baby, what was Cassandra doing when she called him 'Master'?"

I turned to him and wrinkled my nose at the memory.

"It was sexual, wasn't it?" Bash answered for me as he studied my face.

I nodded. "It was."

Tristian gagged, Aden cursed, and Bash looked like he was going to throw up.

I held up my hands. "Besides the fact that your ex is hooking up with your father, which, by the way, is disgusting..." I moved toward him and grasped his hands. "Sebastian, I just have a feeling it's him, or if it is not, we know he is involved. And he can lead us to The Wishmaker."

Bash looked down at me, seeing the truth in my eyes. His eyes flashed red as the fear—and anger—settled into him.

His father was The Wishmaker, and he wanted us all dead.

Chapter Thirty-Eight

I now knew why Daniels would always say it was the quiet before the tempest. I sat on the front porch with a cup of coffee as the dark clouds rolled in from the sea. The bright sunny morning had morphed into a grim afternoon. It felt thicker and smelled like the salt from the ocean.

Dyna sat in my lap as I lazily petted her white fur. I couldn't help but chuckle at the ironic parallels I could draw from the sky to my life. Highs and lows, love and grief, joy and sorrow. I wondered what my parents would think about this life for me. Would they be thrilled about my adventure or scared for me?

The door creaked open as Aden stepped onto the porch in athletic pants and a long-sleeve shirt with a towel wrapped around his neck. He sat down next to me, his arms on his knees as he leaned forward.

"You're deep in thought, baby. I've been standing in the doorway for five minutes."

I looked at him and gave him a small smile that didn't quite reach my eyes. "Just thinking."

Aden took my hand in his. "I think we all have been. There is light in the end."

I looked into his eyes and saw the pain that sat behind them. I ran my hands down his back. Perfectly smooth, not a scar on him, but sometimes, our scars aren't on the outside.

"Aden, Ella told me what your father did." His whole body stilled, but I continued. "You don't have to talk about it, but if you ever want to, I'm here to listen."

Aden blew out a breath. Sitting up, he cupped my face in his hands. "You want to know how I survived?" His steel-gray eyes peered down at my blue ones. "You. You got me through those moments when I was so lost. I would close my eyes, and there you were, your face, your touch, your soft voice telling me it was okay. Only you, it has only ever been you."

I pulled him in for a soft kiss, my tears falling and landing on his cheeks.

He put his forehead to mine. "Don't cry for me. I don't deserve your tears." He wiped them away and kissed my temple. "Come on, the boys and I are heading to the gym to clear our heads and think about what we'll do about Morgan."

"A long-distance shotgun is one thing that comes to mind for Morgan," I muttered, and he smirked.

"Let's try to avoid murder and jail time, baby."

I stood with Dyna in my arms and walked into the house. "Fine, but let's not cut it out completely."

I strolled into my room and changed into a pair of bike shorts and a loose tank. I grabbed my shoes as my phone rang with a text.

"Princess, hurry!" Bash called from the living room.

"Hold on. Coco is texting me. I'll be out in a minute."

Coco: *I heard about it last night. Are you okay?*
Lexi: Nothing I couldn't handle.
Coco: *Rumor has it that you and Grayson got cozy.*
Lexi: Nothing happened besides harmless flirting. Let's just say it was to make three alphaholes and one magical witch uneasy.
Coco: *Evil little siren. Morgan is an ass inviting you to that. I heard Franklin was a miscreant, as usual.*
Lexi: Butt-faced miscreant, as always. He is the least of my concerns. I can handle him. Just stay away from Morgan. I overheard a few things last night, and he is dangerous. Keep your distance.
Coco: *I am not scared of that pretentious three-piece suit asshat. Damn vamp thinks he sparkles.*
Coco: *Hey, how about some drama-free dinner? Here at the estate?*
Lexi: Actually, yeah, I could run a few ideas by you and Jason. I think we have a lead for the mermaids. Crows Hallow. Do you know how to get on the island?
Coco: *Lexi... Crows Hallow is full of dark magic. Why the hell do you want to get on that godforsaken island?*
Lexi: I will explain later, but maybe ask Jason.
Coco: *I will, and be here by six.*
Lexi: Love you. See you soon.

I pulled on my shoes and ran to the living room to meet the guys. They all looked in my direction.

"Everything okay?" Tristian asked.

I nodded. "She heard about last night."

They were quiet as I walked past them. Bash and I were still barely talking. I knew we needed to have it out, but right now, my gut had a pit that I couldn't shake. "Let's go before the rain hits."

Tristian opened the door, and we headed out.

I walked to the car, and Bash sped to my side. "Princess, we need to talk about last night."

I turned to him and inhaled sharply. "Bash, not now, later. I need time. Let's clear our heads so we don't say things we don't mean."

His eyes searched mine, and he grasped my neck, gently pulling me into a searing kiss. "Okay, but we will talk later about you and that damned wolf-dragon."

I rolled my eyes. "Grayson is a friend, and I was helping him out."

I slid into the front seat as Aden hopped in the driver's seat. Once Tristian and Bash were in, we sped away to downtown.

Tristian owned three gyms in Providence Village. His newest and most popular one was Vulcan's Fire. It was a luxury gym with a spa and a restaurant, and it had condos on the top floor that overlooked the entire Village. Bash and Tristian co-owned it together, only catering to the super-exclusive clientele.

We walked through the marble-floored foyer and made our way to the modern elevators. Bash pulled out a black slate card engraved with a gold flame, the *v* and *f* snaking around each other on the card. It was simple but gave off an air of importance, which I guess was the point of the gym. He touched the card to a small keypad that sat to the side. A pair of sleek black-gunmetal doors opened to reveal a pure-white marble floor with dark benches running along its sides. Gilded mirrors gleamed as the soft light reflected off them.

"This place is ridiculous. You realize that, right?" I pointed out.

Bash smirked as he pressed his thumb to a button labeled 'penthouse.' "Well, Princess, we call it home."

I turned to him, mouth agape.

I pointed to the surrounding area. "You mean…"

Aden laughed. "Yep, baby, we all live here. We have a set of apartments that overlook all of downtown Providence Village."

I rolled my eyes. "Of course you do." Then I turned to Aden, batting my eyelashes. "When do I get to see your bedroom?"

Aden wiggled his eyebrows. "Fuck the gym. Let's go now."

I laughed, and the door dinged open to the gym's main floor.

The first thing I saw was floor-to-ceiling windows that overlooked the entire downtown. It was stunning.

"Weights and machines are over there," Tristian pointed out. "Private dressing rooms and spa up there. It's about three stories, so the gym is on the first floor, the spa is next, and then a restaurant and bar on the top floor. It's a full experience." He gestured across the way. "Pool is outside through the doors there. We have a private room for us today. Do you want to come with us, Lil' Star, or will you go to the pool?"

I looked out the door and saw the massive pool.

"It's salt water, too." He gently nudged me.

I grinned. "I'll meet with you later."

He smiled. "I figured. Be careful, Lil' Star." He kissed my cheek, and they walked off.

I walked to the pool and shed my workout clothes, my suit underneath them. I dove into the pool, feeling my power restore as I swam my laps.

Once I pushed myself until my arms and legs were sore, I got out and dried off. I changed back into my clothes and went in search of my Devils. I found a few rooms where trainers were with clients. As I wandered, a deep, thumping noise came from the end of the hall.

I opened the door to see my Devils dripping in sweat. Their shirts were discarded in the middle of the room as they did pushups. They leaped to their feet in unison and moved into jumping jacks. Then they began to do circuits of exercises. It was as if they were dancing. They moved with each other so eloquently that it was no wonder they were as dangerous as everyone said. I leaned against the wall, watching them, and I couldn't deny how much I wanted to go to them.

Aden's eyes flicked to mine, and a cocky smile grew on his face. He whispered something to the other two, and they whipped their heads in my direction. They smirked as they moved toward me.

"Princess, want to see if you can keep up with the Devils?"

I moved from the wall and walked gingerly over to a pair of boxing gloves lying on the floor. "No thanks, I'll just work the bag."

I winked, slid the gloves on, and moved to the punching bag, thanking the stars that Ella convinced me to take kickboxing classes for the past four years with her.

I wrapped my hands and put my gloves on. I started with a basic combo punch and moved into throwing kicks at the bag. I let my mind concentrate on the bag and its movements. Soon, I was moving into more complex combinations, adding in kicks.

My mind wandered to that dark space where I second-guessed everything I knew. I kept thinking about Morgan and how he must have had a hand in my parents' murders. With each punch to the bag, I became angrier and angrier with him and myself. Why did he kill my parents? Why Daniels? Why take every good thing away from me? Why is he still trying to take away everything—my coven, my friends, and now my Devils?

I pounded the bag with all my might and screamed my fury into it. I wanted to make someone hurt as much as I did right now. I wanted someone to feel the pain I felt and had lived with all those years. The grief that lived within me, never wanting to escape, but desperate to be free.

The music stopped, and I was pulled into someone's arms as they whispered my name. I looked up and saw Bash, and his green eyes held mine.

His voice came out hoarse, and he brushed my hair away from my face. "Don't let them win, Princess. You're forged from the depths of the ocean itself. Show them your wrath."

That wrath weighed heavy on my soul; I needed to get it out.

The thing with relationships was that they weren't perfect. They were messy and complex, and you had to compromise a lot. That was the one thing I was learning with my Devils. We could be angry with each other and fight, but at the end of the day, our love for each other meant the most.

I looked around. Aden and Tristian were near, their eyes intense as they watched us. I held out a hand, and they came over. They wrapped their arms around Bash and me, enveloping us in one big hug.

"I'm sorry, Princess. I want you safe, and the thought of losing you... it feels like claws are trying to rip you away from me."

Aden whispered, "For us, we wouldn't survive, baby. I wouldn't survive."

Tristian ran his hands up my back, soothing me. "So, if it comes down to it, Lil' Star, we will sacrifice ourselves for you first and foremost. You are our world, Lexi Rose."

Without a doubt, I felt the same. My Devils were becoming my world too, and the thought of losing one of them made my soul ache and my heart shatter. I would burn down the world for my Devils, knowing they would do the same for me.

Chapter Thirty-Nine

We showered and headed over to my family's estate. The night was oddly quiet as the moon cast its light on us. The fog seemed thicker the closer we got to the house. I looked out the window and up to the sky. A tinge of red was on the moon tonight. A lot of humans thought red on the moon was a bad omen. It only meant a shift was in our future. This could be good or bad.

"Hmmm, signs of a change." I looked at Tristian, a frown contorting his features as he looked at the moon.

"Could mean anything, Lil' Star." He reached for my hand.

"Still doesn't change this knot I have in my stomach."

Bash kissed my temple. "We'll figure it out."

"We have to." I leaned back in my seat, closing my eyes as we drove through the neighborhood.

"Coco should really get a gate," Bash said under his breath.

"Agreed," I whispered back.

Coco and Jason were waiting for us on the porch, drinks in hand. Coco waved like a maniac, and I rolled my window down to wave back.

Coco yelled to us, "Come on, it's a beautiful night to eat outside, and I made my famous cheesecake for dessert!"

Tristian grinned. "I love you, Lil' Star, but that cheesecake is mine!" he yelled as he flung the door open and leaped out of the moving car.

My jaw dropped in surprise as I watched him roll out and spring up like a damn ninja. He dusted his pants off as if it was nothing and jogged up to Coco. Once he reached the porch, he wrapped her in a bear hug.

"Hey, hey, stop getting handsy with my girl," Jason said as he pulled Tristian off, laughing.

Aden parked the car, and we piled out.

As we walked up, I pointed to Tristian. "What the hell was that?"

He winked, chuckling. "That cheesecake is mine. I take cheesecake very seriously, and when Coco says desserts, I come a runnin'."

Coco pulled me into a hug. "Hello, my darling girl."

I stayed in her arms for a moment. "Hey, Coco."

She pulled back, looking into my eyes. She examined me for a minute and pursed her lips. "Hmm, Let's eat. Then you and I need to talk, Lexi."

Jason wrapped his arms around my shoulder. "Now, talk to me about what you learned at the Ryder's, and do I need to kick Morgan Ryder's ass?"

I laughed half-heartedly. "I hope not, but if you do, my money is on you."

He smiled and took a sip of wine. "Coco said something about Crows Hallow?" His voice held a serious tone.

I looked over at him. "I need a strong drink and Coco's dessert before we dive into that."

He nodded. "Me too, Lex, me too."

We gathered around the patio table and talked, ate, and drank throughout the evening.

Jason leaned back in his chair, his hand relaxing on his stomach.

"Crows Hallow. What do you want to know about the island?"

The table conversation stopped suddenly, and I swallowed the bite of food in my mouth. "Everything. How did it come to be? What makes it so dangerous? What kind of magic is on the island?"

Coco sighed as she brought out a tray of tea. "Just like your mother. She was obsessed with the island."

I looked to Coco. "She never mentioned it before."

Coco shook her head. "Your father didn't want you looking into it."

Jason sighed. "The island has been there forever. Going back to the first founders of Providence Village, they talk about an island in the distance full of dark magic and the demons trapped there." He went back inside, walked to a bookcase near the fireplace, and pulled out an old leather-bound book.

"Here, this will tell you what you need to know. I don't know how to get on the island, Lexi." He looked down at me. "Some things are better off left alone. Not even magic can stop the evil that lives on the island."

I took the book and held it to my chest. "Yeah, but if I can save the mermaids, isn't it worth it?"

He smiled sadly. "It is. The Silver Pearl is lucky to have someone who cares as much as you."

I stood and hugged him with one arm. "Well, here are to adventures of the unknown."

Coco raised her glass as we toasted. "To adventures."

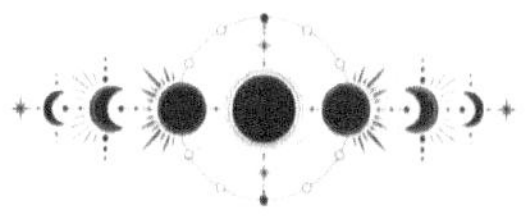

The night air was cool as Coco and I talked outside under the garden gazebo with a cup of tea. Jason and my Devils were playing a game of pool and trying to drink each other under the table. I smiled, looking at the stars and feeling at peace for a moment.

"Okay, spill, tell me all the juicy deets that went down at the party."

I took a sip of my tea and told her everything. Her eyes widened, but she listened and didn't say anything until I finished.

Coco took my hand. "Morgan Ryder has always been egocentric, proud, and, well, he's an asshole." I snorted a laugh. "But something doesn't feel right."

I nodded. "I thought that, but what I heard all lines up perfectly. I can't imagine it could be anyone else."

She sipped her tea carefully. "Well, here is some advice: The most dangerous thing in the world is a silent one. The most dangerous people are the quietest."

I looked down. "You don't think it's him?"

She shook her head. "I'm saying I don't know, Lexi. Get solid evidence first before you set the fire." She patted my hand. "As for Crows Hallow, I'll help you get on the island, but promise me you'll be careful. The island is said to be cursed to all fae." Her voice went soft. "I don't want to lose you, my love. We're all our family has left."

She hugged me close, and I felt like I was sixteen again. I didn't let go of her for a while.

"I love you, Coco."

She pulled back and smiled. "And I, you, my darling girl." She cleared her throat and stood. "You know, I found a bunch of boxes upstairs from the attic. A few were your mother's. She was obsessed with that island when she was young. Your grandfather forbade us to go there, so, naturally, your mother learned everything she could about it. Do you want them?"

I perked up. "Please, can I go look at them now?"

She pulled me to stand. "Why do you think I brought it up?"

We walked to the house, and Bash spotted me. "Jason, Aden, and I are going to the conservatory to see if we can find anything to help us with the island."

I headed to the stairs. "Coco found a few of my mom's old boxes.

I'll see if she says anything about how to get on the island. Where's Tristian?"

Aden came up behind Bash with Jason laughing. "On his third slice of cheesecake."

A muffled voice came from the kitchen. "It's like crack, Coco. What the hell do you put in it?!"

I laughed and yelled to the kitchen, "Be careful, or you're going to make yourself sick!"

Jason laughed. "Bash just said the same thing."

I looked over to Bash, who was trying not to smile but failing. "He'll be asleep in twenty minutes anyways. Let's go, *frère*."

I smiled and watched them leave.

We walked to my parents' old room. I froze as the flashbacks from the night they died played in my mind. My mother's eyes stared at mine. My father was face down on the carpet, and the blood, goddess, there was so much blood.

Coco's hand found mine. "We'll do this together."

"Okay, together."

She pushed the door open, and the room had been cleaned and redone. Their furniture was still there, but now the carpet was gone, and a plush rug sat on the wooden floors. Four boxes sat in the middle of the room.

I walked to them, dusting off the top of one and opening the lid. Inside the box were thin black notebooks. I pulled one out and opened it to the first page. My mother's handwriting stared back at me. I ran my fingers over the letters, as if I was touching her.

June 1981 was written on the top of the page. Her journals were filled with typical problems of a fifteen-year-old teenager—school, friends, and of course, boys. I flipped through more, and it seemed like my mom had a love triangle going on between my father and someone named Nic.

A loud rustle came from the kitchen, and Coco sighed.

"I'm going to go check on Tristian. I'm worried he found the cookies I was hiding." Coco stood, brushing the dust off her pants. "You okay for a bit?"

I smiled. "Yeah, I am."

She squeezed my arm before leaving the room.

As I thumbed through the notebooks, it was like my mom's voice was in my head. The stories were as if I got to keep a little piece of her with me. I read how she met my father and how they fell in love. I got a glimpse into their life, and I knew I would hold onto these journals forever.

I opened the last box and pulled out a few more notebooks. One was wrapped in a beautiful blue-and-gold silk scarf. I tried to unwrap it, but no matter what I did, the knot wouldn't come loose.

I examined the book closely, and it felt like it was pulsing in my hands.

"It has to be magic," I mumbled.

I stood and went downstairs with the book in my hands, calling for Coco.

When I heard nothing, I looked around and noticed the wide-open door.

"Coco! Tristian!" Fuck, where were they? My stomach twisted.

"Lil' Star." A strained voice sounded from behind me.

I turned, and Tristian lay on the floor, blood flowing down his temple.

"Tristian!" I ran to his side and helped him sit.

"I'm okay."

I looked at his head and found a deep slash across the back.

"Here, put pressure on it. I'll be right back."

I ran to the kitchen and grabbed a towel. I turned to run back but stopped in my tracks. A black envelope sat on the counter, and my heart pounded. I took the envelope and ran back to Tristian.

Once I reached him, I pressed the towel to his head. "Hold it."

He took the towel and continued to apply pressure. I put my hands over his and pushed my healing magic into him. The subtle light filled the room as I felt the cut begin to close.

"You should be okay, but be careful. You lost a lot of blood."

His eyes didn't meet mine but instead were looking at the envelope. "Wishmaker," he said in a low voice.

I opened the envelope with shaky hands and pulled out a white paper in elegant red ink. I read it slowly.

My sweet Rose,

*I warned you what would happen. Now the price will
be paid. Find me where the angel's black tears are
dried. You might save a life.*

–The Wishmaker

Four lines. That was it. I screamed in frustration and threw the damned letter across the hall. I heard a whoosh as Bash and Aden came running in, guns out, looking around.

"What happened? Tristian, fuck." Aden moved over to him.

"I was sleeping, heard a struggle, went to see what was going on, and the next thing I know, boom, I was out like a light. Fuck, Lil' Star, I am so sorry."

I looked up, and Bash was instantly at my side.

He spotted the envelope and looked down at me, whispering, "Wishmaker."

One word, that's all he said. Jason came darting in, looking frantic. "Lexi, are you okay?" I nodded as tears filled my eyes, and his went wide as he looked around. Jason bent and picked up a wooden rolling pin coated in blood. "Where's Coco?"

I shook my head, and the tears fell. Bash pulled me to him.

"Lexi, where is Coco?!" Jason dropped to his knees, and I saw his

heart breaking. I felt his agony as it washed over me.
My own heart split as I said the words.
"The Wishmaker has her."

CHAPTER FORTY

The whole room erupted in commotion. I stayed on my knees and stared at the floor, trying to piece together something—anything—to make this make sense.

"He wants us to meet him," I croaked out, and all four turned toward me.

"Where?" Bash asked.

"Where the angel's black tears are dried."

He closed his eyes. The look of defeat cast a shadow on his face. He knew. He knew where we would have to go.

"Where, Sebastian?" I stood, holding the journal close to my chest.

He opened his eyes, and a red glow bled from them. "The Ryder Family Crypt."

"We need weapons," Aden said as he helped Tristian stand.

"Trist, until you're better, you can't come," Bash said.

He scoffed at Bash. "No offense, *frère*, but take a flying leap into a pile of unicorn shit, because there is no way I'm missing this."

Bash was about to argue back, but I put my hand up. "Tristian, you need blood."

His head snapped to me. "Lil' Star, I'm not drinking from you right now. You need your strength."

I nodded to Jason. "I'm not talking about me."

Jason came to him, his arm out. "Take it, but promise you'll bring her back to me."

Tristian bowed his head. "I swear it to the stars."

Jason gestured to his wrist. "Take what you need then."

Tristian gripped his arm tight, and I turned as his fangs sank into Jason's wrist.

"Aden, call Grayson. We'll need backup."

Aden pulled his phone out and spoke softly when Grayson answered.

Once he hung up, he turned to me. "He said that he, Hudson, and Brigitte will meet us on the outskirts of the cemetery."

Tristian walked over. "Cillian should know."

Bash pulled his phone out. "Anderson knows now too."

"Good, let's load up. We have a witch to save and a Wishmaker to kill," I said to the group.

"Come on." Jason waved us over to the living room.

He pulled back a rug and revealed a small door. After he grabbed a key from his pocket, he clicked the lock open. He began to pull out knives, swords, cases with guns inside, and even an axe.

"It's like Mary Poppins's bag." Tristian nudged Aden, who gave him a glaring look. "What? You can't tell me that you don't think that."

I shook my head. "Tristian, it's not the time nor the place."

Sorry, Lil' Star, dark humor is how I deal."

I handed him a gun and a few short swords, which he began to strap across his back.

Jason stood and gave me a small leather case. "It was your father's."

I opened the case, and inside was a white marble dagger. The handle was in the shape of the sun, and I felt the magic in the dagger as I ran my fingers over the sun's rays.

"It's charmed to never miss. I think it'll go well with your onyx blade. Light and dark are the perfect combination. Like you, Lexi."

I hugged him. "Thank you, Jason."

He pulled back with a small smile.

Bash pulled my onyx blade from a small chest of drawers, walked over to me, and pulled it out of its sheath. "Perfect." He strapped my knives to my side.

I turned, ready to go, and handed Jason the journal. "Keep it safe. I think it has answers we'll need."

He took it and looked at the front and back before meeting my gaze. "I'll keep it safe. Go get our girl."

We parked on the road before the cemetery and walked through the woods silently. The fog was so dense, we could only see a few feet ahead. Luckily, we knew these woods like the back of our hands.

"The gate should be right ahead," Aden pointed out in a low voice.

Sure enough, the tops of the iron gate came into view, and a low whistle caught our ears. We stopped, and three figures came out from the side of the woods. Grayson, Hudson, and Brigitte came into view, and a wave of relief washed over me. I felt better knowing our friends were here to help.

Grayson nodded to the guys, but Hudson came and hugged me. "We'll get her out, Lexi."

I hugged him back. "Thank you for coming. All of you." I looked to Brigitte, unsure how she felt about me since the dinner.

Brigitte came to me. "Lexi, we're here for our allies and friends. Remind me to thank you for helping us see things clearly." She winked at me. "Let's go get your aunt back."

Bash said, "We should spread out. Grayson, you and Hudson take the south side, Aden and Tristian will take the west, Brigitte the east, and Lexi and I will go to the north side. This is a rescue mission. Do not kill unless it means your life or theirs."

We all agreed and began to spread out.

I pulled on Aden's hands. "Wait, you two." Tristian stopped and came to me. I pulled him into a hug. "Please be careful."

He smiled and kissed me. "Cross my heart." He took my fingers and laid them on his chest, where I could feel the sturdy beat of his heart.

I turned to Aden, and he ran his fingers into my hair, pulling me into a searing kiss. I pulled away breathlessly.

"To the stars, baby." He rested his forehead against mine.

"To the stars," I breathed back to him.

I stepped back and watched them as they walked away from Bash and me.

"Princess, we need to move."

I turned to him. He was wearing a soft look, and a blush crossed my cheeks. "Let's go."

We walked silently through the cemetery. I concentrated on a silencing spell that expanded around the two of us so our shoes would not make a crunching sound against the grass and trees. The mausoleum came into view, and it stood creepily in the fog. I looked up at the angel, and her face showed the pain of her loss. Bash held up a hand for me to stop. He held his gun in his other hand, pointing it to the ground, and we circled the marble building to find the door open.

We walked up the steps and through the open door into a large room, with the only occupants being the dead. A marble statue of the angel of death with burned wings stood in the middle, reaching out a hand, as if to guide you to the afterlife. A colorful stained glass window with the Blood Moon's symbol etched into its glass was behind it.

"No one's here, Bash." Dread twisted in my stomach.

"I know where they went, Princess." He moved to the statue,

grasped its hand, and twisted.

The wall next to it shifted and opened, revealing a set of stairs leading farther into the mausoleum. He turned back to me and extended his arm. I pulled out my father's dagger and slipped my hand into his.

"Hell of a date," I muttered.

He smirked. "I promise to take you on a real one once we get Coco back."

I smiled. "I'm holding you to that."

We walked down the stairs, which were lined with torches that lit the way. Once we reached the bottom, we entered a round crypt with three doorways that led to darkness, but I focused on the center of the room. Lying on top of a sarcophagus was Coco. Her eyes were closed, and she looked at peace. I swallowed a gasp. She didn't move, but the rise and fall of her chest told me she was still alive.

"Careful, Lexi, it could be a trap."

I nodded at him in understanding as I quickly moved to Coco. I hit a wall of air and cursed. "Damn you. It's spelled."

I turned back to face Bash, but he was looking behind me.

"Of course it's spelled, darling Rose."

I spun around to see Franklin emerging from the darkness of a tunnel just beyond where Coco lay.

He examined his fingers and then looked up at me with a bored expression. "Your aunt is quite the firecracker. Luckily, the ténèbres helped."

"Let her go," I hissed.

He tsked. "Now, why would I do that? My master is going to love the fact that I took the last of the Rose family. He wants you broken." He pointed to me. "You should have just stayed broken. I tried to warn you." He pulled out a deadly-looking blade.

"I will never bow to you or your master, Franklin. How do you think this will end?" I pulled my blade out and smirked. "Your choice. We do this the easy way or the hard way."

"Please say the hard way. I've been dying to teach this weasel a lesson," Bash said from behind me.

Franklin's lips pulled back into a snarl. "You both think that just because you own the right to lead, you should? Let me tell you something, there is a new wave of fae coming in, and we will rise to our rightful place beside The Wishmaker." He smiled widely as he spun the blade in his hand. "Your blood will fill the streets."

"What makes you think fae will follow you?"

His smile didn't falter, and he lifted his other hand. A gold swirl of pixie dust was in his palm.

"The pixie dust. You're going to control everyone through it."

He laughed maniacally. "You're smarter than they give you credit for, siren, but that's not just it. We have members willing to do whatever it takes to ensure the new era will begin. Just need a little blood of the original siren's line to complete the spell. Then not only will pixie dust become addictive, but your magic will be lost. No more witches, just us fae. The balance will be restored."

"If you take a witch's magic, they'll be lost! A part of them will be missing. Why would you take their magic?" I choked out in disgust.

Franklin walked around to me, and Bash shuffled behind me. "Come closer to her, and I'll put a bullet in your brain," he growled.

Franklin laughed. "You kill me, and I have a fail-safe." He snapped his fingers, and ténèbres appeared above us. They moved along the ceiling, creeping along the edges, waiting to wrap around us. "There are so many that you won't survive, but please kill me so the ténèbres can end you. To be responsible for the deaths of the Prince and Princess of Providence Village would make me a god!"

Bash took a step forward, but I held up a hand, shaking my head at him. I turned to Franklin, glaring at him. "Let The Weasel talk."

Franklin pouted at me. "Ahhh, thanks, bestie." He smirked like he thought he had won.

"So, why mermaid tears, and why kill Nyx?"

He sighed and leaned against the sarcophagus. "Master thought we might not need your blood. They didn't want you dead, they wanted to lead with them… but then you had to go and fall for the three Devils. Mermaid tears helped the addiction, but they needed a siren's blood, a vampire's tears, and a wolf's fang from the original families of Providence Village to eradicate witch magic."

I took in a sharp breath. "The three leaders. We wouldn't be willing to give you anything."

He smirked. "I have my ways. See, I had an insider." He swung his gaze to Bash. "Your father is so easily manipulated. A simple potion gave me his tears. Grayson was tricky, but Hyde helped me with that. Did you know your Grayson loves to fight? A few knocked-out teeth, and boom, there was my tooth. The only thing I need now is your blood, my Rose."

I shook my head. "Over my dead body."

He frowned. "That's what Nyx said too. Before I killed her. I thought maybe mermaid blood would work, and when I tried to get some, that bitch escaped and ran for help. Of course, she was high off her rocker. We keep them doused with pixie dust. They're much more manageable."

I growled, "If you have done anything to harm them, I swear…"

He shushed me. "I'm talking now, not you."

I tightened my grip on my blade.

"Good, now, where was I? Oh yes, I killed her, but her blood didn't work. It wasn't strong enough." He turned to Bash. "Framing you was sweet justice, though." He chuckled as he walked around me. "To see your heart fall when they took him away. I thought you hated him, Lexi?"

I ground my teeth, not letting a word out.

I may have thought once that I hated Sebastian Ryder, but I was broken then. When I looked into his eyes now, all I saw was our love for each other and our covens. We had a true partnership, and it wasn't easy, but who said love was easy?

Franklin whispered in my ear, and I shuddered at his closeness.

"Now, if you can just hand me your wrist, I'll take that blood, then Coco is free to go, but you, my dear, are coming with me."

I jerked back from him, ready to attack, but when I looked at Bash, he shook his head.

"Lay one finger on my girl, and I swear, ténèbres be damned, I will end you."

Franklin grunted. "You don't have a foot to stand on, Sebastian. To the stars, I will enjoy killing you, Devil, but first, I will let you sit and watch as I torture your siren. She will be such a good pet."

Bash growled, and movement drew my attention to the doorways. A pair of yellow and white eyes gleamed against the darkness, and I smiled because I knew our backup was here.

"The least you can do is tell us who The Wishmaker is," Bash said in a rough voice.

Franklin put a finger up to his chin and thought about it. "Hmmm, no." He snapped his fingers, and a group of ténèbres shot down from the ceiling and wrapped Bash in shadows, pushing him to the wall. His face was scrunched up in pain.

Franklin turned to me, smirking. "One Devil down. Two to go."

He wrapped his cold fingers around my wrist and pulled my arm toward him. I yanked against his hold as I felt the air wall drop around Coco.

"Shh, give me what I want, or poor Coco will suffer." I stilled, and he pulled me to his front, hissing, "Good little siren." He held out my arm but dropped it. "Let's just be sure there will be no funny business..."

Before I knew what he was doing, he snatched my father's blade from my hand and slammed it into Coco's stomach. She gasped, but her eyes were still closed, spelled into sleeping. I saw the blood pool on her stomach.

"No, no, Coco!"

He yanked my arm away from my body. "This is going to hurt."

As soon as the tip of the blade dug into my skin, I screamed. He dragged the blade down my arm, and the pain was so much more excruciating than a regular cut. It burned from within, and the blade slicing into my skin felt as if it was made of fire.

"It's spelled. I know it's painful."

I whimpered and looked into Bash's eyes, knowing this might be my last chance to tell him. "I love you, Sebastian."

I closed my eyes and dropped my hand to the onyx blade. My blood ran down my arm, and it became slippery in my grasp, but I held onto it tighter until my knuckles turned white, with red trails trickling down the black handle.

I turned to Franklin, who was smiling like a lunatic as his black-pit eyes searched mine. He moved his hand down to mine, holding my arm to see the blood. A hazy look came over his face. "It's like your blood is a thousand sparkling rubies, Lexi, so pretty. We could have been perfect together. We could have ruled the covens together. We still can." His other hand grasps my chin and lifts me up so I am only inches away from his mouth. He moves in closer, as if he is going to kiss me.

"Goodbye, Franklin," I sneered in his face. I slammed the onyx blade into his stomach and pulled it back out, coated in his blood.

His eyes widened in surprise, and he fell back to the floor, holding his stomach. "Guards!"

Movements from the hall filled my ears, and I grinned widely. "I think your guards have been detained."

Grayson, Brigitte, Hudson, Aden, and Tristian walked through the door with Hyde in tow. The light from the torches danced across their faces. Each of them were covered in mud and blood, but the look of victory glinted in their eyes.

"Sorry about the guards, Franky boy, but it looks like they lost their heads." Aden smirked as he tossed a severed head at Franklin's feet.

He screamed in rage as he scrambled to his feet, "You will not destroy us! We are everywhere and everything, the shadows that claim the darkness!" He shot a stream of shadows to the ceiling, and the magic moved among the ténèbres as they began to descend.

The ténèbres screeched out a war cry and dove toward us.

The entire crypt was filled with darkness, and I feared that Death had finally knocked on our door.

Chapter Foty-One

I formed a ball of fire in my hand and rushed to Bash. I sent it flying around him as he broke free of the ténèbres. Grayson growled and threw a ball of light above Coco.

"Grayson! Tristian!" Their heads snapped to me. "Heal Coco and get her out of here!"

Tristian took a torch and rammed it through the shadows. "On it, Lil' Star!"

Grayson responded with a grunt and shot a flame of fire at the shadows that were trying to wrap around us.

I ran to Bash, and he grabbed two torches to battle the shadows. Brigitte and Hudson were back-to-back. Brigitte formed a ball of light so bright, the shadows cowered from her. Hudson threw a punch at Hyde, who was trying to escape, and I searched for Franklin. The worm had weaseled his way to the exit. I looked around to find a way to stop him. A trickle of water ran down the wall beside me, so I laid my hand against the cold stone wall and blasted a shot of water at him, sending him flying back to the ground.

I ran to Tristian as he started to heal Coco. The blood had pooled around her, and her breathing was shallow. I threw fireballs at the shadows as they crept down from the ceiling and reached for Tristian's arm. They shrieked in fright, and the sound was like music to my ears. The ténèbres were beyond evil—their only purpose was to wreak havoc on us fae—so to hear them suffer was a beautiful sound.

The healing light from Tristian's hands spread over Coco, and her breathing steadied.

Grayson was by my side in an instant. "Brigitte! Use your light as a guide!"

She smiled, and her eyes turned white as she murmured a spell under her breath. Rays of light sprung from her fingers as the ténèbres screamed and fell into the closest shadows, cowering from the mighty priestess. Grayson lifted Coco, and he looked back at me.

"Go! Keep her safe."

He nodded and held Coco close to his chest as Brigitte and Hudson followed him out.

A body rammed into me, knocking me to the ground. Before I could get away, Franklin climbed on top of me, wrapping his hands around my throat. "You little slut! I will destroy you!"

I put my knees up and pushed into his stomach. He grunted and locked his hands around my neck, squeezing. He was crushing my throat, and it was hard to pull in air.

I saw my Devils fight to get to me, but the ténèbres were relentless. Aden's eyes were wild, Tristian screamed like a warrior, and Bash was the Devil incarnate, fighting with everything he had to get to me.

I knew it would be too late as I felt the light fade, but I wouldn't stop fighting. I pounded my fist into him. I would not die this way. I refused to. I dug my nails into Franklin's hands and clawed my fingers down. He only tightened his grip, and I saw spots in my vision. I was going to pass out soon, and I thought, *Fuck, this is not the way I want to go. I don't want to go. I don't want to leave my friends, family, and Devils.*

Franklin was jerked back and thrown near the exit. I blinked, and when my vision cleared, Agent Rengard and Cillian stood above me.

Cillian wrapped his hand in mine. "Are you okay?"

I gasped in a big breath of air, welcoming the sting in my lungs.

"What the hell are these things?!" Cillian yelled as ténèbres tried to attack us.

Rengard growled from behind me. "Ténèbres, they're the shadows of the dark fae. They'll destroy your soul inside and out."

Cillian looked at me, his eyes ready for a battle. "Good thing we brought backup."

Fae and human FBI agents swarmed into the room, ready to battle. Witches had fire and light ready to strike down the ténèbres. We all worked in sync as we battled through the ténèbres—a common enemy—destroying the shadows as we went.

From the corner of my eye, I saw Franklin climbing the stairs, and I growled, "Not today, you little worm."

I shot a fireball near him. He turned to look at me, and the little bastard smiled.

"Go after him!" Cillian called, and I looked back at him. "End this, Lexi!"

I nodded.

Agent Rengard smirked. "Looks like you need a way out, Ms. Rose. Allow me." He threw his jacket down and threw himself into the ténèbres.

I gasped as a bright light escaped him and a path was formed.

"Run, Lexi!" Cillian called as he made his way through the shadows.

Tristian came to Cillian's side, fire ablaze in his hand. "We got this, Lil' Star. Go get him."

I found Aden, and he was battling Hyde. He sent him flying back with a kick and threw himself on top of him.

"Lexi!" Tristian called. I looked back at him. "Go! Don't let him get away!"

I ran to the stairs that led up to the cemetery.

Bash grabbed my arm. "Come back to us, Princess."

I looked into his green eyes. "I won't make any promises, but I'll try my damnedest. I love you, Sebastian Ryder."

He swallowed, and I saw the pain flare in his eyes. "And I, you, Lexi Rose."

I turned and ran. I ran away from my Devils, knowing we would find our way back to each other. I climbed the stairs, taking them two at a time. Outside, the fog had lifted, and the night sky was clear. The stars were bright as I looked around the cemetery. Franklin was running with a limp, and I chased him. He ran in front of a group of trees near the back and fell to the ground.

I stopped above him, pulled my black blade out, and put it to his throat. "Give me a reason not to kill you here and now."

He turned to me and smirked. He rasped out, "I told you, fail-safe." He flicked his fingers, and candles appeared on the ground and lit. We were in a circle with a protection spell. A skull sat to the side with a burning black candle.

A book, my father's dagger, and a bowl with ancient symbols engraved on the side sat next to Franklin. He stood and moved. I tried to lift my feet, but I was rooted to the ground.

I struggled for a minute before Franklin's voice came from next to me. "See, that is what happens when you refuse your magic for so long, Lexi. Any witch would have known to look for a death circle. A skull of a fae, black candles, and a protection circle."

He took the knife and a small bowl, sliced his palms, and let his blood fill the bowl. "*Les spirits sombres et sombres, je vous appElla. Apportezmoi le pourvior des aciens. Apportez moi le pouvoir du premier et commandez ma volonté.*"

I gasped as I realized he was calling on The Dark Ones. It was said that they were no longer here, extinct from our world ages ago.

If he used them to control us, we were all doomed.

The ground rumbled beneath me, and a ring of fire surrounded us. I looked at Franklin as his eyes turned solid black, and inky smoke seeped from his mouth. Thunder rolled across the sky, and flashes of lightning cracked in the air as rain began pouring down on us.

Franklin's hands turned black, and he walked to me, my father's blade raised above his head. "All will know your sacrifice. Goodbye, Lexi Rose!"

I screamed and held up my hands as a flash of green magic burst from them. Franklin stumbled to the ground. I watched in shock as flames of green danced along my wrist. I never performed that kind of magic before, but it moved through me as if I had always possessed it.

I lifted my leg, willing it to move. It felt heavy, but I still managed to move toward him.

He sneered at me. "It is really sad that you think you still have a chance. I have the magic of The Dark Ones. A pathetic earth spell won't stop me!"

I snarled at him and lunged. "What I have is something you'll never have, you weasel!"

He stumbled back, but I followed. I threw a hard kick to his stomach and watched him fall to the ground. I jumped on him and leaned down to sneer in his face.

His eyes were full of surprise as I hissed. "You might have the power of The Dark Ones, but I have my own."

I summoned my air magic and threw a punch to his face to break his nose.

"*Whore!* You filthy little blood whore!" He picked me up and threw me.

As he stalked toward me, I jumped up and wrapped him in a water bubble. He smirked and touched it, and it sizzled out.

"Fine, fight fire with fire." I sent a ball of flames toward him and ran at him, swinging and kicking him as he fell to the ground.

I threw a stream of vines out, and they wrapped around his legs. He answered with a flash of black smoke, and the vines withered and died.

He smiled. "I am Death itself! I can touch anything and choose its life or death." He laughed. "My master will grant me the highest honor, and I will rule with power."

Thinking outside the box, I wrapped the vines around his arms and bound them tightly with the earth's mud. He struggled to escape. I tilted my head to the side and ignited flames to surround him. "I wouldn't move if I were you." I arched a brow as he screamed, the flames licking at his hands. "Hurts, doesn't it? I told you not to move."

I placed a water bubble over his mouth, and his eyes widened in fear of drowning as I walked toward him. I could see the truth in his eyes—he knew he was about to die.

"No, Franklin, you won't rule. Because no one will know your name once you are dead."

He struggled against the vines, and his eyes begged me to show mercy. He didn't show mercy to Daniels, Nyx, or anyone else. I wasn't going to show him mercy now.

A shadow walked out of the trees, and I saw Aden. He was bloody but alive. I smirked. My Devil found me. But then I looked into his eyes. They were filled with something I'd never seen in him before: regret.

Hyde stepped out behind him with a gun to his head. "Release him, or I'll end your Devil's life now."

My magic struggled as I wrestled with the choice of my coven or my Devil.

"Lexi, don't," Aden begged.

I let my magic fade away.

Franklin spoke from behind me, his voice muffled, "Blood or Devil, your choice."

I closed my eyes and said, "Drop the gun."

Hyde smiled. "Nah, I'm gonna keep this on him so you don't go back on your word."

I glared at him. "Oh, I'm not worried about me, more like what he will do to you once he decides how to kill you!"

Franklin's arms tightened around me. His manic voice crackled out, "Let's finish this, my pretty Rose." He pulled me back to him, and I felt nauseous as his hands tightened around me. I growled as he took the knife and my arm, slicing it again, deeper and harsher than before. My blood poured into the bowl.

Aden threw his head back and cracked Hyde in the nose. A sickening snap sounded as Hyde fell back, and Aden moved so fast, he was practically invisible. He grabbed the gun and aimed it at Hyde. But then he changed his mind, growled, and bashed Hyde over the head with the butt of the gun.

He turned and ran to me. Franklin cried out as he released the ténèbres on me. They surrounded me, quickly concealing me in darkness.

"Let me borrow that onyx blade, baby!" Aden yelled.

I tossed the blade to his feet. He plucked it from the ground and walked through the ténèbres as they separated for him, screaming into the night.

Aden reached Franklin and threw a punch to his face. Franklin wrenched back and lunged for Aden. They rolled to the ground, throwing punches at each other. The onyx blade was tossed to the side as Franklin screamed, calling for the shadows to cover him again. They swooped down from the sky, and Franklin moved quickly as ténèbres captured Aden, encircling him and moving through him, feeding off his magic and power.

I screamed. "Let him go! You have my blood. Let him go!"

The ténèbres were vicious as they poured down his throat, and the darkness encased him. I screamed his name as I tried to find any power, but I was so drained and weak that I could barely stand. The blood still dripped down my hand as I tried to rush over to Aden.

Franklin flicked a wrist, and I fell to my knees as I tried to reach for Aden—my dark knight, my Devil.

Franklin walked to him, wiping blood from his mouth, and the ténèbres cowered away from him. "My Rose, maybe this will keep you in line with The Master from now on."

He moved behind Aden, who looked defeated and slumped on his knees, holding his stomach. Franklin held him back by the throat, and Aden's eyes widened as a trickle of fear seeped through them. "Let this be a lesson you won't forget."

He brandished the onyx knife in his hand.

"*Nooo!*"

I struggled to move quickly to them, and a spark blazed from within me. I screamed as I used the last of my magic to throw a blast of light at Franklin.

Franklin's sinister laughter filled the night sky. "Oh, you love him, don't you, Lil' Rose?"

The rain fell in sheets around us, the droplets hitting my face. "Franklin, please... I'll go with you if you leave him alive."

Aden shook his head violently.

Franklin smiled and stalked over to me. "You will be mine, Lexi Rose. The Master promised I could have you if I did as I was told." He traced his fingers over my cheek, and I had to bite my tongue from the feeling of his hands on me.

"I said I would go, but know you have signed your own death. My Devils will find me. They will hunt you to the ends of the earth to find me."

Franklin turned and twirled the blade in his hand as thunder boomed overhead. "Ahhh, that's such a sweet notion, Lil' Rose, but you forgot I'm part of something more. I'm more powerful than any other witch here, and now I'll gain the power of The Dark Ones to help me steal more souls and become what I was truly meant to be." He grinned as the ténèbres wrapped around Aden again. His grunts echoed around us. "Say goodbye to your darling Devil."

Aden's face came forward, and he mouthed, "I love you, baby."

Franklin slammed the onyx blade into Aden's chest. The ténèbres released him, and he fell to the ground. I screamed his name, and something inside me broke. I threw my pain out, and a flash of light flew from my hands. Franklin fell back, and his eyes showed fear for the first time since the circle. The blade fell to the ground beyond the ring. The ténèbres surrounded him, and he disappeared from the ring with nothing left but the smoke of his body.

I turned to Aden and ran to him. My knees fell to the ground, the wet grass seeping through my clothes as I pulled him onto my lap. I pushed my magic through and tried to heal him, but I knew the onyx blade was lethal. Tears filled my eyes, and I hugged him close to me, kissing his face. "Shhh. You'll be okay."

His fingers reached for me, softly skating across my cheek. "No, Lexi, go find Bash and Tristian now. Leave me."

I shook my head, my tears blinding me as I tried to catch my breath. "I'm not leaving you. Please don't leave me. Aden... I..."

Aden reached for me, pulling me close. "I don't want to go, baby. I love you too."

I sobbed, pulling him into a kiss, and as his lips found mine, his breath shuddered. I pulled back to gaze into those steely eyes. "You can't leave me. You can't. You promised me forever. You promised me. You can't take that back. You can't leave us, Aden. Please fight. Just hold on."

My tears fell onto his face as it paled. A sense of hopelessness filled my chest as the air thickened into a cold blanket around us. I tried to push more of my magic into him, but it didn't work. I was completely drained.

I closed my eyes and prayed to whoever could hear me. I offered my life for his own, but no one answered my plea. I opened my eyes, and I looked down at his, which opened at the same time.

"One more look at you, my beautiful girl." They flickered closed as a tear fell down his face. "Baby, I will always be with you. Don't stop fighting. Don't let them win. Promise me this."

I shook my head and bent down, pressing my forehead to his. This was not a goodbye—I would not give up on him.

He cupped my cheek, and I opened my eyes. "Promise me, baby."

I shuddered and felt my entire world break. "I promise."

"I'll meet you in the stars, baby." His eyes fluttered closed.

Aden Charmante, my prince, my Devil, took his last breath. It was a nightmare I couldn't escape from as he lay still, growing colder with each second. I sobbed, pulling him to my chest, and the boy who loved me when I was young and began to love me again... was gone.

I didn't want to let go. If I let go, then I knew he would be gone forever.

The rain lightened, and a sprinkle fell as the sun began to rise. I looked to the hill near the Ryder Estate. Two shadows came climbing up, and I raised my head to see Tristian, bloody but unharmed, and Bash was holding his side but still alive. They looked at me, and when they saw me cradling Aden's body, they sped toward us.

Bash got to me first, and his head fell as he saw Aden's lifeless body in my arms. I cried harder, holding onto him.

Bash turned and screamed as he cursed the night skies.

"*Mi frère*," Tristian said as he sank to his knees next to me. He took his hand and held it to his chest. "*Repose en paix, mon frère*." I reached for Tristian as our hands clasped together. What happened?"

My voice cracked. "Franklin, he did this. He killed him." Tristian walked over to the spot where Franklin had disappeared in a puff of smoke. "Hyde! He helped. Aden knocked him out back there." I gestured to where he had landed.

Bash nodded and headed to look for his body. He came back quickly and shook his head. "Gone."

I frowned and looked back to Aden, and my heart broke again. The tears didn't stop, and I wanted to keep him warm.

Bash looked at me with so much pain in his eyes, I wanted to reach out. "We need to get his body back to the Blood Moon Coven's temple so we can mourn him properly. Like a true warrior." His voice sounded miles away, but I nodded, letting him take Aden from my arms.

My sobs came uncontrollably. Tristian lifted me into his arms and kissed my temple but said nothing. We needed to mourn the loss of a friend, a lover, and a brother. I felt the loss of Aden deep in my bones and knew that my heart would never be the same again. The stars dimmed, and the clouds swallowed the moon as our hearts broke for our Devil. Brigitte's words echoed in my head.

"With death, there is always a price."

Chapter Forty-Two

Hyde was quiet as they left. He'd hidden farther back when the Ryder ass came looking for him, but as the woods grew silent, he stood and walked to the circle, getting the siren's blood.

The Master will be upset that we lost our dear Franklin, but now it's my time to earn a spot on the Master's guide.

"You did good, Hyde." A cloaked figure emerged from the shadows. "Sadly, Franklin won't be able to help anymore." Walking toward the circle, he whispered a spell under his breath as the earth shook, and Franklin's dead body began to form in the ring. The Wishmaker knelt, his hands glowing as he pushed them into Franklin's chest with ease, pulling out a completely intact still-beating black heart.

"Aww, tainted souls are so refreshing. Let's hope you can live up to your destiny, Hyde."

The Wishmaker headed to Hyde, sliced his shirt open with their fingers, and slammed the heart into Hyde's chest. Hyde convulsed and fell to the ground. The pain and agony that filled him was unbearable. He felt like he was on fire and drowning at the same time.

He screamed as The Wishmaker stood and watched with a twisted face of enjoyment. "Our work is not done, do let us go forward with the plan, and soon, we will rule the covens, and we will have the power that is rightfully ours."

Hyde lay still on the ground as The Dark Ones filled his soul, turning everything from light to darkness.

Now I know why Franklin enjoyed the kill, because it's the only time you can be free.

"I want that siren, Master. I want to watch her life drain as I take away everyone she ever loved." He stood up, looking at his master.

"Yes, her time will come, dear friend. Now, we have many tasks at hand. Let us go and rest. Then we will plan our time, because my Rose *will* be mine soon."

This isn't the end for Lexi and her Devils.
Book Three of the Covens Series will be out in early 2024.

THREE CROWS HALLOW

"With death, there is always a price."

Brigitte's words echoed through my mind as Tristian held me close to his chest, tears flowing down my face. Bash's shadow loomed in front of us as he carried our friend, warrior, and *frère* back to the Ryder's estate. The estate looked like some sick joke as it sat mocking us, taunting our pain and drinking it in.

Tristian stepped with purpose, but with each movement, his breathing waned, and the pain spilled out of him. He desperately tried to control his anger and sorrow as I clung to him tightly, never wanting to let go. I was praying that this was some kind of nightmare, and I needed to wake up. If I let go, I would break into a million pieces, and I didn't think I would survive it again. My heart and my soul wouldn't survive this loss.

I lifted my head to see a group standing off to the side. Cillian and a group of FBI agents were gathered around Hudson, Grayson, and Brigitte as an ambulance loaded Coco up.

Cillian noticed us first and ran before he yelled, "Medic!" His deep voice bellowed through the air as he screamed, "Medic! Medic!" He stalled in his steps as he looked at Bash, who shook his head.

Cillian bowed his head in defeat and looked at Tristian. "Is she okay?"

His voice was thick with tears, and his guilt and sadness washed over me, making me whimper in Tristian's arms.

"Cill, get it together. She's not strong. She tried to heal him and is completely drained of power. She can't even shield us right now, so fucking lock it up."

Cillian looked at him and nodded.

Grayson, Hudson, and Brigitte ran up behind Cillian and stilled. Grayson saw Aden lying in Bash's arms and let a wolfish howl echo through the night. Hudson and a few other FBI agents followed. Brigitte murmured something to Bash, who nodded, hanging his head as he waited for us. Brigitte met my gaze and moved toward us, as if she was walking on air. Her eyes faded to black orbs, and she moved close, brushing my hair from my face. Even after a fight, she was the calm in all of us.

She frowned as her black orbs looked down at me. "Siren, your heart sings with sorrow for your Devil. We all hear her. Let me take some of the pain. Let me help you, Lexi."

I wanted to protest, but Tristian's voice broke as he pleaded, "Please, Lexi, let her help take some of the pain away, Lil' Star. Let her help you."

I opened my mouth, and a shaky whisper escaped, "Okay."

Her eyes closed, and she pressed her hand to my chest where the shadow's handprint sat.

Her power flowed through me like someone caressing my body. It pulled at my emotions. I felt a string-like magic pull through me, and my heart didn't want to jump out of my chest now. She didn't take all my sorrow, but my tears stopped, and the despair of wanting to join my Devil lessened in my soul. I still felt the sting of his loss as she pushed her magic into me. I gasped, and Tristian held me close.

I found my voice. "No, don't take it all. I want to feel it, Brigitte. I want to feel the pain, because when I find The Wishmaker, I'll use it against him." I whispered the words, but my voice was still hoarse from crying.

Her eyes narrowed with the understanding of my words and my pain. "Do not live in your pain forever, siren, for it can destroy even the purest souls."

I gazed up at her, hearing her words but not heeding her warning, because I would find The Wishmaker, and when I did, he would pay for what he did to my Devils.

Turning my head to Tristian, I whispered into his ear, "Tristian, put me down. I can stand."

He held onto me for a second and placed a lingering kiss on my temple, as if I might disappear from him. "Okay, Lil Star. Stay close."

He set me down, but I held onto his arm for support, my knees still feeling like they would give out any second.

Grayson came up to Bash. "Let me take him, *ami*."

Bash shook his head. "No, we... we will bring him home."

Grayson opened his mouth to argue with Bash when the front doors swung open, and Morgan approached us. His hair was a mess, and his suit was disheveled. He looked like he'd been running his fingers through his hair repeatedly. His eyes searched for us. Finally, he spotted Bash and sped over using his vampiric speed.

His eyes widened in surprise. "Sebastian!" He looked down at Aden and then at his son. His eyes were fiery with anger as he walked to us, but I could taste his distress.

I moved with Tristian to stand beside Bash to show a united front.

His eyes closed as he whispered, "*Je Suis tellement désolé, mon fils de mon sang.*" He placed his hand on Aden's chest.

A soft glow flowed through his hand, and I gasped, about to stop whatever he was trying to do.

But instead of screaming at him not to touch Aden, I felt a tug on my arm as Tristian pulled me closer and murmured, "Lexi, it is what our coven does when we lose a warrior. It is tradition for our leader to share his power with the deceased." He grunted the last word, and his tears hit my hand.

I wrapped my arms around him as he pulled me against the side of his body. My hand landed on his chest, and I ran my fingers over where his heart lay. We held on to each other, as if it was the only thing we could do as we saw the power pour through Aden.

Morgan's head fell forward, and he let a bellow of pain escape his lips for the loss of a boy he had helped raise.

He lifted his head, his fiery red eyes meeting mine. "Franklin, what of him?"

I stood straighter, finding the courage to tell him what his little pet did to us. "Dead and burned. I killed him. He was working for The Wishmaker. He wanted to take my power. Aden tried..." I couldn't finish the sentence as tears threatened my eyes again. "I destroyed him," I snarled, letting him see the rage that lived in me.

His eyes tightened as if he wanted to argue with me, but with one look at Aden, he nodded. "In the name of the covens." Morgan turned to Bash. "Bring him into the sacrament room. I will call on the earth witches to start the transformation, to begin our coven's ritual."

I stepped toward Morgan without realizing it, placing a hand on his arm. "The thought of another witch performing magic for Aden makes my skin crawl." Morgan looked between Tristian and me. "Let us do it." I looked back at Tristian, and his eyes were set in a hard stare at Morgan. "Tristian and I will do it."

Morgan shook his head. "Lexi, you will drain your power. It's already low. You can't. It is too much for the two of you to perform it all."

My hand tightened on Morgan's arm, and Tristian stepped up to me. "We can do it, sir."

Morgan's eyes flicked to Tristian, and he regarded us momentarily. "Fine, but if you feel drained—"

I held up a hand. "We will call upon the coven's earth witches, but you owe us this, Morgan."

He narrowed his eyes at me and backed away. "Follow me."

We walked past Grayson, Hudson, and Brigitte, who were in a deep conversation. Grayson was arguing with Brigitte, but with one touch of her hand, Grayson swung his head to me as I approached them.

"Has anyone contacted Ethan?" My voice tried to sound strong, but it came out meek.

Grayson's eyes softened. "I'll make the call, Lexi."

I started to walk away but turned and hugged him. I murmured, "Thank you."

He held me. "Of course, seductress, we'll take care of it."

Hudson was looking at us with red-rimmed eyes and a look of hopelessness on his face.

I pulled away and mouthed, "Thank you" again to them as Tristian tugged my hand.

"Let's go, Lil' Star, and take our Devil home." His voice sounded rough as we moved through the crowd.

Members from all three covens gathered around the estate as police taped off the surrounding area.

News of what happened here tonight must have spread, because I saw witches and fae of all shapes and forms, from nymphs with their willowy forms as tears fell like rivers down their cheeks to a group of goblins hanging their heads low, bowing as we walked by. The Devils might have been feared, but they were respected, and the Blood Moon Coven had come out to show their respect to a fallen soldier. Ice frosted the grass from the early morning, and I began to shiver. Tristian pulled me close as we walked up the stairs into the estate.

Morgan waited for us as we entered. "I sent Bash down. Tristian, show Lexi the way." His voice was etched with concern.

Tristian didn't say a word as he moved through the long halls. We reached a circular room with a hidden door on the floor that opened outward, and underneath were stone stairs leading down in a spiral pattern.

"Lexi, be careful. The steps are steep. I'll go first. Follow me, and stay near me." Tristian's hand ignited in flame, casting a floating ball of fire above us as we walked down the deep-gray stone steps.

With each step, I felt my power grow within. It was as if the solid walls of this house were full of emotions. I was drowning in power by the time we reached the bottom.

A small hallway made of smooth black stone lay before us. Red torches lit our way, and a black Gothic door with an inlay of gold celestial charts created a soft glow throughout the room. I paused at the entrance, not wanting to enter, not wanting to realize this was real.

"Lexi," Tristian called my name, and I wasn't sure if I could move. "Lexi," he called again. My eyes snapped to him. His hand was extended. "We do this together."

I swallowed the tears back and took his hand. "Together."

We moved into the room, which was round like the tall turret we were in earlier. A large enchanted globe with all the elements scrolling through the roof curved into the ceiling, a glow emanating from within each of them. Earth, Air, Water, and Fire. I even saw the symbol for the spirit. The constellations, planets, and moon phases were sprinkled throughout the room along the walls and ceilings to make it look like they were slowly moving through time. Five massive windows arched over us as the image of the night sky shone above us.

"How?" I said in a tired voice. "How do you keep the magic... so alive?"

"Father has a group of witches that continue to push power into our sacrament room. Does your coven have something similar?" Bash's soft voice cut through the room as he laid Aden on a stone altar made of the same black stone as the door. He looked like he had aged years, his skin ghostly white, eyes sunken into his face, and his chiseled jaw even sharper as he looked down at Aden.

I walked to the altar and saw the dirt smudges on Aden's face and dried blood covering his perfect Cupid's-bow lips. His eyes were closed, as if he was sleeping. He was still beautiful. Even as a kid, he held a beauty no one could rival. I swept his hair to the side, wishing he would open his eyes.

"One more time, please open them!"

Bash was at my side in an instant, pulling me into his arms, and then the warmth of another body wrapped us together as Tristian came to us.

"Lexi, he can't. He's gone. He isn't coming back, no matter how much you beg." His arms held me tight as if holding my heart together to keep it from breaking.

"He can't," I pleaded. " I had just told him he was my everything! How is he my everything if he isn't here anymore, Bash? How are we supposed to be each other's forever when our forever isn't done? Bash, please bring him back. Do anything. Bring him back to me, to us. Come back to me, Aden, my dark knight, come back to me, please!" I clung to his shirt as I finally fell apart.

I screamed into the ceiling, and even the stars above us dimmed as they heard my pain. The ruthless world shuddered above us, knowing what it did by taking the one person who brought calm to my storm. My thoughts dug deeper and deeper into my head until I was spinning and wanting to scream at whatever god would listen to me.

"Lil' Star, we would if we could, we would bring him home if we knew of a way; he would never leave us." His voice cracked, and I let them hold me as I broke apart.

Their soothing words and touches quieted me as my tears slowed. I took a shaky breath and listened to the steady beat of my Devils' hearts, missing the third one. It sounded incomplete, like the rhythm was off without Aden. I looked down and saw a grassy meadow below our feet. I untangled myself from each of them, bending down to touch the grass. It was soft and silky as my fingers grazed the tops, and tiny white and purple flowers sprouted up as I pushed more of my magic into the ground. I closed my eyes, and I imagined what Aden would want. The earth moved to my will as it shifted slowly, and the forest grew around us. Mossy grass flowed throughout the room.

Tristian worked on one side of the room, twirling a hand to create a large tree with a canopy of leaves fading into different shades of green that hung over Aden. Vines climbed from the ground to stand tall, making the altar look more like a bed. I stood, and Bash observed me as I moved to the other side.

I looked at him and held out my hand. "Help me create a place for him to be. Give me your power, so he has a piece of you with him, not just me and Tristian."

Bash's eyes softened as he moved close to me and wrapped an arm around my shoulder, leaving my hands free. "Thank you, Princess." He kissed my temple as he opened up, allowing me to take his power.

My hands bloomed with fire, and I concentrated on separating each flame so it looked like a thousand fireflies were dancing above our heads. Bash looked up, and a tear rolled down from his eye. I wiped it slowly away.

"It's my fault. I made him go after you. I was so worried. I thought... I should have known you would have been able to take care of yourself, Lexi."

I shook my head. "No, Bash, he..." I struggled to get the words out. "He thought what he was doing was protecting all of us. You can't blame yourself."

He looked down at me and rested his head against mine. "I don't know if I can do that."

I cupped his cheek and kissed him softly. "We have to for him, Bash. We have to keep going."

He nodded over at Tristian, who had created arches of wood with three small waterfalls collecting into a pond. Tristian was kneeling on one knee. His head hung as his tears fell into the water, collecting the magic. I walked over, and the water swirled with magic as a movement of fish appeared beneath him.

"They're made out of water," he answered before I could even ask.

Bash clasped his shoulder. "*Frère*, he would have loved it."

I stayed silent as something passed between them, pain, understanding, and finally, acceptance. I threw a hand in the air, creating the lightest breeze to keep the room cooler. Leaves rustled in a peaceful song, and a sweet scent of pine and sandalwood filled the air.

"It smells like him." I smiled and moved to where our warrior lay his head.

My Devils followed, and I reached out my hands to both of them. We stood united in front of him to say our last goodbyes. Tristian cleaned his skin with his water magic. I placed a hand on his cheek and pushed fire magic into him to keep him warm.

I bent over and kissed his cheek one last time. "I am so sorry I couldn't save you." I let my tears fall as they hit his long lashes and sank into his skin.

I looked back at Tristian. "Ice to keep him preserved as he is forever?"

He nodded. "Exactly, Lil' Star."

I closed my eyes, holding Tristian's and Bash's hands in mine as our magic twisted together and formed ice around him. The crystal-clear ice covered him, but you could still see his face, as if he was peacefully asleep.

"I'll tell Father we're ready."

I nodded, and Bash moved away as Tristian pulled me into a hug.

Morgan, Ethan, Ella, Grayson, Hudson, and Brigitte entered behind Bash. Ethan's eyes met mine, and he pulled away from Ella, walking toward me, his eyes never wavering from mine. I reached out and took his hand, and his pain exploded from within him.

"Let it go, Ethan."

He looked over at Aden, and his face collapsed as Ella's hand intertwined with ours. He walked closer, placing his hand on top of the ice. "Always the savior, brother. Damn you. Damn you, Aden."

We watched in silence as people came in and paid honor to the fallen soldier.

Ella was on my other side, next to Ethan and Bash. Tristian came up to me with a large wooden box. He opened the lid, and salt, candles, and a small jar of darkened ash lay inside. I touched each item, feeling the magic dance beneath my touch. "Salt for protection, candles to guide his way, and ashes of our warriors to guide him through the Veil."

Tristian, Bash, and Ethan performed the ritual with care and precision. Bash laid the salt around the altar, Tristian placed the candles on the ground, lighting them with ease, and Ethan took the ashes of the fallen warriors and made interactive patterns on the sides of the ice coffin that sparkled like the night sky. Once they were all done, Ella moved to the coffin and placed a bouquet of flowers—buttercups for friendship, hydrangeas for protection, iris for respect and honor, rosemary for remembrance, and a single sunflower for lighting the way.

Though I couldn't protect him in this life, in his death, I would protect him every day. The Wishmaker should have known one thing: we would come for him one day soon, and I would make sure he felt the pain of a thousand deaths before I sent him to the fiery pits of hell.

Author's Note

And that is the second one! I hope you all enjoyed Hemlock Falls, and no, our adventure isn't over just yet. I told you all that Franklin was a weasel! And poor Aden! I cried so hard writing that scene. My own was heartbroken just as much as yours! We will have to see what book three holds for us in the future but truly thank you for following my story of The Covens.

Thank you to my friends, Megs, Megan, Hailley, Crystal, Melinda, Katie, Renee, and the rest of my girls, for always supporting me. To my hubby, my partner in crime, Tom, thank you for listening to my problems and making sure all of my scenes make sense. To my son for the endless hugs when I am down and the sweet words you give me when I feel lost. To my Mom and Dad for being my number one fans and supporting me through this whole process. To my niece Jayde I know you can't read these yet, but thank you for just being you. You are so bright and loving. It makes my darkest days bright. To my brother, the reason I started writing I know you are looking down from the stars, just cheering me on, and damn it, I miss you every day. To the rest of my family for the support you all give.

To my Team, Nikki, Ben, Jeannie, Tara, and Kristy- you guys are the best and make the book so much better. Thank you for bringing my dream to life. Without you, I would be lost.

To Henry and Wayhues for the illustrations: Bringing a character to life from a book is hard to do, but you guys did it. I appreciate the hard work you put into your art.

To my readers, you guys keep me going, your love for the series means so much, and every video post and like, heart, and comment makes me smile every day. To Kim, Jennifer, Candi, and Michelle Gosh, ladies, the support and love from you amaze me every day.

About The Author

CiCi was born and raised in Texas but now resides in sunny California. When she is not writing The Coven Series or her other works, you can find her spending time with her family, drinking wine with her girls, singing way too loud and off key in the car, or snuggling up with her cat, a cup of coffee, and a good book.

cicimyersbooks.com

Loved this book? Tell us about it!

Reviews are a great way to support your favorite independent authors:

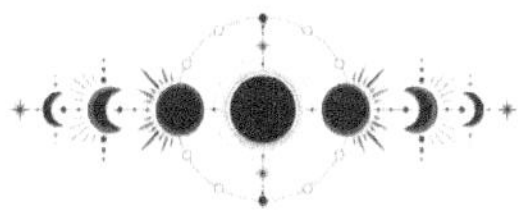

Want more of The Covens Series?

Listen to the Official The Coven Series Playlist on Spotify!

www.ingramcontent.com/pod-product-compliance
Lightning Source LLC
Chambersburg PA
CBHW031436160726
47994CB00005B/1744